The Boy Next Story

AMULET BOOKS
NEW YORK

Library of Congress Cataloging-in-Publication Data

Names: Schmidt, Tiffany, author.
Title: The boy next story : a Bookish boyfriends novel / Tiffany Schmidt.
Description: New York : Amulet Paperbacks, 2019. | Summary: "Rory likes Toby, but Toby likes Rory's sister Merrilee, even though Merrilee is already dating Toby's friend Fielding—and it's all about to get even more complicated at Reginald R. Hero High"—Provided by publisher.
Identifiers: LCCN 2018038523 (print) | LCCN 2018043439 (ebook) | ISBN 9781683354895 (All Ebooks) | ISBN 9781419734366 (paperback)
Subjects: | CYAC: High schools—Fiction. | Schools—Fiction. | Dating (Social customs)—Fiction. | Books and reading—Fiction. | Sisters—Fiction.
Classification: LCC PZ7.S3563 (ebook) | LCC PZ7.S3563 Boy 2019 (print) | DDC [Fic]—dc23

Text copyright © 2019 Tiffany Schmidt
Lettering copyright © 2019 Danielle Kroll
Book design by Hana Anouk Nakamura

Printed and bound in U.S.A.
10 9 8 7 6 5 4 3 2 1

Amulet Books are available at special discounts when purchased in quantity for premiums and promotions as well as fundraising or educational use. Special editions can also be created to specification. For details, contact specialsales@abramsbooks.com or the address below.

ABRAMS The Art of Books
195 Broadway, New York, NY 10007
abramsbooks.com

FOR ALL THE OLDER SISTERS
WHO LEAD THE WAY AND ALL
THE YOUNGER SISTERS WHO
BLAZE THEIR OWN TRAILS.

ALSO, FOR RASCAL—MY SNUGGLY
TODDLER SIDEKICK.

"SHE PREFERRED IMAGINARY
HEROES TO REAL ONES . . ."

—Louisa May Alcott, *Little Women*

1

wasn't one of those artists who thought you had to be a tor-
tured soul to create. I could concentrate on a painting while
still remembering to eat, sleep, and shower. I liked both my
ears where they were, so there was no risk of me going Van
Gogh, and I was just as inspired when I was in a good mood as
when I was in a funk.

But if I did require torture, I was pretty sure driving to
school with the boy I loved—and the girl *he* loved—qualified.

Especially when the girl he loved was my sister.

"Rory, come on," Merrilee called from the front hall.
"Toby's beeped twice."

For the first two weeks of school, I'd been the one nudging her—and helpfully reminding her about things like
coats, backpacks, and the annoying crossover-tie part of our
uniform—but Merri had a whole new motivation for Hero
High mornings: The faster she got out the door, the sooner
she got to see her boyfriend, Fielding Williams.

Have I mentioned she was oblivious to Toby's feelings?
And obliviously never shut up about how happy she was, dating his friend.

"Come on! Come on!" she called from the open shotgun seat of Toby's car. "Today's the day Fielding's wearing the socks I picked out for him."

That didn't mean anything to me. Merri, my oldest older sister Lilly, and I had gone out for manicures two nights ago so Merri could fill us in on her newest boyfriend. But if she'd said something about socks, I'd missed it. Or it'd happened while I was in the bathroom. I was still surprised I'd been invited at all. Mom always said that three was the hardest number for including people—"It's all points and corners"—and the default duo in our house was Merri plus Lilly.

Fielding was an impressive upgrade from Merri's first emo-jerk ex, Monroe expelled-from-school-already Stratford, but I had no idea why she was excited about his socks. Maybe my sister had a foot fetish? Ew, gross.

I mentally deleted that thought as I opened the car door and slid into the back seat, passing Merri her forgotten cross-country bag. "Hey, Toby."

"Morning, Roar." The flash of a smile he directed at me as he turned around to back out of our driveway was better than any cup of coffee. Toby's grin was 99 percent perfect, but the 1 percent that would keep him from starring in ads for orthodontists was my favorite part: His second tooth was just the teeniest bit crooked. The type of crooked you'd notice only if you'd sketched it dozens of times. Like, if maybe you had a portfolio hidden in the back of your closet that contained nothing *but* drawings of a certain olive-skinned, dark-eyed, dark-haired Latino boy whose eyelashes made your heart race and whose long fingers gripped the steering wheel of the car driving you to your new school.

"What do you mean, socks?" he asked Merri as he turned down the stereo's volume and pulled onto our street. It was some movie's musical score—always. I don't think Toby owned songs with lyrics. Sometimes I recognized which film and sometimes Merri commandeered the radio. This time she clicked it off.

"Didn't I tell you this story?" And, just like yesterday, I got to watch from the back seat as Merri—the copilot of Toby's dreams, the girl with a permanent claim on shotgun and his heart—twisted the knife in his back. "It's so cute—who knew *Fielding Williams* could be cute? But I don't know if it'll be funny to anyone that's not me. Or him. It's an inside thing—but make sure to compliment his socks today, okay?"

She giggled. I wanted to growl.

Because here's the thing about my "big" sister: She was a peanut. *Maybe* five whole feet if she had on shoes and used her best posture. Her height paired with her personality (think sugar rush, no sugar needed), her looks (a complete checklist for adorable: freckles, perky nose, huge blue-gray eyes, pointy chin), and her intelligence (hello, Mensa) meant that she was irresistible. Merri was the type of girl people instantly *loved*. And it was a good thing she wasn't evil, because she would've made an alluring cult leader. People leaned in when she talked, squished closer to her in crowds, raced for the seat beside hers at tables. Everyone got sucked into her orbit, because it was a place you felt entertained, safe, *cherished*.

Watching her giggle, wrinkle her nose, then reach in her backpack for breakfast bars I hadn't known she'd packed for Toby *and* me—"Yours is vegan, Rory, I checked"—made me understand why everyone loved her. Why *he* loved her. Toby looked at the foil wrapper on his bar like he wanted to bronze it. Instead he ripped it open and took a big bite. There was a purity about Merri, a sweetness beyond all the sugar she consumed.

I wasn't bitter; I was exhausted. Because every time someone said, "Merri's your sister? I *love* her," they followed up by expecting me to be like her. I wasn't. We had the same brown hair, but mine was six inches shorter, cut at my chin. And height-wise, I was six inches taller. I got the double take "You're *younger?*" not just because of our heights but because I had none of the bounce and perk that radiated from Merri. She giggled; I laughed. She chatted; I fretted. She was impulsive; I was introspective. She was comfortable as the center of attention, and I was much happier standing in the corner. Preferably facing the corner with an easel in front of me.

I loved her, but I didn't want to, and couldn't, be her. No matter how much our parents, teachers, and customers at the family dog boutique, Haute Dog, expected it.

Toby didn't though. He'd known us both since the day he arrived next door. Back then, Merri and I were the same height *and* our mom dressed us alike. His adoptive parents had joined the long list of people who assumed we were twins, but tiny Toby could tell us apart. He built sandcastles with me—and stomped them with Merri. Sidewalk art with me—hose nozzle eraser with Merri. We swung on swings and sang songs—they jumped from the monkey bars and got ice packs.

He wasn't the first person to compliment my drawings, but his compliment was the first to make me feel special. I still had, hidden in the same back-of-my-closet portfolio, a crooked three-legged green cat painted in watercolors on warped paper. In the upper left corner, he'd stamped his approval with a prized Batman sticker.

"Oh, we're not getting Eliza today," Merri said when Toby flicked on his blinker to turn down her street.

"This day's looking up already," he said.

"Be nice." Merri poked him in the upper arm and he snapped his teeth playfully at her finger.

"I'm always nice." Toby couldn't stand Eliza, Merri's other best friend, but he still gave her a ride every day to make my sister happy. And Eliza, she *hated* Toby. Though I wasn't sure she liked many people besides Merri and maybe her teachers. Eliza looked like the flippin' snow queen from *Frozen*, which was fitting because her icy attitude was capable of giving anyone in a three-mile radius frostbite. And that was after her brains and beauty had given them inferiority complexes. I was firmly on Team Toby, but Eliza's fierce protectiveness of Merri and refusal to allow any female around her to be trivialized was pretty endearing.

I looked away and hid a yawn against my shoulder. We hadn't even gotten to school and I was already tired.

"Late night painting, Roar?" Toby was an artist himself—a musician—and he understood night owl creativity. But because he was practically perfect, I didn't want him to know the truth. I'd been up late studying and staring at the bright yellow academic warning I'd gotten in math the week before. I was supposed to have returned it on Monday. But Monday at Hero High had been mayhem. The entire school had been dealing with the fallout from the Rogue Romeo party thrown last Friday by Merri's ex-boyfriend. It was the type of party that was *already* part of Hero High lore—*Remember that time Monroe Stratford broke into the school theater and stole the costumes from the school play, and got in a fight with that new girl onstage, and then the party got busted?*

Unlike most of the people who lied and said they'd been there, I *did* remember, because I'd had the starring role of idiot new girl who threw paint on him. I had two Saturday detentions to prove it.

Eventually Mrs. Roberts was going to remember to ask for the academic warning. I could easily forge a signature—handwriting wasn't that different from line drawing. But forgery was purposefully deceptive. Forgetfulness was passive. So I'd been crossing my fingers through every sixth period and hoping it was contagious.

"Hey, sleeping beauty!" Merri turned around in her seat and held out her *I like big books and I cannot lie* travel mug. "You awake back there? I'm out of princes to kiss you. Want my coffee instead?"

"No, I'm fine." I tucked my hair behind my ears and gritted my teeth. Rory might be short for Aurora, but Merri knew I hated *Sleeping Beauty* jokes.

"You sure? It's good." Merri shook her mug, which would've been a better idea if she'd had the lid closed. Instead it splashed all over my uniform, landing in fat milky plops on my white blouse and gray-red-and-navy-plaid skirt. She wrinkled her nose. "Whoops."

"Are you serious, Merrilee?" But while I seethed, Toby groan-chuckled.

"There are paper towels under the seat, Roar. Rowboat, turn around before you do any permanent damage to your sister."

"I'm really sorry, Rory," said Merri. She paused to take a sip, then frowned when she realized her mug was almost empty. "Good thing Eliza's not here—she would *not* have been happy about that."

"Yeah, good thing," I snapped. But it was too late for her to avoid doing permanent damage to me. Not because I was now modeling the latest in caffeine fashions, but because there could be no winner in the race of me chasing him while he was chasing her.

2

The best portion of Merri's morning began as mine was ending. Waiting to open her car door was the headmaster's son. A perfect specimen of dignity and decorum—at least until my sister launched herself out of her seat and into his arms.

"Mer-ri-lee," Fielding sputtered as she twined her arms around his neck and nuzzled into his cheek, messing up his perfect hair and hugging wrinkles into his blazer. But for all his (weak) protests and throat clearing, he grinned down at her like she was some sort of impish miracle. A week ago they weren't dating, and a week ago Toby would've been smiling as he greeted one of his closest friends and talked lacrosse strategies and weekend plans.

Toby sighed behind me, and a better person might have given him privacy to wear whatever emotion he needed to. I wasn't a better person. I was a self-punishing one. I wanted to see his face as he watched them. I wondered if it mirrored my own watching him.

With a grimace, he turned away from the world's most infatuated couple. "Ride home?" he asked me, pointing to the knee brace he now wore over his khakis, courtesy of an idiot from St. Joe's lacrosse team last week. "I'm out for the season, so I can leave whenever you're ready."

"Yes, please." This Friday was looking up. All I had to do was make it through seven periods and I'd get to ride home with *just* him.

Toby scooped his faded red backpack out of the trunk and closed it with white knuckles. Not looking at Merri or Fielding in a way that felt purposeful, he called a hollow "Bye, guys" before gifting me a small smile. "Have a good day, Roar."

"You too." I waved, then curled my fingers in tight, like I could hold on to that smile and use it to float me through my first two obstacles: Advanced Art and English.

The first should have been my favorite class; I couldn't remember a time when art *hadn't* been the axis my life revolved around. While most of my elementary school classmates had been dressing up like superheroes and Disney characters for Halloween, I'd been Degas's *The Star* dancer, Singer Sargent's *Madame X*, Vermeer's *Girl with a Pearl Earring*, and, on the last year Merri let me tag along with her and Toby, Picasso's *Dora Maar*—I'll admit, that one was a mistake. It required way too much explanation and cut down on our candy haul.

From the days of crayons and Batman stickers until my first few days of high school, I'd never doubted my artistic ability. If you gave me an easel and almost any medium, I'd give you something worthy of appreciation. Creating was what I did; it was who I was.

But this was Hero High, where even art betrayed me.

Mrs. Mundhenk had told me that being the only freshman in Advanced Art was an honor and a privilege. She hadn't informed me that every upperclassman in the studio would see it as an invasion.

At first, I'd shrugged off the silent treatment. The muttering that always began a few steps after I passed. I figured I'd prove I belonged among them and win them over. But when Mrs. Mundhenk displayed my drawing from the first week of class as an exemplar, the mutterings grew louder.

I could tune it out. I'd been practicing meditation for years and my bedroom was across the hallway from Merri, who liked to put on headphones and sing. I could tune out most anything—especially when I was drawing. But no amount of meditation was effective against these cold shoulders. Especially once they became actual shoulders and feet knocking into my easel.

I'd thought—wanted to think—they were unintentional. That once, twice, three times a period someone would accidentally jar the back of my easel with their foot or elbow while I had a pencil or paintbrush to the paper. I'd responded to the syrupy "So sorrys" with a tight smile or "It happens" while I tried to figure out how to undo the damage to my pictures. But the sorrys stopped and the nudges increased. My charcoal drawing started to resemble a cracked windshield from all the jagged lines snaking in wrong directions.

It had gotten to the point where I flinched whenever anyone was near my easel. I was more aware of my classmates' movements around the spacious art room than I was of the Cassatt painting I was supposed to be reproducing. It defeated the entire purpose of me being at this school. I could've stayed at the sixth-to-twelfth grade, all-girls magnet school Merri and I had attended up until this year, but Lilly's future mother-in-law had sold my parents on Hero High's renowned art program and then used her US senator status to secure our admission.

I was supposed to be building a great portfolio to show off with college applications, but so far that portfolio was empty. Even my exemplar painting from the first week had been "accidentally" ripped from the wall the previous night, leaving jagged chunks behind.

"I'm so sorry, Aurora." Mrs. Mundhenk had brought the scraps over to show me as I was setting up. "It was like that when I got here. It must've gotten caught on someone's bag or coat. They must not have noticed, because they would've stopped to pick it up or leave a note. I bet whoever it is would be heartbroken if they knew what they'd done."

"Yeah." I gritted my teeth, because how could a teacher be so informed about her subject matter but so ignorant about her students? "Real heartbroken."

I glowered at the sketch in front of me. It wasn't working. I unclipped the Cassatt print and headed to the front of the room where folders of example paintings were stored. The assignment was "Draw a famous painting with your own spin," and I ignored the crowd bickering around the contemporary folder and picked through the others before selecting Seurat's *Le Chahut*.

Back at my easel, I decided my "own spin" would be replacing the pointillist dots and chromo-luminarism with crisp pencil lines, precise shading, and a monochromatic palette. The result would be less neo-impressionist and more photo-realist. At least that was my hope.

"Hey. Can I work here?" I looked up to see Byron standing at the easel beside mine.

I knew *of* him—junior/twin/popular—from my friend Clara's obsession with creating social diagrams, but I didn't *know* him. He'd never assaulted my easel though, and he shared a name with my parents' dog, so that was enough of a reason to say, "Sure."

"Your painting was kicking, by the way. Sorry it got ripped."

"Thanks," I said. Possibly proving why I belonged at the edges. Was "kicking" good? Or had I just said thanks for an insult? Regardless, it was not an adjective I'd be using; it brought to mind all the shoes that had aimed themselves at my easel's legs.

"So, freshman, what should we call you?"

I put down the tortillon I was crushing between my fingers. "What?"

"What should we call you?" His voice had gone up and slowed down—the way Merri talked to dogs. He pointed to himself. "I'm Byron. So far most people in here are calling you 'the prodigy.' Figured you might want a chance to name yourself."

"Oh." Normally being called a prodigy was a good thing? But it didn't sound like it here. "Um, Aurora—Rory."

Byron unpacked his pencils onto the lip of his easel. "Nice to meet you, Aurora-Rory."

My eyes went wide. "No, it's just Rory."

He grinned. "I got that. I was teasing you."

I could've left it right there. That would've been the end of the conversation and I could've gone back to debating whether I needed an accent color to make my shadows pop. But I didn't. I hadn't spoken to anyone in art in so long and it was like I had a buildup of words piled on my tongue. "Why's everyone obsessed with the contemporary art folder? I thought there was going to be a fight over some of those prints."

Byron laughed—and pointed to the print he was clipping to his easel. It was contemporary.

"Not that I have anything against contemporary art," I babbled. I took a deep breath, ordering myself: *Be impressive! Prove you know your stuff.* Instead I mumbled, "That one's nice."

That one's nice? It was Snipes's *Vanity, Captured*—one of the most evocative pieces of the last few decades. It hung in the Guggenheim, and the last time I was there, Merri had literally dragged me away by my hoodie, saying, "How long can you possibly look at a painting of a peacock?" The answer was "Hours" when the artist was Snipes.

"What do you think of my drawing so far?" Byron asked me. "What would you change?" That question was a minefield and I must've grimaced, because he laughed. "Be honest, I can take it."

I took a deep breath and indicated a few places where the angles were off. When he responded positively to that, I suggested he try crosshatched shading and, at his insistence, demonstrated on his drawing.

"You're going to make this class interesting, aren't you?"

Byron held out his hand, palm up. I was pretty sure we'd all given up high fives back in grade school—at least unless sports or grandpas were involved—but I didn't want to leave him hanging, and I didn't have a clue what was cool at Hero High. Feeling more than a little ridiculous, I smacked my palm against his.

He tilted his head. "Oh, well. Sure. Right on, I guess? But actually I wanted your phone. You know, so I can give you my number."

And if it wasn't abundantly clear I wasn't cool before, it was then. But no one had kicked me all period. The only distractions were Byron's frequent requests for help. It didn't bother me, but apparently Mrs. Mundhenk felt differently. "Byron, enough. Let Aurora do her own painting and *you* do yours. Over there."

He sighed as he packed up his materials to move to the other side of the studio. I thought I was in for another of Mrs. Mundhenk's lectures where she mentioned all my "potential" and then made it clear I wasn't living up to it. Instead, she pointed to the boy standing a step behind her. "Have you two met? You're both freshmen, so you must have some classes together."

I nodded. English. Maybe history? "Chuck, right?"

"Huck," he corrected, and before I could cringe, he added, "Let's pretend I thought your name was 'Dory' to make things equal."

As he spoke, he leaned a hip against a metal stool; only, the seat began to spin down, causing him to stumble. He laughed and I smiled. An embarrassment for an embarrassment—it felt good to find a peer.

"We've moved Huck up to Advanced Art. Since it's two weeks into the year, I was hoping you could catch him up and maybe be friends! I think it will be nice for you both to have another freshman in here."

I stared. Mrs. Mundhenk said, "Great," then tapped her clunky red wool clogs together like a folksy Dorothy from Oz. "All right then, carry on."

I watched her retreating back while Huck clipped a piece of scrap paper to the easel beside mine. Maybe now that there were two of us, I'd be less likely to come in and discover my pencil tips broken every morning, my kneaded eraser full of dirt, my thumbnail sketches missing.

I glanced sideways at him. Huck was tall, with a long-limbed gangliness that screamed growth spurt. He was wearing suede navy oxfords with khakis and a red lacrosse jersey. That was Toby's team. I knew nothing about the game beyond sticks and balls. I'd always meant to watch Toby play, but I'd gotten distracted in the space between intention and action, and now his knee injury was keeping him out for the season.

"Um, welcome. Hi." Why was I so awkward all the time? I frowned at my paper. I wished Mrs. Mundhenk hadn't used the word "friends." It made my stomach knot with loneliness. I didn't even know this kid, but those seven letters made my throat itch like patheticness was pollen and I was covered in it.

"Thanks," he answered, but instead of turning toward his own easel, I felt his eyes on me. Maybe if he stared long enough, he could tell me what was wrong with my piece, because something was. The drawing might be technically fine, but it felt . . . spiritless. Lost. A bit like me. Dangit! Why did she have to say *friends*? Now it was all I could think about.

"Why are you looking at me like that?" I snapped when I couldn't take it any longer.

"I'm trying to come up with a way to suggest we be pals without sounding like a creeper . . . or a toddler."

"What?" I whirled toward him, panic-eyed. Had I been thinking out loud? Merri did that sometimes.

His mouth lifted in a mischievous grin that made dimples appear in his cheeks. "Just hear me out a sec. Maybe Mrs. Mundhenk is on to something." He held up a fist, lifting a finger for each reason: "One, we're the only freshmen in Advanced Art and that probably means we both *like* art. Two, we're two of the few freshmen who didn't attend Mayfield Middle Academy and haven't been together since kindergarten. Three, we both have all-day detention tomorrow, and I don't know about you, but I've seen *The Breakfast Club*, so I know that's like friendship boot camp."

"Of course I have." Clearly, he hadn't met Merri, because that answer was obvious. She and rom-coms went together like a wrecking ball and flying bricks, which was often how it felt when she crashed into my room and demanded I watch them with her. "You were at the party too? I thought I was the only freshman."

"I was there. Not my best decision." He shrugged in an

exaggerated motion, his square shoulders brushing the tips of his hair. "I've got more reasons if you're not sold."

"Let's hear them," I said, but honestly he could've stopped after the first one. Or even at zero—just the desire to be my friend was good enough. Did that make me a loser?

"Four, we have a lot of classes together: English, history, French—and if we're friends I can look at the doodles you're always drawing without seeming nosy." He gave me a sheepish one-dimple grin and I laughed. He lifted his thumb. "And five, we both love coffee."

I wrinkled my nose. "No. I don't."

"You don't want to be friends?" He cringed, but he was quick to hold up both palms and say sincerely, "That's cool—I didn't mean to pressure you or anything."

He turned to his easel and I fought the urge to smack my palm against my forehead. "No," I clarified. "Yes, we can maybe be friends—but no to coffee. I hate it."

"As your friend . . ." He paused dramatically. I snorted and nodded. "I regret to inform you that you're wearing a whole lot of something you hate on your shirt."

"My sister got a little enthusiastic with her travel mug." I'd put down my pencil somewhere midconversation and fully turned toward him. A strange sensation fluttered under my ribs—not quite hope, but at least not the bleak despair I'd felt since my first week here. "Does that invalidate reason number five?"

He shook his head. "Five, I *really* like coffee, and now I don't have to worry about you stealing mine." I laughed, but his face was earnest when he added, "Seriously though, no pressure on the friendship thing. I can stop working on our friendship bracelets anytime."

I snorted again. I knew he was joking, that this whole conversation was wink, nod nonsense, but dangit, part of me wished it was real. That it was possible to fast-forward through awkward and get-to-know-you and be instant BFFs. I'd never had a "best" friend. I'd been a part of the group but never the other half of anyone's necklace.

Clara, the only other friend I'd made at Hero High, was still mad I'd gone to the Rogue Romeo party without her. It didn't matter that the party had ended with me being escorted home by Headmaster Williams or that I'd be spending the next two Saturdays in detention while she was cheerleading at football games. Apparently not inviting her had violated some fledgling friendship code.

Everything about Hero High dynamics exhausted me: trying to interpret my classmates' subtle changes of expression, inside jokes, secret crushes, and historic rivalries. I'd given up on finding a spot for myself in the preestablished invisible social hierarchy they'd brought with them from their private middle school.

I flicked a curl of pencil shaving at Huck. "Let's call it a friendship test drive."

"I'll take it." He bent over his easel where he'd been making lazy shading gradients. I don't think he meant for me to see how relieved his exhale was. Did it make me a bad friend if I was glad that maybe I wasn't the only one so lonely at Hero High?

3

Huck and I didn't talk for the rest of class. Maybe we were both worried about doing or saying something awkward and scaring each other off . . . Or maybe that was just me.

When the bell rang, I shoved my pencil bag in my backpack and rinsed off my charcoal-smudged fingers. Normally I raced out of the room, like the side-eyes and snide comments were chasing me, but now I paused with my hand on the door. On the wall beside me was a giant display about the school's founder: Reginald R. Hero. He'd been an artist—a famous tile maker—and because of that, the arts program here was endowed and supplied in ways I'd only dreamed about in my charter school classes last year. When Huck caught up, I shuffled my feet. "Um, ready for English?"

My personal answer was *No, never*, but he flashed his dimples. "Let's go get our Gatsby on."

I groaned and my fingers tightened around the strap of my bag. "Don't tell me you're enjoying that book."

Huck pulled a water bottle out of his backpack. "So far it's a story about rich people and parties. What's not to like?"

Well, my family certainly didn't qualify as the former—not with all the loans for Lilly's college, the bills from her upcoming wedding to the senator's son, and the Hero High tuition that wasn't covered by financial aid. And from "Ring Around the Rosy" through Rogue Romeo, I'd never fit in at parties. So, there was quite a lot not to like in Huck's statement.

"I just don't get the book."

"I'm sure you'll figure it out," said Huck as we reached the classroom door. "Besides, I don't think it matters *what* Ms. Gregoire makes us read; she's always going to make it sound fun. It's pretty much a consensus on the lacrosse team—if Ms. Gregoire's not your favorite teacher on campus, you're doing something wrong."

I'd had a similar conversation with Clara last week. She'd practically inserted Ms. Gregoire's name in the first cheer she'd learned on her new squad. And at every family dinner, Merrilee practically levitated while talking about how great she was. Merri thought she was magical. "Like, *literally* magical, Rory. She makes stuff from the books happen in her students' lives. Eliza doesn't believe me, but pay attention and see what you think."

I was paying attention. I was paying such close attention that my notes were practically a transcript of her lectures: *"I don't want you to analyze, I want you to invest—put yourself in the story. I want you to immerse yourself in these words, then give me your personal reaction."*

What did that even mean? Because whatever it was, I was doing it wrong. I'd be lucky to make it to Halloween without getting a second yellow academic warning.

Huck winked at me and headed to his seat halfway around the circle. As I sat at my desk, Clara did the same thing she'd done all week—averted her face and sighed loudly.

I was way too exhausted to endure another period of her silent treatment. Except, here in this classroom, wishes had a way of coming true in weird, warped outcomes, because Clara turned and spoke to me for the first time since Monday's *"I don't understand how you could go to that party and not bring me!"*

"Oh, it's *you.*" Her words were neither quiet nor logical. Who else would be in my assigned seat? It didn't make her disdain hurt less. I liked Clara. I liked her a lot. She'd been the first person to smile at me when I'd been hovering in the corner during last summer's freshman orientation. She'd excused herself from a conversation and come over, saying, "You're new! Come sit with me. I know most of this stuff already because my brother, Penn, is a junior here. Plus, I already know practically every other freshman in this room. I'll tell you about them if you tell me about you!"

We'd texted all summer. She'd hugged me on my first day and saved me a seat in every class we shared. Until the Rogue Romeo party, we'd sat together at lunch and in Convocation, which was a whole-school assembly at the end of every day. This week I'd been back to chilling with the dust bunnies in the corners. I was over it.

I leaned forward and whispered, "Are you ever going to forgive me? What if I promise to never go to a party without you again? Or just never go to a party?" The second option was way more appealing.

"Did someone say 'party'?" asked Ms. Gregoire as she breezed in from the hall in a jewel-green sleeveless maxi dress. The fabric was printed with gold foil eyeglasses, which matched the gold sandals peeping out below the hem. The colors complemented her dark red hair perfectly; the bangles on her wrist added a tinkling punctuation to her gestures. I had to give it to her; no matter what I thought of her assignments, she knew how to dress. And make an entrance.

She reminded me of a more stylish Ms. Frizzle from *The Magic School Bus*, only instead of science, she got way over-enthusiastic about books. One day in class I'd kept track of the number of times she'd made comments about "seeing ourselves in the story"—by the time the period ended, I was at seventeen.

So far, we were two chapters into *The Great Gatsby* and the only thing I saw was confusion. I didn't need more than thirty-eight pages; I was over this book already. It annoyed me as much as Merri's dog—also named Gatsby because my sister *loved* this novel as much as her drooly, shedding mutt. But then again, she'd chosen Fielding over Toby, so clearly her taste in all things was questionable.

"Thank you all for your beautiful reaction pieces on the opening chapters," Ms. Gregoire enthused once we'd all settled in and unpacked for the period. "Some of you are *there*! And some of you are *almost* there." Our desks were arranged in a ring, which made the center feel like a stage and always made her speeches feel like theater-in-the-round. She had a habit of walking in circles as she spoke, and she was leaning against my desk when she added, "Some of you haven't quite made it to West Egg yet, but I have high hopes."

I knew that was a story reference—the book took place on two imaginary islands off Long Island: East Egg and West Egg. And from the way she was discreetly tapping a finger on my desk as she spoke, I was pretty sure I was the "some of you" who was too dumb to get it.

I'd been the slowest in a class before. I'd been the one who needed extra help. But usually I could identify what it was I didn't understand. With *The Great Gatsby* I felt lost. So much of what filled the pages didn't seem to matter, or if it did, I couldn't figure out why.

Did we need a whole page describing a billboard for an eye doctor? Was that important? What about the dog Tom buys for his mistress? Merri said any time there was a pet in a story, it was significant. She could give whole speeches about Hedwig. But this dog didn't even have a name.

In the first chapter, Daisy had said she hoped her daughter would be "a beautiful little fool," and that's how I felt while reading. But unlike Daisy, I didn't think that was "the best thing a girl can be in this world." Or maybe Daisy didn't really think that? I couldn't keep up with the lies and posturing of these characters.

"Today, let's read together." Ms. Gregoire proposed this with breathy enthusiasm, high eyebrows, and a dramatic inhale, like she was waiting for us all to clap or cheer for her suggestion.

And dangit, when I looked around the classroom, everyone else seemed ready to pull out pom-poms or do the wave. Clara was hugging her book to her chest. Dante was drumming his dark fingers on his cover. Huck had already flipped to the page.

"Do I have any volunteers to read?" she asked. Every hand in the room went up. Well, every hand except for mine. "How wonderful. Let's see . . ." She tapped her lip and rotated as I slumped down in my seat. "We're going to read a few pages, then stop and discuss. How about Keene, Clara, Dante, Elinor, Gemma, and Huck. Does everyone remember who's reading before them? Huck, I'm going to stop you before you get to the bottom of your page. Don't be surprised when I interrupt."

Keene's page was a description of Gatsby's party prep. Clara took over for even more description—an endless thread about his juicer and its two-hundred-orange capacity. Was that exciting back in Fitzgerald's day? Was that their small talk? Instead of showing off their latest cell phone, they'd brag about the size of their juicer? I sighed and tried to follow along, but what even was "yellow cocktail music"?

I didn't belong in this classroom. Not with them all grabbing pens to underline and annotate *while* we read. I could either move my finger along *or* try to process it.

At least something had finally happened. By the time Elinor read, the narrator—new boy in town, Nick Carraway—had been invited to one of Gatsby's famous parties. He spent the whole of Gemma's page walking around and feeling uncomfortable. Maybe this was it? Maybe this was me finally having my moment of textual connection? Because painful awkwardness at parties was my MO. Nick's description of the way people stared at him when he asked where to find Gatsby—that's exactly how I'd felt at the Rogue Romeo party last week when I was given endless *Who are you and why are you here?* looks.

"Annnnnd, stop," Ms. Gregoire told Huck. "Good class today, people."

But wait. We were forty-four pages in and hadn't met Gatsby! Was that what made him "great"? Did he not appear anywhere on these 180 pages?

Was this one of those trick endings to make the reader feel dumb? Like that play Merri dragged me to where they waited the whole time for that guy Godot to show up and he never did?

"Aurora?" Ms. Gregoire stopped by my desk as everyone else packed up. "I'd like to speak to you after class. I'll write you a pass for your next teacher. Or would you rather talk after school?"

I'd rather not do it at all. Was that a choice? I picked C: *Let's pretend this conversation never happened.*

I stared at a smudge of charcoal I'd missed on my pinkie. "After class is fine."

Clara paused to give me a grim nod of support. Huck gave me a salute with two fingers from the forehead. I managed a half smile in response before Ms. Gregoire shooed them out the door. "Aurora, let's talk about you and how you're handling this book."

I gripped the cover with both hands, feeling the paperback's corners curl under my fingers. "What about it?"

"When we met after school on Monday, we discussed the trouble you were having connecting to the short stories."

"Yes." What more was there to say? I'd been there for that conversation on my failings; I didn't need to relive it.

"I've since read your paper on Shirley Jackson's 'The Lottery'—and it almost seemed like you were equating being admitted to Advanced Art to being selected for the titular lottery."

"What? No. I want to be in Advanced Art. I don't think anyone wants to be chosen to be stoned." Which I was pretty sure was what happened to the lottery winner in the story. And I was telling the truth, or at least mostly. Unless subconsciously I was writing about how awful art class was? "I—I didn't mean it?"

"Uh-huh," said Ms. Gregoire. "Well, regardless, I'm hoping to see you form a stronger connection with *this* novel. How do you feel you're doing?"

"Fine?"

"Good." She smiled at me. "So which characters are you identifying with the most?"

"Um . . ." I was not prepared for this pop quiz. She'd leaned forward. With her folded hands and her eye contact, she was a portrait of attentiveness and interest. Now I just needed an answer.

Who was I supposed to identify with? Nick Carraway—the newbie in town, an outsider with plenty of privilege and connections but not nearly as much money? Daisy Buchanan—the pretty girl who whisper-talked and was either vapid or fake-vapid? It certainly wasn't Tom, Daisy's racist, abusive, cheating husband.

"What if I don't identify with any of them? These characters all feel the same. Everyone's rich, white, and beautiful.

I mean, I'm white, but . . ." I trailed off, cheeks blazing. Did that sound like I was fishing for her to say I was beautiful? Not what I meant. *Dangit.*

"Fair point." She nodded. "Thankfully the books we read throughout the year will contain diverse characters, but I'm also not asking you or your classmates which one you *look* the most like. I'd hope that regardless of gender, race, appearance, orientation, background, or abilities, there's a shared level of humanity and common ground you could connect with. Or even reject." She paused. "That's a reaction too. I don't expect your default to be agreement."

"Oh." I fanned the pages with my thumbnail. "Then maybe Nick Carraway? I'm new too and definitely an outsider."

"Really?" Ms. Gregoire gave her head a small shake. "That's unexpected. Hmm. *Nick?* Are you sure?"

So clearly there had been a right answer and I hadn't given it. "Who were you thinking?"

"While I see where you're coming from about the outsider perspective—Hero High is a tough assimilation—Nick isn't the only outsider in the book." She leaned back and waited for me to connect the dots. When I didn't, she spread her hands like she was lifting up a tray. "Gatsby!"

"Gatsby?" I gave a short, uncomfortable laugh. "But we haven't even met him." Had we? Was I so confused that I'd missed the part where he appeared?

"Exactly!" Ms. Gregoire thumped her hands on her lap like I'd made a brilliant point. "And most of your classmates would say the same thing about *you*. It's that enigma piece—you both have it. Lots of intrigue and dazzle, but no one is allowed too close. And the speculation—well, it just swirls about you both."

Speculation? About me? That I hadn't heard, but my teacher had. Great.

She was still looking at me expectantly. "Um, I hope no one here thinks I killed a man." I swallowed and clarified. "You know, like how the party guests whisper that about Gatsby?"

Ms. Gregoire tittered. "So you *were* listening. I wondered. You looked a million miles away during class."

"I don't get this book," I confessed. "Yellow music, orange juice . . ." I flipped to the page where we'd stopped. "What does 'spectroscopic gayety' even mean? And if I don't understand the words, how am I going to get symbols and stuff?"

Ms. Gregoire waved away my question with a graceful swipe of gold fingernails. "I'm much less concerned about your vocabulary or grasp of symbolism than I am about what this book *means to you*. You've got so much to say. You just need to be willing to risk trying."

I reached up to cup my forehead with both hands while I stared down at my desk. "I'm not smart like Merri. I'm going to disappoint you if you expect that."

"Oh, Aurora, no. That's simply not true." She sat back in her seat like she was stunned. "There are so many ways to be smart." I caught the pointed look she gave at my charcoal-stained fingers. "Your talents aren't lesser, they're just different. And I know you Campbell girls are going to do extraordinary things here."

I wasn't sure about *this* Campbell girl, but maybe Merri could be extraordinary enough for both of us. The bell rang and I shoved my book in my bag. "I need to get to science, but I'll do better. I promise."

"Rory." Ms. Gregoire put a hand on my arm as I stood. "All you need to do is be yourself. People are here to know you, help you. You just need to *be*."

I scrunched my face up. I would not cry. I wouldn't. "I'm trying so hard."

"Maybe you're putting all your effort into the wrong things," said Ms. Gregoire gently as she handed me a pass. "Using it to keep people out instead of letting them in or letting them help."

"Maybe," I answered, but her voice sounded hopeful and mine did not.

4

My math classroom was a circus of color and posters, each begging to be that day's distraction. It was like an inspiration factory threw up on the walls in the form of kittens and athletes and fancy hand lettering and *You've got this* clichés.

This fountain of encouragement all flowed from the kindest teacher on my schedule. I glanced at the smiling black woman who was currently crouched beside Elinor's desk, nodding and pointing. Despite what Mrs. Roberts *and* all the posters said, I didn't "got this"—I hadn't the faintest grasp of geometric proofs or linear equations.

Mrs. Roberts had given us fifteen minutes to complete fifteen problems. There were two minutes left. I was on problem number four. I was pretty sure the first three were wrong.

I frowned at a poster of a joyful bee. It read *Failure only starts when you stop trying.* No, actually, failure "started" when you scored below sixty-four. I knew this from experience.

I wanted to be in my bedroom so badly I could practically feel the texture of my doorknob beneath the fingers I was clenching in my lap. The brass circle was dotted with daubs of paint, dried in layers and smears until the metal barely peeked through. The walls behind my door were white—not that they were visible. I'd started tacking up my own sketches and prints from my favorite artists long before I had permission to do so.

I kept my art supplies organized in the turret. Each of our bedrooms had something that made them *ours*. Lilly's had its own bathroom. Merri's had a balcony that she used as an escape route for visiting Toby. Mine had a tower. The windows on all sides meant I had a ton of natural light. The low perimeter shelves that Merri claimed were begging for books—I used them to store canvases, brushes, paint, pastels, charcoal, ink, nibs, palettes, and a lifetime's worth of sketchbooks.

And that's where I wanted—no, needed—to be. Wearing yoga pants and one of Dad's old dress shirts as a smock, with my fishbowl burbling cheerfully. A blank page in front of me, a pencil in my hand. The freedom to take everything explosive and suffocating inside me and turn it into lines and shapes and shading.

Drawing wasn't a physical release in the way Merri described running or the way Clara said she felt after kickboxing. Toby would sag with relief after pounding out a particularly demanding piece on piano. My art was escape. It was centering. It wasn't possible to spend hours focusing entirely on creating while *also* stressing about real-life problems. Like how I had enough trouble with math when it was just numbers. Once they threw letters into the mix, I was over my head.

One minute left. I was still on problem four. *X* and *Y* still taunted me.

They straight-up laughed two minutes later when my answers weren't close to correct. Though, according to the top-hat-wearing monkey on a poster by the pencil sharpener, *You lose the same points if you're wrong by one or wrong by one hundred. Check your work!*

"Let's get an answer from someone we haven't heard from yet." Mrs. Roberts's gaze roamed across the rows and I ducked. My math survival plan was *Keep your head down and write everything down.* The first so I wouldn't be called on, the second in the hope it'd eventually make sense.

"Miss Campbell, what do you have?"

And like my score on my last pop quiz, my survival plan was zero percent effective.

"Um, I'm still working on it." Technically, I was working on problem four. She'd asked for number eight.

"We can wait." Mrs. Roberts drummed the electronic marker she was holding against her navy slacks. She favored dark, solid colors but paired them with gorgeous broaches or statement necklaces. Today's pin was a hammered copper dragonfly that glowed against her dark skin and burgundy blouse. Her lip stain matched her shirt and her lips stretched into an encouraging smile as she said, "Go ahead and finish up."

I opened my mouth to protest, then snapped it shut when I thought I might vomit instead. There were twelve other students in this class. Add in the teacher and that made twenty-six eyes staring at me. See, I could do *some* math. Just not this stupid geometry. I didn't need to prove that a triangle's angles added up to 180 degrees. If the textbook told me it was true,

I'd believe it. "Go on now," said Mrs. Roberts, a hint of some faded southern twang creeping into her voice.

I picked up my pencil, but my hand was shaking so hard it created a seismograph reading in my notebook instead of a diagram. "Can you come back to me?" I squeaked.

"Why, sure." Mrs. Roberts's brown eyes were sympathetic, but how could she not see this was torture? "You keep working, we'll circle back."

I looked at the book again. At the example on the board. At the shoulders of the guys who sat on either side of me. One was scratching the back of his neck, and the other kicked the desk in front of him as he crossed and uncrossed his ankles. Clara was behind me, but there was no inconspicuous way to turn around, and I doubted she'd help me anyway.

"Aurora?" Mrs. Roberts prompted. "You ready with number eight?"

"Thirty-six?" I crossed my fingers.

She shook her head. "Not quite. Why don't you take another crack at it and I'll be over in a moment to help you. The rest of you, start problems sixteen to twenty."

I drew a slash through my calculations and flipped to a clean page, where I dutifully recopied the problem and tried again. Thirty-six. The posters mocked me—*Never stop asking questions.* Well, I'd mastered that part. It was understanding the answers that baffled me.

Mrs. Roberts caught my eye and held up a one-minute finger, then bent back over the notebook of the kid she was helping.

I stood and crossed the classroom. By the door, right above the hook holding the bathroom pass, was a poster that read *You can't be a smart cookie with a crummy attitude!* I wondered where *tossing* your cookies fit in that equation, but I wasn't going to stick around to find out.

The last thing I saw as the door shut behind me was the rainbow-hued poster on the back: *It's a good day to have a good day.*

I tried not to gag on the irony: Every day at Hero High was . . . not good. I rushed into the bathroom. Not the most creative of hiding spots, but I didn't have many options. I spent five minutes doubled over in a stall trying to get into a meditative headspace and slow my breathing. My eyes traced the lines of the tile grout and fixated on the one that was set slightly crooked. I was that crooked tile, the one that stood out in a row of matching perfection. The mistake.

Hello, rock bottom. Because why else would I be comparing myself to bathroom tiles?

"Rory, are you in here?" If I couldn't tell who it was by the voice that managed to be both bubbly and authoritative, I would've been able to tell by the shoes outside my stall. Only Clara paired her Hero High uniform with designer sneakers covered in navy blue glitter. I was pretty sure they'd come presparkled from Fifth Avenue, but I wouldn't put it past Clara to glitterize them herself. "Mrs. Roberts sent me to check on you. There's only three minutes left in class."

I slowly slid the latch and peeked out the door. "Does this mean you're talking to me again?"

Clara had a curl twined around her finger. She straightened her hair on Tuesdays and Thursdays. On Mondays, Wednesdays, and Fridays, she "let it do its own thing," which was perfect blond spirals. She gave it a tug and let go, then pointed a manicured finger at me. "Fine. I'm talking to you again. But next time, you'd better tell me when you have the good gossip. I could've warned you Monroe Stratford was trouble. He's had a mean streak since elementary school—I totally would've called him using you to get back at Merri for their breakup."

"Well, then you would've been right."

"And what was up with using me as a party-alibi without letting me know? That's, like, sneaking around 101." She pushed the stall door open and pulled me out. "Face it, Rory Campbell, you need me."

"You're right." I rolled my eyes but gave her a smile.

"Good." She gave a sharp nod of her chin. "Also, could you pay attention? Bancroft and Dante are about to pull a muscle or fall out of their desks trying to give you the answer."

"Give me what?" Was she referring to the same two guys who sat on either side of me and had spent the whole period avoiding eye contact?

"Hello! Scratching their necks, crossing their ankles, left sleeve above the elbow?" Clara raised her eyebrows. "Don't tell me you forgot the— Oh wait!" She smacked her forehead. "You weren't in fourth grade when we made it up. Well, don't worry about that now. I'll teach you the code later."

"You all cheat?" This was surprisingly satisfying. Maybe the whole class was as clueless as me. I guess at least *one* kid had to get it, but maybe all the answers rippled from them.

"Not really. Never on tests. Just during class so things like today don't happen. There are rules. I'll teach you them along with the code. Now wash your hands so we can head back."

They'd wanted to help me. I pumped soap onto my palm and rubbed it into lather. My classmates had tried to help me. Of course, because I wasn't one of them, I hadn't understood their help. But they'd tried! And that was enough to make me not want to escape down the drain with the soap I was rinsing off.

Clara watched me in the mirror as she adjusted her headband. She handed me a paper towel, then she swung the bathroom door open wide. "By the way, the answer is X equals one-twenty."

5

"A re you going to the club fair?" asked Huck. He'd drifted over from his locker as I struggled to open mine. I hated all numbers right now—the ones on my lock's dial, the ones in math class answers, and especially the ones that made up my class averages. Huck bumped my hand out of the way and gave the lock a twist and a tug. It fell open, no combination necessary. "Are you a joiner?"

I laughed as I thought about all the things I was failing to juggle: schoolwork, artwork, work-work at the family dog boutique. "I don't have time to be a joiner, but feel free to join away."

"So, that's a no. Between orchestra, school, and sports, I don't know if I do either. Speaking of, if you feel like going to a lacrosse game, I'll actually see playing time today."

I pointed to my chest. "Grounded. And I don't do sports." It wasn't the first game of the season, but it was the first Toby was missing. There was probably some symbolism or irony or something literary in this, but I was barely passing English, so I wasn't going to attempt it. "But good luck."

"Thanks." He held up a hand for a fist bump, one he finished with fireworks and explosion sounds when my knuckles made reluctant contact with his—thereby destroying any fears I had of him thinking nonplatonically. "See you bright and early, detention buddy."

I started to walk away, then turned back. "If you do go to the club fair, don't sign me up for anything."

His dimples popped out in a devilish grin. "It's like you know me already."

It only took the walk across campus to undo the smile Huck had gifted to me. Around me people were calling names across paths, meeting in hugs, texting on phones. Tables lined the walkways and the students behind them manned clipboards and chatted as they recruited classmates. Everyone was part of this place and making more connections by the moment. They all gave each other pieces of their days, of their time, of themselves. I didn't have any pieces to spare.

Like the parties at Gatsby's house, everything at Hero High whirled faster and faster. A glittering swirl of *Look over here, disaster on your right, humiliation on your left, social isolation dead ahead.* Spinning out of control until I was a dizzy top starting to wobble, about to fall. What would happen if I stopped for a moment? Would I ever be able to catch up again?

Anyone who said "Just ask for help" didn't understand there was nothing *just* about that sentence. Thinking about it in class made my hands damp and my head spin until I was missing even more information. The one time I *had* tried, pausing at the end of math class to ask Mrs. Roberts to reexplain the last problem, she'd opened her mouth and talked and written numbers on the board, but all I'd been aware of was the blood pounding in my ears, the rigidness of every one of my muscles as I stood there pretending I understood. My throat grew tighter and tighter, so I could only nod frantically when she wrote $X = 12$ and asked, "Does that make more sense?"

Toby wasn't waiting at his car. I sank down on the asphalt of the parking lot, leaning against his tire and unzipping my backpack, like doing something would make me feel less conspicuous. Not that anyone could see me sitting between Toby's Audi and the Bimmer one spot over—but there were people and voices all around. My backpack was crammed with every book and notebook from my locker, and each was equally untempting. Did I start with the classes I was still passing or with the one I was failing? If I spent too much time pretending I could figure out math, my other grades would suffer. If I didn't figure out how to "connect" to *Gatsby* soon, I'd be moving from West Egg to Academic Probation.

I closed my eyes and picked a notebook. Geometry. How was it possible that I could draw all those shapes, but the math of figuring out their areas and angles baffled me?

Toby *had* promised me a ride home, right? Maybe he'd decided to board the team bus and ride along to the lacrosse game as a spectator. Or maybe he was at the club fair signing up for replacement activities. Or waiting outside Merri's detention. Since she hadn't actually attended her ex's party, just been there to pick me up when it got busted, she had after-school detentions instead of all day Saturday.

Or Toby could've forgotten me. The notebook in my lap blurred as tears rolled off my cheeks to add watermarks to my geometric proofs.

"Hey, sorry I'm late." I hadn't noticed Toby approaching, but now his feet were right in front of me. The white soles of his sneakers—shoes that he hated pairing with khakis but that his doctor insisted he wear while in the knee brace—were an inch from my knee. "Merri asked me to swing by the club fair and sign her up for lit magazine and creative writing club. Only, she asked Eliza too, so the two of us got into it above a clipboard. You know how it is."

I nodded, but with my chin down, sniffing back tears and hoping my face hadn't gone all splotchy.

"Rory?" He crouched down as much as his knee brace would allow and flipped through the splattered and doodled pages of my notebook. I bit the inside of my lip to stop it from quivering. But he saw it anyway. He saw everything . . . except for the thing that mattered most. "What's going on?"

"I'm . . . lost."

He stood and held out a hand to help me up. "We're not talking about just math, are we?"

I shook my head. A dangerous motion with eyes that were pooling wet again. "It's everything about this school. It's the classes, the students, the studio—everything."

He tugged me into a hug and I tried not to turn into a blubbering mess that left tear and snot marks all over his shirt. He already saw me like I was five—no need to give him visuals to back that up. He rubbed my back and asked, "Do you know how to navigate at sea?"

I laughed against his shirt, inhaling the mint and lic-orice smell of him and letting the adorable randomness of his thoughts make me smile. "No."

"Sailors need three fixed points. Then no matter where they're going, they know where they are." He pulled back and gripped both of my shoulders, studying me in that way that no one else did. Like he saw me, not as a tagalong or an incon-venience but as a person. "Well, Aurora Leigh Campbell, let's find you some points. You have a family that loves you. You're a super-talented artist. You get motion-sick on the teacups."

I made a face. Not at the last one—that was sorta charm-ing, because I couldn't believe he remembered—but at the first two.

And he caught it. "Not feeling the family/artist thing right now?"

"Not so much."

"Okay. You're Aurora Leigh Campbell. Teacups, a weak-ness for anything key lime flavored, and you pick the third. Something that's not going to change."

That was easy: *I'm Aurora Leigh Campbell. I get sick on the teacups, key lime is my favorite flavor . . . and I'm hopelessly in love with Tobias May.*

6

My first detention landed on the last weekend of September. Did that mean fresh starts and blank slates applied Monday morning? If so, I only had to make it another forty-eight hours.

I was standing in front of the kettle waiting for it to whistle when Mom picked up my empty mug. "I'm holding this hostage until you look at me, Aurora."

I turned and met her eyes. They were stern inside slightly crooked eyeliner. Her lipstick was pressed into a thin line of disapproval. Mom never went anywhere without makeup. I don't know that I'd recognize her smile without the peach hue she'd been wearing for years. Her smile was like Merri's— the type that was charming and welcoming—but she hadn't smiled at me much lately. I looked around for Dad. All three of us were daddy's girls; Mom was the disciplinarian. "Good morning."

"Is it?" She arched an eyebrow. It was the same look I'd seen Lilly practice in the mirror when she was trying to look stern or lawyerly. "Saturday detention. This goes on your record. Are you taking this seriously? Do you know how lucky it is that you weren't expelled?"

Okay, I made a bad decision letting Monroe talk me into attending his Rogue Romeo party. But at least I didn't *date* him. If we were ranking lapses in judgment, Merri's was worse . . . even if no one else in my family saw it that way.

I nodded solemnly to acknowledge Mom's lecture, but I guess that wasn't contrite enough because she shook her head. "Have you thought about the consequences of your actions? Including that your sister ended up with a week of detention because she came to rescue you?"

"I didn't ask her to!" I snapped. And Merri had gotten a new boyfriend out of the deal. She and Fielding started dating somewhere between our midnight ride home with his father and whatever the two of them did to end up in separate detention halls. Plus, I never would have *gone* to the party if it weren't for Merri needling me about how all the boys liked *her*, with a pointed jab at Toby. Like I needed that reminder.

Merri flounced in and plucked a box of store-brand Pop-Tarts from the cabinet. "If you ask me, Rory didn't need rescuing."

Of course I did. I needed a literal lifeguard to save me from myself right now. But saying that in the kitchen with Mom in lecture mode, Merri humming while getting a sugar high, and Lilly slumped against the counter didn't feel right. I didn't have time for the fallout. Didn't want to expose my screwups before I'd done damage control.

Everyone was still looking at me. Right. Because I needed to answer. I needed to say something clever that combined gratitude with *Don't look too closely*. And I needed to have thought of it about thirty seconds sooner. A combination that was guaranteed to make my mind go blank. Merri stopped bouncing and removed the Pop-Tart wannabe she'd been holding between her lips while she poured orange juice. She tilted her head in concern. "Rory?"

Say something. Anything! I exhaled in a rush. "Well, who asked you? Not me."

Merri's face went blank and she shrugged like she'd expected that. Like *Why wouldn't Rory lash out and act mean?* But that's not what I meant. Not at all. Seeing her face from the stage at the party had been the one minute I'd felt safe all night. I needed a conversational mulligan.

"Well, I don't care if anyone asked me," said Lilly. She was pouring coffee into two travel thermoses. She put one in her purse and started drinking the other immediately. "It's super inconvenient that Rory decided to go wild-child party animal right now. It throws off everyone's work schedules. I've had this appointment with the florist for two months. Do you know how hard it is to find someone who can match whites?"

I didn't know about matching lilies to dress fabric, but mixing up paint colors and trying to get a perfect match? I was very familiar with that. Not that hers was an actual question. "Whoa, bridezilla. Next time I get a detention, I'll consult your schedule first."

"Next time?" The arc of Mom's headshake went from one shoulder to the other. "There better not be a next time, Aurora Leigh Campbell."

"Next time doesn't help me *now*," Lilly muttered into her travel mug as she snatched up her planner full of fabric

samples and business cards and bridal magazine clippings. "I
can't believe I have to go to the store before this appointment.
No one better get dog hair on me! Because you know Lucinda
will make it A. Thing."

I didn't apologize again. It wouldn't matter. I was serious
about the bridezilla thing and sick of *Lucinda Caulkins this*
and *Lucinda Caulkins that.* The wedding planner her fiancé's
mother had hired fed Lilly's expectations that everyone
should bend over backward because she wanted to wear a
puffy dress and change her last name. Or maybe *not* change
her last name. I didn't know, but now wasn't the right time to
ask. Not when she was still grumbling into the bottom third
of a very large and rapidly emptying thermos of coffee and
making angry notes that looked like a hit list in her planner.
She wrote Ask Lucinda!!! on top in ransom note letters and
underlined it three times.

"You okay?" I asked her, because she wasn't the Campbell
most likely to go nuclear. That was . . . I glanced at Merri,
who'd finished her toaster pastry and was sitting on the floor
eating a bite of dry cereal, then tossing the next scoop to her
dog, Gatsby. Yeah, that was me.

"I'm fine. I mean, why wouldn't I be? Just because there's
more things on my to-do list than hours in the day and
Lucinda keeps emailing me *Just checking if you've made a
decision about this or that,* when *this* or *that* hadn't even
occurred to me as a thing that needs deciding! Comparing
three nearly identical napkins to the curtains in the dining
room? Who does that? Well, besides *me,* since that's how
I'll be spending my night. And don't get me started on her

comments about 'foundation garments' and 'controlling the jiggle.'" Lilly took another gulp of coffee and smoothed her hands over her hips.

Should I remind her that she looked like a plus-size Jackie O and that Trent loved her jiggle? Or would that be obnoxious coming from the sister who had fewer curves than a ruler? Normally Lilly was super body positive. Maybe it was a joke? Ugh, Merri would know how to respond, but she was busy getting Gatsby to balance a Cheerio on his nose and had missed the whole exchange.

"When will you be home from detention?" asked Lilly.

"Um, three?"

"I should be back from my cross-country meet by one. I'll come right to the store," offered Merri.

"If you take a picture of the curtains, I can help with complementary napkin colors," I offered. "The bridesmaids' dresses are burgundy, right?"

"Mine's MoH gold," added Merri.

Every time she flaunted her maid-of-honor status—or, as she called it, "MoH," pronounced "moe"—I wanted to scream. *We get it, you two are closer. You're her first pick, her best friend. You're the one who gets to give a speech and get a special dress, and you can save her at the store while I make her late for appointments. Message received.*

"Sorry, it's all gone, Gatsby." Merri stood and stretched her arms above her head. She had on the red shorts of her cross-country uniform, but they disappeared beneath the hem of an oversized Hero High sweatshirt when she dropped her arms back down.

"Is that—" I bit my lip. "Whose sweatshirt is that?" Because Merri had a habit of collecting Toby's too-smalls and repurposing them as her own, but this would still fit him. And seeing her collarbone peek through the neck hole as the sweatshirt slid off one of her shoulders made me want to tear it from her body.

"Fielding's." She beamed and bounced. "I stole it. Figured it might bring me luck today."

"He's coming to cheer for you, right, Mer-bear?" asked Dad. He kissed us each on the top of our heads as he entered the kitchen, then beelined to the coffeepot. "I'm sorry I can't be there."

"It's no big deal. I'm actually *not* a fan of people cheering for me. It's too much like being yelled at—all that 'Go faster, Merrilee!' 'Catch her!'—it sounds so . . . disapproving and aggressive. Besides, Eliza will be there and Fielding is coming. I've given him a list of things he can cheer."

"Next race, promise," said Dad while Mom took their Pomeranian, Byron, out for one last pee break. Dad refilled Lilly's mug, and I wanted to warn him she was already over-caffeinated and a stress mess. "I wish I could come to the florist too, silly-Lilly. It kills me when you girls all go in differ-ent directions. Rory, you, however, are on your own. I didn't get any detentions in high school, and I'm not about to start now. Principals scare me."

It was said with a chuckle and a fake shudder, but good humor didn't mask the meaning underneath: *You* got in trou-ble, but *I* never did.

Mom breezed back in, tossing sets of car keys to Lilly and

Dad. "We need to motor. Agility training class starts in an hour and the cones and hoops aren't set up."

"Have fun with that," I snarked at the same time Merri gushed, "Oh fun! I love when the puppies wriggle through the tunnels!"

I left the kitchen before all the *I know, right*s could begin. It was time to be done with the *One of these things is not like the other Campbells* portion of my morning.

"Hey! Rory." Lilly chased me into the foyer. "Sorry for being such a troll. I know, I know, I'm a grown woman who's scared of her own wedding planner." She sighed and plucked a petal off the vase of stargazers Trent had delivered last week. If she was waiting for me to contradict her, I hadn't been planning on it.

But I did say, "You don't need foundation whatevers."

She rolled her eyes. "I know, right? But I'd love your input on colors. You have such an eye for that. Thank you."

"Plus, she's rejected all my suggestions," said Merri, nudging Lilly out of the way so she could sit down on the foyer's bench to put on her sneakers.

"I'm sure paisley with rhinestones would be lovely," Lilly started—behind Merri's back she made her eyes wide and shook her head. "But that's not quite the aesthetic I'm looking for."

"Not *with*, or. This is an either paisley *or* rhinestones suggestion," said Merri. "I read about them being trendy."

"Maybe that will work for Fall Ball with Fielding," I suggested.

Ah, and there was Merri's Fielding Face. That smile

exploded from one cheekbone to the other whenever he was mentioned.

"I wonder if he'd wear a paisley bow tie?" Merri wandered off muttering and daydreaming. Lilly mouthed *Thank you* to me and headed out the door.

School was a twenty-minute walk. I spent it thinking about our styles. Lilly's was classic—pearls, pumps, plus-size tailored lines and muted colors. She was always fully pulled together and completely gorgeous. Merri's was paisley and polka dots and rhinestones and ruffles. All sorts of things that shouldn't go together, but she called it "toddler chic" and combined them in adorable and unexpected ways that worked for her.

I preferred clothing I didn't have to think about or stress over if I wiped paint or charcoal or clay on myself. I wanted to be able to move and bend and stand for long periods without anything pinching or binding. I liked colors—bright colors— but rarely had to worry about anything matching or clashing, because I paired everything with black. Not for clichéd *Look I'm an artist!* reasons, but because it hid stains.

Detention was the first time I'd gotten to wear non-uniform clothing on campus, but because we were doing manual labor, I hadn't needed to come up with anything impressive. At least I hoped not? I glanced down at my lime-green yoga pants and worn sneakers. I had a long black T-shirt and a black sweatshirt over these and I'd pulled the front of my chin-length hair back with a few haphazard bobby pins. Was everyone else going to be in designer jeans and flannel shirts? Would they be labor chic while I looked sloppy? My hands began to sweat as I second-guessed everything. Was I not supposed to pack a lunch? Did the cool kids go off campus? What should I have done? Gotten Huck's number so I could call him and say, "I know we just met, but what are you wearing? No take-backs on the friendship!"

This felt like the sort of thing other people just *knew*. The kind of thing where they'd say, "Who cares, wear whatever." But the reason they could say "who cares" was that their "whatever" would instinctively be the same as everyone else's.

I'd been told to report to the main office, and even stranger than walking across an empty campus was listening to my footsteps echo in the empty hallways. I paused before the dark oak doors, taking a deep breath and swiping my damp palms on my pants before I pushed it open.

"Sign in." A bored-looking woman slid a clipboard across the receptionist's desk. I hadn't noticed her the only other time I'd been in this office—the day I'd gotten this punishment—but I couldn't imagine she normally wore a teal sweat suit to work. Her weekend casual wear made this whole scene feel more like a fever dream. Past her desk, through the large windows that overlooked the south hallway, I could see students forming groups and huddling up. I wasn't late, but apparently I hadn't known everyone else was showing up early.

"Hey!" I looked up from my shaky signature to see Huck leaning in the door from the south hallway. I exhaled my relief at seeing *any* familiar face, but then my stomach clenched as I crossed to him and noticed he was frowning. "Listen, I'm sorry if I came on too strong with the whole *Let's be friends* thing yesterday. I hate being *the new kid*, and it was ten times worse being the new kid in a class full of resentful upperclassmen. I thought you might too." He paused, waiting for me to contradict him, say anything. But I was too dumbfounded. Was he withdrawing his proposal of friendship? No. Wait. Stop.

Huck sighed and gave me a small dimpleless smile. "Anyway, you said you didn't drink coffee and I saw you had this at lunch, so . . . peace offering."

I didn't look to see what he was holding. I was too busy rehearsing what I'd say. It came out as a blurt, the words smearing together. "I-want-to-be-friends-promise!"

"Oh." Huck brightened. "Good."

I took the bottle of my favorite brand of kombucha and clinked it against the glass of the second one he was holding. "No peace offering necessary. But thanks. Also, you're really observant, aren't you?"

He shrugged sheepishly. "So they say. I don't mean to notice things; I can't help it. Also, what is this stuff?" I heard a crinkle of plastic, then a *pop!* as Huck removed the cap from his bottle. The telltale hiss of carbonation was lost underneath the other students' chatter. Before I could warn him it was a bit of an acquired taste, he'd taken a huge gulp.

Then there was a bottle being thrust into my free hand, and he was dashing for the bathroom.

I was so aware of every pair of eyes that swiveled toward our spectacle. *Thanks for that, Huck.* My nails made quick work of the labels on the bottles and rang against the glass underneath in a rhythmless jittery beat. I studied the floor. In the administration building—the fanciest on campus—it was marble or some other hard stone that was mottled and swirled in shades from white to gray to black. My nervous habit was to figure out how I'd draw things, and I did that now, picking out shapes and gradients of color, starting at the slab beneath my paint-spattered sneakers and working my way out in ripples.

"Is he okay?" asked a girl with delicate features and dark skin and hair.

"I hope so?" I answered, my voice too soft.

Apparently that was a good enough answer, because people resumed their conversations, only to turn back when Huck reappeared. He gagged and pointed to the bottle he'd handed me. "That's gone bad."

I unscrewed the top. It smelled fine to me, but maybe it had fermented too much? Chancing it, I raised the bottle and took a sip. "It's fine."

"No." Huck shook his head. "That *can't* be how it's supposed to taste—like ginger, vinegar, and dirty tea. You *like* that?" He screwed his mouth into a grimace. "Not judging you, just . . . Ugh, I want to scrape it off my tongue."

Before I could defend my favorite drink, *or* tell him he'd basically gotten it right, it *was* fermented tea, another door opened and out stepped Headmaster Williams. Unlike his receptionist, he had not dressed down for the weekend: navy suit, crisp white shirt, shiny shoes. Even his tie was knotted firmly in place. I'd have to ask Fielding if his dad even *owned* clothing without creases. He cleared his throat and folded his hands in front of his stomach, waiting for everyone to stop talking and acknowledge his presence.

"Good morning. I trust you all came ready to work and atone for your misdeeds at the party last weekend. You'll be working in pairs on a variety of tasks. Line up with your partner and I'll assign your job."

I wanted to stop and say a prayer of gratitude for Huck being dropped into Advanced Art and my life yesterday, because my anxiety was screaming with the *could have been* of searching for a partner among strangers—but there was no time because the line was forming and he and I were at the end of it. He was still scraping his tongue against his teeth. "They should call it *kom-dontcha*."

I snorted. "That was terrible."

He looked pleased with himself. "It really was, wasn't it? I'm practicing for my distant future as king of the dad jokers."

The pair in front of us moved, and suddenly I was face-to-face with Headmaster Williams. One last giggle slipped out before I had time to flip my expression to dread.

"Miss Campbell, it's good to see you're looking properly penitent." Was that sarcasm? Were headmasters allowed to be sarcastic with their students? I wasn't sure, but it didn't matter—I no longer felt like laughing. "I've saved the perfect task for the recalcitrant freshmen." He looked between Huck and me and amped his disapproval. "You'll be cleaning the spilled paint off the stage. I've had the custodial staff unlock the theater's janitorial closet. Make sure to test the solvents before you use them. Wouldn't want you making things worse, would we?"

I bit the inside of my cheek. Worse? Was that possible?

If so, I was pretty sure I was capable of achieving it.

7

uck was in charge of testing the different cleaners. He did this by sniffing them and rejecting the ones that smelled the worst. I was pretty sure the one he picked was glass cleaner. Or maybe car wash? He dumped the bright blue liquid in a bucket, then filled it with hot water until bubbles cascaded over the top and sloshed with each step as he carried it down the aisle of the theater. He plopped it on the stage, causing suds to slop over and pool beside the dried puddle of yellow paint.

I followed with an arsenal of brushes, rags, and sponges.

"Let's get our scrub on." Huck clapped once, then paused. "Oh, wait—" He pulled a pair of bright yellow rubber gloves from his back pocket, slipped them on, then clapped again. They matched the paint.

I shifted restlessly on the stage. Just standing in the same space where Monroe had been so cruel brought out goose bumps on my arms. I'd been a moron for buying into his charm and believing that he'd needed my help to paint backdrops for his Rogue Romeo performance. *I heard you're the best artist on campus. Merri brags about you nonstop.*

I kicked at the dried paint. Monroe had wanted me at the party to be a pawn, not an artist. I was part of his revenge plan, payback for my sister breaking up with him. This paint stain was my proof I'd fought back.

Huck used a scrub brush to push the spilled water onto the paint. It splashed onto my sneakers, making me jump and bringing me back to the present. He grinned up at me. "Want to play the question game?"

"I have no idea what that means."

"I'll ask you a question, you answer, I answer. You ask me a question and I answer, you answer. Simple."

"Sure." Anything that replaced me having to come up with hours of small talk was an excellent idea. I knelt and picked up a rough sponge, dipping it into the sudsy water and bringing it over to one of the paw prints Gatsby had tracked across the stage during Merri's rescue mission.

"Favorite artist— No, that's too hard. Let's work up to that." He tapped a yellow-gloved finger against his lips. "Favorite pasta shape."

I laughed. "Angel hair, I guess. Or farfalle, because they look like butterflies."

"Cool. I'm a fusilli guy. Your turn."

I settled onto my knees and began to scrub. Glass cleaner or car wash, whatever it was might work. "Favorite place on earth?"

"I'm pretty partial to where we just moved from: Rio Grande." I made a face and he laughed. "Spelled like the river it's nowhere near, but pronounced like that, I promise."

"Rye-o Grand." I tried it out and nodded as his outsider status made more sense. "Where is it?"

"Ohio. Until last month I was a Buckeye. It's weird coming from a really small town to this. My parents worked at the local university, but they got jobs at schools out here. Mostly because they have tuition reciprocity with more colleges. I bet they wished they'd figured that out before my brother graduated from NYU last year." He shrugged. "What's your favorite place?"

"New York, the city." My parents loved our town. Merri too. She knew the name of our mailman, of practically every customer who walked through the door of Haute Dog. She definitely knew the names of their dogs. If we went to Cool Beans, they wrote her name on a pink cup before she placed her order. She wanted to grow up, go to college, then come back here—like my parents had.

I didn't. I wanted skyscrapers and steel bridges. I wanted subway cars that were too cold in the summer and stifling in the winter and the subway platforms that were the reverse. I wanted galleries and pop-up performances and street art that made me cry. I wanted to get to the point where I could give directions to tourists because I considered myself a local.

"My turn," said Huck. "Why were you at the party?"

"Ha. Um." Which version of the truth did I share? That Merri had mocked my ability to make my own friends, so I went to spite her? That her ex had flattered me? That *Rogue Romeo* had sounded like the sort of avant-garde art I wanted to see in New York? Or that I wanted Toby to see me as cooler and older and thought an upperclassman party might help?

I had dozens of reasons for going, but none of them were *Because I wanted to be at the party.*

"Um," I repeated, studying the bucket of suds, like the answer might be in the bubbles.

"How about I go first." He cleared his throat and drummed his yellow gloves on his knees. "I wasn't invited. I overheard some guys on the lacrosse team talking about it—and I couldn't deal with another Friday night at home. My friends in Ohio were talking about how great high school was, and my dad was getting on my case about 'putting myself out there' . . . so I party-crashed. Whoops." His voice was light, but the sponge in his left hand was squeezed dry. "The good news is, after getting busted at an upperclassman party and being bumped up to varsity lacrosse, my dad thinks I'm super popular and he's stopped bugging me." He turned to the floor and scrubbed it with a vengeance that moved paint. "Your turn."

I sat back on my heels and put down my brush. His words had earned some sort of reciprocal honesty and the idea of spilling a truth wasn't horrible. Because everyone around us had great friends, best friends—people who already knew all their secrets and flaws and had a shared history. I'd always had a collection of acquaintances. I'd spent my life being a really good third wheel. The chance to be someone's first choice was so tempting it made my throat ache—like friendship was a thirst that confession could quench.

"I don't have a good reason. I don't like meeting new

people. Or making stupid small talk. And I mean, I *really* don't like it. I have nightmares about the day I'm old enough to work in my parents' dog boutique alone, because waiting on customers leaves me in a cold sweat. I won't go get the mail if Mrs. Shadid across the street is watering her plants, because I know she'll talk to me. Walking into the office this morning—that was way worse than any cleaning task. And every day in art class? I hate it so much."

Wait. That was more than I'd meant to share. Once I'd gotten started, I couldn't stop. I bit my lip to prevent anything else from spilling out.

He grimaced. "So, the combination of social anxiety and starting at a new school where most of the kids aren't new to each other . . . that sounds super fun."

"It's the best," I said with a fake smile. And he didn't know the half of it, that Merri and I had only been accepted because Lilly's future mother-in-law had pulled strings. "Especially when in my family, anything less than being super outgoing is classified as an 'attitude problem' or 'being antisocial.'" I swallowed and sat back. "'Surly' is another favorite."

"Well, I find surly interesting. And you've already tried to poison me with kombucha and I'm still here, so . . ." Huck blew a handful of soapsuds at me.

"I don't even like parties," I added. *Dangit, Rory, let it go! New topic.* "I don't know why I'm telling you all this. I promise I'm not always this awkward." *Shut up. Shut up. Shut up!*

"I've got that thing—that Nick Carraway thing from *Gatsby*—people are always telling me secrets. It's the dimples." He flashed them as he dumped more water on the stage and pushed it around with his brush, not noticing the mess he was making. "You and Gatsby have that in common, by the way—the parties thing. Oh, that was a spoiler." Huck cringed. "Sorry. I read ahead. Should I warn you I'm a nerd like that?"

"Gatsby, the character we still haven't met? The one who throws parties that need endless description—*that* Gatsby doesn't like them?" I rinsed my scrub brush, then started on a new section of the stain. "How soon until we learn that?" Maybe Ms. Gregoire would think party-hating was an acceptable personal connection?

"Not too much longer. I thought I'd get ahead before exams. I heard the first round is killer for freshmen—Dante told me they use it to weed out the kids who can't cut it."

Well, that was just fantastic. Maybe once I flunked out of high school I could get a job in paint removal, because my ferocious-anxious scrubbing was pretty effective.

"My turn." I was taking this conversation to safer, non-academic topics before I went full-panic. "Favorite animal?"

"Cat—specifically *my* cat. Her name is Luna."

He won all the points for not being a dog person. "I have a fish and a snail. Klee the Fifth and Ariel the Eighth."

"Klee sounds heartier," Huck commented. "I'm assuming he's a goldfish?"

I nodded, loving that he knew the reference. The original Klee and Ariel and the bowl itself had been eighth-birthday gifts from Toby. I'd been obsessed with Paul Klee's *The Goldfish* . . . and Disney's *The Little Mermaid*.

Huck rubbed his gloves together; they squeaked and he dimpled. "Celebrity crush?"

I groaned. I was so bad at all things pop culture. I tried to think of the name of any cute actor or the last movie I'd enjoyed. It was some superhero thing last spring with Toby. "Um, the guy that played Captain America."

"Ah, one of the Super Chrises, good choice. I'm more partial to a dark, broody Dr. Strange. Also, Wonder Woman."

"My sister has her costume," I admitted, which was all I knew about the superheroine. "And I can't remember which guy was Dr. Strange . . . but maybe we could watch it sometime."

Huck frowned and my stomach dropped. This was why I never put myself out there; if I never tried to make friends, I could never be rejected.

"You can't remember Benedict?" he asked. "That's a crime against humanity. Name the time and place. I'll bring the snacks."

I exhaled my relief into a handful of soap bubbles. Maybe sometimes taking a risk paid off. "Deal."

8

The afternoon was a repeat of the morning, only with prunier fingers. By the end of the day, Huck had me laughing until I was tearing up, and it felt like maybe we could actually be friends, *real* friends, not just lifeboat friends who bonded out of necessity. The thought made Hero High a little less menacing.

"They may need to change the fall play from *Romeo and Juliet* to *Macbeth*," said Huck as he tossed his scrub brush in the dirty water. "Because this stage has got 'Out damn spot' all over it."

I snorted. "Are dad jokes cool in Ohio?"

He winked. "The coolest."

The stain *had* shrunk. It had gone from being Hula-Hoop size to Frisbee. Well, Frisbee plus paw prints, plus spatter. "Good thing we have another week to work on it," I chirped with false enthusiasm.

Huck rolled his neck and it cracked and popped like Rice Krispies. "I like paint more when I'm applying it, not removing it."

"Agreed." I was going to have to spend some serious time on my yoga mat to counteract all the hours crouching. I bent over and dangled my arms, and the relief as my muscles unlocked was almost painful. Still upside down, I asked, "Are you walking home, or is someone picking you up?"

"Hey, um, Rory? Do you know Tobias May? Because I was JV until he got injured, so I'm pretty sure he's not here to see me."

"What?" All the blood rushed to my head when I flipped upright and I staggered from dizziness. Toby. Right there at the foot of the stage. Boosting himself onto the stage next to me. "Oh. Yeah." If I aimed at pathetically bored, maybe I'd manage to hit somewhere close to not-swooning? "He's my next-door neighbor. Um, hey?"

"Ouch." Toby slung an arm around my shoulder and any hope I'd had of faking indifference exploded into a racing heart and flushed cheeks. "'Next-door neighbor'? You classify me by geography? Not by friends since before you were potty-trained? I can still sing your tinkle song if you need proof."

"Not necessary!"

He began to hum the opening notes of "Twinkle, Twinkle, Little Star" and stepped out of reach when I tried to cover his mouth. "Tinkle, tinkle, Aurora Leigh—time to go in the pot-ty."

I groaned and covered my face. "Is this drive-by humiliation?"

"It can be. Or it can be a ride home." Toby scooped my sweatshirt and lunch bag from the corner of the stage. "I was bored and wanted to see how you were holding up."

"You were bored? Thanks, I'm flattered."

Toby grinned. It was my favorite grin, the one that

stretched his mouth wide and displayed his slightly crooked tooth. It was a belly-laugh grin that warmed me up like soup in winter. "That's a funny way of saying, 'Toby, my hero, you're the highlight of my day.'"

Ha. I joined him in laughing, but not for the same reason. If only he knew how true that statement was.

"C'mon, it's three o'clock—go sign out. Then meet me in the parking lot, because technically, you're not allowed visitors." He glanced over my shoulder to where Huck was coming back in the theater. I hadn't noticed he'd left—but the stage was clear of brushes, buckets, and cleaners. "Does your friend need a ride?"

"Do you?" I turned to Huck. "And also, Huck, Toby. Toby, Huck."

"Hey." Toby held out a hand for Huck to shake. "I heard you did great in the game last night. Congrats."

Huck ducked his head to look humble, but I could still see his dimples. "You left some tough shoes to fill. And thanks, but my dad's picking me up."

Toby nodded. "See you in a few, Roar." I watched as he headed up the aisle. The knee brace made his gait the tiniest bit unbalanced, but I was pretty sure I could watch a GIF of him walking for hours. Toward me would be better, but the view from the back wasn't bad either.

Huck pointed at the door. "How long's that been going on?"

"W-what?" I sputtered. "There's nothing— Nothing's going on. He's . . . Merri's." In more ways than one. In all the ways that counted he was hers. "He and I . . . we're friends."

Huck arched an eyebrow. "Whatever you say." I was about to protest again when he started for the door. "Come on, the Headmustard awaits."

I forced a laugh and followed.

Headmaster Williams wasn't in the office, and the receptionist was waiting with her purse on her desk and her keys in her hand. We were the last two who needed to sign out. No one had bothered to tell the freshmen that detention ended early.

"Enjoy the rest of your weekend," Huck told her as she locked the door behind us. She responded by turning off the lights.

When Huck said the same to me before climbing into his dad's car, I smiled and said, "Ditto," while thinking ahead to weekends where he and I might hang out for reasons other than school punishment.

Toby was leaning against his car looking at his phone. The frames of his rarely-worn-but-frequently-daydreamed-about glasses and the metal of his knee brace glinted in the sun. His gray, long-sleeved T-shirt was pushed up to showcase the lingering glow of his summer tan on his olive skin and wrists that were heavy with muscles. These were the lines I loved to draw most, because they reminded me of how those hands moved across piano keys or guitar strings. He looked like a movie poster. A book cover. An advertisement of everything I wanted.

He looked up from his phone and smiled. I'd had a dozen years to grow immune to that grin, but it still knocked the breath from my lungs.

I stopped short of his car and asked, "Did Merri tell you to come get me?" Because that would be a very Merri thing to do. Especially after the guilt-laden kitchen chaos that morning.

"Nope. Every once in a while I have my own ideas." He tugged a strand of my hair. "I knew everyone was at the store and you were upset yesterday. I wanted to check on you."

"Oh." I looked down at myself. The bright green knees of my yoga pants were dimmed with dust. I'd lost my bobby pins at some point, and now my hair flopped around my face. My hands were dry from the cleaning products and smelled like chemical lemon. "I'm pretty gross. You want me in your car?"

"It's about time. Have you seen me after lacrosse or your sister after cross-country? This is only fair. I was convinced the only time you ever got messy was with paint."

"Clearly not."

"Really?" He lifted one of my hands and turned it over. It was stained yellow from the paint we'd scrubbed off the stage. My face had changed colors too—red—because we were so, so close to holding hands. I bit back a sigh when he let go. "And you still smell good. Do you even sweat? Like, ever?"

"Of course I sweat. I sweat all the time. I stink after yoga." Why was I arguing this point? Who brags about their sweatiness?

"I stand corrected." Toby pushed off the car and opened the passenger door for me. "C'mon, stinky, let's get you home."

He turned on the car and the stereo came to life. It was midsong, one I didn't recognize but that matched the lilting joy I felt around him. "What is this?"

"The *Amélie* soundtrack." He glanced sideways. "Do you like it?"

I nodded and he exhaled and turned to me. "Isn't it great? Music makes or breaks a movie."

"I haven't seen it, but it sounds . . . happy. Hopeful?"

"It is!" He looked so pleased, I mentally gave myself a gold star sticker. "If I could do anything, that's what I'd do—compose for films."

"That would be a cool job." And a very *him* one. Toby carried around blank sheet music like I carried sketch pads. "You should."

"Yeah, *you* try telling my dad that." He shook his head. "I know it's ridiculous, but I'm always mentally composing a score for my own life."

"No more ridiculous than me constantly mapping how I'd draw everything I see." But now I was lit up with curiosity. What did this moment sound like to him?

He grinned as he backed out of his space. "I should've known you'd get it."

"Um, yeah." My cheeks were way too hot and I was way too flustered by that comment. "So . . . how was Merri's race?" I hated to bring up her name because my time with him was almost always divided in her favor, and right now she wasn't even here and I was still competing against her. Except—he'd know how she'd done and I didn't. It wouldn't occur to Merri to update me. Lilly, yes. Me, never.

You'd think being only ten months apart, Merri and I would have a relationship as close as our birthdays, but the sibling social dynamic had been shaped before my ten-week-early arrival—during the two months Mom had been on bed-rest and seven-year-old Lilly had had to take on much more responsibility for baby Merri. It gelled during the six weeks I was in the NICU, where neither Lilly nor Merri was allowed to visit. By the time I was brought home—"the smallest, reddest, most wrinkly little thing, with an ear-piercing shriek that was shriller than the alarm on your apnea monitor," thanks, Dad—Lilly and Merri were a team. An indivisible team that didn't have room for a third player. Sure, they included me sometimes, and it was rarely malicious when they did their own thing and forgot to invite me. But they still *forgot*, and being the one who was forgettable . . . sometimes it was easier to exclude myself than to wait to be excluded.

I stopped fiddling with my lunch bag and looked at Toby because he hadn't answered. A vertical worry line was digging in between his eyebrows. "I'm sure she did fine. She would've let me know if everything wasn't fine."

"I don't think she cares about her times," I added. "Knowing Merri, she loves practices and hates racing."

"Well, yeah, because she runs with Eliza at practice—there's no way Eliza's slowing down so Merri can keep up in meets." Toby said this like it was unreasonable. But then again, he thought everything about Eliza was automatically unreasonable. Normally I'd defend her—I was lovesick, not dumbstruck—but today I was too tired to do anything but tip my head back against the seat and crack my sore neck.

"That guy—" Toby cleared his throat before he continued. "The one you were with—"

"You mean Huck?"

"I don't know him. Is he trouble? I mean, he was at Saturday detention."

I laughed. "For attending the same party as me. He's fine. He's practically my only friend on campus—don't scare him off." I had a frightening vision of Toby's friends Lance and Curtis cornering Huck in a locker room for lacrosse hazing. Except Curtis was too goofy to be threatening. "Huh. And that"—I pointed out my window to the girl perched on my front step—"is my other, sometimes-friend."

"Penn Highbury's little sister? He's team captain. She's good people."

"Yeah, but what is Clara doing here?" She was in her cheer-leading uniform and raised her arms and waved when I got out of the car. For a brief, terrified moment I thought she was going to do a cheer with my name in it or something, because Mrs. Shadid would definitely hear that and then there'd be no escaping her small talk. But once Clara had my attention she dropped her arms. "About time you got home. Headmaster Williams has no pity, does he?"

"Nope." I smiled at Toby over the roof of his car. "Thanks for coming to get me."

"Anytime, Roar. See you later."

He headed up the walk to his house and I tromped toward my lawn, but my eyes kept darting back to him. To that gray Henley that hugged his shoulders and showed a hint of the muscle he'd packed on from lacrosse and basketball. To the dark hair on the back of his head that was starting to get shaggy, but he'd wait at least another two weeks before getting it cut.

"Man, he's gorgeous, huh?"

I jumped. I hadn't noticed Clara crossing the grass to meet

me, her words an echo of my thoughts. "Yes. I mean, no. I mean— Wait, what?" I stumbled over nothing. Seriously, there wasn't even a hose or rock or lawn gnome to blame. Maybe it was an internal stumble, because my stomach felt like it was free-falling to my feet. "You like him?"

"No," Clara said. "You do."

"I'm sorry, *what*?"

"I brought you a cupcake." She pulled a small pink box from behind her back and opened the lid to reveal a shockingly blue mound of frosting. It was larger than my fist and covered in sprinkles—if there was cake underneath, I couldn't see it. "But then I remembered you don't eat— What are you again? Dairy-free? Gluten? Vegan? I forget."

"Vegan-ish." Normally I hated explaining the what and why of the things I did and didn't eat, but if it steered the conversation away from Toby and feelings, I'd draw her a whole dang plant-based-diet diagram.

"So I'll eat it while you tell me all about you and the hottie next door. You've been holding out on me." She turned toward our front walk and waited. "Aren't you going to invite me in?"

"I can't. I'm grounded." As soon as the words were out of my mouth, I wanted to take them back. Because Clara was a parent-pleaser, and there's no way she'd break the rules. But I'd only just gotten her to talk to me again and I missed her. Ugh, I couldn't believe I was going to suggest this. "But we can take my parents' dog for a walk?"

Dogs slobbered. They chewed up your favorite paintbrushes. They barked when you were trying to concentrate, and they shed on wet paint. They had accidents if you were in the zone and forgot to take them out. But worst of all, when you took them for their walks, dogs were conversation-magnets for strangers, neighbors, anyone who crossed your path.

I mean, where was it written that it was wrong to pass a girl with a four-legged, two-eared drool depository without asking, "What kind of dog is he?" "What's her name?" or "Awww, cute bows." Thanks for those, Merri, really.

And then you were stuck standing there talking about dog fashion and weather while holding a little blue poop bag and wanting to die.

"Oh, that works! And believe me, you want my advice. I'm an expert on matchmaking." Clara dragged a finger through the ocean of butter and sugar, then stuck that scoop of frosting between her pink lips. "Go get the doggo, I'll wait out here."

I unlocked the door and whistled. Byron didn't come running—my parents must've brought him to the store—but Gatsby did, nails skittering on the tile floor and tail windmilling.

"Fine," I told him. "I'll walk you. But no eating anything you find on the sidewalk. And it doesn't mean I like you or your book."

That was good enough for Gats, who licked my knee and chomped on the leash handle while I clipped the other end to his collar.

Clara had finished the frosting and was nibbling on the cake when I came back outside. "Oooh, pupper! What's your name? Aren't you the cutest? I could just steal you right away."

"Meet Gatsby—yes, Gatsby." I held out his leash. "Be my guest."

She laughed but took a step backward. "Don't I wish. I'm allergic. We've got twenty minutes until I blow up in hives. I'll text my brother and tell him to come in fifteen." She began to talk about the game she'd cheered at, the girl who'd gotten bus sick, and her plans for that night when she took the train to visit her dad. She waited a whole two houses past Toby's before she transferred her neatly folded cupcake wrapper to her other hand and grabbed my arm. "So?! What are we doing about this crush?"

"We? Doing? Nothing." I stopped walking.

"That's ridiculous," said Clara. "Of course we're doing something. I can come up with a plan. I'm so good—"

"No, you don't understand. There's nothing to do. He's in love with my sister."

"Oh." Clara let go of my arm and began to scratch Gatsby's head. To him, she said, "Don't tell my mom I'm touching you . . . but who can resist that face? Not me. Not me!" He melted into a furry sidewalk puddle and she crouched to rub his exposed belly while looking up at me and tilting her head. "Okay, we'll need a different type of plan."

A Mustang pulled over and honked. Clara waved at the boy behind the steering wheel. He looked vaguely familiar. I'd probably seen him on campus. "That's Penn. I've got to go, but I'll give this some thought." She leaned in for a hug, then blew Gatsby a kiss. "You're a complicated cookie, Aurora Campbell."

Was that better than a tough cookie? I wasn't quite sure, but I didn't have time to ponder it since Gatsby decided to protest his loss of belly scratches by dragging me down the street.

9

Being grounded had become a form of psychological punishment. I had no Saturday night plans. No one was texting or calling to see if I wanted to join them for dinner or bowling or whatever it was Hero High students did on the weekend.

Which should have meant painting or drawing or sculpting. Those were always my weekend plans. Even before Hero High, those had been my weekend plans, with the occasional movie or trip to the mall when my old friends Molly and Greta had dragged me out. But I hadn't heard from Molly and G in weeks. The last text we'd exchanged was **Good luck on your 1st day!** And some version of **talk soon**. But we'd said **talk soon** and **let's get together** since the day after middle school graduation. And for all our promises, we'd met up only once all summer, spending an afternoon crammed in Greta's bathroom while she and Molly dyed each other's hair. I didn't want blue streaks—and apparently being an audience, not a participant, made me "judgey," which wasn't even close to true. Also, there wasn't much for me to contribute to a conversation solely focused on *their* upcoming freshman year.

Maybe I was an awful friend, but I didn't miss them much.

What I missed was feeling like I knew what I was doing. Like you could drop me in any room with any art supplies and I could create something I'd be proud of. And not just create—I could enjoy the act of creating, get lost in the process and come up smiling. It was why grounding had never felt like punishment. Why sometimes I used to purposely get caught breaking the No Cell Phones During Homework rule so I'd have an excuse for going off-grid.

But that was back when people had actually contacted my phone and missed me when it was taken away. Now my phone was an expensive paperweight and art was a series of disasters.

First, I'd dropped a tube of cadmium-orange oil paint. An uncapped tube. Then, while I was attempting to clean it off the floor and my throw rug, I'd stepped on a paintbrush. It'd snapped in half—the pointier side stabbing into the bottom of my foot. While hopping to grab a tissue, I'd dripped blood on an open sketchbook.

Yeah, art was not happening.

One Band-Aid and half a roll of paper towels later, my floor was no longer orange and my foot was no longer bleeding. I glanced at my backpack and sighed as I pulled out *The Great Gatsby*. Maybe I'd like the book better today?

Nope. I shut the book at the end of the next chapter and pulled out my notebook to summarize: Nick meets Gatsby. Party is wild. Gatsby tells Jordan a secret?? Nick describes his boring life. I shut the notebook and kicked it off my bed. I'd had no reaction except a mild case of secondhand embarrassment for Nick when he realizes the man he's been describing Gatsby's mysteriousness to—*is* Gatsby. Nick was as awkward at parties as I was—maybe there was a journal entry in that? Only, Gatsby immediately reassures Nick, whereas that sort of thing would haunt me all night. Dangit, why did response journals require you to have a *response*?

I left my room and headed downstairs. I needed tea or an apple or maybe I'd get my secret stash of key lime candies from their hiding place behind the canister of steel-cut oats. Maybe I'd steal one of Lilly's fancy bath bombs and hog the bathroom for an hour.

I rounded the corner into the kitchen and was hit with a wall of giggles.

"The butter to kernels ratio is *not* one-to-one, Mayday." Merri was sitting on the counter, swinging her legs and attempting to hold a stick of butter out of Toby's reach.

"I don't see why it can't be," he countered, feinting left, then going right and closing his hand around her wrist. He triumphantly held up the butter, Simba-style. Or Simba-style, if the cub-lifting monkey from *The Lion King* had worn navy sweatpants, an unbuttoned beige Henley, and a black vest that looked like it belonged to one of his father's suits. "Let's try it."

I hesitated in the doorway and tried to decide if I wanted tea more than I wanted to avoid seeing the two of them together. "Hey, Rory," Merri called. She pointed to the popcorn maker and then herself. "Movie night."

"I figured." Because Merri and Toby didn't just *watch*

THE BOY NEXT STORY | 75

movies, they dressed up. It was a whole thing. When I was little I'd spend days begging or blackmailing for an invite. Around ten I started pretending not to care, then creeping up to my room to cry. But they hadn't had one lately. Eliza had been extra clingy at the end of summer and Toby had been away at lacrosse camp and in California visiting his mom.

Merri had her hair twirled into two buns and was wearing pajama pants with some sort of sci-fi bears. Her T-shirt read *Who stole the Wookie from the Wookie jar?* It was unbearably adorable. Toby was leaning against the counter beside her, his hip pressed against the outside of her leg, flipping that stick of butter over in his hands.

He smiled at me. "I don't have a blaster, but I still make a pretty good Han Solo, right?"

"You look ridiculous," I lied. He looked adorable in that way someone can be when you look at them and see their seven- and seventeen-year-old selves simultaneously. The same black hair, but now he wore it cut short instead of in wild curls. The same expressive dark eyes and tan skin. The same mouth that pouted as easily as it laughed. He was chuckling now, a sound that echoed through all my best childhood memories.

"You mean, ridiculously *Han*-some," he corrected.

Soon they'd be in our basement, sharing a couch and a bowl. Fingers brushing. And my sister was the opposite of an idiot, so how long could it possibly be until she realized that Fielding may be great, might even be the second greatest guy in the universe, but the absolute greatest was waiting patiently for his turn?

Yeah, tea was not worth it. "Well, wharf speed ahead," I said, then pivoted to leave.

"Wrong movie." Merri laughed.

"Wait, Roar." Toby was smiling as he crossed the room. "Did you just say 'wharf speed ahead'? *Wharf?*"

"Isn't that a thing in *Star* . . . something?" I wasn't a big film person—I tended to be dragged to movies instead of choosing them. Merri leaned toward romance and Lilly toward historical. Neither of my parents were sci-fi people. The only things with aliens I'd seen were *Lilo & Stitch* and *Home*, and those were with Molly and her little sister. Toby was shaking his head at me, his eyes bright with amusement. "No, it makes sense," I protested. "Like, they're taking the boat or spaceship or whatever to the wharf. Docking it on a new planet."

He shook his head again, his eyes and nose scrunched up before he glanced at Merri and they both exploded into laughter. *"Wh-wha-wharf?"*

I never should've left my room, where the biggest threat was art supply impalement. I ducked my head and turned. "And on that note, good night."

"No. Wait." Toby slung an arm around my neck to stop me. "That might be the cutest mistake in the history of mistakes."

Merri grimaced at the word "cutest," but not all of us were pocket-size and had an aversion to it. For some of us, the word made our hearts race.

Toby steered me into the kitchen, then went to the cabinet and got me a mug. He brought the box of tea bags too. "You'll want a drink during the movie, right?"

"Movie?" I asked, trying to keep my cheeks from revealing my glee over him knowing my tea habits.

"Of course," he said. "Clearly I've been derelict if you know that little about *Star Wars* and *Star Trek*. Sit next to me and I'll fill you in."

"I don't want to interrupt if you're having special friend time or whatever." Which was a lie, because that was exactly what I wanted.

"No, stay!" It was Merri who insisted at the top of her lungs, and I could only imagine this meant she was using me as a nonplatonic feelings shield, which, whatever—if Toby needed to redirect those nonplatonic feelings, I volunteered as tribute.

Downstairs in the basement Merri pointed from me to the couch. "Rory, sit. Toby, get the movie set up. I'm going to go make the popcorn—some with extra butter, and some"— she looked at me—"without any."

"Thanks," I said.

While Toby did his thing with the remote controls, I played some solo form of Twister on the couch. Right knee cushion? Or both feet floor? Butt on middle cushion? Or back pressed against left arm?

"Think Merri's lighting the kitchen on fire? Should I go help her?" Toby asked, his eyes going from the TV, where the menu waited and a song played on a thirty-second loop, to the door at the top of the stairs.

"I'm pretty sure she can handle it. Put your knee up." I pointed to the coffee table I'd shoved closer to his side of the couch.

"Thanks." He dropped the remotes on top, then rearranged his knee brace.

"How's this movie rank, score-wise?" He watched all movies twice—once for plot and once for soundtrack. *"The plot and characters may interest you, but the score owns you."* He'd told Merri that over the summer while I was eavesdropping from the top of the stairs. She'd laughed and disagreed, and he'd countered with *"A good score controls your emotions. It'll make you cry, make you scared, make you feel like you can take on the world or fall in love. Listen."*

They'd gone silent and I'd slunk away. But now *I* was the one on the couch beside him, and he was grinning like I'd asked the best question in the world.

"It's by John Williams—which means it's amazing. Definitely in my all-time top ten—but hold that thought for later. Ready for a short history of *Star Wars*?"

But I paid a lot less attention to his summary than I did to the ten inches of couch cushion separating us.

"Got it?" he asked.

"Magic twins. Bad guys. Spaceships. Robot hand. I think I'm good."

Toby groaned and poked my leg. "Magic twins? Roar, you're butchering this."

"Yeah, well you should see what I do to classic literature," I joked. "Are the space bears from Merri's pants in this too?"

"Space bears?" He covered his eyes. "No. No. No. Those are Ewoks."

"They're cute," I said. "I like them."

"You're cute," he joked back. "The Ewoks are fierce fighters who help the Rebel Alliance save the planet. And, fine, they're freaking cute too."

"Can you both stop saying 'cute' and start the movie?" Merri plopped a bowl of popcorn in each of our laps before taking her own bowl and retreating to the love seat.

"Hey, do you want some—"

Merri was already wrinkling her nose before Toby'd pulled the candy out of his pocket. "If the name starts with *lick*, you know my answer is forever no."

"Licorice is delicious, Rowboat. One of these days you're going to figure that out." He held the package out to me, but I waved it away.

Merri pretended to gag. "I don't know how you like that. Even the smell is gross!"

I disagreed. The scent was quintessential Toby. And while I'd never, ever admit it, when he was away at lacrosse camp and in California, I'd bought a pack and hidden it in my dresser drawer. On the nights when I missed him most—when I could hear his voice on speakerphone in Merri's room and knew that was the closest I'd get to him—I took it out and smelled it. And though I'd deny it until my last breath, I may have slept with it in my pillowcase.

"Are we doing this?" asked Merri as she cranked the surround sound unnecessarily loud.

Toby nodded and hit play. The two of them immediately launched into a recitation of the words scrolling across the opening screen. They had the same serious voice, the same inflection and pauses. I burrowed deeper into my corner of the couch: conspicuous, costumeless, and excluded. A trio of outsider qualities that added up to feeling like this was a very bad idea.

"You ready to be indoctrinated, Roar?" Toby asked, reaching across the cushion between us to squeeze my foot. Maybe this wasn't the worst way to spend an evening after all.

10

was watching the movie. Sorta. I'd tried, but it didn't feel like the type of movie you could half pay attention to, and once I got lost, well, then what was my motivation to *not* switch all my attention to the boy beside me? Which meant I noticed the first time his lips parted in a noiseless sigh. And the second. And every time he adjusted his leg on the coffee table or shifted in his seat. He was inching his finger beneath the top strap of his knee brace, scratching underneath.

I hadn't noticed that Merri had fallen asleep. Not until he ripped open the Velcro on his brace, then grimaced and flashed his eyes over to the love seat where she was softly snoring with her legs tangled in a blanket. She didn't move, and the tension melted out of his posture, only to return when he shifted his leg while trying to smooth the fabric bunched beneath the strap.

"How much is it still bothering you?" I asked in a whisper.

"I'm fine," he said. But when I didn't turn back to the screen he elaborated. "It burns by the end of the day, and I'm still taking Motrin before I go to sleep. Mostly it's just . . . irritating. The brace pinches and rubs. Nothing fits over it, and it's just so *there*, for everyone to see. I know these aren't international tragedies, but I miss lacrosse. I miss my team. I hate . . ." He shrugged. "Everyone's busy, you know? And now I'm not."

I wondered if his dad, who I secretly called "Major May" because he was strict and neat and had rules for things I'd never dreamed of, knew Toby was unhappy. He'd always worked long hours, but I hadn't seen his Mercedes coupe in the driveway for . . . days?

"Me either," I admitted. "Not busy, I mean."

Toby paused the movie. On the screen a spaceship was frozen midexplosion. I knew that feeling. My life had already detonated, but all the pieces hadn't jettisoned and caused max destruction yet. I heard the remote hit the coffee table before he shifted to face me more fully. "Everything okay, Roar?"

Which would be worse—if he cared but not in the way I wanted or if he didn't care at all?

I swallowed and raised my chin to nod, but Toby continued. "And since I already know the answer is no—why don't you save time and tell me what's up?"

"It's just—" He was looking at me with those eyes that made me feel like I was the only person in the room. In the universe. And like my problem was something he'd move mountains and popcorn bowls and throw pillows to fix—or at least so he could pick up my hand and squeeze it. And while that didn't solve anything, it *did* create all the breathless sensation of an asthma attack. You know, without all the danger and inhalers.

"You can tell me anything, Roar. You know that, right?"

He squeezed my hand again and I managed a horribly

incoherent jumble of sounds. "Ya-gah." Then took a deep breath and exhaled out. "I'm kinda failing math."

"Hey." Merri stirred sleepily and yawned like a kitten, all pink tongue and stretches. "Why's the movie off? Is it over?"

Toby didn't look in her direction. His eyes were still pinned on me, full of concern and hurt. "What do you mean you're kinda failing math?"

"What!" It was a question word, but there was no question mark on Merri's exclamation. And though she had lopsided buns and creases on her cheek, she'd bounced immediately to wide-awake. "What does he mean, 'What do you mean you're kinda failing math?'"

"You're the genius," I grumbled at her. "It's not that hard a concept." I pulled my hand from Toby's and picked up a throw pillow to use as a shield. I also glanced from the couch to the stairs—was it possible I could make it up them before they caught me? I mean, Toby was in a knee brace . . . but Merri was now a runner. Dangit.

"But how did this happen?" Merri was practically falling off the couch as she tried to untangle her legs from the blanket. "How bad is it?"

"F bad," I answered, my annoyance rising at both of them. It was a secret for *Toby*, not for public consumption. And not for Merri to use as a weapon to make me feel dumber. "Does it get worse than that?"

"And you haven't *done* anything about it? What's wrong with you?" She came to stand in front of me. Glaring down with hands on her hips.

"Hey!" interjected Toby.

"You sure *you* don't want to answer that?" I snarked back. "You have plenty of experience telling me exactly what's wrong with me."

"Does this have to do with that academic warning I saw last week? Tell me you had Mom and Dad sign it. Tell me they know."

"Do *not* say anything to them. Seriously, Merri, I'll go *Fahrenheit Whatever-It-Is* on your bookshelves if you do."

"Hey. Campbells!" Toby put two fingers in his mouth and whistled. "Time out. Rowboat—go sit on your couch and shut up for a minute. Roar, take a deep breath. So, retests?"

I took incredible delight in Toby telling Merri to shut up— it almost made up for the rest of this. Except not really. "Mrs. Roberts said I could retake the last quiz."

"Great." Toby scrubbed a hand through his hair. "And the first round of exams is in a few weeks—so you'll need to go all in on some tutoring. I can do that."

"You don't have to do that." My stomach had been pretzeled with humiliation this whole conversation, but the thought of Toby being a firsthand witness to my inability to do things with numbers made me want to vomit.

"Yeah, she's my sister," said Merri. "I'll tutor her."

I shook my head vigorously. "Um, no."

Toby was also headshaking. "I got it."

"Hey," Merri squeaked, standing. "I currently check *your* math homework, Toby. Clearly it should be me."

He carefully lowered his knee and stood too. "To quote Rory, 'Um, no.'"

I looked between their standoff and tried not to let the

fact that they were fighting *over me* go to my head. Because, (a) the end result was going to be math tutoring, and (b) this is what they did. They fought. They yelled. They slammed doors. They stomped away. Then Toby climbed Merri's balcony with a chocolate bar or ice cream or a book and apologized. Merri forgave him and he was relieved. They'd go sit on the roof and talk about *best friends forever*. And then the cycle started all over again next time she got mad.

They may be fighting *over* me, but Toby had never cared enough to fight *with* me. He'd never stood outside my door with a present tucked under his arm and a look of soul-deep devastation on his face while waiting for my forgiveness. I sighed and considered escaping again.

"She's *my* sister. If anyone's going to be stuck tutoring her, it should be me."

"Stuck? Thanks, Merri." Not that she heard me, not that I was part of this conversation.

"Knock it off. I'm tutoring her. She's my Knight Light adoptee. I've taken her math class, and you haven't. She might be your sister, but she's my . . . She's Roar. I got this."

I'm his . . . I would've given up every one of my paintbrushes for the ending of that sentence to be different.

"Besides," continued Toby, stacking our empty popcorn buckets and collecting water glasses. "You two will kill each other. And, Rory, didn't I do a good job teaching you about *Star Wars*? I can do this."

"Magic twins and Ewoks," I said—but I must've missed the part with the sci-fi bears. Or the part where Luke and Leia realize they're twins—because I was pretty sure they kissed

each other? I'd have to ask Toby to clarify later. But first I nodded emphatically, because he'd made a valid point—Merri and
I would turn tutoring into a blood sport. "True. I pick Toby."

Merri melted. Her bottom lip pouted and her shoulders
drooped and I felt my own posture do the same, because what
if Toby gave in? He always gave in—if Merri wanted coffee, we
detoured to Cool Beans on the way to school. If she wanted a
bite of his brownie, he broke it in half. If she wanted to be my
tutor . . . he'd surrender all claim to the job.

"Come on, Rowboat," he said softly. "It's the week after
I lost lacrosse and . . ." He didn't say the word "you," but he
looked at her with eyes as heartbroken as my own must've
been. I was a distraction. A boredom cure. "I've got piano lessons and physical therapy . . . that's it. I need this. I *want* to
do this."

"Fine," Merri conceded before turning to me for the first
time in the argument. "But don't think this means you get out
of telling Mom and Dad. Come on, Mayday." She scooped up
the popcorn bowls and flounced up the stairs—Toby limping
after her.

I was left behind to stare at the blank TV screen and try to
process what had happened.

11

After church on Sunday I was scheduled for six hours at the store. I brought *The Great Gatsby*, French, and earth science with me. Earth science was fine. I currently had a B. I planned to keep it. But French and Fitzgerald were equally foreign. I plowed through our second assigned chapter, trying to make sense of the pieces Huck had told me.

I couldn't, so Monday morning found me in front of Ms. Gregoire's classroom, knocking on her door with a sweaty hand.

"Oh, Aurora, come in." Ms. Gregoire stood up and put down the purple and green pens she'd been drumming on the edge of her desk. Walking around to the front, she leaned against it, blocking my view of the stack of papers she'd been grading. I wondered if one was my last reaction journal and how much purple and green ink had been bled on the pages.

Her dress today billowed on top and was more fitted through the thigh to knee. It was navy with brassy trumpets printed all over. Her shoes were red. Her lips too. And yet again I joined the legions of students who'd sat at these desks and wanted to adopt her as a style icon or personal shopper.

"I had a follow-up question about our conversation on Friday," I said.

"Go ahead."

"Well, it's just that . . . I can't be like Gatsby. He's all about parties. I . . . am not." I knew I was contradicting Huck's conclusions, but he had to be wrong; Gatsby was party king.

Ms. Gregoire tilted her head and smiled at me. "Is he? Think about it. Does Gatsby *love* parties, or does he just *throw* parties? Does he attend them? Does he enjoy them?"

"Why else would he . . ."

"Why else indeed? Follow your instincts. You're almost there!" She drummed her fingers on the desk behind her. It felt like the buildup to some big announcement, like I was supposed to punctuate her drumroll with some genius-level breakthrough.

Instead I sighed and mumbled, "Thanks. I'll see you in class."

"Anytime. And, Aurora, I don't want you getting discouraged. If this book isn't you, we'll find one that is."

I waved limp fingers and left, but it was nice to know that Ms. Gregoire made mistakes too. She'd meant to say, *If this book isn't* for *you*. Whatever, it was a minor one-word difference, but it was something and I'd take anything at this point.

Especially since I arrived in art to discover that someone had slid a piece of paper on top of mine in the drying rack. I'd think it was accidental—that someone had put their own painting in without noticing mine was already there—except the paper that had hopelessly smeared mine was blank.

I blinked and blinked. Like that would change what I was seeing or help me hold back tears. Someone bumped my shoulder and I turned with murder in my eyes—not that there was anything left to ruin on the painting in my hands.

"Whoa. Rough Monday, Campbell?" Huck took a step back and held up his hand. "Holy Warhol! What happened to that painting?"

"This class happened to it! Everything I do here gets knocked or dropped or . . . this!" I crumpled the paper and tossed it in the trash. "It's fine. I'll start again. It wasn't that good."

Huck's eyes were wide and full of questions, but my own were still glistening, so he intelligently zipped his lips—literally mimed using a zipper like in kindergarten—and grabbed me a new paper. He clipped it to my easel, then dropped his pencil bag on the easel next to mine.

"I thought you were a potter," I said. He'd told me so on Saturday. How he couldn't wait to get on the wheel on Monday.

"Not today," he answered.

That class no one jostled my easel. Probably because whenever anyone came near me, Huck would call them out by name. "Hey, Jocelyn, what are you doing back here?" "Craig, do you want to get by? Let us know if we need to move out of your way." "Need something, Oliver?"

"How do you know all their names already?" I asked Huck.

He tapped his temple. "Steel trap . . . but also, I'm making some of them up."

I laughed and joined in. "Hey, Nadia. Those are some *kicking* boots." I still wasn't sure if "kicking" was cool, but my use of its double meaning was intentional, because Nadia had aimed them at me in the past.

Huck offered me a discreet low five when she mumbled something and walked away. I beamed at him, feeling he was very much the guardian angel his dimpled smile mimicked. You know, if there wasn't so much mischief in that grin.

It was effective but not productive. Regardless, I was feeling *good* about art for the first time in weeks. Or, at least I was until Mrs. Mundhenk stopped by to check on us. "Oh, Aurora. When are you going to show me what you're capable of? It's so much more than this." She looked at my paper again and sighed.

After she walked away, Huck tried to joke. He even broke out knock-knocks, but I cut him off. "I'm better than this."

"I believe you," he said.

"No, I really am—I just—I just need to *show it*." But the thing about desperation and creativity is they're not compatible. They can't coexist in the same person—at least not when that person is me. Instead of being brilliant or even decent, I spent the last five minutes undermining everything I'd started. I ended the period the same way I'd begun, by crumpling my paper and tossing it in the trash.

❧

Things finally got interesting in English class that day. We read more aloud and learned *why* Gatsby had all those lavish parties—Huck was right, he didn't like them. We also learned why he was fixated on the green light he could see from the end of his dock. It was a light on Nick's cousin Daisy's house.

And Gatsby—he was in obsessive love with Daisy.

His mansion. His wild parties. They were for her. It was an elaborate setup, because Gatsby wanted her attention . . . and her affection.

"Now, I'm sure some of you have done some pretty wild and maybe ill-conceived things to try to win the heart of your crushes, but no one pines quite like Gatsby," said Ms. Gregoire. "Or do they?"

She stumbled slightly and hip-checked my desk. But when I looked up from her feet—which didn't seem even slightly wobbly in her four-inch red heels—she winked.

No. Not cool. If I pined like Gatsby, well, that was my own private humiliation. I didn't throw parties to broadcast my unrequited love, or ask his friends to set us up, or change my name and the way I talked, or any of the charades that Jay Gatsby was neck-deep in. Not that Daisy had noticed— she hadn't come to any of his parties, so what good were all his efforts?

Ms. Gregoire tapped a happy beat with the pads of her fingers on my desk. I wanted to squash them with my book. "Pair up!" she called, and I'm sure there were words after that, but who ever heard anything over the roar of partner-work panic?

"I was thinking," began Clara as she wound her arm around mine and used that to pull my desk toward hers. "This could be the solution to your little neighbor problem."

My desk tilted as Huck sat on the opposite corner, almost tipping it over. "What neighbor problem? Is it like the art class problem?"

"Aurora, are you three working as a group, or are you still choosing a partner?" Ms. Gregoire asked.

I said, "No," at the same time Huck and Clara both said, "Yes." Though it wasn't quite clear what any of us were answering.

Ms. Gregoire nodded sagely. "Good. Carry on."

"What does she mean? What problem are you having, Campbell?"

"*She* is named Clara," said the girl still attached to my arm. "And she doesn't know why you're interrupting our group. So, goodbye." She waved her hand and turned back to me, like Huck would disappear from the front of my desk if she stopped watching.

Clara was usually the opposite of rude, but she'd been trying to corner me to talk about Toby all day. Maybe she wouldn't if he was here?

"Be nice," I said. "Huck and I are friends. He's in my art class."

"See?" He shrugged. "We're friends. And by 'neighbor problems,' do you mean May?"

I groaned and Clara let go of my arm to throw up her hands in exasperation. "Yes! You know about her epic, lifelong crush on Toby?"

"Clara!" I hissed, looking around the room and only exhaling once I saw everyone else was too busy doing the assignment to overhear her declaration.

"I do now," said Huck, but with such obvious dimpled glee that she smiled at him. "Campbell, you were holding out on me. This makes so much sense. So, Clara, you've got a plan? Because I'm thinking"—he dragged his desk over and then sat backward on its attached chair—"that Rory should go full Gatsby on him."

She gave a crisp nod, the kind that would earn her props in cheerleading. "Exactly."

"I liked you better when you were strangers," I mumbled. Clara patted my hand and Huck rolled his eyes. I wondered if I should excuse myself to go drown in the closest water fountain or toilet. Did that require a bathroom pass? "I want nothing to do with a plan about him."

"Him, Gatsby? Or him, Toby?" asked Clara.

"Shhh!" Objectively I knew that no one else in this room cared. No one was sitting on the edge of their seat waiting to hear about my pointless infatuation, but I'd held this secret close for years and had zero desire for it to be public.

"So what's your current plan?" asked Huck.

"Seriously, you too?" Why was Ms. Gregoire spending so much time talking to Keene and Dante instead of noticing that we weren't working? Normally she was all over me like dog hair on black pants. "My plan is to not do anything."

"But Gatsby doesn't sit there and passively wait for Daisy to find and fall in love with him. He's chasing her. He's doing everything he can think of to get her back—the parties, the plotting. He's not leaving anything to chance," said Huck.

"Exactly!" said Ms. Gregoire. She'd approached our

group from behind, making me jump and so glad she hadn't arrived seconds earlier. But something about the way she said "Exactly" felt personal. It made my toes curl inside my yoga flats.

Clara had started speaking, probably making a brilliant point—one that was teacher pleasing and not about my nonexistent love life—but I interrupted to ask Huck, "You're saying Gatsby *makes* things happen so that he'll see Daisy?"

"Well, yeah. He's spent the past five years reinventing himself into someone he believes would be worthy of her—he's not going to leave the rest to chance."

"Oh." Because I was. I was expecting some magic trick where Toby woke up one day and saw me differently and forgot everyone else.

Ms. Gregoire put a hand on my chair and one on Huck's, creating a bridge for the static electricity that crackled across my skin. "I like the way you're complementing each other's discussion—building a shared comprehension. It's very Nick and Gatsby, isn't it?"

I didn't know. Was it? I thought Gatsby already knew it all. But if he had, he wouldn't have needed Nick's help to get access to Daisy.

I waited until Ms. Gregoire walked away to join Elinor and Gemma's group, then turned to Clara and Huck. "Fine. Help me. Tell me what to do."

12

Clara and Huck's strategy session was full of bickering and brainstorms that made me want to hide under my desk or escape out the window.

"We're not giving her a makeover," Huck said firmly. "She doesn't need one."

"Fine," snapped Clara. "But some things aren't about *need*, they're about *fun*. We're agreed about the rest of the options, yes?" She waited for his nod before they both turned to me. "So you have three choices, Rory. Pick one and we'll launch our plan of attack."

"We are not attacking anyone," I answered, my head spinning with pictures of me post-horrific makeover being twirled like a top and thrown at Toby. All three of their plans sounded equally disastrous. The first required me to ignore Toby, which I didn't think I was capable of. The second, to act like a mini Merri, which I couldn't pull off. And the third was absolutely a no-go . . . I just wasn't that good an actor.

"Figure of speech." She waved off my concern. "We've got that Knight Light meeting after lunch—that's your deadline."

Huck rubbed his hands together. "Project Green Light has been green lit."

"Don't call it that," I protested. Attacks? Deadlines? "This is such a bad idea."

They laughed like I was joking. I drew panicked doodles all over my notebook, carving my pen into the red cardboard cover until I revealed the white fibers underneath.

The Knight Light mentor meeting was directly after lunch, which meant I was too nervous to eat, so I talked Huck into heading to the art room.

"Only if we work with clay," he answered. "C'mon, it's like grown-up mud pies."

I wondered if he joked to distract from his talent, because if I had any question why he was in Advanced Art, it disappeared within minutes of him sitting down at a potter's wheel. I chose to sculpt free-form and had barely begun planning and pinching off pieces before it was time to clean up. In the same amount of time, Huck had managed to make his lump of clay bloom from an orange into a graceful melon-size bowl. It had a narrow base, then tapered out in thin, even walls. While I watched, he used a flat tool to add a perfect wide brim. He slowed the wheel, then grabbed his wire tool and deftly cut it off. Covering it loosely in a bag labeled with his name, he tucked it on a high shelf in the drying room. I wanted to fast-forward to when it had reached leather hard, when he'd flip it upside down and put it back on the wheel to trim and cut a foot. I wanted all his secrets and skills.

"Five minutes," Huck called, and I finished rearranging the other pottery projects so mine was hidden in the back. I didn't label it. Maybe if no one knew it was mine it would escape destruction?

While I scrubbed clay from beneath my nails, Huck told me updates he'd gotten from his Ohio friends over the weekend. I suspected he knew I wasn't really listening, but he was chatting at me to calm my Knight Light nerves.

It was Hero High's mentorship program—each sophomore chose a freshman or transfer student to "adopt" for events and activities throughout their first year. Merri had been Toby's first choice, of course. But she'd already paired up with Hannah Kim, so she'd forced him to take me as a consolation prize. I'd been waiting and waiting for this first meeting, but now I stood frozen outside the door to the dining hall.

"Come on," said Huck with a gentle poke in my back. "Let's go in."

Instead of entering the lunchroom, we took the stairs up to the Knight Light Lounge. Some fancy alumni had donated the room. It was large enough to hold the whole freshman and sophomore classes. The lighting was all exposed Edison bulbs and the walls were dusky purple; seating was high stools, low couches, and floor pillows. There was a tiny stage—a black painted platform the size and height of a double bed's mattress—and on it was a single stool. The program's motto was painted in block letters on the wall above: *Knight Lights—they guide your way.* It looked like the sort of place that would be famous for latte foam art and slam poetry nights, but instead of beverage service we had Mr. Welch, who taught media classes. He was sitting on the stool with a clipboard, checking everyone off as they entered. He nodded at us and Huck gave him a tongue click, double-fingergun combo that made the teacher chuckle.

"How did you get so good on the wheel?" I asked to distract myself from Clara and Huck's looming deadline.

"I've been throwing since I was . . . I dunno, maybe eight? My mom's a hobbyist potter. I spent a lot of weekends at craft fairs before I started playing lacrosse. If I had to be there, I figured I might as well have my own stuff to sell. It's fun."

"I hate the wheel. I feel like all my instincts don't work there. I get too tense and end up collapsing anything I throw."

"And the master becomes the student." Huck flopped down onto one of the giant foam-filled cushions, then grabbed my elbow and yanked me down next to him. "Don't worry. I can teach you. And I won't make it all *Ghost* for you, because, you know . . . platonic."

I shook my head. "Not following."

"Wait a minute." He leaned up on one elbow and stared at me. "Your sister, the one you described as a rom-com queen, has never made you watch *Ghost*?"

"Um . . ." I didn't really hear the question, because the rom-com queen had walked in. It wasn't her who distracted me. Nor Eliza, Sera, or Hannah. It was the fifth member of their small pack—the guy who *should* have been looking for me but was instead glued to her side. I leaned closer to Huck and forced a laugh. It wasn't premeditated, it wasn't even a full thought, but when Toby did remember I existed, I wanted him to—

"Okay, serious question," said Huck. "Is this how we're going to play this? You're choosing option C? Jealousy? I need all the necessary info, Campbell, if I'm going to be an effective boy-*faux*-rend."

"Um—" My cheeks flamed as I scooted back a few inches and my eyes shot to Toby. Not that he'd noticed me yet. Not that he'd even looked. From all appearances, he was still entranced by whatever story Merri was telling.

Clara paused behind us and hummed the *Jeopardy* theme song. I reached up and whacked her leg. "Fine. Plan C."

"Oh!" I'm not sure which of us was more surprised, but she recovered first. "Okay then, I'll get out of your way, lovebirds."

"May is an idiot," said Huck. His voice was uncharacteristically quiet as he pulled me closer. "And I am so here for this scheme." He brushed a piece of hair off my cheek as he leaned down and whispered, "But you've got to pinkie swear you won't fall for me. I know my animal magnetism is intense, but resist."

I laughed when he held up a pinkie, but he raised his eyebrows and waited until I hooked my own around it.

If this were one of Merri's books, this would be the moment when I'd feel a frisson. The music would slow down, we'd get all caught up in intense eye contact, and I'd realize that my new friend was the one who gave me tingles. Instead I looked in Huck's face and grinned. "You have Doritos breath."

"Cool Ranch, baby."

Over laughter and joined fingers I saw Toby glance in my direction. He started to turn away, then did a double take. Abandoning my sister and her story, he headed my way.

13

"oday Knight Lights and their adoptees will be doing get-to-know-you surveys," said Mr. Welch. He waited out our collective groans. "I know. They were cheesy in elementary school and haven't gotten less so. Sophomores, you survived this last year; I have every confidence there'll be no fatalities this time either."

"Unlike Gatsby." Huck leaned close and whispered in my ear, "Sorry, spoiler." He and I were still on the same floor cushion, but now Toby was sitting on a stool behind my shoulder. Huck's Knight Light, Curtis, was sitting next to him, swinging his flip-flopped feet so that his brown toes passed just inches above our heads. Fatalities? Gatsby? Was Jay going to pine to death? Ugh, if so I wanted a new ending pronto.

Toby nudged me with his sneaker and I looked up at him. He put a finger to his lips, and I felt like a toddler getting a scolding. I shifted on the pillow, trying to sit up straighter, but Huck poked me in the side and I collapsed half on top of him. He settled his arm around my shoulder and tipped his head to lean on mine as he whispered, "Don't blow it now—he hasn't looked at the teacher once."

Across the room, Clara gave me a below-the-table thumbs-up. At least she was being discreet. I wouldn't have put it past her to post a bullet-point plan on the room's chalkboard wall: Rory's Guide to the Guy Next Door.

"Hey, Roar." Toby bent forward on his stool. He waited until I pulled my head off Huck's shoulder and looked up at him. "These get-to-know-you things—think it's unfair we have such a big advantage?" He shifted his eyes to Huck, who'd leaned his chin on my shoulder when he turned toward Toby too. "No one in this room knows you as well as I do."

"Um, except for my sister?" I countered.

Toby's ears turned red. "Well, yeah. But after Merri—"

"Then maybe we should trade partners," interrupted Huck.

It was a good thing Mr. Welch had stopped talking and was handing out papers in the front, because even with the increased buzz of forty pairs of students making plans, Toby's "What? No! Rory is *my* adoptee" sounded super loud.

"M'kay. I'll let you borrow her," said Huck. He stood and I was suddenly staring at three hands in my face as he, Toby, and Curtis all reached down to help me up. I decided Curtis's was safest and also that Huck needed to check if it was too late to join the drama club. He was way too good at this.

"I'll see you after, Camp . . . bear."

Or maybe *good*, but not perfect. I mouthed *Campbear?* at him and he grimaced. I laughed and said, "Later, Huck. Curtis."

Toby frowned at everyone who greeted us as he strode across the room to get our packet, then trudged to a pair of stools in the back corner. Digging a pen out of his faded red backpack, he turned to the first page and pressed the tip to the line beside the top question. "Let's get started. Maybe I don't know everything about you after all."

Huck and Clara were going to be way too pleased—but for however long this moment lasted, I had Toby's full attention, despite the fact that Merri was in the same room. Maybe it was time to take a page out of Gatsby's book and attempt to be alluring and mysterious. I arched an eyebrow. "But wouldn't it be boring if you did?"

We didn't finish even half the questions, mostly because Toby insisted on writing down my answers word for word. It was like a high-intensity version of the question game Huck and I had played at Saturday detention, only stranger because Toby was acting like his life depended on my answer to *Favorite sports team*. "Um, none? Does Olympic figure skating count?"

About forty minutes into the interrogation, he asked, "What was your scariest moment?"

I tilted my head. "You know this one. That time with the basement door? When the knob came off and I couldn't get out and you couldn't hear me banging because Merri had dragged you off to play circus on the swing set." Super-wonderful memory, that one. Slamming my fists against the rough door until my hands had splinters. Screaming until my voice gave out. Mom found me slumped against the door after I'd wet my pants and sobbed myself sick. I'd been six. I'd refused to go into the basement again until it had been finished.

"Why don't you tell it from the beginning," suggested Toby, his pen at the ready.

"No." I laughed. "Toby, you know all this. We could blow this off, talk about anything."

He clicked his pen twice. "It started when you were going to get a quilt from the dryer, right?"

"We were going to build a blanket fortress." I was surprised he remembered that much—the day hadn't been nearly as scarring for him.

"And then you never came back," he said at the same time that I added, "And then you forgot about me."

I glanced up from my hands. I'd been knotting them together in my lap, thinking about how long it had taken Dad to dig out the splinters. Toby looked up from his paper. And I'd always heard about falling into eye contact—like it was a pothole or a puddle. But there was something trapping about that moment. About the way we were really seeing each other and seeing perhaps we didn't have the same memory of that day. It was like Toby said earlier: Maybe we didn't know each other as well as we thought.

"Annnnd, time," called Mr. Welch from the front of the room. "The lesson plans I inherited from last year's Knight Light supervisor instruct me to have you all come up here and introduce your adoptee—but I vote we skip that part."

Toby and I faced him. We provided our part in the obligatory laughter, but I wasn't really seeing what was in front of me. I was too deep in my head, trying to deconstruct Toby's expression the way I would if I were drawing it. Had he looked as vulnerable as I felt? Had there been something wistful or eager in his eyes?

"We can finish these up tonight," said Toby.

"Tonight?" I swung back toward him.

"Tutoring." He flipped his pen and caught it. "I'll come over after dinner."

"Wait—" I wanted to delay or cancel, but Toby had gone to find his friends and Huck and Clara had popped up like the smuggest prep school jack-in-the-boxes.

"Come on, heartbreaker," Clara said, steering me by the wrist. "You can tell us about it on the way to history."

I had a response journal due for English the next day, and as I stared at my computer that night, it would've been so easy to write about Toby or Daisy or anything that ended in an "ee" sound, but that was never happening. Instead I wrote about New York, about Nick Carraway's observation that "the city seen from the Queensboro Bridge is always the city seen for the first time, in its first wild promise of all the mystery and beauty of the world."

I could relate to that. Each time I stepped out of the train station in New York City, it took my breath away. It was easy to fill a page about New York, especially when I made the font as big as my NYC dreams.

New York is a combination of breathless beauty and soul-stealing sorrow. But even its poverty and garbage can be picturesque with the right framing and backdrop. As an artist I'm trained to look for compositions. It's enough to make me forget for a moment that that pile of trash bags is someone's belongings, or that that blackened toe peeking out from tattered cardboard is someone's foot. Those are the types of reminders I need—the ones that cancel out all the promise of mystery and beauty and force me to consider things with rational thoughts. Because New York City does that—it teases you with ambition, the type that's swept up Nick Carraway. But it also doesn't hide the carcasses of other people's smashed dreams. The trick is to force yourself to see them.

I read it over. It was pretty bleak. But bleak was good, right? Merri always joked that upbeat things were commercial and depressing things were called "literary"—I wondered if I could sell Ms. Gregoire on this being a "literary response journal" versus one fueled by stress.

It was after dinner—granted our dinner had been early so Mom could head back to the store and relieve Lilly, but it was still *after* dinner—which meant Toby could arrive at any time. And I wasn't ready.

I spent the next half hour storming all over my house to try to figure out where we should work. Not the living room, because there was nowhere to put books and papers besides

Mom's low coffee table, which was covered in porcelain dog figurines. Not the dining room, because it hadn't been cleared from dinner and Gatsby and Byron would beg and bug us. Dad was doing dishes and listening to podcasts at ear-killing volume in the kitchen. My bedroom? No, the thought of Toby in the room with all my secret sketches was enough to make my hands shake.

So that left the basement. I lit a mint-scented candle to cover the burnt-popcorn smell. I vacuumed up the kernels and dog hair tumbleweeds. I put away the remote controls, plumped the throw pillows, restocked the mini fridge with Toby's favorite root beer and waters for me—and hid Merri's cream sodas so the sight of them wouldn't snag his attention. Pencils had been sharpened, mechanical pencils reloaded. There were erasers and paper and calculators lined up. If I'd had time, I would've bought his favorite brand of licorice or made a playlist—but this was the best I could do on short notice.

And it was stupid. This was *Toby*. We'd spent hours and years together. But that didn't mean I wanted to fail in front of him. My phone rang a half second before I picked it up to call him and cancel. "Hello?"

"Hey, Roar." Toby hesitated, then added, "I saw Fielding's car in your driveway and was thinking—maybe you'd better come over here instead."

And if I'd needed any sort of demonstration about why stressing out was worthless, there it was. I wasn't Gatsby. I had no allure or power or fancy orange juice machine—there was no way I was winning him over. While I was worried about what to wear to learn sine and cosine, he was worrying about seeing Merri with her boyfriend.

Was he avoiding Fielding *all* the time? Or just when he was around my sister? And how long until Merri noticed and tried to mediate? Yeah, that was not going to go well.

"Sure," I said as I snuffed out the candle. "I'll be right over."

14

Gatsby was a moron. There were other girls. Ones unattached. Forget green lights. Find a red one. A blue one. Any other color to obsess over.

Daisy Buchanan didn't deserve him. She wasn't loyal or smart. And what was up with him and his whole stupid fancy car? I hated cars and shotgun seats and the fact that Toby would always be my green light, but Merri was his.

Merri, who was sitting in his passenger seat making him laugh and smile and totally oblivious to the way he'd watched our driveway out his kitchen window the whole time we sat at his table and trudged through my homework last night. His posture hadn't relaxed until Fielding's car backed out, and he hadn't noticed when I'd said, "And that's the last one. Thanks, Toby," with half a dozen problems still to go.

Daisy. Toby. They sounded stupidly similar and that was probably the type of thing I was supposed to confess for English. Ms. Gregoire would likely give me an A-plus if I ripped up the response journal in my backpack and submitted nothing but the lyrics for the song about a bicycle built for two with Toby's name swapped in.

"I'm half crazy, all for the love of you . . ."

"What are you humming?" Toby turned around at a stop sign to give my knee a playful flick and my heart turned over. Or, it did until he gave Merri one too. "You Campbell girls and your mysterious humming. This one does it whenever she's bored or smug or has a secret."

I slumped down. Of course he knew every one of her moods and tells. He probably had spreadsheets where he analyzed her smiles. Which were totally different than my sketchbooks full of his expressions . . .

"What is it for you, Roar: bored, smug, or secret?"

"Secret," I said. "But unlike *This One*." I reached forward to flick her too, only I aimed for her neck and the wrong side of gentle. "I won't crack and tell six seconds later."

"Ow!" said Merri. "Everyone stop flicking me!"

I watched Toby's eyes narrow in the rearview mirror and braced myself for a rebuke for harming poor Merri. "But I'm your Knight Light," he said. "You can tell me anything."

Merri snorted. "You're letting that title go to your head. It doesn't actually come with a badge and privileges. Leave poor Rory alone."

Normally I'd object to "poor Rory," but today I was too grateful. Or cruel, because the easiest way to make her happy was also the easiest way to hurt Toby, and that didn't stop me from saying, "So, has Fielding asked you to Fall Ball yet?"

⌒⌒

Ms. Gregoire ended class on Thursday by telling me to stop by after school. Which meant I stressed and sweated and squirmed through my afternoon classes. All that work Toby put into trying to cram math into my brain—wasted. I spent the whole period staring at the clock and the light bulb-shaped poster above it: *Genius is 1 percent inspiration and 99 percent perspiration.*

Well, I had the sweat part down and totally needed a new deodorant, one that was Hero High panic-proof.

Another consequence was it cost me my ride with Toby. I texted him while standing outside the classroom: **Meeting with Gregoire. I'll walk home after.**

She was waiting with a smile, a coffee mug, and my response paper—or what was visible of it beneath her scribblings. "Grab a seat. I want to talk grades and support and making sure you're getting enough of the latter to improve the former. I don't want you missing out on things here."

Eye contact while being lectured was always tricky, but even trickier was trying to pay attention while also stealing peeks at her upside-down comments on my paper. "Um, I've got a math tutor now. I'm taking a retest tomorrow."

"Oh, that will be good. Mrs. Roberts had expressed concern about you. Who is it?"

"Toby." My cheeks turned pink just saying his name.

"Interesting . . ." She crossed her legs and tapped the paper in front of her. "Well, since I can see you're curious, let's talk about this. You're still not showing me any connections."

I slumped down in my seat. Apparently, I hadn't managed to pull off "literary."

"Nothing about this book feels personal? Nothing about the parties? Or feeling like a fish out of water? New to a social scene?" I kept shaking my head and she kept giving me a dubious look. "No . . . green light?"

There was a knock on the door and both of us shifted our gaze to the guy standing there. "Hey, Roar, sorry to inter-rupt. But, I got your text. Ride home, you-me? I don't have piano until four thirty, so I can wait. Twenty minutes? Thirty? An hour?"

I went dazed and dizzy, because he'd shown up with no warning. My nod was slow, like a bobblehead with a rusty spring.

"Thirty should be plenty. Thanks, Toby." It was Ms. Gregoire with the answer, since I hadn't noticed he needed one. After he left, she was all "Hmmm" and head tilting and glances from me to the door. If one more person guessed my crush, I was going to find a place that gave poker-face lessons and enroll immediately. "If I recall, I was asking about any green lights in your own life."

"It's . . . not green?" Nope, not green. Toby—like everyone in a Hero High uniform—was wearing navy, gray, and red. The only thing green about it was my envy of how he looked at Merri in ways he'd never looked at me. As for lights? I was grateful my room didn't face his house, because there were far too many times I'd glimpsed the glow beyond his bedroom balcony doors and been glued in place, wondering what he was doing. Wishing I had half the access to him that Merri did.

The nights where he had his door cracked and I could hear him playing his keyboard were the hardest. I'd spent hours sit-ting on the side of the tub below the bathroom window listen-ing to his compositions cross the narrow strip of lawn between our houses. Every time I'd walked out of that room while he was still playing—usually because Merri banged on the door and announced she needed to pee—it was physically painful.

"Come on, Rory. Give me something to work with. What words do you think of when you think of Gatsby?"

Did she mean the character or the book? And would it be okay if my answer wasn't positive or PG? I swallowed. "Um, it's a cautionary tale."

"Good. More. Cautionary against what?"

I was probably supposed to say "capitalism" or "excess" or "reckless consumption" or who knows what. Something smart, with quotes to back it up.

I looked around the room, wondering which of these seats was Toby's. "Love."

"Well, there's a start." Ms. Gregoire dusted off her hands. "We're done here."

"Wait. What?" Hadn't she told Toby thirty minutes? But why was I protesting her letting me leave? "I mean, thanks! I'll try harder."

"Don't try harder—try not to not try so hard."

Whatever that meant. But I had a feeling the explanation would use all those minutes I'd gotten back, so I nodded and left.

I practically ran from the humanities building to the art studio. I needed a hideout. A place to wind down from that meeting and vent some of the creative energy and anxiety crackling beneath my skin.

I had only twenty-five minutes, but it was one of those days where everything felt enchanted. The lines I drew flowed like magic from my pencil. Within a few minutes, I'd roughed out a sketch and was ready to paint. The colors I mixed matched the ones in my head and the connection between my brain and my paintbrush was flowing at autobahn speeds. I hadn't gotten a smock. I hadn't pinned back my hair. Which meant both my face and my uniform were speckled in gold and gray and green, but I didn't stop and I didn't care.

I'd finally found my way back to the art zone and I was never, ever leaving.

"I hope you haven't missed your ride."

I jumped and screeched. But luckily, the only thing I spattered with my paintbrush was my shirt. I made things worse by pressing my hand—still clutching the brush—to my pounding heart as I turned to face the door.

Ms. Gregoire had spoken, but she was standing with Mrs. Mundhenk. "Didn't we tell Toby thirty minutes? It's been more than an hour."

"It has?" I put down the brush and pulled out my phone. The screen was covered in texts I hadn't heard. Toby looking for me. Merri looking for me because Toby had called her. Toby worried. Toby calling Lilly. Toby threatening to call my parents. Toby giving up and driving home to look for me there.

"I lost track of time. I need—" I texted one-handed as I walked my brushes to the sink. **Sorry! I'm fine. I'm safe. Be home soon.** I looked up from the screen a step too late, already midcollision with the sink. I bobbled everything I was holding, almost giving myself and my phone a bath in paint water.

"Let me help," said Mrs. Mundhenk.

"Ahem," said Ms. Gregoire. "First, you should come see

this." She was standing in front of my easel, studying the painting I hadn't had a chance to stop and take in yet. I'd been so focused on each individual part that I didn't know if it worked as a whole. But I knew those parts well. I knew what they added up to. I knew it wasn't a painting I'd intended for public consumption. I'd planned on this one joining all my recent projects in the recycling bin. It had just been good to paint. Good to remember that I could.

And portraits of Toby had always been my gateway to the art world.

"The likeness—it's remarkable," added Ms. Gregoire.

"But it's more than that—" said Mrs. Mundhenk as she joined her. "I know you're talented, that's always been obvious, but I didn't want to see you playing it safe. I want people to be able to walk into a gallery and ask 'Is that . . . ?' and hear 'Why, yes. It's an Aurora Campbell.' Because that's what you're capable of. That's what I've been waiting for. What's on this easel—it's captivating. It's vulnerable. I want to hug that boy or hug the artist because of the emotion you've provoked with his expression and your choice of colors. Aurora—this, my dear girl, this is you. This is your voice. It's unique. It's powerful. Don't ever hide it."

No. It wasn't me. It was what I wanted. It was what I didn't have. It was what was private, and I didn't want it to be discussed any longer.

"I'm going to need to keep this," said Mrs. Mundhenk.

I shook my head and dropped my phone. Thankfully on the counter and not in the sink. "Absolutely not. You can't— No one can see—"

"I won't show it to anyone. At least not anyone at Hero High." I was still shaking my head when Mrs. Mundhenk added, "And I'll count this toward your grade—give you an A-plus."

My mouth dropped open as I slumped against the sink. I had so many incompletes in here. I needed the grade. "You can't show anyone. Really."

"Will it help if I also count this as your last response journal and give you an A?" asked Ms. Gregoire. "Don't think I didn't notice your use of color—he might as well be standing under a green light."

I rubbed my hands over my face, leaving behind streaks and smears that I couldn't bother to care about. "Green doesn't just stand for Gatsby. It's also jealousy, and calming, and greed. And it's been shown to improve creativity." I was pretty sure I wasn't making that last one up.

"It can be all those things. And I have no doubt that there are people who will say green symbolizes money or the earth or rebirth." Ms. Gregoire smirked and pointed to my easel. "But in *that* particular painting, green means something else."

Any of the responses in my head were going to either cost me my grade or earn me a detention, so I bit my lip and grabbed my phone from the counter, my bag from the coat hooks, and ran.

I was two blocks away from home when a familiar Audi pulled over and a familiar boy in a leg brace jumped out, the musical arrangement to some movie's epic battle scene spilling from his car's speakers.

"Are you okay?" he asked, limp-running over and grasping

my upper arms. I wasn't sure if he was going to hug me or shake me. I don't think he was either. "What happened?"

"I texted."

"Yeah, but it didn't say anything. I was freaking out. Merri and Lilly are freaking out. The only reason your parents aren't freaking out is Lilly decided not to call them yet. Where were—" He dropped his arms and stepped back. "The art room. Look at you. You're covered in paint. Why didn't I check there? I'm such an idiot."

"I lost track of time. I'm really sorry."

"I swear, Roar, all I could think about was those Lifetime movies about the missing kids Merri's always watching."

I bristled at his use of the word "kids." "I was only missing for thirty minutes."

I don't think he heard me. He was tugging on his hair. "And I was going to be the last person who'd seen you alive— and how would I live with that? And they'd bring in the sniffer dogs and I'd give them the sweatshirt you left in my car . . ."

I snorted and opened his passenger door. "You really went all in on this fantasy, huh?"

He slid into the driver's seat. "It's not funny. Text your sisters."

"Yes, sir."

"And don't ever do that to me again."

I wanted to laugh. The euphoria of Making! Art! Of hearing it complimented! Of seeing that Toby cared! It all went to my head like the bubbles in seltzer water, tickling the inside of my nose and curving my lips into a smile. "Hey, cranky. Your race-car bed is calling. It says you need a nap."

The scowl on his face dissolved so quickly I was a step behind when he paired a full-throated guffaw with that grin that always hit me like a sucker punch. "You know about my race-car bed, huh? When are you going to stop peeking in my windows?"

Okay, that was a bit too close to accurate, but since he didn't know that, it felt safer to sass back. "Can you blame me? Those footie Superman jammies are hawwwt."

"Superman?" He gasped as he shifted the car into drive. "Blasphemy, Aurora Leigh Campbell. You know I'm a Batman guy." Toby handed me a bottle of kombucha from his cup holder. "Here, I got this for you before you went AWOL."

"Thanks."

By the time we reached our street—a whole two minutes later—I'd texted Lilly and Merri and called off the search party. Toby pulled into his driveway. "You busy tonight? I'll be home from piano by five thirty. Want to come over and see my race-car bed?"

The thing they don't tell you about spit-takes is that the amount of liquid in your mouth magically multiplies before you aerosolize it and spray it everywhere. This is especially true when the person on the receiving end of your spit spew is the unrequited love of your life. I scrunched my eyes shut so I didn't have to see the kombucha dripping off his chin, the droplets on his glasses, the places his shirt collar was wet.

"I am so sorry," I mumbled, wiping my chin on the back of my hand.

"I see how it seemed like I needed a cold shower, but I was just asking about tutoring."

"Tutoring?" I opened my eyes just to cringe again.

"It may have sounded like the world's cheesiest pickup line, but *come on*, it's me and you. I was joking—" He grinned and my stomach lurched; yeah, me and him. So funny. "You know, since you're not into this whole tutoring thing? But if you promise not to spritz me again, I promise not to make it torture."

"Sure. My quiz retest is tomorrow and the exam's coming up. I'll take all the help I can get."

"Let's work at my house. It'll be less . . ."

"Chaotic?" I supplied. "Between the dogs and Lilly's daily wedding drama and Merri being Merri . . ."

"Yeah." Toby's voice turned bitter as he added, "My house is good at silence."

I wasn't sure how to read that comment, except to notice once again that I hadn't seen Major May in a while. I made a mental note to ask him about it when he wasn't dripping with my backwash. "Sorry again for scaring you. See you at six?"

"Can't wait," he said. And I thought he actually meant it.

❧

Race car shaped or not, I didn't get to see Toby's bed. He led me to the kitchen again and put my books on the table in the most boring room on earth.

"Does Major May know that colors besides white exist?" Because there was monochromatic, and then there was *This is what the inside of an all-white snow globe looks like.* The walls, floor, countertops, cabinets, and backsplash all matched.

"The place mats are beige." Toby looked around and laughed. "It's pretty awful, huh?"

"Merri calls it the 'stain-temptation room.' I want to buy you red cups, or orange curtains, or yellow towels. Or even just a plant or a fridge magnet." I opened a cabinet and shut it quickly. The interior was white and the dishes matched.

"How about you stay here?" Toby teased. "You're the most colorful thing I know."

So what if my yoga pants were purple and green stripes and my tank top was yellow. I had on a black hoodie and black shoes. If you ignored the fact that both were polka-dotted with paint spatters, they were practically plain.

"I'm a thing now?" My words were a little breathless, because Toby had crossed the kitchen to stand in front of me. His arms snaked beneath mine to cage me against the counter. I could smell his pine bodywash and the licorice he must have had after dinner. The urge to turn my head into his hair and sniff his shampoo was pretty overwhelming. I might have given in if he hadn't suddenly lifted me up so I was sitting on the island. It was a maneuver right out of my childhood when I'd begged for boosts or piggybacks.

"You look good up there. Can you stay and be the centerpiece?"

For a second my heart clenched with hope. This was flirting, right? It felt like flirting. My smile wavered when I glanced over at the math books stacked on the table and remembered the joke he'd made in the car, where the pairing of him plus me had been the punch line. My stomach soured.

It didn't matter if he smelled like heaven and this sounded like flirting. It wasn't real.

"I'll feed you juice boxes and Jell-O. You can even drip if you want."

Those had been two of my favorite foods—when I was eight. My shoulders slumped as I leaned away from him. Is that how he still saw me? Because I hadn't eaten either in years. I slid down from the counter on the side across from where he was standing. "How about you show me how to do some of this math?"

He blinked. "Right, math." He flipped the lid of my textbook open and shut a few times. "Want tea or anything first?"

"Maybe later." I looked around the empty kitchen, suddenly curious about what I'd find if I opened the fridge. Toby used to eat dinner at our house a couple days a week—he hadn't since Merri started dating Fielding. I wasn't quite sure how their friendship dynamic worked anymore. He seemed to openly pine when Merri wasn't looking, and when it was the two of them—or the two of them ignoring me—they were the way they'd always been. But as soon as Fielding entered the picture, Toby got stiff and awkward. Did Merri know how Toby felt? I hadn't heard them on the roof in weeks, but Toby was in a knee brace, so maybe that was more about self-preservation than the state of their relationship?

Right now, in this kitchen with zero personality and zero dishes in the sink, I wondered how often he was alone in this house and if Toby had had licorice for dinner.

15

was humming *Jurassic Park*'s theme when I got to art the next day—a remnant from my morning drive with Toby. It was Friday. Mrs. Mundhenk no longer thought I was a mistake. Huck worked wonderfully as an easel bodyguard. To top it off, based on yesterday's studio session, I had my art mojo back.

Also, spending ninety minutes the night before with the guy who made my heart race *and* who explained math in ways that made me feel less like a moron could've had something to do with my good mood.

It was time to go oils. That type of paint required a level of commitment I hadn't felt ready for in this room, but now I was. Get me a paint knife, get me some turpentine, bring on the tubes. Ultramarine blue, titanium white, Mars black, yellow ochre, cadmium red, alizarin crimson—I wanted them all. I was going to mix and layer them until the finished product was something breath-stealingly good. It would be exactly like Mrs. Mundhenk suggested, something that was undeniably *me*.

This wasn't a portrait, and the composition was simple: red rubber boots sitting in a puddle. But water was never easy to paint. The sketch would be fast, the rest of it slow. I began to work in the negative space, beginning with the deepest black and adding in tones of blue as I progressed. The shape of the boots was just beginning to emerge when suddenly the white space they would occupy turned sludge gray.

I was so confused by the change that it took me a moment to realize the cause—or to recognize that the same dirty paint water dripping off my paper was also splashed across my shirt.

"Whoops," said a girl in a tone that didn't sound *whoopsish*. It didn't sound accidental at all, and there was nothing apologetic about the way she twirled her empty cup on her finger. "I guess I didn't see you."

A surge of rage pounded against my teeth and tongue. Weeks of silence were cracking and all the emotions I'd repressed spilled out in one word: "Enough!"

I yelled it so loud that someone dropped something. I listened to it clatter in the instant silence in the room. But one word wasn't enough. Especially when the girl in front of me—Maya—seemed to think it was funny. She was definitely choking back laughter. Or, at least she was until I kicked my easel. Not the sideways shove that she and all the others had engaged in. No, I kicked it over, causing the easel beside mine to fall too. Luckily it was empty because Huck was working on the wheel. I stepped closer to Maya, waving a paint-stained finger in her face. "It is *not* okay!"

"What in the world is going on over here?" asked Mrs. Mundhenk. "Rory, Maya, explain yourselves."

"It was an accident," said Maya. All her missing contrition suddenly appeared on her face. "Rory must've moved her easel when I was walking by and I tripped."

"No!" I shouted. "This wasn't an accident. It wasn't an accident when my sculpture got smashed, or any of the times that my drying paintings were smeared. Or ripped. Or the fact that no one in here seems to be able to walk by my easel without bumping it. And my supplies disappearing or breaking. None of this is accidental. I don't know what I did to piss everyone in here off, but—"

"It's the Snipes thing," called out Byron from the crowd that had formed in my corner of the studio, everyone openly gawking at the silent freshman who'd finally found her voice. I whirled toward him and he held up his hands, stepping away from my easel, which he'd been fixing. "That doesn't make it okay—but it's because of the Snipes workshop. No one wants to compete with you. If you don't produce anything, then no one has to."

"I don't even know what that is!" I roared.

"Is this true?" asked Mrs. Mundhenk. "You've all been sabotaging a classmate's art for your own gain? In *my* studio? In this school that prides itself on the student body's integrity? I'm ashamed of you all. And I'm sorry, Aurora. I can't imagine what this has been like. I wish you said— No, I wish *I'd noticed* earlier. Or that someone else had spoken up. I owe you a bigger apology than that, but for right now, go to your next class. The rest of you will be staying. And Headmaster Williams will be joining us."

"Not everyone," I clarified. "I don't know everyone who did or didn't—but definitely not Huck or Byron."

"Very well. Byron, Huck, and Rory, you're excused." Mrs. Mundhenk turned to the remaining students with a look of furious disapproval. "The rest of you, I don't know what to say, except—"

I shut the door on "except." I didn't need to hear the lecture, I just needed the harassment to stop.

"Hey, wait," Byron called. "You really didn't know about the workshop with Snipes?"

I studied his face. It was super pale, but he always skewed that way—he didn't seem to be joking. "Andrea Snipes?"

Of course I knew who she was. I had postcard prints of her work hanging on my bedroom wall. She'd been an artistic wunderkind in the eighties. Took the art world by storm and had paintings in the great museums all over the globe. In third grade, I'd asked Santa for a lunch box printed with her *Girl, Rising*. Incidentally, that was the same year I stopped believing, after I caught Dad in the basement with a glue gun trying to attach a print of the painting to a Minnie Mouse lunch box.

Huck gestured impatiently. "So what is this Snipes workshop that has everyone so worked up?"

Byron rolled his eyes and grumbled, "*Freshmen.* Every four years she does a workshop in New York over winter break. She accepts a dozen students from around the country and works intensively with them for a week. It's this year. You can't apply—you have to get nominated by your art teacher. But teachers can only nominate two students."

He turned to head toward the upperclassman lockers. "No one wants to compete with you. Can't say I blame them."

⌇

"Can I ask a question?" Huck and I were walking from our lockers to lunch. Some days I ate with him. Some days I ate with Clara and her group, and some days—when the morning had asked too much and I needed to regroup—I ate in the art room. But after that morning's showdown, I wasn't quite ready to step foot in there.

"I suppose," he answered. "But I don't know any more about the Snipes thing than you do. And I don't think I *need* to learn about it. I'm not a contender. And that's cool."

"It's not about that. It's about English. Does Gatsby seem great to you? I don't mean to make you my own personal SparkNotes, but . . . is that part still to come? Or is it a sarcastic title because he's really a dud?"

"I think . . ." Huck was clearly choosing his words carefully. It was a new look on him and one I appreciated. If he'd had this answer on the tip of his tongue, I would've felt more stupid than I already did. "It's going to be good for you when we finish this book. I don't know why it stresses you out. Did you hear what Gemma said about champagne bubbles being a metaphor for the brevity of life? Or Dante's theory that Tom has a crush on Nick? Half the time everyone's making stuff up."

"Even you?"

Huck raised an eyebrow. "Well, of course not. Everything

I say is brilliant and canonical." He flashed his dimples. "It's just a book. Don't let it get to you this much."

I'd gone back last night and looked up when Gatsby was first described in the novel. It was on page two when Nick admires Gatsby's "extraordinary gift of hope" and "romantic readiness." But I couldn't decide if those qualities made him exceptional, or exceptionally foolish. I couldn't decide what they made me either.

I grabbed the cafeteria door, but Huck put a hand above mine and stopped me from opening it. "I never answered your first question. No, I don't think he's that great. That's the point—that he's not what he seems. His reputation is built to impress, but it's all a facade." He dropped his hand. "You, Aurora Clementine Campbell, are guileless and honest and wear your heart on your face—you're the opposite of a Gatsby, and I think that's pretty great."

My cheeks heated. "My middle name's not Clementine."

He nodded somberly. "It should be. Now come on, let's eat. Rumor has it they're handing out study guides in sciences and math today. I don't know about you, but I need to start carbing up."

I hadn't heard that rumor, but I *had* looked up my averages last night. If we needed study guides three weeks before midterms, I was dead meat. I had to do well on today's math retest *and* get at least a B on the exam to bring my average above passing. Ugh, Ms. Gregoire might have been right about there being different types of smart—but they weren't all equally helpful in high school.

16

refused to have a birthday party. I rejected the idea of a birthday dinner at a restaurant because I knew my family would coerce the waiters into singing. No thank you. I was celebrating my fifteenth birthday in a much less tortuous way—wearing my favorite ratty sweatshirt and leggings, holed up in my room surrounded by sketch pads and paints. I'd completed my second Saturday detention the week before, and this was my first free weekend—I wanted to spend it submerged in art. But despite my insistence and resistance, when Mom called me down to the kitchen Sunday afternoon, she snapped a paper party hat on my head and yelled, "Surprise!"

The room was semi-full of all the people I knew at Hero High. "We tried calling your friends from your old school, but it's homecoming weekend," Mom explained. "They all said to wish you happy birthday."

Wow. I hadn't thought of them in weeks. Which had to make us truly awful friends, but I was also secretly relieved they weren't here. It was strange enough looking from Merri to Fielding to Huck to Toby to my mom and dad, plus Gatsby and Byron sniffing hopefully at everyone's feet, tails flailing.

"That sweet Clara is coming later," Mom told me.

Great. Hopefully by then we wouldn't be standing in an awkward silent circle admiring Mom's taste in decorative dish towels and the dogs' ability to lap water out of their bowls.

The doorbell rang and everyone watched me answer it. Merri's dog came with me to bark at and lick the new arrival. "Stay, Gatsby," I ordered as I opened the door. Byron from art class stood on the other side.

"Um, hi?" I said.

"Happy birthday. Your sister invited me—is it weird I said yes? I felt cornered." His eyes darted from me to the pathetic party over my shoulder. I bet he was regretting that decision.

"It's weird she asked you." I'd mentioned him a whopping one time to Merri, but in her mind that meant we were best friends, because in her world she was on birthday-party-invite status with people she'd just met. "You might as well come in."

"Thanks?" He handed me an envelope. "It's a gift card. I didn't know what to get you."

Why would he? We'd talked only a few times. The main thing I knew about him was he *hadn't* been a bully in art.

"This is Boy Byron?" asked Mom. She offered him a plate and pointed to the snacks. I wanted to die. "Have you met your namesake? Oh no, he didn't pee on you, did he? Byron has a bad habit of peeing when he meets new people."

"He does?" Clara asked with a laugh from the open doorway. She joined the group and poked him in the chest. "Well, learn something new every day. I'm glad I've known you since we were little. I'm not a fan of being peed on."

"No, she didn't mean Boy Byron, she meant this one." Merri knelt and whistled, and my parents' Pomeranian came scampering from under the dining room table where he'd been hiding from the doorbell. Let's be honest, he'd likely peed under there too. Merri waved one of his paws. "Byron, meet Boy Byron."

The dog took one look at all the strangers in the foyer and barked furiously while retreating into his tablecloth lair.

Clara shoved a gift at me and squealed, "And where's my favorite doggo? Gatsby!" He came running and laid down at her feet, belly up. She gave him a hasty scratch, then turned and ran out the door, calling, "Be back—need to grab my meds before my mom leaves. Allergic!" I wondered if she'd actually come back, or if I could convince the other guests to use that excuse and leave.

"Why does he get to be Byron and *I'm* 'Boy Byron'?" He didn't look offended, just bewildered. He'd curled the paper plate in his hand so it looked like a taco.

"We can't call him 'Dog Byron'—that sounds ridiculous." Merri said this like it was completely logical, adding, "Plus I've known him longer."

Boy Byron—ugh, now she had me doing it—laughed. "If you say so." He cleared his throat. "I didn't realize how much a height difference there is between you two. How often do people think Merri's the little sister instead of the other way around?"

Because shorter and cuter must make her younger, and that totally didn't make me feel like a gangly troll in comparison? Especially when Fielding and Toby both stepped closer to Merri in reaction to the insult on *her* behalf. Fielding was holding her hand and Toby's was twitching at his side, like he was trying to stop himself from reaching for her too. Instead he glared daggers at Boy Byron. At least that meant he wasn't glowering at Fielding? Progress, maybe?

I wanted to glare too. But all eyes were on me since I was the involuntary host of this disaster. I gritted my teeth. "Well, she *is* my little sister. Older, but littler."

Merri scoffed. "Just wait. I'm one good growth spurt from catching up. Plus, since I eat meat and dairy, I'm the one getting all those growth hormones and chemicals Ms. Vegan is always talking about avoiding. They've got to be good for something."

I'd never, ever been that type of vegan—the one who lectures other people on what they eat. I didn't even tell people I ate a plant-based diet unless I had to. I'd eat around sour cream on fajitas or pull cheese off pizza. It wasn't my job to police what anyone put in their mouth, and yet all Merri had to do was use the v-word and I was the bad guy.

I wasn't sure what my face looked like, but now mine was the hand getting a squeeze. Huck had come to stand beside me. And Toby—he didn't move from Merri's side, but he frowned. "I've never heard Rory say anything like that."

Huck squeezed my hand again, a subtle warning that Toby's weak defense was not a reason for me to beam like the sun shone down on me alone.

"Oh, girls, stop fussing at each other for five seconds." Mom bustled through the clump of us and set a tray of vegetables on the table. "It's my fault Merrilee is such a munchkin."

"How?" asked Merri. "You're taller than Dad."

"My gorgeous Amazonian." Dad pressed a loud kiss on her cheek as he followed behind her with a bowl of red pepper hummus. It was a bowl I'd made, which meant it was lop-sided. I hoped Huck wouldn't notice.

"I didn't get to nurse Merri as long as you two." Mom pointed from me to Lilly, who had just come down the stairs. She had a purse over her shoulder and was clearly on her way out but stopped short when she saw the crowd and heard Mom's words. "The doctors strongly suggested I stop when they put me on bed rest for the birthday girl. Didn't help though. Six weeks later, Aurora made her impatient debut, two months early."

"You were a preemie and you're still taller? Maybe I should go vegan."

Merri and I exchanged eye rolls—way to hit us *both* in sore spots, Boy Byron.

Mom shook her head. "I really think it has less to do with what Rory eats *now* than it does with what she ate back then. I swore that girl was never going to wean—"

"And that's enough of that topic," Merri interrupted Mom. Her cheeks were light pink, mine felt blazing. I turned and hid my face in Huck's shoulder. He patted my back.

"What?" I could picture Mom blinking innocently. "Eliza was just saying the other night that we should normalize topics like breastfeeding and—"

"Okay!" Lilly clapped her hands before Mom could dig in deeper. "How about we have a new conversation before Rory gives a live enactment of 'It's my party and I'll cry if I want to.' Also, on a completely unrelated note: Mom, I'm going to need to see a script of your toast before the wedding. And maybe don't consult Eliza while writing it."

"I'm just saying there might be a connection between height and breastfeeding. I bet Eliza *would* know that."

Huck raised the hand not patting my back. "I've only met Eliza once—but she left a pretty strong impression. I'm fairly certain she'd object to any conversation that shamed mothers for their feeding choices."

"Oh, true. Hmmm. I take it back. Well, eat up." Mom paused to pinch Huck's cheek. "This one's a keeper, Rory!"

Dad chimed in with "Hear, hear!"

I pushed away from Huck's shoulder and waited for him to correct them. He didn't. Right. The plan. I'd forgotten because there hadn't been any need or opportunity to parade around as a fake couple in the past few weeks. He traced a lazy line along my back with his thumb and grinned at me like we had an inside joke. Which I guess we did—if the punch line was the zero chemistry between us and my pathetic feelings about Toby.

Toby, who was currently glowering at Huck instead of Byron.

Clearly one area where Gatsby and I were not alike was in the ability to throw a party. We both managed to collect an array of interesting and talented people in the same room— but his guests had fun and mine had staring contests.

"Hey! I'm back. Sorry, I had to chase her down the block. I swear my mom is oblivious when she drives." Clara popped into the room, the silver ribbons in her hair sparkling in the overhead lighting and glittering as bright as her smile. "Happy birthday, Rory!" She crashed me out of Huck's hug and into her own. "Ohh, is that hummus? I'm starving."

Within thirty seconds she'd rearranged the energy in the room, creating conversations and pairings that left Huck and me with some breathing space. "Think I can pull a Gatsby and sneak off from my own party?" I leaned into his shoulder while my traitorous eyes tracked Toby across the room. Merri was sitting on the edge of the dining room table, and he was standing in front of her, smiling at whatever story was making her lips move a mile a minute and her gestures grow enthusiastic enough that he moved his water glass out of range.

"Lovesick and pining isn't a good look on anyone," Huck whispered. "So avert your eyes and wipe your drool."

I elbowed him in the stomach and he laughed, drawing the eyes of everyone else. Toby's lingered the longest, confusion and curiosity in their angles.

Huck pivoted so his back was to the room and he was fully facing me. He leaned forward and whispered in my ear, "Your boy's been asking about me."

"Don't call him that, and what do you mean?"

"He went to Curtis and Lance and asked them about me. 'Grilled them' was actually Curtis's choice of words. He found it hilarious."

"It's got to be a big brother protective type thing," I said. "Right?"

Huck opened his mouth, but before he could answer there was a new shoulder pressed against mine, nudging me a step away from Huck and expanding our huddle to accommodate another person. The same person we'd been whispering about. Toby asked, "What's the birthday girl doing hiding in the corner?"

I snorted. "This birthday girl is happiest in the corner and has been trying to get out of birthday parties since she turned six."

"Oh, right." Toby stole a carrot off the plate Mom had filled for me. "The year we discovered you're scared of clowns."

"Yes, thank you for the reminder." I turned toward where Huck had been standing to explain how that party had flipped from frolic to nightmare as soon as the performer stepped out of her van, balloon animals at the ready. But Huck was gone. Toby and I were alone and he was giving me that smile that made the rest of the room disappear.

"Fifteen. How do you like it so far?"

I laughed. "Did you turn into my great aunt Aida? Because that sounds like something she'd say."

"It was pretty bad, wasn't it?" Toby leaned against the wall beside me, his shoulders blocking my view of the rest of the room. If everyone else decided to leave us alone, well, then they could take the cake and keep their presents and I'd still be the happiest birthday girl ever. His smile dimmed. "Huck seems okay."

"He's not bad," I said. "I hear you've been checking up on him."

Toby's ears turned red. "Curtis has the biggest mouth, I swear."

Before I could follow up with a question that lead toward the why of this, a dog came shooting in from the dining room with something in his mouth. He dove between my legs and knocked me off balance. "Whoa there, birthday girl." Toby steadied me with an arm around my waist, which, let's be honest, only made me dizzier. "Your sister wants me to join a band."

"What?" I was disoriented by his touch and the topic change.

"Lance is forming an indie rock band. Do you know Lynnie? She's Byron's twin and dating Clara's brother? She's in it too. Merri wants me to try out. She's worried I'm bored."

"But . . ." A band might mean no more rides home, no time for tutoring. More important, "That's not the type of music you play."

"Exactly!" He beamed and squeezed my waist before letting go to raise both hands to his hair. "See? You get it. Is it that hard to tell the difference between what you'd hear on the radio versus what plays in the background of a movie?"

"Um, no?" Was that a rhetorical question?

"Thank you." He laughed. "Sometimes I think you're the only one who gets me"—my heart surged!—"music-wise, at least. It must be the artist thing."

Was this the time to argue that maybe it was a *Me plus him* thing? That our compatibility went way beyond the arts?

"Toby!" Merri called from across the room. "Come tell Fielding about that time with the frog and the toothpaste."

He went—of course—but at least he was talking to Fielding again? It was hard to be excited about that when I was left alone with a dog who had a mouthful of napkin. *Happy birthday to me.* I lifted the corner of the tablecloth and commanded, "Drop it, Byron!"

There was a clatter across the room and I looked up to see my art classmate let go of a carrot stick. It bounced to the floor where Gatsby was waiting to swallow it whole. His face was wide-eyed and *What'd-I-do?* He put his hands up as he backed away from the platter. "I thought those were fair game. My bad."

"No." I tried not to laugh. "Not you, Boy Byron. Him, Byron." I pointed under the table to where my parents' dog was calmly ignoring me and shredding the paper napkin into drool-darkened strips of red confetti.

"I've got to change my name." He reached for another carrot, pausing with his hand above the tray and looking at me for permission.

I laughed and nodded as my dad hit the kitchen lights and my mom came around the corner with the blazing cake, already beginning the birthday song. Luckily everyone joined in quickly, because Mom was many wonderful things, but musical was not one of them. Toby was right over her shoulder, his face glowing in the candlelight, his smile brighter than the flames.

"Make a wish, my baby girl," said Dad once the song ended and the cake was set in front of me. Across the room, Huck met my eyes and tilted his head toward the guy I'd wished for on my last five cakes.

None of those had worked, so I watched the candles sputter and drip as I tried to think of something new. Finally, I took a deep breath and blew: *I wish I was enough.*

17

ey, Roar!" Toby called across the parking lot on Monday morning a week after my party. He started to jog toward me but only managed a few strides before he looked down at his knee brace and slowed to a walk. His jaw was tight when he reached me. "I forgot to ask in the car. Math date?"

I blinked at him. "I'm sorry, what?"

"You. Me. Your textbook. Some calculations going down. Sound good?"

Was it wrong that I was still hung up on his use of the word "date" and how cruel it was to combine that with "math"? Especially immediately after a car ride where he'd practically made moony eyes at my sister while Eliza gagged in the back seat and I tried not to bang my head against the window. "You don't have to tutor me every day." Because if I didn't have to work and he wasn't busy with piano lessons, we'd been filling our time by meeting over pencils and protractors.

"I asked you, remember? Come on, I need you. You're the only thing saving me from cereal for dinner—again—and moping around my house. Plus, you've got exams next week."

"Next Friday." The cynical part of me focused on the fact that he was bored, but my stupid, stubborn heart only heard that he *needed me*, that I could *save him*. What could I possibly do but open my mouth and say, "Sure."

"Great. I'll pick you up at five?"

"Aren't we meeting in your kitchen?" I'd started to get used to the place—though I still mentally redecorated whenever one of his explanations got long-winded.

"Nah, I need to get out. Plus, there's this restaurant I've been dying to take you to in Galwyn. You haven't been to Mockingburger yet, have you?"

I shook my head but bit the inside of my lip. New restaurants were always tricky. I hated asking the waiter or waitress which menu items were meat-, dairy-, and egg-free. Maybe I could search their menu online?

"Relax, Roar." Toby gave my arm a squeeze, which meant he was touching me, which was the opposite of relaxing. "It's a vegan restaurant. Get it? *Mocking*-burger? Their fake burger is supposed to taste just like real meat. I'm psyched you haven't been yet. I've been meaning to tell you for weeks."

Even the cynical part of me didn't have a retort for that. It was a lovely distraction to think about while I spent the first hour of my day in an art studio that was still super silent, super awkward. The only real noise in the past weeks had been when Mrs. Mundhenk made the class apologize to me one at a time. I'd never played soccer, but I'd watched Lilly's team a few times—and at the end of the game, the two sides worked their way down the opposite team's line, shaking hands and saying, "Good game. Good game. Good game."

It felt like that. "I'm sorry. I'm sorry. I'm sorry," with the same rote lack of expression. Only Lilly had had a whole team behind her, and this class was twelve of them and one of me. A huge part of me wanted to duck away from a dozen sets of eyes and run and hide, but I shoved down that anxiety and covered it with my anger. The only good that came out of all this was my determination to prove them all right—they *should* be scared of my talent! I was going to create something so wonderful that I'd be one of Mrs. Mundhenk's Snipes workshop nominees. And then I was going to get picked.

18

t wasn't a date. It was tutoring. *Tutoring.*

Which didn't explain why I spent an hour getting ready, blow-drying my hair instead of letting it do its volumeless air-dry thing. I got out my makeup, all fancy-pants hand-me-downs from Lilly, and did my whole face. Makeup was easy; it was just painting and shading on a 3-D canvas—but looking in the mirror and seeing myself through the highlighter and eyeliner never felt right. The only paints that seemed natural on my face were accidental acrylic, watercolor, and oil smudges.

But under Lilly's powders and creams I looked older. And reminding Toby I wasn't still in overalls and pigtails wouldn't be the worst thing that ever happened.

Except it wasn't a date, and that girl in the mirror wasn't me.

"Whoa." Merri was headed toward her room as I came out of mine. "Look at you."

"Yeah." I ducked my head. "I was playing around."

"If you ever want to 'play around' on me, I'm in. You look amazing." She grabbed my chin and angled my face in both directions. "Lilly! Come see this!"

I jerked my head away. "I was going to wash it off."

"Not until Lilly sees it," ordered Merri. "Lillian! Get your buns out here! Now!"

"What?" asked Lilly, her bedroom door cracking open. "I was on a conference call with Lucinda and the florist. This better be important."

"Look at Rory."

Oh, I really didn't have time to be the butt of whatever teasing Merri was coordinating. I covered my face with both hands. "Leave me alone."

"No, wait." Merri grabbed my arm, and for someone so little, she was formidable. "Lilly, her makeup is exactly what you were saying you wanted for the wedding."

Lilly stepped in front of me, blocking the hall. "Can I at least see it?"

I sighed and dropped my hands, making a face as I said, "See?"

"Wow, Rory—you look . . ." She beamed at me. "Amazing."

I tugged my hair, trying to pull it forward over my face. "When you say it like that, I wonder how horrible I normally look."

"No. It's— You look like you're going to look in college. It's like getting a peek at future you." Lilly's eyes were wide and hadn't stopped scanning me.

I rubbed at my cheek with my sleeve. "It's not like I walk around sucking my thumb."

Lilly shook her head. "I don't mean it that way—and this is exactly the natural look I want for the wedding. Whatever you did made your eyes look huge and pop."

"It's not that hard. I can teach you."

"Can you just . . . do it?" Lilly was circling me like a judge at a dog show. "Maybe we could do a practice run and if I look as good as you do, I'll cancel my makeup artist and you could do it instead?"

Merri shoved her phone in my face. "Let me get a picture so we don't forget." She wouldn't stop snapping until I obeyed her command to "smile," but once she was finally satisfied, I ran to the bathroom and washed it all off. Just in time for the hall clock to strike five and the doorbell to ring.

&

It wasn't a date. Really.

I had my math book on the floor beside my shoes. Granted I was wearing non-paint-spattered black flats, so that was fancier than normal, but my textbook definitely wouldn't be riding shotgun on a real date. Toby had on the *Dunkirk* score. I didn't know the movie well, but the war premise didn't sound romantic and the music just made me anxious. Not a date.

But Mockingburger *was* adorably date-worthy, all reclaimed wood and earth tones and mason jars. The lampshade over our small table was the color of pine needles. I was literally sitting across from the love of my life under a freaking green light. Seriously though, I didn't need a book's stupid symbol of pathetic pining to tell me my crush was hopeless; I'd figured that out all on my own.

Gatsby was the worst.

The food, however, was delicious. Toby praised the number of broccoli-free options—"Not gonna lie, I was worried"—
and said his mockingburger "tasted like real cow."

Since I turned down his offer of a bite, I wasn't sure if it
was true; but my butternut squash risotto was plate-lickable.

While there was plenty of chewing and swallowing, there
wasn't a whole lot of math accomplished on the nondate,
which was a thousand percent my fault, not Toby's. I was
distracted by his flannel shirt, by his wrists, by his jaw when
he chewed, and by the way he wiped his mouth. Every explanation went in one ear and evaporated before we hit the next
problem. He didn't get mad, just more determined.

Me? While I wasn't sure what to do with the tiny numbers
hovering to the right of X and Y, my own humiliation was
exponentially increasing with each new failure. Why couldn't
I be home painting? Or torturing myself with math away from
all the witnesses? Or reading *Gatsby*—because things weren't
looking too great for Daisy or Jay. I'd stopped with two chapters between them and what I was pretty sure wasn't a happily
ever after—despite all of Gatsby's efforts. Maybe there was a
moral or a response journal in there somewhere. Maybe Merri
was right and Ms. Gregoire's lit lessons were life lessons if I
only looked at them the right way.

"Roar?" Toby touched the back of my hand and I jumped,
nearly stabbing him with my pencil. "You stuck?"

"I've hit a wall," I said. "Sorry. Dinner was great and I appreciate all your help—but everything's confusing me tonight."

"I know that feeling." He looked at me for a long minute.

He'd been doing that a lot tonight—at first I kept discreetly wiping my mouth, licking my teeth, but I hadn't found any food to dislodge. "That picture . . . on iLive?"

"What picture?" I asked, closing my notebook and textbook.

"The one Merri put up of you."

"Oh no." I was going to kill her. "Show me."

He pulled out his phone and unlocked it. That was all he had to do because the photo was already on the screen—one Merri had taken in the hall "so they'd have an example for Lilly's wedding." One where she'd made me smile. I didn't look at her caption or the comments or how many stars and hearts it'd received. I looked from my face on the screen to Toby's.

"I didn't recognize you right away." The confession made him uncomfortable; he was fidgeting with his fork. "I'd scrolled past it, scrolled back—then realized it was you."

My cheeks were warm and growing hotter. Was that the scrolling version of a double take? "I was just messing around. I didn't know she'd post it."

He ducked his head. "I didn't know if you'd show up looking like that—and it's gorgeous, you're gorgeous . . ."

Did it count as a compliment if there was an invisible "but" tacked on the end? I waited him out, knowing that if I didn't hop in, he'd be forced to fill the silence and finish his thought.

"But, I hated that I didn't recognize you."

"Still me." I forced my voice to sound light. "Still right here and the girl you see every day. Often at unholy early hours for the drive to school."

"Yeah," but he stretched the word out and shook his head.

"Seriously, Toby, it's just makeup. I'm the same person. You see more of me than Major May—don't get weird on me."

Toby laughed bitterly. "Well, that's certainly true."

His voice made me want to tiptoe with my response. "How is the major? I haven't seen him in a while." Not that we were coffee buddies, but we got along. Better than he and Merri did. At least he used my name. He called her "the wild twin." I'd been "the quiet twin" before he switched to "Aurora"—though I was fairly certain that sometime in the past decade he'd figured out we had separate birthdays as well as personalities.

"He's—" Toby cleared his throat, and something about the way he was holding his mouth made me put down my water glass. "He's seeing someone. It's getting pretty serious, I guess."

"Oh." The former Mrs. May had moved out when Toby was eight, so I didn't think that was the issue here, but the angles of his chin and jaw were all stiff and wrong. I didn't know how to draw this version of his face. "Do you like her?"

"We haven't met. My dad says there's no point. I'm leaving for college soon."

"Three years," I clarified, in case there was some plan for him to skip a grade that I hadn't heard about. "And it's not like college is shipping you off to war—you'll come back for holidays and summers."

"Just telling you what he said. Maybe he's hoping I'll go to college in California near my mom or something."

"Please don't." It slipped out before my head could catch up with my heart.

He gave me a brief smile and spun the last sweet potato fry in a circle on his empty plate. "Anyway, he doesn't bring her to our house. He's been working more out of the Manhattan office, so he stays over at her apartment a few nights a week."

"So you're . . . alone?"

"Sometimes." He sat back in his chair. "It's not like he ever worked normal hours. And I've gotten real close with the pizza guys. And Chinese food. And the one sub place that delivers. So this . . . this is a good change. Vegan food is surprisingly tasty. Maybe you'll convert me." He paused to eat his fry. "Except for ice cream. I'm keeping real ice cream. Is licorice vegan? 'Cause that's a deal breaker."

I crossed my arms. "No idea. I'm not a real vegan."

"You mean you're imaginary?" Toby asked with a grin.

"No, I just— I don't ever call myself that. I know Merri does, but . . . I'd say 'plant-based diet,' but then people want a whole explanation and it becomes a thing. And I cheat sometimes. I like honey in my tea. I'm not—I'm not in it for the animals. I mean animals are fine, but . . ." I shrugged, not wanting to fall into the trap of using the same stereotypes I resented.

"Okay, so what are you in it for?" He pointed to the remaining risotto on my plate and I pushed it over. I was already six bites past full.

"Myself."

He took a bite and groaned his pleasure. "Good ordering, Roar. Also, explain."

"If I eat this way I sleep better. I focus better." And neither of those had ever come easy for me. "See, it's selfish."

"The cow on the menu—in other restaurants—doesn't care why you're not eating it."

"The cow on the menu is past caring either way." I leaned forward. It felt good to get this out, especially since all the judgment I'd been expecting hadn't come. "But you know when I'm the worst? Right before bed. Sometimes I just crave milk chocolate or a bite of cheese."

"Ah, yes. The bedtime munch." Toby waved his fork at me. "I'm guilty of that too."

The bedtime munch? My heart was, as Merri would say, squishing in my chest. Could he be more adorable? "Yeah, but if you give in to yours, it's not a big deal. It's not . . . cheating. No one teases you for it."

"When I get the bedtime munch, no one's there to even notice. But, yeah—I can see how Merri would be . . ."

"Obnoxious?" I suggested. "It's not just her. People assume that vegans are moralistic and when they find out I'm not one hundred percent committed . . . you'd think I'd gone out and slaughtered the animals myself, or that they'd just won some big victory because I ate butter."

"Hey." Toby reached across the table and put his hand on top of mine. Forget fancy cars and their zero to sixty, my heart had gone resting pulse to sprint in the space between beats. "If you want, I'll take you from here to get bacon ice cream with a side of fried chicken. It's not 'cheating'—it's your choice. You get to decide what you put in your body, and that's no one else's business."

I smiled. I mean, I'd been wanting to since he touched

my hand, the hand he was *still* touching, but at least his comment warranted one. Maybe not the radiant beaming I aimed in his direction, but there was no toning it down. "That sounds like a speech Eliza would give."

He pretended to frown. "Stupid carpool. She's rubbing off on me. But since she's the smartest person either of us will ever meet, maybe I'll take it as a compliment. Is that a no on the ice cream?"

"It's a no. And a thank you."

His hand squeezed mine before he pulled away to flag down our waitress. "Could I have the check?"

19

Merri was waiting in the kitchen when I got home. She was sitting on the floor with her back against the cabinet, Gatsby's head on her lap, a book in her hand, a cup of tea beside her, and the most ridiculous orange and blue tie-dyed robe draped around her shoulders. She used a napkin to mark her page and nudged Gatsby to move. "Where were you?"

"Out with Toby. He's tutoring me, remember?"

"Right, because you wouldn't let me." She fell in step beside me as I headed for my room. "Did you forget it was your day to work in the store? Mom came home to get you and you were gone."

I dropped my head. "I totally forgot. How much trouble am I in?"

"Lilly covered. You owe her." Merri paused between steps. "Rory, Mom and Dad have signed your academic warning, right?"

No, but they could sign the next one if my exam went poorly. I fidgeted with a picture of the three of us in snowsuits. "Hopefully it's a nonissue after next Friday. Toby's been trying his best to make me less stupid."

"You're not stupid." Merri stomped her slipper sock. "Also, I can help too. Did it ever occur to you that I *wanted* to tutor you? That I like spending time with you when we don't fight?"

"No," I answered honestly. "That didn't occur to me even a little."

"Well, I do, you jerk."

I pushed past her and finished climbing the stairs. "Then maybe you shouldn't have said Toby 'didn't deserve to be stuck with me.' Or that I was your responsibility and you 'had' to help me."

Merri's eyes went doll-wide. "Oh. That does sound bad."

"You think?" I lowered my voice as we passed Mom and Dad's room. "I know you've got this whole *Rory is prickly and it's her fault we're not friends* story. But it's not all on me. This is not one-sided. You can't blame me for not wanting help from someone who makes it clear she doesn't want to spend time with me."

Merri's head fell until her chin hit her chest. "I do so want to."

"When would that be? When you're not hanging out with your boyfriend? Or your best friend? Or your other best friend? Or your whole new group of friends? Or doing wedding stuff with Lilly without me? Or running with your cross-country team? Or your new lit club and writing thing? When exactly do I fit in your busy social schedule?"

I hadn't meant to make her cry. I just wanted to be heard, to be seen, to matter. Merri's eyes were shiny, but she blinked. "Right now. Get your notebook."

While I struggled through the first problem she assigned, she doodled. Hearts, of course. Strings of them cascading and ballooning all over the page. "Equations are a lot like relationships," she said softly.

I didn't look at her, but I stopped writing.

"They need to be balanced. The variables—the people—on both sides need to be equal for it to work. They have to *both* want it equally. If they don't . . . well, there's no solution for that."

I knew she was talking about us. About my X effort needing to match her Y. And that was true and fair and something I'd think about later. But that algebra didn't just relate to sisters.

"If you subtract from one side, you add to the other. They have to work together. It can't be one variable doing all the heavy lifting. The other variable needs to . . . care. Equally."

My pencil dropped from my hand and rolled off my bed. I didn't look to see where it landed, but I folded my arms across my twisting stomach.

"Does that make sense?" she asked.

I nodded because I didn't trust my voice. Maybe that's why math and I never got along—I wanted the least balanced relationship in the world to work. I kept trying to force the variables into a solution, but really was there any combination that made sense when I was putting in all the feeling and Toby was reacting with friendship?

"I'll try more if you will too," Merri added.

"Promise," I whispered.

And maybe she was expecting me to be snarky, because it took her a moment to accept the arms I held out for a hug. "Good," she said. "And you've got this. Get some sleep."

I didn't. Instead I stayed up and finished *The Great Gatsby*. And after that—I didn't know if I'd ever sleep again.

20

Campus during exams looked like something out of a zombie movie. Everyone was sleep-deprived and distracted. Well, everyone but Eliza, who still looked like an undercover movie star, one who viewed exams the way elite athletes do the Olympics. In the car on the way to school, we gave her free rein to lecture us about studying and caffeine and the latest scientific articles she'd enjoyed. Not because we were interested— or at least I wasn't—but because everyone was too tired to make conversation.

I arrived in art to find Huck double-fisting cookies. "Want one? Man, Curtis can bake. It's some Egyptian recipe of his mom's and I swear they're made of magic." I shook my head at the sandwich baggie he held out, and he spoke around a mouthful. "I love this Knight Lights thing. What did Toby get you?"

There hadn't been a good-luck box in my locker, but then again, did I really expect one? Merri had been the adoptee Toby had wanted. I was the one he'd settled for. Plus, he didn't cook and I was tricky to bake for anyway. And better than any cookies or sparkly pencils like Clara had gotten, Toby had given me *his time*. I lifted my chin and answered Huck, "A passing grade in math."

I hoped it would be true.

It felt ridiculous to spend six hours in class when the only period I could focus on was the one containing that day's actual exam. Earth science was Tuesday, history Wednesday, French Thursday, math Friday. Oh, and my final Gatsby paper was Wednesday too. English class discussions had done nothing to change my horror at the ending or to make me feel more inspired to write about it.

After school on Tuesday I changed out of my uniform and into pj's, made popcorn, and hurried down to the basement to pull up the movie I'd rented online. It wasn't cheating since I'd read the book.

The basement door creaked open. "Roar, you left your history notebook in my car," called Toby as he started down the stairs. "You're watching a movie? I thought you'd be in a fortress of flash cards."

"I'm seeing if the movie clarifies the book. My final paper's due tomorrow."

"Ahh. I've been there." Toby dropped my notebook on the coffee table and whacked me with a throw pillow. "Move over."

"You sure? There's no spaceships, guns, or magic . . . though it might have a good score? It's by Craig Armstrong." Was it weird to admit that I'd looked it up? Should I tell him that now that he'd pointed out how music influenced a movie, I couldn't stop noticing it?

"Oh, I'm in! He's a genius." He leaned back and loosened his knee brace. "What is it?"

"*The Great Gatsby*. Wait." I turned to face him. "You must've read this in Ms. Gregoire's class last year—can you save me from F. Scott Fitzgerald?"

"Nope. Sorry. Never read it. She teaches new books every year. Something about the texts having to match the students."

"Of course she does." I slumped back on the couch, hugging a pillow to my chest.

He snagged one and shoved it behind his head. "Hit play. Maybe we can figure it out together."

Two hours later, almost every character was on the screen—the temperatures and tempers were rising in a New York City hotel room. Gatsby was about to reveal his and Daisy's affair, about to demand that she choose him over her husband. My hands were fidgets in my lap, ready to cover my eyes if it was too painful to watch. Next to me Toby had gotten more and more rigid. His jokes about the parties and fast cars had faded after Gatsby's green light infatuation with married Daisy was revealed. He'd swallowed audibly when they started to have an affair—sat forward through the euphoric montage of Daisy and Gatsby bliss.

But now—he snatched up the remote and pressed pause. "This book, it doesn't have a happy ending, does it? Daisy's not going to leave Tom. She and Gatsby don't run off together."

I shook my head slowly. That was the ending I wanted too.

"Turn it off," said Toby, though he was the one holding the remote. His face had gone chalky beneath its olive tones. "I don't want to see the end. I'd rather think it stays in this place where there's still hope." He stood and backed away from the couch. Pulling his phone from his pocket, he typed in a text with wide eyes and frantic fingers. He barely paused at the bottom of the stairs to blurt out, "Sorry, Roar. I just— I can't," before fleeing up them.

Hope, like Gatsby's great hopefulness. Like my own. Except it was all misplaced, and if I pressed play I knew the disasters that would play out on the screen because I'd already read them on the pages. Gatsby had gotten Daisy back, but only for a moment, only in words and dreams. She was about to slip through his hands and choose her husband over his hope. She was about to get behind the wheel of his car and kill a girl. He was about to lie to protect her. He was about to die.

I sat frozen for long minutes. Toby's plan was better—to walk away while hope was still an option. But I wanted more than hope. I wanted more than this torturous limbo I'd been living in. I wanted knowledge, and the only way I'd get that was if I asked.

I stood.

I paused twice on the stairs to take deep breaths and ground myself in the feel of the carpet beneath my feet and the imperfections of the banister beneath my fingers. I shut my eyes as my hand curled around the knob on our front door, inhaling and holding it until I saw stars. There were still stars when I opened the door and my eyes—only these were hung in the late October sky. The brightest light of all was behind a pair of balcony doors—my own North Star. The lawn was cold and damp beneath my bare feet as I crossed from ours to his. I left footprints on the slate path to his front door. His dad's car wasn't in the driveway, so I let myself in.

I didn't turn on any downstairs lights, so all that blinding white was a study in grays and shadows that would make a haunting charcoal drawing. I paused to mentally frame interesting angles and pieces. Just long enough to calm my breathing before I started up the stairs.

Toby, I rehearsed under my breath, *there's something I need to tell you. I don't want you as a tutor. I don't see you as a chauffeur. I don't want you to see me as the kid next door or your Knight Light adoptee. I want you to see me as me. I want you to love me.*

Eh, maybe I'd walk that back a bit. Save the declarations for after I saw his face and knew if there was anything worth hoping for.

I was at his room, raising my hand to knock on the slightly open door when I heard my sister's voice. "You can't keep doing this." Merri was pissed. When she got mad, her words lost their shape, blurred together in a sludge of emotions that trembled in the same way she did. "Toby, we've had this conversation. We've had it more than once. You can't just send me texts saying you have feelings for me."

"I was going to just come over." His voice was still as desperate as it'd been when he fled from the movie. "But I didn't know if you were home."

"You're missing the point!" Merri's voice was shrill. "That wouldn't be any better. I don't want you just showing up in my room."

Toby laughed, but it sounded nervous. He wasn't as oblivious to Merri's anger as he was pretending to be. "Like you just showed up in *my* room? And I've always been welcome in yours."

"Not anymore," said Merri. "Privilege revoked. Also, Fielding is your friend. Doesn't that count for anything? You're hurting me *and* betraying him. Hello, do you want to tick off a nationally ranked fencer?"

The last line was so typically Merri. Her anger burnt itself out quickly and she always tried to build jokes from the ashes, like she couldn't bear to stand in the aftermath and deal with the feelings that were exposed and damaged. "Toby, you know I love you . . ."

I bit my lip until it throbbed, any pain to distract from the one that was building in my chest. *She loved him?* Was Merri a true Daisy? A cheating, playing-both-guys Daisy?

"I love you too." Toby's voice soared and my heart crashed.

"No," Merri said softly. "That's not what I mean. I love you, but I'm not and will never be *in* love with you. And I miss the boy who wasn't afraid to make me angry. Who didn't hesitate to call me out when I messed up. You could never lose me as a friend because you made me mad—but you will lose me if you don't stop trying to be more. I need you to hear me when I say I don't feel that way. I'm sorry that hurts you. You mean so much to me as a friend, but, Toby, my feelings aren't going to change and"—her voice quivered—"I hate that you're trying to force them to."

I lowered my forehead to rest against the hall wall. My heart broke for both of them and for myself as well. There might not be car crashes and bodies in the road, but there was some Gatsbian damage here as well.

"I wanted that country song," said Toby, his voice as torn as ripped paper.

"Which one?" Merri asked.

Toby laughed and tapped out a few notes on his keyboard. "Any of the ones that start with a scabby-kneed boy and a girl with hair ribbons and end with them sitting on a front-porch swing with their own kids."

"I want that too—" I couldn't see Merri's face, but I could hear the earnestness in her voice and knew how pinched her forehead would be, how her bottom lip would tremble and her eyes would look enormous as she gazed up at him. "But I want it with us living next door, trading off whose porch we sit on and who supplies the Popsicles. Someday in the *very* distant future, you'll be my kids' Uncle Toby. I'll be your kids' Auntie Merri—aka, the fun aunt. I want you in my life, Toby. For forever. But not if you can't hear or respect my feelings."

He inhaled so brokenly that I didn't care if I exposed myself. I needed to see him, see if he was okay—because Merri's vision for the future left no room for his own. All that hope he'd been harboring for so long had been drowned. I shifted slightly, silently. Through the crack in the door I saw her standing with hands on her hips. His were shoved in his pockets as he studied her face. Finally, he shut his eyes and sighed. Opening them, he reached out and put a hand on each of her shoulders. Twisting his mouth into a bitter smile, he asked, "Am I supposed to teach my kids to call him 'Uncle Fielding'? Is he who you see yourself with?"

"Gah, Toby." Merri leaned her cheek on his forearm in an attempt to hide the enormous smile blooming there. Her Fielding Face. "It's only been five weeks."

"Doesn't matter," said Toby. "Look at your face. I know you too well. And he's too smart not to realize how extraordinary you are and how lucky he is."

"I don't think Fielding's the Popsicle type." Merri giggled the words into his skin and I pressed my forehead so hard against the doorframe that it hurt. "They drip and make messes—you know how he feels about messes."

"He'd tolerate them for you." Toby and Merri stepped back simultaneously.

"Yeah, I think he would." She rubbed her arms, then hugged herself. "He makes me so happy. I'm not saying that to hurt you. I'm saying it because I desperately want that for you too. Someone who makes you this happy. That person isn't me. It's never going to be."

Toby had turned away—from her, from me. He was facing his keyboard when she said, "I'm sorry."

He was still facing it when he answered, "Me too. And I won't . . . I heard you. I'm sorry."

She slipped out his balcony and into the night. That should've been my cue to leave too. My plans for coming here had been torpedoed, and the only thing I had to offer this scene was more hurt and humiliation. But then his fingers crashed on the keyboard. Not in chaos but in a crescendo of such strong emotions that my eyes immediately filled. This was his soundtrack for this moment.

It wasn't a happy song. It was longing, it was wistful, it was coveting. It was ambition and searching and green light yearning. His fingers played the melody like he knew it by heart, like it came from his heart. Like it *was* his heart breaking in those mournful notes. I slid down the wall and listened. Because no one should be alone in that much pain. Because even if he didn't ever know I'd been there, I wanted there to be an audience to his talent, an acknowledgment of his hurt.

The notes trickled to a stop. A new sound filled the air— ripping paper. He tore and tore and tore, and I could only imagine the pile of sheet music at his feet. I stood when the sound stopped, pausing long enough to hear him breathe out, "Goodbye, Merrilee May." Then I left to say some goodbyes of my own.

While I'd been huddled on the floor in his hallway listening to his compositions for my sister, I'd realized that I had never, could never, would never be Jay Gatsby. Because Gatsby had had Daisy to lose—he'd had a moment when she was his.

Toby had never been mine. And he never would be.

It was time.

I tiptoed out of his house. Up in my room with the door shut and music on to mask my tears, I copied his lead, tearing up sketch after sketch after sketch of a grin with a slightly crooked tooth, of eyebrows that fanned over the kindest brown eyes. I tore up each dream, each promise I'd made myself, each hope I'd held for the future.

Then I went back down to the basement and forced myself to watch the end of the movie. Gatsby floating dead in the pool he'd never taken the time to swim in. A funeral with no mourners, because he hadn't let anyone know him. No one but Nick and Daisy—and he hadn't been enough for her.

I wanted to be enough. I wanted to be *more* than enough for someone.

Upstairs I deleted the paper I'd started and began again, typing out the quote ringing through my head: *"They were careless people, Tom and Daisy—they smashed up things and creatures and then retreated back into their money or their vast carelessness, or whatever it was that kept them together, and let other people clean up the mess they had made . . ."*

Merri and Toby were both so careless—both so clueless. They weren't malicious, but that didn't make our collective hurts any less. We loved and we lived and we rowed side by side like the "boats against the current, borne back ceaselessly into the past" that Fitzgerald used to close his book. But I was putting down my oar. I was changing the constellations I used to navigate.

If I stayed stuck in the past, it would destroy me. It was time to move on. It was time to let go.

21

The windshield wipers dragged against the glass with a rubber scrape. It was an in-between rain, and Toby had spent the whole drive adjusting their speed. Having never been in the driver's seat, I wasn't sure if it was actually that complicated, or if it was easier for him to focus on them than on my sister seated beside him.

Merri was chattering about classes. Making bio and Latin and, ugh, math sound like they were gossip. I wanted to shake her for being oblivious to all the tension in the car, until I really looked at her—her stiff posture and knotted fingers—and realized she wasn't. She was overcompensating.

All three of us had matching puffy eyes ringed with dark circles—though I was the only one who knew the whole story.

Merri's fingers fluttered like nervous birds. "And that, Mayday, is why—"

"Can you not call me 'Mayday' anymore?" Toby's voice was rough.

I'd always hated their stupid exclusive nicknames, but watching the color drain from Merri's face made my stomach flip. I wanted to reach forward and hug her. I'd heard her crying last night. I'd been psyching myself up to comfort/

join her, but Lilly beat me to it. Since Lilly didn't have her own Toby heartbreak going on, she was the better choice. But that didn't make it any easier to be the odd man out. The one sobbing alone in her bedroom.

I watched Merri's mouth form the word "Why" twice before she managed to whisper it.

"Because it feels prophetic now. I don't need to be reminded how I crashed and burned." Toby bashed his hand down on the blinker before pulling his car to an abrupt halt in Eliza's driveway. He reached for the horn as she came out the door.

I wasn't sure which one of them broke my heart more, but both halves of the front seat were curled into themselves with pain and betrayal. I dug into my backpack and pulled out a notebook and pen as Eliza opened the car door. "Good morning."

Toby *hmm*'d in response and Merri's "Happy Halloween" was a pathetic, spiritless thing. Eliza turned to me in confusion and I passed over the note I'd scrawled: Friendship armageden went down last night.

I was sure I'd spelled "Armageddon" wrong but trusted Eliza was smart enough to figure it out and come up with a plan to fix this. It's not like she wasn't prepared. One morning back in September, I'd grabbed her arm so she couldn't follow Toby and Merri and Fielding to their lockers. "Why do you hate Toby?"

The question had made me nervous—I hadn't wanted to know anything negative or critical about him, but I'd asked on a morning full of giggles and him smiling like each of

Merri's playful pokes was the best present he'd ever received. I'd thought maybe if I knew Eliza's reason, I could adopt it for my own and it would hurt less to be around him.

"I don't *hate* him," Eliza had said. "I hate that one of these days he's going to make some big declaration or ultimatum and Merri's going to be hurt when she has to reject him. I hate the inevitability of that outcome and his refusal to acknowledge that his feelings are unrequited."

My stomach had twisted. "You don't think she could learn to like him back? They're best friends. Isn't that the foundation for a good relationship?"

Eliza had shaken her head. "First, *I'm* her best friend. Also, their friendship dynamic would be toxic in a relationship. What happens when they fight? Merri pouts, Toby forgives—or grovels if he's at fault. She asks, she receives. There's a power imbalance. She's never going to care as much as he does. He's never going to say no to her. Someday he'll resent her for it. They'd make each other worse people, not better."

At the time, I'd laughed. "That's your idea of romance? Someone who will say no to you?" But her comment about making each other worse people had been looping in my head—it had made it into last night's paper too. Gatsby, for all the ways he'd changed himself for Daisy, hadn't become a better person. Not a happier one. Daisy's fleeting attention, Daisy's affair—those weren't love. And his one-sided adoration wasn't either. He hadn't seen past his idealized obsession to notice her flaws.

I added a quick upside-down sketch of a nuclear cloud to the notebook. Eliza closed it with a grimace. She added her silent sigh to a car that was full of them, then leaned forward between the seats. "Yesterday was my half-birthday," she began.

Merri's face creased. "Oh, that's right, day before Halloween. I knew that— How did I forget?"

Great work, Eliza. Merri looked closer to tears than before.

"I didn't expect you to remember," said Eliza dismissively. "However, it means I have my license test today. If I pass—"

"Of course you'll pass," interrupted Merri.

"*When* I pass, I'm allowed one passenger for the first six months."

"We know," snapped Toby, because Eliza had been enlightening us on the rules of driving since school started. Critiquing Toby's hand and mirror positions and offering bits of instruction like he hadn't had his license for seven months.

"My point is, Merri, would you consider becoming *my* copilot for a while? Not that I expect you to navigate."

"Yes!"

Normally Toby would've fought this. It would've been Merri-tug-of-war and she would've committed to some ridiculous shared custody plan.

Now he nodded. "Good idea." He met my eyes in the rearview mirror. "Sounds like it'll be me and you, Roar. You'll get what you always wanted."

I almost choked on my tongue. "Excuse me?"

"Shotgun? It's yours." If there'd been any bitterness or cruelty in his voice, I would've rejected him in an instant. I'd been used as a pawn by Monroe to hurt Merri and I wasn't going to make that mistake again. But Toby just sounded tired. He tried to offer me a rearview mirror smile, but it wouldn't stick to his face. "Unless you'd rather go with someone else too. Or walk?"

What would it take for me to walk away from him? I wasn't sure I could. But staying couldn't be healthy either. I wasn't going to be a Gatsby, chasing disaster. I stared out the window at the rainy day—the sky had darkened and the air felt thick. Weather as uncomfortable as all our moods. "Well, at least not today. Maybe tomorrow."

"Cheeky, no-good brat."

It was a joke, but he only pretended to smile and I didn't bother.

22

My history exam was fifth period, which meant all those dates and wars and names had to stay in my head until then, hopefully not dislodging any verb conjugations for tomorrow's French test or formulas for Friday's math. Most everyone on campus was sitting by their locker or in the library or a classroom cramming last-minute notes. I should've been joining them, but my feet brought me through the rain to the humanities building, and I raised a damp hand to knock without any plan for when Ms. Gregoire answered.

She took one look at me—pale skin, dark circles, dripping hair—and nodded. "Just as I predicted. It's time."

"Time for what?" I took a step backward, because the lights in the room had flickered, and for a moment she'd been outlined from behind—her red hair down and curly, her dress long and black, ruffled in ways that caught the eye when she moved. It was the first time I'd seen her not in colors or prints. It could've been a couture mourning gown—if English teachers grieved for fictional characters. But it was Halloween and I'd seen enough Merri-movies to know about plots with witches and spells that were supposed to fix people's lives.

Ms. Gregoire looked like she'd stepped right off one of those sets. If she'd replaced her desk with a cauldron, I was out of there. Except maybe I'd do the opposite—maybe it'd be nice to drink a potion or accept a spell and have someone else steer my life for a while. Since the only way I knew how to drive was to crash.

"Come in." She gestured with a hand heavy with gold rings that glittered with stones I didn't recognize. "It's time for you to be done with Daisy—" She paused to shut the door behind me. "And Gatsby and Nick and the rest."

"Aren't we already done with him, er, *The Great Gatsby*?" I'd submitted my paper via the class Dropbox last night.

"Yes, but don't think I didn't hear the sarcasm on the word 'great' there." She smiled and spun a ring on her finger. "What I meant was that *you* are done with that story. You need to let it go."

My heart sank. If Merri was right about Ms. Gregoire being teacher-magical—and millions of romantic reminders about how she'd fixed up Merri with Fielding via a book implied that she was—and if *I* was right about *The Great Gatsby*, then I was also right about Toby. It was time to move on.

"But I can't let you move on—" The lights flickered again as she spoke.

"What?" I gasped. My knees felt weak, so I sat. The unnatural darkness outside made the classroom shadowy and sinister.

"You're not moving on to Wright. I mean, you'll read that too; but we need to do something about that grade of yours. I'd hate to see you put on academic probation and miss out on

Fall Ball, or the Candlelight Concert . . . the Snipes workshop. You need to pull these grades up."

"Oh." My cheeks burned. Of course she wasn't psychic. What was wrong with me? I steadied myself by placing my hands flat on the desk. "Right."

"Now, I've read your paper . . ." She brought a hand to her heart. "It made me cry."

I bit my lip so I wouldn't add, *"Me too."*

"It's a good start, but we still need some GPA repair, and you need this assignment for other reasons too." She winked and spun her rings again. They were catching the light in dizzying ways, then disappearing into her palm. "Sometimes students need a book that's not part of the general curriculum. A book that's just for *them*."

Fear rose in my throat like a burp. "What are you suggesting?"

"Some extra credit." She bent to rummage through her desk drawer. "I've been keeping it here until you were ready."

"You already picked out a book for me?" That was how Merri said it started—Ms. Gregoire chose a book *for her* . . . and the plot details bled over into her life. My eyes were drawn to the windows again—forked lightning streaked across the sky, making everything a sickly green.

"No, the book picked you. I've been waiting for the right moment to present it." She plucked up a novel with a sunny yellow cover and held it out on two palms.

The book was massive, the type that could be used as a doorstop or hammer or bug killer. "You want me to read that *on top* of schoolwork?"

"There's no rush. I want you to set your own pace with this one." She bobbled her hands, making the book dance between them. "So, are you ready to see what it is? Any guesses?"

She was so excited, and I was so . . . not. We were in rip-off-the-bandage territory. I wasn't going to be able to fake enthusiasm, so the faster the charade ended, the better. I plucked the book from her hands and turned it over.

"*Little Women.*" The title and four silhouettes were embossed on the cover in orange. When I brushed my hand across them, they were cool to the touch—except, *Ow!* The fourth one, the smallest girl, was scalding hot. It made no sense, but my fingertip was bright red.

But Ms. Gregoire had had the book cover down on her palm and she didn't appear to be in any pain as she clapped her hands together. It was the same moment the thunder caught up—making her clap supersonic. The reverberations pounded in my chest. "This is going to be good for you, Rory."

I looked from her eager face, to the book, to the creepy weather—touched the cover again: cool, cool, cool, *ow!*

I shifted my grip so I was only touching the corners. I wanted oven mitts or a hazard suit . . . or an explanation. But everything about this scene was surreal, and when I opened my mouth to ask, the words that came out surprised me. "What do I need to do?"

"Let's make a deal," Ms. Gregoire said, and an eerie note began to fill the classroom. It stretched into a melody that belonged on the score of any horror movie, full of suspense and quickening heartbeats. I held my breath as she reached in her drawer—

And turned off her cell phone.

"Sorry about that." I wanted to laugh or ask about her creeptacular ringtone, but my tongue still wasn't cooperating. She continued. "You can submit artwork instead of response journals—as long as you include a brief written explanation of each piece."

"Oh, I can do that."

She laughed. "I know you can. Aurora—" She paused as lightning flashed again, this time the thunder following immediately. "You're going to surprise yourself with what you're capable of—and I can't wait to see where the book takes you and what you find once you're there."

23

The book fell out of my bag at lunch. I kept meaning to leave it in my locker, but every time I got in front of that stupid dial, I forgot.

"Are you reading *Little Women*?" Clara scooped it up and hugged it to her chest.

I nodded. "You've read it?"

"Oh my stars, I loved this book—" I tried to decide if her endorsement was a good thing. She hadn't hated *Gatsby*. Clara turned to the rest of the table and held it out. "Elinor, Gems, Iris—remember *Little Women*?"

Iris, a petite blonde who gave Merri a run for her money in cuteness factor, squealed. "The best! We were all obsessed."

Okay, that made me feel better about the assignment.

"Remember how Mr. D kept threatening to confiscate our copies?" Gemma had the faintest trace of her mother's British accent. Her brown cheeks stretched in a wide smile as she reached for the book and thumbed through the pages.

"No, it wasn't Mr. D—it was Mr. Khan. Sixth grade, not seventh," corrected Clara.

Clara was all about precise details, so of course she was right—but I stopped listening to their conversation about copies hidden in desks and rereading until pages fell out. Sixth grade? Is that the reading level Ms. Gregoire thought I was on, since *Gatsby* was too hard for me? I snatched the book from Gemma, making everyone at the table stop talking and turn.

"Sorry." I crammed it in my bag and stood. "I forgot . . . something in the art room." I turned and ran out of the cafeteria.

Clara cornered me in the hall before math. "What was that about?" she demanded.

"The history test?" I'd known when it was in front of me, but any information I had retained was now dumped into a blue test booklet, leaving my head empty and the rest of me exhausted.

"No, not the history test. *You*. In the cafeteria. You know you left your lunch there?"

"Oh." I spun toward the door. "I did?"

Clara grabbed my sleeve. "I packed it up and it's in your locker, but you must be starving. I have a protein bar in my bag—want it? Are you okay?"

"Test anxiety," I fibbed. "Wait, how'd you get my locker combination?" I flipped over the bar she'd shoved in my hand to scan for dairy and to make sure it didn't have candy-bar levels of sugar. The last thing I needed was a surge and crash in math. I ripped the corner open. "Thanks."

"I ran into lover boy. Our Knight Lights have our locker

combinations, remember? Hasn't he left you any exam prep presents?"

I stiffened, and I'm sure the bar didn't actually taste like cardboard and rotting leaves, but the bite in my mouth had become unchewable and my throat and stomach vetoed the idea of swallowing. Darting across the hallway to the trash can, I did my best to subtly spit the bite into my hand before tossing it in.

"You weren't joking about test anxiety, were you?" Clara's eyes were wide. "Want me to take you to the nurse?"

"I'm fine. It's not that. It's just . . ." I couldn't tolerate her calling Toby anything other than his name. Not "dreamboat," not "stud muffin," not "Captain Sizzlepants"—all of which she'd used in the last week. Actually, I couldn't tolerate her saying his name either. Our friendship needed to be a Toby-free zone. "I'm over him. I'm not wasting any more time thinking of him that way."

There. Maybe if I said that often enough, it might come true.

Clara staggered against the wall. "You can't give up on him. What about true love?"

I shrugged, but my muscles resisted the movement as much as my heart did, and the words that followed tasted like soap. "I guess it wasn't."

"But . . ." She was quiet. Her hands scrabbled at the poster hanging behind her back: *Fall Ball—Get your tickets today!* I'd drawn the art last week at lunch as a favor for Mrs. Mundhenk, who was an adviser for the student council, and Clara, who was the freshman class rep. "What are we going to talk about now?"

I snorted. "If stalking Toby was the glue to our friendship, that doesn't say a whole lot about us."

Her cheeks turned pink. "I didn't mean it that way. We will always have me trying to recruit you for committees and your doodles making Convocation tolerable and us both wishing I could dognap your pupper without it causing my literal death by hives. And—"

The bell rang, cutting off her list, and Mrs. Roberts leaned her head in the hall. "Miss Campbell, Miss Highbury, come join us."

"Apologies, Mrs. Roberts." Clara smiled at her. "Just having a mini strategy session. You know how it is during exams."

Mrs. Roberts opened the door wider. "I promise you'll find the study session *inside* the classroom more productive."

I foolishly hoped the subject was closed with the classroom door, but five minutes into the review Clara kicked the back of my chair. This wasn't an entry on the super-secret answer code—I knew that because she'd taught me after my birthday party. "Rory, psst. Rory."

I wanted to put my head down on my desk until I had the patience to deal with whatever came out of her mouth next. Instead I stared at a poster that graphed *Places you'll go* against *Willingness to try*.

"Rory." Clara leaned forward until her mouth was at my ear. "I have a great idea. Let's set you up with Huck! You guys could just switch from faking to real."

I turned so fast I almost bashed my head against hers. "No. Absolutely not."

"But he's sweet and you guys get along," Clara insisted.

"Not interested."

"So we're back to Toby?"

"No!"

"Aurora? Did you have a question?" asked Mrs. Roberts. Frankly I was surprised it had taken us so long to get caught, but that didn't make it any less humiliating to have the entire class look at me. All those eyes on my bright red face. Could they see my throat and lungs tightening? Because I had no oxygen in me, which meant I could get no words out.

"We're a little lost on that last problem. Could you go over the second part again?" Clara effortlessly used her smart-girl privilege. There was no shame in admitting you were confused when you were confident you wouldn't always be. Or admitting you were wrong when you were usually right. If I stopped class each time I got lost, we'd make no actual progress. My tutoring sessions with Toby helped, but it was like once I stepped back in this room, my brain decided to prove all the *You can do it* posters wrong.

24

There was one hour between me and a drive home where I'd get to practice mentally friend-zoning some-one who had friend-zoned me a lifetime ago. Then my bedroom. A nap. Some sketching. French flash cards. Dinner. French flash cards. Bed.

Except, *dangit!* I had to work at Haute Dog. Scratch the nap and sketching. French flash cards would take place between customers. Hopefully the store would be quiet. How many people needed dog supplies on a rainy Halloween evening?

Huck and Clara sandwiched me on the walk into the Convocation Hall. One of these days, I was going to find time to get in there and sketch. I didn't usually go for buildings, but this one was all angles and arches, huge stained-glass windows of flowers and books and maps. It had all the orna-mentation of a church without any actual religion, though I'm sure students had spent time on these benches praying for passing grades and reciprocal crushes and athletic wins. I could count myself in the first two categories.

Normally the headmaster spoke at Convocation. Some-times coaches or club advisers. Monday, the nurse had given flu prevention tips and demonstrated handwashing techniques. Two weeks ago, we'd had student government speeches; last week, the winners had talked about the Fall Ball.

I sat and pretended not to notice the concerned looks from Clara and Huck. Between leaving math and lining up to enter the hall, Clara had found Huck and informed him, "Rory is claiming to be over Toby."

"It is true?" Huck scratched the back of his head and frowned.

I nodded and prayed they would let it go or Headmaster Williams would hurry up and begin. Before he could, there was a commotion up front.

"Isn't that your sister?" asked Clara.

Isn't that your sister? Those were the words I'd heard before Merri cannonballed off the high dive at the town pool for the first time. We were five and six, and she hadn't passed the swim test but had "borrowed" the deep-end bracelet off someone's picnic blanket. Toby had dared her. They were the same words I'd heard in fourth grade when Merri decided to go rogue in her fifth-grade chorus concert—*"Because 'Jingle Bells' is more fun as a mash-up."* And in seventh grade, when eighth-grade Merri decided to protest the cafeteria's use of nonrecyclable cups by wearing an outfit made from them— not realizing how quickly Styrofoam would crumble.

Nothing good ever followed the words *Isn't that your sister?*

I tracked Clara's pointing finger across the aisle and up a few rows to where—yup, my sister—was standing on a bench. A hush had fallen over the room, because who doesn't want to witness a good scandal? I slumped down and added a new prayer: That since I was largely invisible on campus, no one knew she was related to me.

"Fielding"—for someone so tiny, Merri could project—"you asked me this once, and I was stupid enough to say no to you. This time I want everyone to witness me asking you—" Her boyfriend's shoulders were stiff, and his brows raised, but he couldn't take his eyes off her, and he had both hands up, preparing for the inevitability of her slipping.

Reaching out, she clasped one of those hands between both of hers. "Will you make me the happiest girl on campus and go to Fall Ball with me?" She did a little nervous dance when his stunned silence stretched. Adding with an impish grin, "Or you could humiliate me in front of everyone by saying no—that's an option too."

He freed his hand and used both arms to lift her down. But instead of placing her on the ground, he held her close and whispered in her ear.

Merri twined her fingers around his neck and kissed him for three long seconds before hopping *back* on the bench.

I'm sure she was going to shout his obvious answer, but Fielding didn't need a pint-size spokesperson. Shocking probably everyone in the hall, he joined her on the bench. He cleared his throat and, straightening his tie, stated, "Of course I've said yes."

The room exploded with whoops and applause and good-natured ribbing. Over it all was the sound of Headmaster Williams tapping his microphone. "Fielding, Merrilee, if you're done with your antics, I'd like to begin."

Merri nodded. And curtsied. Then hopped down into

Fielding's arms. His ears were red and his posture stiff, but these were the only indications of how massively far outside his comfort zone he'd just leaped. He kept an arm around Merri, looking down at her like she was the most precious person in the room. And to him, she was.

I hadn't looked at Toby. I wanted a merit badge for that. Because I'd wanted to see if he was okay or measure how much this had hurt him. But, no. He had to handle his feelings. I had my hands full with my own.

Walking with Toby across campus to his car, even with neither of us talking, felt like the best noise-canceling earphones. It not only muted my awareness of the rest of the world—everything beyond the sidewalk and the guy beside me—but also cranked down the volume on my brain. It hit pause on all the worries and insecurities and racing thoughts that constantly shouted for my attention, and the million other nameless anxieties that were lining up and waiting to announce themselves. Because Toby didn't make me nervous. My feelings *about* my feelings for him were obnoxious, but when I didn't focus on them, I enjoyed being with him. We'd been friends since before I knew what a crush was; I hoped we'd be friends long after I got over my infatuation. I could do this.

"We should go to that," Toby said, interrupting my contented musings. I blinked and followed his finger to a flyer on a lamppost. It was one I knew well, having watched Clara pose in front of a larger version in the hall before math *and* having drawn the illustration myself. "I'm dateless. If you are too, we might as well."

My feet stopped. Like the poster needed closer inspection. It didn't. I could re-create the falling leaves that gathered into a ball gown in ten minutes. But my feelings did. I *should* have felt elated—*Toby asked me to a dance*—but I couldn't manage an exclamation point on that thought.

"No," I said, my stomach twisting in knots. "Thanks, but no."

"Do you have a date?" he asked. "I should've—"

"Nope." I started walking because he was looking at me a little too closely and the corners of my eyes were starting to itch. Stupid boy. Didn't he know I had a million daydreams about a moment like this? He was ruining them all.

"Hey!" He caught up and stopped on the path in front of me. "Roar, why not?"

"Because—" was all I managed before my voice wavered. "I deserve to be asked on more than a whim. I want better than *We might as well go together*—like someone who wants to go with me and made me their first choice."

"Rory. Roar, I—" He shifted his weight on and off that stupid knee brace and opened and closed his mouth.

"It's fine," I said. It wasn't, but I wasn't either and I couldn't stand here and listen to him backtrack or offer words in ways that didn't mean what I wanted them to. Because I'd never be his first choice, the girl he was nervous about asking. I was done being *might as well*. "But I'm going to walk home."

"You don't have to. Let me drive you."

"It's stopped raining. I'm good."

"Please don't be mad, I didn't—"

"I don't want to be around you right now," I snapped.

His mouth shut and he took a step back. I'd never yelled at him. Merri did all the time, but I was the smoother-over, the peacemaker. Maybe I'd lob a snarky comment occasionally, but never with the heat I'd injected into each of those words. I adjusted the strap of my bag and tried to remember if there were tissues in the pockets. Tried to guess how far I could get without breaking.

He didn't stop me, but he did meet my eyes and say, "I'm sorry," before stepping out of my way.

I was tempted to call Huck or Clara or even Lilly. Let anyone's voice crowd out my thoughts so I wouldn't have to be alone with them. We'd finished *Gatsby* today, and now this felt finished too.

At least I'd let go of my green light without the whole murder thing. Jay Gatsby should've learned some limits.

I'd reached mine.

25

'd barely made it off campus before Toby pulled up beside me and lowered his window. "Roar, can we talk?" I stopped walking and he continued. "I get it . . . I mean, I don't get it completely, but I get that I hurt your feelings and I'm sorry."

"I know." I wasn't quite sure if his explanation made things better or worse.

He put on his hazard lights, then leaned forward and rested his head between his hands on the steering wheel. "I'm messing everything up lately—Merri's barely talking to me and I hurt *you*. I never meant to do that, Roar."

But he *had*. And I was done. It didn't matter what my heart felt watching his agonized face. I'd decided. And I was stubborn; once I made my mind up, I didn't quit. Just ask ice cream. I may have cheated sometimes, but I didn't quit. I couldn't tell him all that, so I did the next best thing. I walked around his car and got in.

Toby's face went soft with relief for the space of an exhale, before he tipped his head back against the seat and asked the ceiling, "What's going on lately? Everything's changing."

"It's called growing up," I teased. The last time I'd seen him sit in that posture, with the same *I won't cry* expression, he'd been seven, I'd been five. We were on his back patio and Major May had cooked us dinner. Toby had been forbidden from leaving his chair until he cleared his plate. But there was a green obstacle in the way—Toby's personal nemesis: broccoli. He thought he'd have to live in that chair from then on out: *"Will you bring a blanket when it's winter, Roar?"*

I'd done one better. I'd eaten his broccoli when Major May went to get matches for the citronella candles. Toby had caught me lightning bugs as thanks.

"I don't want to lose you." His eyes were as wide and vulnerable as they'd been when he'd talked about his dad at Mockingburger. "Am I going to?"

"You couldn't if you tried—don't you remember what a good tagalong I am? Merri says I'm like burrs on a dog's coat."

"Thank God for that." Toby gave me a half smile and a half hug, leaning over the console to put an arm around my shoulder and rest his cheek on top of my head. He might have been thinking about me, or the people he'd lost lately: his dad, my sister, his team . . . Either way, I stiffened and pulled away. There were limits to what I could handle while forcing my heart to play this friendship game.

"Want to do something? Let's go somewhere. A movie. Mockingburger—it was good, let's go back. We can dig out old costumes and trick or treat, or you can keep me company while I hand out candy—I promise you don't have to answer the door."

I shook my head, then reached over and unpressed the

hazard button. "You can drop me at the store. I have to work tonight."

༄

My shift started with me working beside my parents. Mom asked about my day and hummed as she flipped through the unsold Howl-ween costumes. "These'll get marked down tomorrow. Might as well pick one for Byron. What do you think, pirate or pumpkin?"

I'd learned long ago that the correct answer was not "Neither," plus there was the strange fact that both Byron and Gatsby *liked* wearing clothes. Well, Byron did. Gatsby liked it for a few minutes until he decided to eat them. I glanced at Byron, who was currently sleeping on a bed Dad had strategically positioned in sunlight. "The lobster."

"Good call! I think I have one in his size out back." She hurried off to check, sliding her feet into the loafers she'd taken off while crouching beside the display.

During slow times, Dad quizzed me on French. His accent was dismal, but he made up for it in enthusiasm. "Jay nest says pass." He pointed at me and started a timer on his phone. "You know this one! I bet it's the first thing every French student learns."

"Can you spell it?"

He looked disappointed that my tip to not pronounce the last sound on every word still hadn't made him fluent. "Here—" He held up the card to show me my scrawl.

"Je ne sais pas," I said with a laugh. "I don't know."

"But you *did* know," he joked. "And I knew you would."

Dad's jokes were the best—in small doses. And I was more than ready when Lilly arrived and he handed over flash card duties. Cheeks were kissed and "See you at homes" exchanged. The bell over the door chimed with my parents' exit and Lilly shoved the cards aside and pulled out dinner.

Technically, we were supposed to take turns and eat in the backroom, but I refused to be the only staff on the floor. "Black bean soup—dairy-free, I checked—baked potato topped with salsa, and a side of green beans sautéed in olive oil and garlic. Did I do okay?"

"Perfect," I said, and she beamed. "Thank you." It'd been two years since I'd gone down my plant-based nutrition path, but Lilly had been at college—and going through her own food issues. No one ever told me directly, but I'd overheard her and Merri and my parents talking about "disordered eating" and "treatment." Not that I'd been oblivious—all my sketches from that time captured her hollow face, dull hair, cracked nails, patchy skin.

I scanned her now: rosy, round, beautiful, healthy. But underneath her perfect makeup, I'd bet her eyes and nose were as red as mine. Last night after Merri's epic crying session, I'd heard Lilly pacing her room until one o'clock in the morning. She'd been on the phone with Trent, and I couldn't tell what they were talking about, but her voice was pitched high and her footsteps fast.

I was about to ask—for an update on the wedding, if she was okay, if I could help—but before I could find the right words, Merri bounced in. "Sorry I'm late, cross-country ran long—I got lost. I got my whole running group lost. This is what happens when Eliza goes for her driving test and leaves me behind." Merri took a sip of whatever was in Lillian's to-go cup, then frowned. "Gah, that needs sugar. Then I stopped at the senator's office to pick up more buttons to bring to school. It's too bad three-fourths the Hero High population isn't old enough to vote. She's way more popular on campus than Mr. Stratford." Merri grimaced like the taste of her ex-boyfriend's father's name was bitter—though that could've been the second sip of Lilly's coffee she'd tried to choke down. "I bet you can't wait until the election is over. Senator Rhodes looked *stressed*. Oh, and she said to say hi to her favorite future daughter-in-law."

Trent was an only child and Lilly was her *only* future daughter-in-law, but I didn't point that out because the lines on Lilly's face looked more pronounced. I yanked the coffee out of Merri's hand and gave it back to Lilly.

"Only one week and the election will be over. Then no more talk of polling numbers and canvassing." She sipped from the cup I'd put in her hands. "Six. More. Days."

"Then it'll be all wedding, all the time!" Merri whooped. Lilly gulped until the cup was empty.

I picked up my flash cards, because I didn't want to see the clash between Merri's excitement and Lilly's stress. I made it through a dozen before Merri got around to describing her Convocation adventures. I knew it was coming. She was squirming with impatience like an un-housebroken puppy, and finally she climbed on the counter and swung her legs as she announced, "So, I have news."

Which was my cue to leave. Anything Fall Ball related

made me want to dive headfirst into a box of tissues. After last night, my nose couldn't handle another cry fest—not unless I wanted to be Rudolph for Halloween.

I stacked the cards and dug out an elastic band from the drawer below the register. There were plenty of things I could do—check inventory, neaten displays, sweep, decorate. Anything that had me not here, hearing "And then I climbed right up on the bench—they're a lot higher than they look. And Fielding, he told me later—"

We were almost out of the small size of Indestructibones. It'd be irresponsible for me to stay and chat instead of saving customers' couches and shoes from teething puppies.

"Headmaster Williams is starting to like me. Rory—" Merri called, and I froze at the stockroom door.

"Yes?" Maybe she wanted me to fetch her a cream soda. I crossed my fingers.

"Did you notice Headmaster Williams didn't interrupt until *after* Fielding answered? And he came up to us after Convocation and invited me to dinner this weekend. That's got to be progress."

Lilly squeezed her arm. "It sounds promising. Want me to make a manicure appointment for us?" Merri nodded and Lilly grabbed a coupon from the stack on the counter and jotted down Nails with M.

I waited for my name to be added. I mean, sure I complained about the smell and the sitting, and I'd end up chipping them in art, but they'd at least ask, right? Instead, Lilly folded the note and stuck it in her planner and Merri bounced and added, "His dad asked what I'm allergic to."

"Maybe so he could cook it," I suggested, because Headmaster Williams reminded me of the Grinch. His shoes and heart were definitely too small and his smile looked rancid.

Lilly shot me a *Not helpful* grimace.

"Well, it's good I'm not allergic to anything then!" chirped Merri. "Imagine if I were *you* with all your won't-eats."

"Yeah, imagine." I dropped all pretense of socializing and wandered over to the comfy chair by the front window. Digging out the sketch pad I kept in the drawer beneath, I began to draw the Dalmatian that was scampering after his owner as she examined different bags of dog food. He was actually pretty cute. The mom was holding her dino-suited toddler by one hand and had the dog's leash looped around the other. Each time she bent over to read the ingredients on a bag, the two of them would meet behind her back for kisses and giggles. It was probably just the dog cleaning off whatever Halloween candy was smeared on the boy's face—but still. Cute.

The sketch turned out well enough that when she'd picked her bag and dragged it to the register, I ripped off the page and carried it over too. Stammering and red-faced, I said, "Here," and retreated as soon as her fingers had closed around the paper.

I was halfway across the store before she'd turned it over. "Wait! You drew this?"

I froze. "I hope that's okay?" Dangit, was it a childhood privacy thing? Was I supposed to ask permission first? Had I offended her?

She stared at me and I curled my toes in my shoes. Finally, she blinked. "This is amazing. I can't believe you did this."

She shoved the receipt Merri held out into her wallet, then thumbed open the billfold. "How much do I owe you? This is the perfect Christmas present for my husband."

"Oh, I couldn't—" I took a step backward, stumbling over air and knocking down half a rack of leashes.

"Yes, she could," interjected Merri. "Pay whatever you think is fair. And thank you."

"No, thank *you*," the woman said to Merri and again to me on her way out. "How often are you here? I'm going to tell all my friends to come by."

"Um, usually Wednesday nights and sometimes on the weekend." I was kicking past-me for my stupidity. Couldn't have turned to a blank page. Nope, had to be an idiot and do the nice thing, and now I was getting the well-intentioned third degree and Dalmatian fur and sticky handprints on my pants, since the toddler latched on to one leg as the dog rubbed against the other. Hello, claustrophobia in the middle of an open-floor plan.

"And what's your name?" She held the drawing out to me. "Can I get you to sign this?"

"Aurora Campbell," I mumbled and scrawled, before handing the paper back and disentangling myself from pudgy hands and leashes. "Have a good night."

Merri handed me the cash but I didn't count it. I shoved it in the register the next time I checked someone out. She'd gone to bat for me even though I'd been too busy pouting to compliment her Convocation spectacle. So what if it wasn't something I'd do? No one asked me to.

Mom always said, "Spitting in someone else's tea doesn't

make yours taste any better." The same was true for cashew cheese and meatless hot dogs. Well, maybe not the hot dogs—there really wasn't anything that could salvage those.

But, whatever, Merri was happy. She and Fielding were happy. It wasn't her fault I'd held on to this crush, or her fault Toby didn't return it. I'd meant it when I told Merri I'd put some effort into fixing our relationship.

I cleared my throat and called her name. Then hated myself for how quickly she dropped her broom and scampered over. "Hey, what's up? What are you drawing now?"

"Um, nothing really."

"You should draw the bed display, then add in the next dog that comes in the store."

"Yeah, um, sure." I added a bed. "Sorry if I was a jerk about Headmaster Williams. I'm sure he's warming up to you. I mean, everyone does. And congrats on Fall Ball. Do you know what you're going to wear?"

"Thanks!" Merri did a graceless pirouette. "Wear to Fall Ball? Or dinner at the Williamses'?"

"Um, either?"

"Not a clue. But will you do my makeup?"

"Sure," I said. "And someone once recommended paisley and sparkles—maybe start there."

She laughed and Lilly joined in. I basked in the moment, fiercely proud of the sound of those giggles echoing off the floor, windows, and rafters and deeply aware that these moments were fleeting—this time next year, Lilly would be married and off to law school. Two years after, Merri would be at college. While we had them, I wanted to hold on tight.

26

On Thursday morning, I arrived at art to see Mrs. Mundhenk had written Snipes Nominees on the chalkboard. One of Boy Byron's paintings was on an easel in the front of the room. It was the one he'd worked on next to me. A Snipes reproduction—which, thinking back, had been pretty popular. The obsession over the contemporary art folder suddenly made sense. Well, if copying a Snipes painting was a requirement, then I'd disqualified myself and I didn't have to stress anymore. My footsteps were lighter as I hung up my coat, adding my congratulations to the tide launched at Boy Byron.

He preened like the peacock in his painting—a cubist rendering of *Vanity, Captured*. "Is it too early to start worrying if I'll get picked?"

Instead of attaching myself to the group around him, I continued to the back corner where my painting in progress waited on the drying rack. I'd salvaged the rain boots. Maya's paint water added a dingy gray overlay, which worked with the mood of the piece.

Huck was already setting up on the easel beside mine. "I'm fuming it's not you. He's good; you're better." He paused and reclipped his paper so it hung straighter. "In case you were wondering how I felt about this whole thing."

"Noted," I answered with a laugh. "But I'm fine."

"Okay, class." Mrs. Mundhenk came out of her office, clapping to get our attention. "As you can see, I'm ready to announce my nominees for the Snipes workshop. Now, there's no guarantee that either of these artists will be chosen, but they're both worthy. As are many others in here. This is a very talented group, but"—she paused to grip the back of a chair—"many of you did not qualify. Any artist who would tear down or sabotage another artist's work in an attempt to get ahead doesn't deserve this opportunity and couldn't handle the supportive community Ms. Snipes builds within her workshops. The art world is too difficult for artists to view each other as competitors or enemies. Look for chances to lift each other up—like Ms. Snipes has with this workshop—not tear each other down."

Throughout her speech, I watched my classmates do one of two things: look away or look at me. Those who lowered their eyes were ashamed and apologetic. Those who glared were pissed.

Basically, by being here I'd disqualified the bulk of the class. I'm sure that wouldn't make them at all resentful and that my popularity award would be arriving in the mail any day.

"Now, you all see Byron's painting up here. Let's give him a round of applause for being our first nominee."

The class clapped, but it was aggressively brief. The

impatience in the air felt thick, humid enough to curl the sketch paper on our easels.

"Our second nominee, well, isn't going to surprise anyone. It's Aurora Campbell." The roar of panic in my ears drowned out any clapping. I wanted to hide behind my easel and never come out. My shoes were lead as I shuffled them and tried to make myself smaller. I flinched when Huck patted my back.

"Congratulations to Byron and Rory. Both of you come see me to sign forms. Everyone else, get to work."

I didn't go see her during class. I waited until after the bell had rung and the coatroom had emptied. "You said you had paperwork for me to sign, but—"

"Here it is. Look at it carefully. There are a lot of places to initial and date. I'm using your painting of Tobias as your entry—but like I promised, no one here will see it."

"Are you sure you wanted to nominate me? It's not because I got picked on, is it?"

"Do you honestly think that?" Mrs. Mundhenk put down the pages she'd been passing me one at a time. "My only reservation was if you were ready, maturity-wise, after that whole party scandal in September. The workshop will skew toward upperclassmen. Freshmen *can* be nominated, but at teacher's discretion." She pointed to another place I needed to sign and I scrawled my initials. "You would get so much out of this experience."

"Thank you."

She smiled and pointed to one last line. "I'm crossing everything that you get picked."

As Mrs. Mundhenk stacked the papers, I hesitated. "One last question." I bit my lip, because this was a deal breaker. "How much does it cost?"

She tapped the paperwork to align the edges. "Did you miss the part about the grants? You just signed it."

"You were talking . . . I couldn't read and listen."

"There are grants for students who need them—so, don't worry about that. Stay focused on your exams."

"Okay." I nodded. "French today, math tomorrow."

"Bonne chance," called out Mrs. Mundhenk. *Good luck.*

I'd need it.

27

Toby's knee hadn't stopped jiggling since I'd opened the passenger door Friday morning and he'd skipped over "Hi" or "Good morning" and gone straight to "How are you feeling about your math test today?"

"About the same as when we finished tutoring last night." Like passing wasn't impossible, just improbable. Made more so by the cumulative lack of sleep I'd gotten all week.

The benefit of stress and exhaustion was that I was too busy trying to remember formulas to swoon. Turns out that while being tutored by my crush had been helpful, being tutored while *not* thinking about how badly I wanted my tutor to kiss me—much more helpful.

"You've got this. You know you've got this, right?" Toby asked me for the millionth time in our five-minute drive.

I smiled into my travel mug, the scent of peppermint tea curling up around my cheeks. "Well, the first seven times I agreed with you were all lies, but since you asked again . . ."

"Sorry." Toby's grin was sheepish. No one did sheepish quite as adorably as Toby. Or mischievous. Or impishly apologetic. Not that I was noticing. Nope. I was pulling out my math notebook and focusing there instead. And it was getting easier.

Without looking up from my notebook's spiral binding, I asked, "Is there a reason you're so invested in my math grade? Do you have money riding on my exam? At least I know you bet I'd pass."

"I heard about the Snipes thing."

"What about it?" My voice had gone sharp, because if he'd seen my painting I was going to throw myself out of this car and pray the one behind us ran me over.

Toby glanced at me as we paused at a stop sign. "Lynnie in my music class was talking about it. Her twin, Byron, is the other nominee. She said he was freaking out about midterms because there's a GPA requirement."

"A what?" I really should've read those forms. Mrs. Mundhenk's warning to stay focused on my exams suddenly had a whole new significance. My grip on my notebook tightened, like I could absorb formulas through my fingertips. "Do you know what it is?"

He shook his head. "I thought you knew. Sorry."

My stomach clenched, my breathing going fast and shallow, my notebook slipping to the floor. How humiliating would it be when my nomination had to be pulled because I couldn't pass math? My fingers scrabbled for something to hold on to. My right hand clamped around the door with white knuckles, but before I could reach for my backpack strap with my left, Toby's fingers closed over mine and squeezed. "But it doesn't matter, because *you've got this*, Roar. I know you do."

Could I get a poster with those words and his face on it,

please? It'd be way more motivational than all the cookies, kittens, and flamingos on Mrs. Roberts's wall. He squeezed my hand again before letting go to flick on the blinker and turn into the school lot.

"I've got this," I repeated in a whisper.

He looked at my pale face and groaned, then pressed a button on his phone. "Here. *Batman* theme. It's my go-to song for when I need to get pumped. *You've got this.*"

He was right about the song. I just hoped he was also right about the test.

❦

All week I'd debated telling Clara about Toby's Fall Ball request. I wanted her advice . . . but only if it matched my get-over-him vows, and she was more likely to shriek *"Say yes!"* and come up with a scheme about a magic, perfect dress that would win him over.

By the time I reached the art studio, I was worn down by lack of sleep, math test anxiety, new GPA-nomination worries, and the echoed sensation of Toby's hand on mine. It was too much to contain—I was like a shaken soda, I needed to let off some pressure and tell *someone.* Lucky Huck. He put his pencil down to listen, but I told the story while facing my easel, my paintbrush moving in frantic swoops and jerks. ". . . And then he asked me. In the parking lot on Wednesday."

"Great. But it'll have to be Clara dress shopping with you. I don't do 'Does this look good on me?' Own the fact that you're gorgeous—wear whatever you want."

"Um, thanks?" I think there was a compliment in there. "But I wasn't asking that. Will *you* go with me? I told him no."

"Are we taking the jealousy game too far?" Huck leaned back from his sketch and frowned. He switched from a 2H to a 4B, then used his gum eraser on the tip of the nose he was drawing. "There's a fine line between making someone pursue you and making someone give up."

"I don't want him to be jealous. I meant it, I'm over him."

Huck turned to me to confirm my words. I nodded. His lips pressed down with sympathy, but unlike Clara, he didn't protest. "And you're asking me?"

"As friends." Because of how Toby's words had hurt me, I clarified. "I don't want it to be a date, but I'm not 'settling' on you. You're the person I want to go with, the one I'd have the most fun with. But if you have a date or there's a guy or girl you want to ask, I get it."

"Nah," he said, and I gripped my paintbrush painfully tight, not sure which part he was rejecting. "There's no one I want to ask. Platonic prom partners it is."

"It's not the prom," I clarified.

"Don't ruin my alliteration, Clementine Campbell."

"If you change your mind, that's okay too. I'm not super sure I really want to go to the dance, but—"

"Let's not go together."

I blinked at him. "But you just said 'yes'?"

Huck dimpled. "You hate things like this, right? So we could agree to not-go." He paused. "Together. We'll do something else that night."

"Oh, that's a much better plan." Just thinking about the dance had me sweating, and I swiped my hand across my forehead, leaving behind a blue stripe. "Though Clara might kill us."

Huck tapped his pencil while he schemed. "Agree to paint the photo backdrop. I bet if we recruit Byron to help she'll get over it."

"Byron?" I glanced across the room to where his auburn head was bent over a drawing board, but before I could tell Huck to elaborate, he asked, "Will you be okay if Toby goes to the dance with someone else?"

My stomach, heart, and thoughts knotted in that math-class panic feeling. And just like when I got called on in there, I didn't know the answer.

28

I didn't trust myself when it came to math. Had some of those exam problems actually been easy, and had others been in hieroglyphics? Because some I couldn't wait to brag about to Toby, but others . . . I swore I'd never seen anything like them.

Mrs. Roberts had patrolled the room while we tested, murmuring compliments and placing encouraging bookmarks on the corners of our desks. Sadly, mine was not Toby's face but a paint palette with each word in a different color: *Don't decide you can't before you discover you can.* The kid next to me got *Think you can* written on a train. I saw his accidentally, but then spent ten breaths panicked that it looked like I was cheating.

The gesture was super thoughtful—but also super distracting. And by the time the bell rang at the end of the period, I slid out of my desk boneless with stress and exhaustion.

"I'll have these back on Monday," she reassured me. I squeaked in response.

Merri was MIA all weekend. If she wasn't at Eliza's or Haute Dog, then she was sequestered in her room with her face buried in her laptop. When I dropped off lunch—because she was in forget-to-eat headspace—I asked what she was doing. She blinked like she didn't recognize her room or her sister, then shushed and shooed me.

"You're welcome," I snarked from the hallway, but she didn't bother responding.

Lilly was home though. She had her sidekick with her. I'd liked Trent from the moment Lilly introduced him to the family a few years back. Merri had not. And since Merri wasn't exactly poker-faced, we'd all sat through many, many tense meals. But she and he had some bonding breakthrough recently—something about his time at Hero High or the time Merri now spent campaigning for his mom's senate race—so she wasn't hiding because he was here.

I liked Trent because he was comfortable with silence. He did small talk too—better than I'd ever master—but he was cool with putting on a podcast or playlist and letting that be the backdrop while we drove somewhere or set the table or did the brunch dishes. All tasks he didn't hesitate to volunteer for. That Sunday I was making a fruit salad and he was peeling eggs, a chore I hated and that would've fallen on me since Lilly was on the phone with their caterer and Merri was upstairs typing.

"Thanks for doing that." I pointed with my paring knife to the pot he was taking off the stove.

"Sure!" His grin displayed perfect teeth. Trent looked like the king of Ken dolls, until he started talking and revealed his deep-seated geekiness. "I just watched this life hack video with a trick for peeling them all at once. Wanna try it?"

204 | TIFFANY SCHMIDT

"As long as I don't have to touch or eat them, absolutely."

He got out a plastic container and filled it with water before transferring the eggs inside it and fastening the lid. Switching on the kitchen radio, Trent began to shake the container to the beat. I bit my lip to try to trap my giggles. It didn't work.

"Oh, you laugh now, but wait until you see the end result," he said.

"Uh-huh." I turned back to the pineapple. "You do you, Trent."

For the most part, his eggs came out perfectly peeled. One had broken in half, but he put it on his own plate. He came back in the kitchen and stole a piece of banana from the fruit salad. "We're good—let's call everyone in."

I'd known something was up all morning. Brunch was normally Dad's domain—he manned the griddle or waffle iron—but today it had been all on Trent and me. Dad and Mom disappeared upstairs as soon as we got home from church. This week's French toast, eggs, and fruit salad were way less extravagant than Dad's usual spread, but he didn't comment beyond saying, "Thanks for cooking."

Merri and Lilly exchanged glances. They exchanged them again when Mom said, "Girls, we need to talk to you about something."

I was tempted to interject, *"Yeah, let's talk about how Merri and Lilly don't include me in their nonverbal communication."* But that made me feel even more pathetic.

Merri bolted out of her chair, tipping her orange juice onto Lilly's empty plate. "I don't want you to get a divorce!"

"What?" Dad patted her back. "No. It's nothing like that, Mer-bear—why would you think that?"

"Because she's her," I muttered, and Lilly kicked me under the table.

Trent carried Merri's cup and Lilly's plate over to the sink. He dumped the juice back in her cup, rinsed and dried the plate, then returned them as Merri sat back down and said, "Gah. Sorry for interrupting."

Mom snorted. "Anyway—as we were saying." She cleared her throat and studied the silverware. "Thanksgiving is in a few weeks and I know it's the season for Christmas lists, but the holidays are going to be a bit . . . smaller this year."

"We wanted to give you a heads-up," Dad continued when Mom's voice trailed off. His eyes were fixed on the bowl of peeled eggs. "It's just . . . between tuition and wedding expenses, things are tighter. We don't want you to worry—" Only, telling me not to worry was like throwing gasoline on a bonfire. My anxiety flared and made it harder to hear his words. "Think about asking for one medium-size present this year. And treat your cell phones carefully, because we're not replacing those anytime soon."

"Is everything okay at the store?" asked Lilly. She was holding Trent's hand under the table—a benefit of him being a lefty and her a righty was they could do this while still eating—but I wondered if it was weird for her to have him hear this conversation. Trent's family—like most of my Hero High classmates—was loaded. The only thing that would dampen the Rhodes's Christmas was if his mom lost her senate reelection race next week.

"The store is fine—maybe not competing as much as we'd like against the big-box store—but it's holding its own. And the new shops opening in our plaza should increase foot traffic," said Mom.

All three of us opened our mouths with follow-up questions, but Dad cut us off. "That's enough of that, let's hear about your weeks. Trent, how's your mom holding up through this final stretch? Merri, when's your next meet? Rory, what have you been painting? Lilly, update me on wedding plans."

Trent looked to Lilly and I followed his eyes, catching the slight wince that flickered across her face at Dad's question. Instead of answering, she said, "We have news. Trent and I have finished our law school applications."

My parents launched into congratulations and Merri questioned, "What if you don't get into the same place? Or have different picks? Who gets to choose?"

Trent pulled a quarter from his pocket. "If it comes down to two schools, we'll flip for it. But we've applied in geographic clusters. I'm not worried."

Lilly was telling Dad about law libraries and "L-one course loads" and beaming in the way she did when Trent walked into a room. I hadn't ever been that excited about school. Even in kindergarten I'd hidden in the painting corner and refused to join the class when they circled up for calendar time.

"I want to see a map of all the schools," demanded Merri. "And let's go ahead and eliminate any that are more than two hours away."

Trent's eyes widened. He couldn't tell if she was serious and looked to Lilly for guidance. I interrupted before this could become A Thing—"Once you've picked, will you buy me a law school sweatshirt? You know it's the closest *I'll* ever get to law school." I tacked on a cheeky grin, and everyone laughed.

But I wished they hadn't. I wished someone had contradicted me. I could feel my shoulders pulling in, the pineapple burning on my tongue. If Toby were here, he'd make a comment like "Because you'll be too busy trying to keep up with the demands of museums and collectors clamoring for your art."

I wasn't guessing—I *knew*. There was fierce absoluteness to Toby's protectiveness. Whether defending Merri against her own scatterbrained-genius reputation, or defending me, or even Eliza—he didn't let the people he cared about be mocked, not even in self-deprecation. I wondered if he knew how grateful I was—and if he had anyone to do the same for him.

After brunch Mom and Dad left for the store, Trent and Lilly got in his car and went to campaign headquarters, and Merri went back upstairs. I pulled out my phone to text Clara or Huck, then put it away and opened the front door instead. I did all sorts of second-guessing as my feet crossed the threshold—but I still turned down the walkway and headed across the lawn. I could do this. Friends hung out. Friends stopped by and complained of boredom. Friends told each other when they appreciated support—and until now I'd been worried he'd read the swooning subtext of any compliment I gave him. That needed to change.

But friends also knew things about their friends, and Major May's car was in their driveway. Seeing the Mercedes felt like an exhale. I'd have been even happier if the car were pulled into the garage like he was going to stay awhile, but at least he was home. I crossed my fingers and said a prayer that his tires would go flat, that his engine wouldn't start, or that he'd realize how spectacular his son was and need no further excuse to stay and spend time with him.

Without an excuse of my own, I went to my room and pulled out *Little Women*.

"Christmas won't be Christmas without any presents . . ."

I snorted. One line in and this book was already more relevant than *The Great Gatsby*. Another character followed up with *"It's so dreadful to be poor!"* and I felt goose bumps prickle across my skin. I settled onto my bed, propping a pillow between my shoulders and the wall. There were four sisters in the book: The oldest, Meg, was sweet. The second, Jo, was feisty. Beth, the third, was a little too saintly. And the youngest, Amy, was an artist—or at least she'd mentioned needing drawing pencils on the very first page.

Unlike the March sisters, we weren't poor. I got that. We had more than a lot of people had, and I was lucky, but sometimes it was hard to keep perspective when surrounded by classmates who lived like Gatsby. Who'd be getting new cars and designer wardrobes for the holidays. Not that I wanted or needed those things, but it would be weird to ask for *anything* after Mom and Dad's disclaimers. I couldn't think about the way they hadn't met our eyes and the tight expressions they'd worn without wanting to curl under my covers.

Maybe if I left Hero High, things would be easier for them. Maybe, depending on my math grade, leaving would be unavoidable. The idea sat sour in my stomach. I twisted my knees up toward my chest and opened the book again, ready to immerse myself in a different set of sisters' problems and leave my own behind for a while.

29

S o?"

I was clutching my test when I walked out of Mrs. Roberts's classroom on Monday, and Toby's sudden appearance in my personal space made my heart jump . . . then race. Because my heart is a traitorous traitor. "Dangit, Toby. You can't spring out of nowhere like Batman lurking in the shadows."

"I'm like Batman?" Toby grinned. "That's the nicest thing anyone's ever said to me. But tell me again later, right now I want to hear about *this*." He plucked the exam from my hand and turned it around to read the score.

People had to be staring, because Toby was whooping, but I didn't know for sure because I had my head tucked against his collarbone. One—so I wouldn't get sick, because his spinning hug was a lot like the teacup ride. Two—he smelled good. Three—I didn't want to see the faces of anyone gawking. This was the sort of thing that happened to Merri all the time. People picking her up—just to prove they could. She hated it. Maybe I would too if it was a daily thing, but Toby hadn't stopped saying how proud he was from the moment he scooped me into his arms.

"I knew you could do it. We need to celebrate! What should we do? Eighty-freaking-three! I'm more excited about your math grade than my own."

When he put me down both of us stumbled a bit, clinging to each other to stay upright as the dizziness passed. And I laughed, a full sound that might have drawn more attention, but I didn't care. I'd gotten an eighty-three, I'd been twirled around like a rom-com heroine, and the thing I was thinking throughout the twirl was how grateful I was for my *friend*—the one who'd worked so hard to help me get that score.

"Thank you," I said against his collar. "I wasn't the easiest pupil, but you were an amazing tutor."

"Were?" Toby shook his head. "I'm not done with you, we've still got more than half a school year, Roar."

"Yeah, but you don't have to—"

"I want to."

I sniffed and focused on my breathing. "I know you're Merri's *best* friend, but you're one of mine too. I want you to know I appreciate you." Maybe it was stupid to bring her into it, and it sounded weirder and weaker than I wanted. I didn't have her gift for words and my feelings made it harder to say what I meant—like, how to make "Thank you" convey all the sincerity and emotion I wanted to cram into those eight letters. How did I demonstrate that *this* "Thank you" was bigger than when he held a door for me or said "Bless you" to a sneeze?

But maybe some of that gleamed in my eyes or glowed out of my radioactive-red skin, because he squeezed my shoulder. "Me too, Roar."

I blinked and blinked, but my stupid eyes wouldn't stop glazing over.

"So?!" Huck's shout reached me before he skidded around the corner. "Why are you crying? Are those tears of joy or I-need-a-better-tutor?" He turned to Toby, who let go and took a step back. "No offense, man. I'm sure she's an unruly pupil. I've seen the way she doodles on class notes."

I snuffled. "Tears of joy."

Huck swiped at his eyes. "Dangit, Campbell, you're going to make me cry too."

"Well, she's already got you saying 'Dangit,' so . . ." Toby muttered, kicking a pencil stub down the hallway.

"On a scale of one to one hundred, how happy are we talking?" Huck thumbed to his calculator app. "What I'm really asking is, Snipes nomination, do you get to keep it?"

I took his phone, glancing at the screen to see the rest of my quizzes and retest scores already inputted. I typed in eighty-three and handed it back over. I wasn't going to be the one to hit equals because I didn't ever trust math not to betray me. Huck took a deep breath and touched the screen. He exhaled and pulled me into a hug. "Clementine Camp-bear's going to New York!" he hollered.

"Um, haven't been picked yet." I laughed and turned to Toby to roll my eyes. Except Toby was now five feet away.

He picked up my schoolbag and held it out. "We should get to Convocation. I bet we're already late."

30

Tuesday night I was climbing the walls. I'd tried sketching and rearranging my prints, but I couldn't be in my room any longer—I couldn't be in my *head* any longer. Not thinking about someone was way harder than thinking about him. I mean, *them.* Gender neutral, because I wasn't thinking about him.

I'd already voluntarily worked extra at the store—packing away Howl-ween costumes to make room for dog coats and boots. I'd done my homework. I'd done yoga. But we weren't doing tutoring tonight because Toby's piano teacher had invited him to dinner, and all I could think about was the fact I wouldn't see him. *Dangit.*

Lilly would've been a good distraction, but she was spending election night with Trent at his mom's campaign headquarters. There'd already been photos of Lilly online from when she went to vote—seeing them had given her hives. She'd second-guessed every aspect of her outfit for tonight while I'd done her makeup, and the only thing that had gotten her out the door was my suggestion, "Trent needs you."

I raised a hand to knock on Merri's door, but when I heard a massive crash from the other side, I skipped etiquette and swung it open, realizing midswing that it was possible she and Fielding were taking advantage of our parentless house and that might've been a make-out crash. Was that a thing? With Merri, it seemed like it could be.

"What are you doing?" we asked at the same time. Her because I was standing in the doorway with my eyes squeezed shut, and me because I was asking if it was safe to open them.

"Can I come in?" I clarified.

"Sure, watch where you step." It sounded like permission to open my eyes. No Fielding, but books *everywhere*. Like a library had projectile-vomited on every flat surface. "Waiting on the election results is the worst. I offered to come to head-quarters, but Senator Rhodes and I decided my anxiety might feed hers."

I bit back a smile. Merri and the senator had the odd-est friendship. Personally, I was never going to get over the time she'd caught me bored-sketching her. She'd loved the drawing—done in blue ballpoint pen because it was the only thing within reach—and it was all over her final round of ads. Every time I saw it on a poster or mailer or commercial, I wanted to pry up the carpet and hide underneath. Not that it was bad or unflattering—but my thoughts while drawing it had been. I'd been so annoyed by her need to give a long speech welcoming our family to hers and stressed by the unavoidable small talk afterward. The fact that she *liked* me and my art made me the worst type of awkward in all interactions.

"Fielding suggested I find an outlet for my stress," Merri continued. "So I'm rearranging my bookshelves by color."

"How were they arranged before?" I asked.

"They weren't." She turned her laptop to face me and pointed to the image search on the screen. "But look at all these rainbow libraries. Aren't they gorgeous?"

That was an aesthetic I could get behind. I bent to sort the pile closest to me. "Let's separate the mattes from the glossies, then integrate them strategically."

Merri raised her hands. "You are now the boss. I bow to your superior artsy intelligence. Keep me away from the *New York Times* election reporting needle, and I'll do whatever you say."

I waited for her to add "Don't let this go to your head" or "For the next hour" or whatever snarky disclaimer made it clear we were only bonding within her parameters.

"Oh," she said, and my stomach clenched. "And can we listen to Christmas music? Fielding has a rule that we have to wait until after Thanksgiving, but that's still two weeks away."

My insides shifted from nerves to bubbling laughter. Shotgun privileges in Toby's car came with two radio buttons of my own. I'd programmed one to the all-Christmas-song station. Most days we listened to film scores, but on Friday Toby had joined me in singing along. Mariah Carey better watch out; he did a mean "All I Want for Christmas Is You." I bit my lip to keep from grinning. "As long as it's not the *Chipmunks Christmas* on repeat."

"I was eight." I raised an eyebrow and Merri rolled her eyes. "And fine, nine through twelve too, but it's a quality album."

I laughed and waited for her to begin a non-Chipmunks

playlist, then picked my way over to the books heaped on her bed. "Let's start with whites."

It was eleven by the time we'd finished. I called up a streaming news channel on Merri's laptop and we watched the camera pan over Lilly's tear-streaked face. "Happy tears or sad tears?" Merri demanded. "HAPPY TEARS OR SAD?"

"Indoor voice," I said. "And, newsflash, Lilly can't hear you. But, look—" I pointed to the scrolling banner: *Senator Rhodes wins in landslide election*. The two of us sank down on the bed, arms tired from lifting and bones weak with relief.

"I'm so proud of her and the voters. Really of our whole state." Merri was now the one crying happy tears. "I know I'm ridiculous since I can't even vote—"

I cut her off. "You're not ridiculous. Don't call yourself that." I hated when she bought into what others said. It was easy for people to focus on her size and smile and enthusiasm and miss the brain behind them. "You worked hard on that campaign, you should be proud."

"They're still using your drawing." Merri pointed to the graphic on a screen behind the podium as balloons and confetti fell. Then she started to boo. For a second I was insulted until I read the new information scrolling across the screen. *Despite fifteen-point margins, Stratford refuses to concede the election and demands a recount*. "I'm so happy he lost. And so, so happy for the senator."

She stood and jumped on the bed, making me bounce. "Plus, look at these bookshelves. Rory, they're gorgeous! Thank you, thank you!" She punctuated each word with a

THE BOY NEXT STORY | 217

jump until I groaned and rolled onto the floor mumbling, "Remember the teacups."

Merri stilled. "You're not actually going to get sick, are you?"

"Maybe?" From my spot on her rag rug, I saw a book we'd missed wedged beneath the shelf. I pulled it out and snorted. Her copy had a red cover but was as thick as the yellow one in my room. "Have you read this?"

"*Little Women!*" Merri squealed in a pitch that made Gatsby howl downstairs. "That was my favorite book when I was ten." Ten, as in half a decade younger than I was. As in the age when she still believed in Santa and slept with a night-light. I was reading a Santa-believer's book. "Didn't you love it? Ugh, I'm never forgiving Amy for that burnt manuscript. And Demi is the cutest. And Beth! How hard did you cry over Beth?"

"Um, I'm on page ten."

"Oh. Whoops. Well, you will. You're not completely heartless."

"Thanks." Merri either didn't hear or chose to ignore my sarcasm. "Ms. Gregoire assigned it to me for extra credit."

"She did?" Merri's jaw dropped. "You know what that means, right? She picks you a book and it changes everything."

I'd heard this before. Merri loved Ms. Gregoire. If she could give her credit for solar power and sliced bread she would. But then again . . . the book had burned me. I still couldn't touch it without tingles.

"Don't roll your eyes!" Merri pointed a finger in my face. "Fielding and I wouldn't have happened without *Pride and Prejudice*. And Trent totally implied he and Lilly were the result of a Gregoirean book pairing. He won't tell me which book though."

I raised an eyebrow, because Lilly hadn't gone to Hero High and hadn't met Trent until college. Right? I was going to join my sister in nudging for that story. "Well, I got *Little Women*—so what's that mean?"

Merri chewed her bottom lip. "It depends. That book is the original sorting hat. Only instead of a Hogwarts house you get a girl. I'm a Jo, obviously. Lilly's a Meg. Eliza refuses to be any of them. She's probably an Aunt March if we're honest. You're an Amy—tell me you know you're an Amy."

I glowered at her. In ten seconds, she'd summarized the reaction paper I'd spent two hours drafting. One I'd thought was so original and clever. "Yes, I know I'm an Amy."

Merri glanced over her shoulder and out her balcony doors. I followed her gaze because I'd take any excuse to look at Toby's room. It was lit up bright, but his balcony doors were shut. Merri rubbed her hands together in glee. "I've got a hunch, but I cannot wait to see how this plays out."

31

On the Wednesday of Thanksgiving break, Trent drove me home after work, teasing, "You might be the only teenager I know who isn't glued to their phone."

"Do you spend lots of time with teens who aren't me and Merri?" I asked.

"Well, no," he admitted. "Just you two and my cousin, Quinn, who'll be a Hero High freshman next year."

I nodded and leaned against the seat. Nodded again when he suggested, "True crime podcast? Funny one?"

I knew there were texts waiting on my cell—Clara requesting my schedule for the next couple of days so she could make plans; Huck's comedic and desperate updates from his eight-hour car trip; a picture from Byron of his latest drawing with a note: **Something's not working. What?** But I was too exhausted to respond to any of them. The store had been packed since Dad unlocked the door this morning, and everyone had been chatty. I was in introvert overload long before my shift ended at three. Trent's podcast was background noise I could ignore, not even curious why the words I caught included: "blood spatter," "anxiety," "vintage housedresses," and "cats."

"Hey, sleeping beauty—oh wait! I take that back. I just meant . . . because you were asleep. I wasn't making a joke about your name. Lilly says you hate that."

I cracked open my eyes to see Trent frowning. "Forgiven." I yawned. "Thanks for the ride."

"No problem. But actually—can you do me a favor?" He got out, then opened the door behind his and picked up an enormous vase of lilies. They were pure white in their centers and on the tip of each petal, but in between they were a purple so dark it resembled black. I wanted to draw one immediately. "Can you put this in Lillian's room?"

"If I can carry it?" I looked dubiously at the fancy vase— was it crystal? How big a deal would it be if I dropped it? "Did you buy every lily they had in the store?"

Trent looked at the bouquet in his arms. "Is it too much? It's the anniversary of our first kiss, and she's closing at the store, then doing something with Merri, and I have dinner at my aunt's—I wanted her to know I was thinking of her."

I was glad he hadn't handed me the vase yet, because it might've melted through my arms at the sweetness of his words, or maybe I'd have dropped it out of bitterness for those plans my sisters apparently had that didn't include me. Most likely it'd have slipped from my startled grasp when a voice behind me said, "It's perfect. I'll carry them in for you."

Trent passed the vase to Toby and the two exchanged *Thanks, man, No problem, dude* head nods. "I'll see you tomorrow at Thanksgiving, Rory," Trent said before getting in his shiny car and backing out of the driveway.

I hadn't seen Toby since our Knight Light meeting Tuesday

morning. The freshman and sophomore classes had worked in their pairs to pack food-drive boxes for the local pantry to distribute—Toby and I had been in charge of adding a bag of potatoes and a can of cranberry to each box—but only the sophomore Knight Lights were allowed to miss the second half of the school day to deliver them to the food pantry. The adoptees spent the afternoon in classes as usual.

It had been only thirty-six hours since that super-awkward moment when Toby had clinked a can of cranberry against the one I was holding and said, "It's times like this that make me realize just how super lucky we are."

And I'd responded with a breathless "Yeah," only to realize—when Lance added, "Seriously, we should be doing more service projects"—that Toby hadn't been talking about being super lucky to spend time with *me*.

My cheeks burned just thinking about it as I unlocked the house and followed Toby inside and up the stairs. "I'm going to give these to you here," he said at Lilly's door. "I don't feel right going in Lil's room without her permission. Meet you in the kitchen?"

"Sure." I braced myself for the weight of the vase and tried not to stagger or splash as I crossed Lilly's pristine room and hefted the flowers onto her dresser. I spent a minute arranging the blooms to frame the card tucked inside. And to take pictures for future still-life drawing purposes. See? I did use my phone—just not to check my messages.

Then I hurried down to the boy waiting in my kitchen. He was standing near the sink, a twist tie held between his teeth as he spun the bread bag shut. There was a peanut butter sandwich cut in crooked triangles and a glass of milk on the counter beside him. I grabbed a spoon and stuck it in the open jar. "Dad made cookies." I pointed with my now-heaping spoon at the bulldog cookie jar on our counter. "Oatmeal raisin, I think."

"Oh, cool." Toby helped himself to a handful and then carried his plate and cup to the table. I filled a glass with water and joined him as he asked, "Where is everyone?"

"Lilly, Merri, and Mom are at Haute Dog. Dad and I opened—so now I'm home and he's at the grocery store stocking up for Thanksgiving." I'd given a hard pass to going with him and dealing with crowded aisles and dodging carts to grab stuffing mix. Thank goodness Trent had stopped by to see Lilly and agreed to shuttle me home.

Toby nodded and took a sip of milk, but he was overly focused on his plate. On his place mat. On fiddling with the metal pug-shaped salt and pepper shakers—which I couldn't imagine he needed for a PB sandwich or cookies.

"You okay, chef?" I asked before popping my spoon in my mouth.

"Are you busy tonight?" he asked in a rush. "There's this thing—forget it . . ."

I put a hand on his arm and held up one finger. Why had I shoved my mouth full of peanut butter? How had my older sisters never warned me about this potential flirting-food fail? But then again, Lilly's dating advice had been: *When you find the right person, you just know.* And Merri's always came in the form of four hundred pages between two covers.

Toby was practically vibrating the table with his tapping foot, and his knuckles were white around the salt-shaker and a cookie. There was no attractive way to get out of this situation—pull out the saliva-slimed spoon with a gob still on it? Not in this lifetime. Instead I desperately tried to work up enough spit to swallow without choking. I stood and dropped the spoon in the sink and chugged half of my water so that I could degum my mouth enough to answer.

"Is 'Forget it' the name of the thing? Or did you decide I wasn't cool enough midsentence?" I'd had a ridiculous amount of time to come up with something to say, and yet that was the best I could do. I paired the words with a smile, but was that peanut butter on my lips? *Dangit.* I was a mess. Covered in dog fur and kibble dust, wearing a wrinkled store uniform and now peanut butter.

"No, it's just . . . You'll probably think it's boring."

"Try me." I blushed at the earnestness of my words, because I meant them so deeply. *Just give me a try, just a little one. I promise I won't disappoint you if you could just see me that way.*

"It's a concert. But not like a radio concert."

"What kind is it?" The more he desperately undersold it, the more I wanted to go; but I was already shrinking down a little, my shoulders coming up. I'd only been to one concert. A Top 40 earworm-attack that Merri had dragged me to after Lillian got food poisoning and had to give up her ticket. Merri had pushed and charmed her way to the front, and I'd tried so hard to follow her, but her fingers slipped from my wrist and I'd been left in a crowd of strangers dancing and bumping into me as they jumped and screamed lyrics at the top of their lungs.

By the time Merri had backtracked to rescue me, the claustrophobia was so intense I could barely breathe.

"Instrumental. It's a visiting orchestra playing the score from the first *Harry Potter* movie. It'll be long and—"

"Chairs?" I asked, my voice a little too hopeful. "We'd have them, right?"

"Yeah . . ." He gave me a strange look. "You'd consider it? I wasn't sure if you had plans with Huck or—"

"Huck's on his way to Ohio for Thanksgiving, but—" I paused and tried to figure out how to phrase my next question; Merri was a huge *Harry Potter* fan. She and Toby had read the whole series together, sometimes sharing a single book, her chiding him to *Hurry up so I can turn the page* and him responding *Stop talking so I can read.* "Am I taking someone's ticket?"

His smile fell off his face at the same speed my stomach plummeted. I'd never realized "emotional roller coaster" referred to how feelings could make you want to vomit. "It was more of the *hope* of taking someone."

I stayed quiet. What more was there to say? I was the backup Campbell; had I really expected anything different? He'd probably planned out their cosplay and prechosen a crescendo to build to a kiss . . .

"When I bought the tickets, I really thought my dad might manage to get home early the day before Thanksgiving and come with me. But he's got a dinner thing."

"Now you've got me," I answered softly, resting my hand on top of the saltshaker in his fist for half a second. "And unlike him, I promise not to make any passive-aggressive comments about the arts being for other people."

"Well, that makes you a huge upgrade." He chugged the rest of his milk, then stacked the remaining quarter of his sandwich and his last cookie on a napkin before putting his dishes in the dishwasher and booking it for our door like if he lingered I might change my mind. "Thanks, Roar. I'll pick you up at six."

The concert was held at the college where Huck's parents taught. Toby had spent the drive gushing about the genius of the composer, John Williams, and listing all the other films he'd . . . scored? Was that the word? Regardless, it was a lot: the *Star Wars* and *Jurassic Park* movies, and on and on and on. Toby's enthusiasm was so infectious that I was still grinning long after he'd gone over my head with technical details. I had no clue what "non-diegetic" meant, but I was glad it made him so happy.

A few seconds into the concert, when the first lilting notes began to dance from their instruments, Toby grabbed my arm. Not in an *I'm trying to scare you* or *Don't run away* way. This was *My feelings are so big. I can't believe this is happening. Let me anchor myself on your forearm.* Selfish or not, I was glad his dad had blown him off so that I could be the one to see his joy.

I spent the ten minutes after worrying that he could feel my pulse racing through my skin and debating whether I could place my other hand on top of his or slide his fingers down to mingle with mine.

And then I forgot. Because even without the wizards and owls and magic and old castle, this music was powerful. Maybe *more* powerful without the film. I was a visual person. My art depended on my eyes, but Toby's didn't. So I shut mine, leaning my head back against my seat as the music flowed around and over me.

There were moments when the composition made my blood race with secondhand suspense. Moments it slowed in sympathy for whatever sadness was being conveyed. And a moment where the music matched my own happiness—I was here, experiencing this with Toby—and in that instant, it was instinct or inspiration, or let's just blame it on the instruments, because I reached over and squeezed his hand.

He responded by pulling away. And I couldn't reconcile my reaction—my extreme personal disappointment paired with a triumphant musical arrangement—until he dropped his arm across the back of my chair, fingers grazing my shoulder. My heart exploded right along with the notes in the song.

When the music ended, I peeled my eyes open to find Toby looking at me. Around us people were standing and applauding and I knew we should join them, but Toby's face was just eight inches from mine and he was studying me the way I studied a person I'd be drawing. No, not impersonal like that. There was nothing analytical about his scrutiny.

"For half a minute at the beginning, I thought you were asleep."

I shook my head. "I was absorbing. That was amazing."

He smiled and at the same time we said, "Thank you for—"

I finished with "inviting me" as he said, "coming with me."

He was studying me again, staring at my mouth. We were a cocoon of privacy in the middle of a standing ovation, applause that felt like it could be happening for *us*, for the fact that we'd finally gotten here. Toby put a hand softly on my shoulder, and it felt like now or never, so when I saw him begin to move closer, I shut my eyes and leaned in—

And collided with something a lot less forgiving than his lips.

Toby grunted, and I blinked to see I'd managed to head-butt him in the stomach. At least I didn't wear lipstick? Because if so, there would've been a clear pucker pressed against the white shirt over his abs. He hadn't been leaning in to kiss me; he'd been standing to applaud. That hand on my shoulder hadn't been a romantic caress, he'd used it to help himself stand up—because, knee brace.

And now he was looking down at me with concern and confusion. "You okay, Roar? Maybe keep your eyes open until the car, but if you want to sleep on the drive home, that's cool."

Could the conductor maybe come stab me with his baton? Or could one of the cellists strangle me with their bow? That had to be less painful than drowning in embarrassment.

I nodded and threw myself into clapping—my hands

much louder than the fading applause around us. I couldn't even clap correctly, let alone kiss.

I let Toby lead the conversation and the way to the car. He recounted all his favorite concert moments while I replayed my behavior and cringed. As we waited in the line of traffic to exit the parking lot, I huddled against the passenger window and he hummed and tapped rhythms on the steering wheel, pausing to say, "I hope Huck didn't mind that you came here with me tonight."

"Why would he?" I blinked, then remembered. It could've been the perfect time to clarify that Huck and I weren't dating—had never been dating—but how could I explain the truth without exposing the stupid plan and the reasons behind it? Just the thought of it amplified all my raw mortification from trying to make out with Toby's shirt.

"Right. Why would he?" Toby parroted my words, but his voice had gone darker, deeper.

My eyebrows drew in at his tone. Was I even screwing up fake dating? Was there a different answer or explanation I was supposed to give? "Huck doesn't care if I hang out with friends."

"Right." Toby's response came out on a sigh and I unglued my eyes from the windshields of other cars, where I'd been trying to analyze the body language of other concert-leaving duos to see if they were currently trapped in conversations that required maps.

I'd done or said something wrong, because Toby was frowning at all the brake lights, and just a few minutes ago he'd been euphoric. "I spend more time with you than anyone. Everyone in my life knows that. Tonight, I hadn't even told Dad where I was going yet, and he said, 'Say hi to Toby for me' when I got my coat."

Some part of this ramble had been the right words, because his eyes lightened and his cheek was twitching from trying hard to keep his grin in check. He leaned over and bumped his shoulder against mine, totally unaware of the shock waves that even casual touch sent through my system. "So what you're saying is, you're going to miss me horribly tomorrow when I'm in New York eating some stupid-expensive catered turkey dinner."

"I'll cry into my cranberry sauce," I joked, because neither of us wanted to hear my honest answer: *Yes. Yes, I will.*

32

dragged my feet and rolled my eyes on Small Business Saturday, but it was for show. I didn't mind working at the store on the nights when Merri and Lilly were there too. When it was Mom and Dad, there were too many sighs over invoices and rising vendor prices for me to feel anything but anxious, but on nights with my sisters—

"Girl talk." Merri said it like a demand, like a threat. And it sort of felt that way, like confessions were going to be removed with a dental drill or pulled out with my fingernails. The crowds had fallen off around five, the shoppers and my parents heading home for leftover turkey sandwiches. Merri was way too eager to fill that void.

"I'll go first," she continued. "I want to know about kisses."

I grimaced; my non-kiss at the concert was too recent for this to be a safe topic. "Does Fielding have bad breath or something? I knew he was too perfect."

"Ha." Merri snorted into her cream soda. "No. There are no problems there. We belong in spots one through ten of the top kisses of all time. In fact, Lills, if you want any inspiration for your church kiss with Trent, I've made Fielding practice and I'm pretty sure we perfected it."

"Noted," said Lilly. "But we're set."

"Fine, but you're missing out."

"Okay, exhibitionist," I teased.

"What about you?" asked Merri with a sudden focused gleam in her eye that made me wonder if this was the point of the conversation. "Have you ever kissed a guy?"

"Or girl," added Lilly.

"I'm assuming sandbox kisses don't count?" I asked. Even though that was the one that counted most in my book. Because my first kiss—or at least the first one I remembered— was a wet, licorice-tasting smack of triumph after Toby and I had scraped the bottom of the sandbox to build what we'd called "Mount Everest." I'd been so surprised that I'd butt-planted right into the mountain, causing a sand avalanche and ruining the celebration.

"No," said Merri, leaning forward with eager eyes. "Only after thirteen. Also, on an unrelated note—where are you in *Little Women*?"

"Still page ten," I answered. "And, yes. I had a Voldemort of a first kiss at art camp last summer. It will not be appearing on anyone's top ten. It's not even on mine and it's the only one I have to list." Lilly and Merri looked at each other with wide eyes and raised brows, and frankly I was insulted. "It's that surprising I've been kissed? It wasn't my fault it was bad. He had egg salad for lunch and there were braces involved."

"No, it's not that," said Lilly.

"You know Voldemort?" gaped Merri.

"Dangit, I *can* read—and I've seen the movies. And *he-who-must-not-be-kissed* definitely earned that name. He made the rest of camp torture for me once he realized I was not down for a repeat encounter." I was stupid to have brought up *Harry Potter*, because now all I could think of was my second failed kiss . . . and all the advice I couldn't ask for. Not about him. Not from them.

"Who is the brace-faced brat? Where does he live? Can I kick his butt? I'm scrappy, and my boyfriend's got swords."

"And my future mother-in-law is a senator. I'll get her to legislate his idiot butt."

I laughed. "I'm not sure that's how it works; shouldn't you know this, Miss Pre-Law?" I turned to Merri. "Let's keep you away from all things sharp and pointy."

She shrugged. "Fair enough . . . But what about now? Fall Ball. Are you going?"

"No. Huck and I are planning to not-go together."

"Huck?" Merri frowned. "So you guys—"

"We're friends. Period." It was a relief to say something honest, even if I couldn't reveal the whole truth or the why behind the lies. "The dance thing isn't my scene. I get why other people like it, but it's like a birthday party on steroids. When Clara helped me paint the photo backdrop, she was talking about dresses and shoes and limos and pre- and post-parties . . . She made Byron and I vote on like ten different hair options. Lilly, I can't even imagine what it's like to plan a wedding."

Her smile grew tight and she opened the drawer beneath the register and began to organize the pens and elastic band jumble inside. "Yeah, it's . . . a lot."

"But it'll be worth it. Trent's going to either cry or wet his

pants when he sees you in that dress walking down the aisle."
Merri was so busy being starry-eyed that she didn't notice
Lilly had gone pale.

"I vote for crying—if it's a choice between that or public
pants-wetting," I joked. Merri laughed, but Lilly had taken
out her massive planner and flipped to the current to-do list.
There were so many annotations, cross-outs, and scribbles
that it looked like secret code.

I wanted to take that thing and hide it. Burn it. Like
removing the target of her stress would remove the source.
But I didn't know what the source was. Not Trent, because
he still made her smile like every day was her birthday. And
while they weren't all about Merri's public declarations, they
communicated in small looks and touches—in the ways I'd
seen my parents do my whole life. I had no doubt that if Lilly
decided to shove the planner in a recycling can and told Trent
she wanted to marry him on a moon bounce, he'd be the first
to take off his shoes and roll up his pants.

My hands were moving over my sketch pad as I watched
her flip pages and jot things down. I was drawing—not the
stress-fried sister in front of me, but the smiling one in my
mind. She was in a flouncy skirt, hand clasped with Trent,
whose tie was askew and shirtsleeves rolled up as they jumped
on an inflatable. It was the barest outline of a sketch, but the
potential was there if I made the time.

"Aurora Campbell?" The door had barely shut behind a
short, balding man wearing hipster glasses and an orange
tweed scarf. He was carrying a bulldog wearing a matching
vest, but alas, no glasses. The man's eyes roamed the store

and settled on me. "You've got to be Aurora. Look at you, sketching already. My friend Marnie showed me that drawing you made of her sweet Octavio and Turner."

I should've asked the woman her son's and dog's names, because this wasn't the first time a referral from her had shown up and I was dying to know which was which. I could've asked this guy, but all I managed to do was nod before he leaned forward to look at my sketch pad, which was a violation of both my privacy and my personal space. I took a step back and he grimaced.

"Sorry! Sorry! That's probably a total artist taboo. Please tell me you'll still consider drawing Mr. Grumpus." Hearing his name, Mr. Grumpus shuffled forward a few feet and opened his mouth. A long string of drool slid out and landed on his owner's loafers. Despite this, and despite the fact that this was way too much enthusiasm for me, the dog looked like he was smiling and he was actually pretty cute. A sketch began to frame itself in my mind.

"Go grab me a few books from the shelf over there." The man started to turn. "Leave . . . Mr. Grumpus."

He handed me the leash and I dropped it to the floor, pinning it beneath my foot so I had both hands free to draw. I sketched in his scrunchy face and big eyes, his open mouth and dripping tongue, the rolls around his collar and the cut of his vest.

The man was back. "What should I do with these?" he whispered.

I glanced at the staggering pile of books he'd carted over.

"Use the hardbacks. Pile three with the bindings facing away. See if you can get him to put a paw on the stack."

Mr. Grumpus cooperated and I adjusted the lines of the drawing to match the new setup, adding in shadows and texture and shading to match the white markings on his fawn coat. "I'm going to need some time." And space if I could get this guy to give it to me.

"That's fine. I'll go shop. Call me if you need me." He bent down and added, "Stay, Mr. Grumpus." Not that the dog had shown any inclination toward moving.

"Oh, wait." I had a sudden inspiration. "Your glasses, can you see without them?"

The man's cheeks turned pink as he handed them over. "I'll manage."

Once he was across the store I peered curiously through them. Plain glass. Yeah, he'd manage just fine. I waited until I had most of the other details finished before attempting to balance them on Mr. Grumpus's nose. He sneezed and tried to lick me but offered no other objection.

Still, I sketched them quickly, then rescued the glasses, putting them safely on the shelf beside me before I added some depth to the books' pages and reflective shine to the buckle on his collar. I looked up from the pad to see Mr. Grumpus had gone to sleep, and Mr. Grumpus's owner was engaged in an animated conversation with Merri.

I returned the dog, handed over the sketch, then let Merri deal with the gushing appreciation while I returned the prop books to their shelves. I slipped the bills in the cash register and slipped my phone out of my bag. Fifteen more minutes until we flipped the sign to *Closed*.

I had texts from Clara, Huck, and Toby. My first instinct was still *Toby, always Toby*, but I ignored it. Toby and I had had plenty of hangouts lately. Huck was in the car again, this time coming home. He just wanted to whine about the drive and his parents' taste in podcasts. I sent him a sad emoji.

It was Clara I texted back once I was home. And Clara I let talk me into a synchronized watch of her favorite movie, *Clueless*, where we sat in our respective rooms and hit start simultaneously, then texted each other real-time reactions. I found myself wanting to discuss the soundtrack, but I saved those thoughts for a different audience and instead responded to Clara's observations about costumes with my own thoughts on the framing.

About ten minutes later, my door cracked open. Merri glanced at my laptop and said, "Great movie. Scoot over."

I moved a pillow out of the way and slid across my bed. "I'm live-watching with Clara."

Merri bounced beside me. "Good, then I'll watch it with Fielding—he can skip ahead—and you."

"And you," I echoed, knocking my shoulder against hers.

She grinned. "Think how much cleverer we're going to sound since we get to practice our commentary on each other before we text it. I give you permission to steal anything funny I say."

33

A month ago, being "just friends" with Toby had felt impossible. But by the end of November we had a routine. We were quiet on the ride to school, but it was the comfortable kind. The type you didn't need to fill with nervous chatter just to beat back silence, but you didn't hesitate to break when you had something to say or wanted to sing along with "Last Christmas." And when we hit the Hero High parking lot, every day I sighed and said, "Back to the salt mines" or "Is it Friday yet?"

And every day Toby replied, "You've got this, Roar."

Every day I believed him.

We met at his car after school. Then homework, sometimes together, sometimes apart. But there was always something: a movie, dinner, walking one of the dogs, tutoring—something. That was what made the difference; each time we separated there was a plan in place for when we'd get back together.

I didn't need to cling tightly to scraps of his attention, because I had so much of it, and by relaxing my grip, I'd cleared my vision. Toby wasn't the perfect boy I'd pretended he was. He was impatient, impulsive, restless—not with me, with himself. His knee made it worse, because he'd lost the physical outlet for his energy. More than once I had to cut him off when he did his physical therapy exercises double or triple the prescribed amount. I'd look up from a math problem to see him white-faced and shaking as he attempted one last squat or lunge.

He could also be lazy. While I didn't go a day without drawing, he'd go several without practicing his music, tell me he didn't feel like it or "My muse is on vacation." He'd build a tower of cereal bowls in the sink, then tell me stories about frantically loading the dishwasher when he heard his dad's car pull into the driveway.

He could be quiet and distant—lost in his thoughts or mental compositions. And he could be entirely present—making me feel like the world centered on whatever I said or did or drew.

"What are you doing?" I asked. I let myself in the door without knocking these days. His piano lessons and physical therapy ended by five, so it was assumed that if I wasn't at Haute Dog, I'd be over sometime between six and seven. I always brought my math stuff, but we only opened it 50 percent of the time.

"Sorting my music." Toby was standing in front of the kitchen table; he pointed to the piles of sheet music on top. "Some of these are awful—it makes me feel really old."

"You've been seventeen for three whole months now—where are the gray hairs?" I went up on tiptoe and pretended to check his head.

"Ha." Toby batted my hand away. "Well, I'm two years older than you, so trust my age and wisdom when I say I used to be a lousy composer."

"Why are you?" I asked, sitting on the table beside his piles and smiling at the changes in handwriting throughout the years. "Older, I mean. And not a junior."

Toby rubbed the back of his neck and I wanted to retract the question. "I was already going to be old for my grade with a late summer birthday, but my parents thought I needed an extra year of preschool after the adoption."

"It bothers you?"

He shrugged and I thought that was going to be my answer, but then he sank onto the chair in front of me. "No one's ever asked me that before. Yeah, sometimes it does."

I held my breath, because I wanted to be his no one. The person he had all sorts of first shares with. But more than that, I wanted to be here and hear him in this moment and not be so caught up in my own daydreams and swoons that I missed the reality. I'd done that before. More and more I was realizing how often I'd done that: projected the Toby in my head onto the guy beside me instead of appreciating the flawed and fantastic person he was.

"It's just—Fielding's always been my best friend at school . . ." I wondered if his pause was full of him thinking about their current awkwardness. "He's a grade above me. Not saying Curtis and Lance and all those guys aren't great, but there are times when I look at Fielding's grade and wonder if I'd fit in better with him and Penn and Byron." He leaned back and stretched out his legs in front of him. It was a surprisingly vulnerable pose for someone who was exposing so much of his inner thoughts.

"I haven't seen you hang out with Fielding much lately." I wasn't tiptoeing into this minefield, I was belly flopping.

He rubbed a palm across his face. "I owe him a call or text or twelve. I'll get on it."

"Good idea." And my good deed for the day. "But I interrupted what you were saying about school and year."

He shoved away a stack of pages. "It's not just that—I feel this way a lot, wondering if I'm where I should be."

"When else?" I reached my foot out until it was grazing the leg of his chair. I needed to be touching him somehow and linking myself physically to this conversation.

"I think probably every adopted kid 'what-ifs' sometimes. Especially if they have no details about their birth parents."

You don't have to tell me this. The words were on the tip of my tongue until I realized why I wanted to say them. I was desperate to say them—because his face was tight with pain, his skin stretched over his bones, making shadows and hollows that haunted me. Would haunt me even after the conversation was over. I wanted to stop his hurting. But if I stopped his words . . . it wouldn't do a dang thing.

Because it wasn't the words that were causing his pain; it was the truth behind them. And me wanting to stop him was selfish. It was about my desire not to have to see this. So I swallowed those words and offered a different set. "I'm here, I'm listening."

"I'm a Latino named *Tobias Bronson May* with a B-minus in Spanish. That just seems wrong. Or maybe it's not. Maybe my birth parents spoke Portuguese or English, or who knows? But they didn't want to, or couldn't, keep me. And I know a lot of kids of divorce wonder if they picked the right parent to live with. Not that all of them get a choice. But I did. Mine were equally apathetic. Neither of them really wanted me either."

"Oh, Toby . . ." I wouldn't lie and tell him his experiences weren't true, because they were real to him and they were raw. I didn't know what his score for this moment would sound like, but in paint it would be all blues and blacks with a splash of red heartbreak.

"Should I have gone with my mom instead? I almost asked her during our Sunday phone call last week."

"But then you'd be on the West Coast! You'd never see us."

"Yeah." He shrugged, oblivious to how the casual dismissal cut me to the bone.

My hand shook, and I pulled it back into my lap twice before I committed to reaching down and squeezing his. This wasn't about sizzle and sparks; it was about sympathy. And when he twisted his fingers in mine and held on tightly, I didn't swoon or falter. I just let us *be* in this moment where he needed his friend. He scooted his chair in until he was right beside me, then leaned his head on my shoulder. My breath caught in my chest, but I exhaled and managed, "I'm glad you're here."

"Right now," he whispered, his words soft against my skin, "me too."

34

Somewhere Merri found a dress that was paisley, sparkly, *and* pretty. I wouldn't have thought it was possible, but proof I was wrong was doing skirt twirls down the hallway. Eliza laughed and pulled her hair up in a simple twist that made her cheekbones impossibly high and her eyes pop. Eliza's dress was "gray" according to her and "like a perfect shimmery dolphin" according to Merri.

I was straight-up eavesdropping. My bedroom door was open and I leaned against the wall beside it, poking at the third chapter of *Little Women* while listening to them primp and prepare. Jo March had burned off her older sister Meg's hair while trying to curl it—which made me want to shout warnings to Eliza. Merri should not be trusted with hot hair appliances. I still wasn't over the time she'd burned my neck with a straightener, causing a mark that resembled a hickey; all of sixth grade had teased me for a week.

But unlike Meg and Jo's little sisters, Beth and Amy, I was not jealous about being left behind. Not even when Fielding showed up at the bottom of the stairs looking like something out of an expensive cologne ad.

I waited for the rom-com moment of him making some grand declaration about Merri's appearance. Instead he drew her close and whispered in her ear, one hand curved softly between her bare shoulder blades, the other holding her hand. Her mouth curled up as her cheeks flushed. Mom and Dad were both flashing cameras around them, but neither even seemed to notice.

Eliza cleared her throat. "Are we ready?"

"Just one more minute," Merri said, still nuzzled in his arms. "I'm busy taking Fielding's breath away."

"I hate that idiom," said Eliza. "It's not biologically possible to steal someone's breath."

Fielding's chuckle was low and light. "As much as I hate to argue with you, Eliza, I'm going to side with Merri. I forgot how to breathe for a moment when Merrilee appeared at the top of the stairs." He paused to look at my sister like he was drinking her in, then added politely, "You look lovely too."

Only Eliza would look delighted to be receiving a lesser compliment. And only Merrilee would respond, "Yes, we're gorgeous. Now let's go see everyone. And dance. Fielding, what's the ratio of slow to fast songs at Hero High? I'm hoping—"

He cut her off with a kiss. Like she was too irresistible to wait even one more word. It was a pretty dapper move.

The three of them waved to my parents and me and climbed in his car—Eliza scowled when Curtis scrambled out of the back seat to open her door. Scowled, but gave him a head-to-toe scan that made her cheeks pink. "I can open my own door."

"Of course you can," he answered, "but if my mom ever

saw that she'd disown me, so by indulging my gesture of respect, you also save me from orphanhood."

I could practically hear her eyes rolling, but she let him close the door for her before he scurried around to the other side and climbed in.

I sat on the steps and watched them drive away, waiting for Huck's dad to pick us up to go bowling. In *Little Women* Jo had met her next-door neighbor, Theodore Laurence, aka Laurie, at the party. But I didn't glance at *my* next-door neighbor's house to see if Toby was walking out the front door with a date of his own.

Two hours later, after Huck had thoroughly trounced me at bowling, his dad dropped me back home.

My eyes darted left out of habit, and all the laughter of the night soured in my stomach, along with the too-salty bowling alley pretzel. Toby's house was dark. His car wasn't in the driveway.

Which pretty, perky, preppy Hero High girl had he taken to Fall Ball? Was he dancing with her right now? Was he mooning over Merri? His jealousy discrete but obvious to those who'd turned studying his expressions into an art form? Clara was one text away—she'd have answers and take pictures if I asked. But I didn't want them. I'd had the chance to be his date for tonight and I'd made the right decision saying no. We were friends. And that was enough.

It had to be.

35

The weekend felt as long as the first few chapters of *Little Women*. I'd stared at one page for an hour before giving up and staring at my ceiling instead. I told myself falling out of love wasn't as fast as falling out of bed—it took much longer and hurt much more. I told myself no news about the Snipes workshop was good news. I told myself I was getting better at math and English and fitting in at Hero High. Basically, I told myself a lot of lies.

I brought the book with me to Haute Dog on Sunday and flipped the cover open and shut while I stared blankly at the empty store. I'd written only two response journals so far; I couldn't motivate myself to read a book others thought was babyish. What did it say about me if I related to it?

Monday, I stayed after class and asked, "Why did you pick *Little Women* for me?"

"You'll see." Ms. Gregoire smiled enigmatically. "Where are you in the book now?"

"Seven chapters in—is that too slow?" I started to duck my head, but Ms. Gregoire was shaking hers.

"No, that's fine. Which girl is your favorite?"

I frowned, because I was pretty sure my answer was wrong. "I'm supposed to like Jo, right? Because she's the most exciting and we spend the most time in her head?"

"I'm not interested in what you're 'supposed' to think. I want your actual opinion."

I hesitated only slightly—just long enough to nibble off a coat of lip balm. "Amy. It's a youngest thing. And an art thing— we even have the same favorite brand of drawing pencils."

"Ahh, Team Amy." Ms. Gregoire grinned. "I like it. And what's your 'hot take' on Laurie—am I using that term correctly?"

"Um, I'm not the right person to ask. Toby says I'm always a couple generations off with slang."

"Oh, Toby." She smiled and sipped her coffee, her expression gentle as she prompted, "But first thoughts on Laurie?"

"I don't know, he seems fine. He's probably a Fielding to Merri's Jo."

Ms. Gregoire sucked in a breath through her teeth and crinkled her nose. "I don't want to give anything away, but . . ."

"But you disagree?" She wasn't even subtle about it. But I already knew I was wrong. Boy next door who gets in trouble and romps around with adventurous Jo? There was no question who he resembled. I wasn't going to say it, though. Putting the words out there made it real.

"Fielding's a wonderful young man . . . but I wouldn't categorize him and Theodore Laurence in the same genre of human."

"Genre?" People had those? Or was this some metaphor/ simile/smart people thing? I flipped the pages of the book.

"There's plenty more to come. Keep reading."

That was true. While *The Great Gatsby* had been 180 pages, this book was five hundred. *Not-So-Little Women* would've been a more accurate title. "Why?"

She put her hand on the book and slid it across the desk to me. "Because you need it."

The novel nudged against my fingers and the contact sent goose bumps down my arms. The "it" in "you need it" didn't mean extra credit; it meant the content between the covers.

"What if I'm reading it wrong?" I asked.

"You know there's two sides to any piece of art. There's the creator's intent and the audiences' interpretation. If one of your paintings inspired sadness in a viewer but you were happy when you painted it, does that make their reaction wrong?"

"No," I said.

"Exactly. What is *your* reaction to this story? I don't want you to try to figure out some 'right answer,' I want *your* answer."

I gritted my teeth, but the words still built behind them, until my mouth was opening without my permission and a riptide was slipping out. "Just once, can't I identify with the star? Why am I always the secondary character? The second choice? Gatsby, Amy—don't I get to be the hero even in fiction?"

"First of all, if Amy were a sentient being, do you really think she would think of herself as secondary? No. She's not and neither are you. She's a heroine. You are the heroine of your own story, Aurora. You're no one's sidekick or second fiddle. Forget that. Now, what else is holding you back?"

"I can't write like Merri. I can't say things on paper the way I want in my head."

"I don't need you to write the world's most polished prose. And writing's like any other skill; it improves with practice. Besides, I approved some drawings. I want you to tell your truths."

"I'm not lying."

"No, I don't mean that—though maybe you are, a little, to yourself. I mean: Go deeper. Find *your* truth, *your story*. I don't need you to tell me your secrets. I don't need to invade your privacy. But I need there to be honest emotions. I think *you* need to find some honest emotions. So tell your truths, even if you just tell them to yourself."

If she wanted truth, I'd find it. I spent the morning lost in my head, then went to the art room at lunch. Not to paint but to pull out my laptop. By the end of the period I'd written something true. So true it hurt.

Is it possible to have PTSD and not realize it? Because I finally found a moment where I connect with the text—Amy and her pickled limes. Side note: That sounds disgusting.

Mine was less revolting food fad and more folded paper—origami stars were the rage of my fifth-grade class. Everyone folded them, collected them, traded them, competed to see whose flew the farthest when flicked through the air. If you were cool, you had stacks in your desk—stored in an origami box if you were Stella, because she was the coolest of cool fifth graders. Did I mention she hated me? When I tried to offer up my own first attempts at stars, she scoffed and rejected them because they were plain computer paper. Hers were origami paper and mine were "boring junk." I tried again the next day—after having spent an hour the night before decorating mine with doodles and cartoons. This time she ignored me. The class followed her lead. "Do you hear something? I don't."

It was September—and the curse of having been born in October is that birthday and Christmas money is long spent by the start of the next school year. I had to do chores around the house and store for two weeks to earn the money to buy a pack of fancy origami paper. In the meantime our teacher, Mr. Rafe, had gotten fed up by all the origami drama and banned all stars from the classroom. Not that it stopped anyone. We just got stealthy. When I finally had enough money Lilly drove me to the stationery store and I picked the most gorgeous, bright, tie-dyed patterned paper—I stayed up way past my bedtime and folded exactly enough stars to give to everyone in my class.

I'd made one for Stella, and it was the most gorgeous of all—blue and green swirled paper on one half, silver foil on the other. But on the way out the door that morning, I decided she didn't deserve it and impulsively gave it away to someone else instead. I still remember the way my stomach twisted and lurched as I watched her stomp up to Mr. Rafe's desk and tattle.

His face turned bright red. He walked up and

250 | TIFFANY SCHMIDT

down the rows of our classroom and made every one of my classmates turn in the stars I'd given them. Then he made me watch as he fed them through the paper shredder.

I cried so hard I threw up on my shoes.

And reading about Amy and her limes brought me right back to that night of hiccuping sobs when I begged my parents to let me be homeschooled or switched to a different class—anything but walk back in there.

I'm glad Amy got her wish to leave school, even if I didn't get mine.

36

ey Roar," Toby called from his living room. We never spent any time in there. It was always the kitchen. And the only other light I ever saw glow in his house was his bedroom's. I followed his voice to find him dressed down in his glasses and basketball shorts and a Hero High lacrosse T-shirt. "Save me from these exercises. My physical therapist accused me of slacking on the stretches, and I made the mistake of mentioning that to Fielding and now he—"

"Fielding was here?"

"Yeah." Toby ducked his head and grabbed his water bottle. "I thought about what you said last week. I've been lousy to him lately and he called me out on it. I let something like not being on the team and . . ." He trailed off and took another sip, his eyes darting in the direction of my house. I shoved thoughts of Merri aside and focused on the fact that he'd listened to *me*.

"How'd it go?" I crossed my fingers behind my back.

"Well, besides his lectures on physical therapy and threatening to come train with me . . . Good. He's a good guy." He winced a bit like that truth hurt. "One of the best I know."

"*I've* been a lousy friend as well." I shifted the focus back to me to save him from lingering on that thought. "And Clara totally called *me* out on it too. It must be national friendship accountability day or something. I bet there really is one of those. It's up there with popcorn day and idea day and all those other invented holidays." Geez, I sounded like Merri in full-ramble mode. But at least he was no longer moping like my sister was true north and he was a compass.

"How have you been a bad friend?" His forehead wrinkled as he sat on the arm of the couch.

"I've been busy. I mean, Clara's busy too—she's in every club—but she's made lots of strongly worded suggestions that I pick one and come to a meeting. I finally did today—progress! And Huck keeps offering to teach me more about pottery."

Toby shifted his water bottle between his hands. He frowned. "Is it because you're always here? Tutoring?"

I shook my head frantically. Was it possible for a gesture to be a lie? I needed to be more convincing. "But, school's important, right?"

"Right!" He jerked his chin in a quick nod, seizing on the excuse I'd provided. Neither of us ever acknowledged that we spent as much time not-tutoring as we did studying. "You're doing so much better in math. We wouldn't want you to backslide. So what's tonight's assignment?"

"Oh." I'd actually done it with Clara while waiting for the president and vice president of the student council, aka her brother, Penn, and his girlfriend, Lynnie, to arrive so the meeting could start. "I—I don't have any?"

Which meant I had no reason for coming over. And we'd both just hinted I spent too much time here already. I tucked my hands into the pockets of my sweatshirt and shrugged my shoulders up to my ears. It didn't make me less exposed or my feelings less transparent.

"Well, I'm done with my PT exercises." Toby scowled and picked at the lint collecting on his knee brace's Velcro. "I'm so sick of sitting. One more week in this stupid thing."

"And that's all you can do? Sit?" Which had been the *worst* form of punishment for Toby when he was little. When his parents got mad they'd say, *"Sit right here until I say you can move."* Always somewhere he could see the rest of us playing. He'd practically shake with the desire to join us and the effort to keep his body still.

"Walks. Stretching. My physical therapy exercises."

His whole fall had been a time-out. The realization hit me in the gut, but I couldn't change that, so I wouldn't let him dwell on it either.

"Oh don't be pouty. It doesn't suit you. Soon enough you'll be back to running five miles and whacking people with lacrosse sticks and all sorts of other barbaric sports things." I smiled when Toby did and rolled my shoulders back, feeling some of the tension release in a series of cracks along my spine. "Actually, I think I can help."

"How?"

"I can teach you some yoga— No, don't make that face. You'll love it."

He raised an eyebrow. "Love sounds like an oversell. I might *tolerate* it."

"C'mon." I dropped my backpack in the corner. "This is my chance to teach *you* for once."

"You sure we can't just watch a movie or something? I promise not to talk about the musical score . . ." He scrunched his mouth to one side and added, "Much."

"After, if you want." I was already twisting my shoulders, loosening my neck. If I could help him with his knee, it gave us another reason to hang out, even if I suddenly became an A-plus math student. He didn't need Fielding to train him—

I cut that thought off and hid my guilty expression by turning to move a decorative vase out of arms and legs range. I wanted Toby to fix things with Fielding. And we'd just acknowledged we needed to spend time with other friends too. But he'd seen Fielding, and I had glitter under my nails to prove I'd made Candlelight Concert posters with Clara. We could do *both*: have other friends and hang out.

Yoga was a me and Lilly thing. A way-too-focused-and-slow for Merri thing. Which was *why* it was a me and Lilly thing versus a Lilly and Merri thing. It was exercise that didn't trigger my asthma. It was a way to *be*, to think and exist that muted all the anxious thoughts in my head. But I never went to class without Lilly . . . and she hadn't gone for months, which meant all my recent yoga had been iLiveStream videos.

Five minutes later I'd shoved the coffee table to the corner of the room and coaxed Toby through a reluctant sun salutation. "This isn't hurting your knee, is it?"

"No, but does this even count as exercise?" he grumbled. "I mean, obviously you're in shape, but I'm not even sweating."

I rolled my eyes. "We'll hold this next down dog for— I

don't know, do you think you can manage two minutes? And then I'll check you for sweat." If that didn't impress him, I'd pull out some shoulder stands and advanced positions.

I talked him into the pose, trying not to get a thrill when I had to touch his back to show him how to shift his shoulders away from his ears, to straighten his spine, and to push through his hands and out his tailbone. When he was finally in position, I peeled off my sweatshirt and slid into the pose. "Now, two minutes. Think you can do it?"

"Sure," he scoffed.

"We'll see." I kept up running commentary for the first ninety seconds. Reminders to keep his heels down and keep his shoulders from creeping toward his ears. Talk about slow inhales and exhales and sinking further into the pose. Phrases my yoga instructor had said so often that they flowed from my lips like song lyrics. It was kinda empowering to be the one teaching *him* for a change. But his responses got more and more sporadic. More and more distracted.

"How are you doing back there?"

"Uh-huh."

I lowered my head to look at him around my legs. He wasn't holding the position anymore. He'd dropped his knees, and was—

"Are you"—*okay/tired/hurting*—"staring at my butt?"

His cheeks turned bright red and he sputtered. "No! What? Um, no."

I didn't know whether to blush or lecture or laugh. Eliza would do the second, Merri the third. I was pretty sure I was already doing the first.

Toby studied the hardwood floor. "Normal people can't bend like you."

I laughed and transitioned from down dog to up dog. His gaze shifted to my chest, which was pressed outward in this pose. "Sorry. Sorry, sorry." His cheeks turned redder and he fastened his eyes on my face like they were glued there.

"So, I'm not normal? Is that what you're saying?"

He sat down, no longer even pretending to copy my moves. His hands were white knuckled as they curled around the sweatshirt I'd discarded. I glanced down at my bright blue yoga top. It was smallish and strappy, but supportive and covered all the things I wanted covered.

When I glanced back up, his eyes were still on my face, searching for something as his mouth stretched into a grin that felt like it was mine alone. "Roar, you are—"

Everything about his expression changed in an instant. His eyes went wide as all other emotions disappeared. He stood, tossing me my sweatshirt as he said, "Dad. I wasn't expecting you home tonight."

"I noticed. Your car is parked to block access to the garage." Major May turned to me. "Aurora!" He said it with a big, swaggering smile but also a note of hesitation, like he was crossing his fingers he was correct.

He looked inordinately pleased when I nodded. "Hi, Mr. May."

"I hear my son is tutoring you in math. It's his best subject, you know. Someday he's going to take the finance world by storm."

I hid my wince by pulling on my sweatshirt. Toby's best

subject was music. The last thing he'd want to do was work for his father's firm.

"But this doesn't look like any math I've ever studied . . ." I emerged from my sweatshirt to find him taking in the disarray in the living room and our flushed cheeks with an amused expression.

"Rory was showing me some yoga poses that will help my knee." Toby fiddled with the Velcro on his brace and wouldn't look at me.

"Ah. I hear that's a thing now—guys doing yoga." He laughed. "Well, whatever gets you back in fighting shape sooner. Aurora, you'll join us for dinner."

I didn't know which of his statements to react to—the sexism, the pressure, or the invitation that wasn't a question. I looked at Toby and his lips were still twisted in the small tight smile that'd emerged at the critique of his parking job, but his eyes pleaded with me to accept.

There was a slight desperation in Mr. May's eyes as well, and I wondered what dinner was usually like in this house— on the rare occasions they both attended.

"That would be nice," I said and watched as relief poured into both of their expressions.

Ordering dinner was clearly a well-rehearsed routine. Mr. May called in "the usual" to a local upscale Italian place—with Toby interrupting to tell him, "Add the veggie antipasto." A request I was grateful for when "the usual" arrived and it was sausage pizza.

In my house, we ate takeout out of containers. I would've been fine with popping the plastic cover off the circular tinfoil dish and digging in, but Mr. May spooned everything out onto a plate for me, then carried it into the dining room. He placed it beside the two other plates he'd carried, each containing a single slice. The pizza box had stayed in the kitchen.

"I'm sure my son meant to ask what you'd like to drink, but since he's forgotten, let me get you something." Mr. May opened the fridge and scowled at the contents. "Or maybe Toby just knew he had nothing to offer you."

"I was going to go to the store tomorrow," said Toby with a sheepish expression I'd forgotten. It was one he'd worn through so many backyard barbecues with our parents. When his parents had still been married, he was the target for their anger at each other, lots of tight *"Dear, I thought you were going to take Toby for a haircut, but if you don't care whether our son looks like a ragamuffin, I guess I'll pretend not to either,"* or, from his mom, *"Do you see that scab on poor Toby's knee? Someone decided to take his training wheels off, though I said he wasn't ready."* The barbecues had stopped after they'd divorced; I guess I assumed the nitpicking comments had too.

"It's okay, I've got it." I'd spent enough time in this kitchen to know exactly where the glasses were kept. I pulled two and got Toby and me water. Ice for him, none for me.

The dining room was gray, its curtains silver to match the mirrors that hung on the wall, the chandelier modern—square and glass. The only white in here was the tablecloth, but the aesthetic was just as cold as the kitchen's. Once we were seated, Toby leaned across the table and speared the mozzarella balls off my plate, dropping them on his own. I nudged the last one from beneath an eggplant slice. He grinned and scooped it right into his mouth. I watched his lips and felt my cheeks heat. That was not supposed to be attractive, right? Watching someone eat cheese? But it was the easiness of it, the way we could communicate so much without even speaking. He pretended to gag when I ate a piece of broccoli. I raised an eyebrow and pointed a fork at my hot peppers. He aimed the tines of his at my plate and began to reach—

"Tobias!" We both jumped. My silverware clattered against the table, leaving a splotch of olive oil on the cloth. "Don't you dare take another morsel off her plate. You were not raised like a zoo animal to steal food from others."

"Dad, she doesn't eat cheese or spicy peppers." Toby looked at me, and I hated that he now wore uncertainty in the crease between his brows. "You didn't mind, did you?"

"Of course she minded."

"I don't," I interrupted. "Seriously. Not even a little. I'm glad you ate them, otherwise they'd go to waste."

"Now you're just being polite," Mr. May said, and I didn't know how to respond. Did I deny politeness? I stared at my plate, but there was no answer among the red peppers and artichokes. I prodded a piece of asparagus to the side, batted an olive with my fork, then glanced sideways at Mr. May. Was I going to get a lecture on playing with my food? But he was looking at his son. "Toby, why are you wearing your glasses? Did you run out of contacts again?"

"I had a headache earlier, so I took them out." I tilted my head and studied him—he caught me. "I took some Advil. I'm fine now."

His father nodded and took a sip of water. "Those glasses make you look like Clark Kent."

Was that a compliment because Superman was not unattractive? Or an attempt at bonding because Toby liked comics? Or an insult because Toby was a Batman fan? Or . . . was I reading way too much into this because Major May probably had no knowledge of his son's fandoms? Maybe he was just saying he looked nerdy?

Toby nudged my foot under the table. When I met his eyes, he rolled them toward his dad. I turned to see him eating his pizza with a fork and a knife. Every bite a perfect geometric specimen. I bit my lip to keep from laughing and looked away from where Toby was doing the same. Because if he broke, I would too.

"So, Aurora, besides yoga and math tutoring, what are you up to these days?"

"Um." I cleared my throat. "Quite a bit of drawing, actually."

"Drawing?" He frowned like he didn't understand the word.

"Dad, she's amazing. You should see her stuff. Here—hang on a second." Toby slid out of his seat, leaving his napkin in a crumpled ball on the table beside his plate. He crossed to the kitchen where his books were piled on the counter and dug through them. He returned with a piece of folded paper in his hands, and I wasn't sure which of us was craning their neck more, because Mr. May might be curious, but I had no idea what sort of drawing Toby had or where he'd gotten it. More important, was he in it and did it broadcast all my feelings?

Toby unfolded the paper to reveal a problem he'd had me solve last week. Just a practice one, a warm-up before I started my homework. I'd kept the paper beside me on the table, doodling while he went over new explanations. Apparently, I'd left behind a drawing of an igloo and a polar bear. I glanced over my shoulder at the arctic white kitchen—geez, what had inspired that?

"Isn't she good?" Toby prompted.

"The arts, huh?" Mr. May aimed a condescending smile in my direction and I could practically hear the words he was itching to say about needing a backup plan or hoping I liked ramen noodles. I'd heard them all before. I'd heard him aim them all at his son.

No wonder Toby never talked about his musical ambitions. I poked holes in a slice of zucchini and searched for a topic to bring up. When I was anxious in the store, Mom always said, *"People want to talk about themselves. Give them an invitation."* "Toby says you've been busy lately."

Mr. May had been wearing a permanent grin since he walked in—but not like always-smiling Curtis, who seemed genuinely happy. Mr. May's was a mask. It slipped for a second as he narrowed his eyes at his son. "Have you been complaining? Is something wrong? Why didn't you say something?" His voice had started sharp but slid into concerned.

Toby's shoulders lifted in a silent sigh before he explained. "No, Dad. I'm not complaining. Nothing's wrong. Rory had just asked why she hadn't seen you during tutoring."

"Oh." He turned to me, charm back in place. "In that case, Aurora, I'm delighted that you were over when I came home tonight. It's been so long, I hadn't realized what a beautiful young lady you'd grown up to be. Isn't she, son?"

I didn't want any compliment from Toby that came from that prompting, so I cut him off. "Thank you. But can you tell me a little bit more about your work? I know nothing about finance."

This time his smile seemed genuine. "Should I let you field this one, Toby?" His son froze with a slice of pizza halfway to his mouth, but Mr. May waved a hand. "No, you go ahead and eat. I've got it."

And for the next ten minutes he reconfirmed what I already knew—that I wanted a career that kept me as far from Wall Street as possible. Though anyone with a Wall Street wallet who wanted to buy one of my paintings was welcome to.

Toby still had his foot pressed against mine. In any other setting, I'd be thinking about the way that felt, but now my focus was stolen by the way his heel was jiggling like a piston and the blank expression and empty eyes that faced me across a tablecloth I'd stained but he'd kept meticulously clean. At the end of the meal when we carried our plates to the kitchen, it would be like he hadn't been here at all. And despite the fact that his father talked *about* him, for how little Mr. May talked *to* him, he might not have been.

"So, school's going well, physical therapy's going well—" these were statements, not questions, like any other answer wasn't acceptable. "The house is passably clean and it looks like you reminded the landscaper about that shrub. Anything else I need to know? Anything new?"

Need to know? I wanted to scream. I wanted to shout out that there were a million things he should *want* to know about his son, and none of them fit on a checklist of one-word answers. I might be a champion at social awkwardness, but the dynamics between these two won medals. And worst of all, I got the sense that this was his dad actually *trying*.

But Toby was saying, "No, Dad," and maybe that signaled the end of the meal and our escape from a prison of flatware and politeness.

I set my fork and knife across the corner of my plate. "It was very good to see you, Mr. May, and thank you for dinner, but I should be getting home." There was guilt in my statement and I couldn't look across the table. Was I abandoning Toby or giving us all an excuse to move on to the separate portions of our night?

But it was nine thirty, and if I didn't show up soon, my parents were going to worry. I still had homework to do; though, this was a convenient reason to put off *Little Women* for another night.

Toby stood and picked up both our plates. Like I suspected, my spot looked like an olive-oil spatter zone, while his was pristine. "G'nite, Roar. I'll pick you up tomorrow."

"It was lovely to see you, Aurora." Mr. May reached over and patted my hand with his cold one. "And what my son means to say is, he'll walk you home."

"I—I live next door?" I pointed in case he forgot. "It's right there."

Mr. May pursed his lips. "I raised my son to be a gentleman. Tobias, go get your shoes."

I shot Toby an apologetic look, but he'd already put our plates down and headed into the mudroom.

"Really, he should've been doing this all along. What sort of man doesn't walk a lady to the door?"

"The kind that's confident she's capable of finding it by herself?" I said softly, but that wasn't enough to quell the fire in my stomach, and now that I'd started, I couldn't stop. I clenched my hands into fists beneath the tablecloth. "Toby is *the best* of guys. And if you don't know that, wake up! He's kind and he's intelligent and he has the biggest heart. And— and I think he looks hot in his glasses!"

"Roar."

I shut my mouth and turned my flaming cheeks toward where Toby was standing in the doorway, holding my shoes and the schoolbag we'd never opened.

Mr. May sounded amused when he said, "Good night, Aurora, and I agree with you. You're a good influence. Son, see if you can hold on to this one."

I didn't know if it was meant to be a jab at him and Merri— but Toby stiffened. He didn't move until I took my shoes and opened the kitchen door.

It was a thirty-second walk across our lawns, but it was the longest thirty-second silence I'd ever endured. My feelings were too big and wild; I couldn't wrestle them into coherent thoughts or words. At my door, he slid my bag off his shoulder and gave me a small smile. It was a totally different species from the grin we'd been sharing before his dad arrived— hollow and brittle, like the robin's eggshells I'd collected as a kid to try to match their color.

My arms were around him before I even recognized the impulse. It was a little kid hug—not forearms on his shoulders, hands in his hair, like when Merri embraced Fielding, but my arms wrapped around his middle, squeezing tight so that my face was pressed against his chest. It was the only comfort I could think to offer, and after a torturous two breaths where he stood rigid, he melted. His arms came up to rest on my back, his cheek nuzzled against the top of my head, his breath stirring my hair in quick pants like he'd finished a run.

My emotions exploded like this art exhibition I'd seen where darts were thrown at paint-filled balloons. Pulse soaring, skin tingling, muscles tightening like I was never letting him go. He had gripped the back of my sweatshirt like I was a life preserver, and he held on until his breathing finally slowed. His fingers loosened, then dropped; he straightened, and we both took a step backward, eyes on our shuffling feet.

"I, uh." Toby cleared his throat, but his voice still sounded hoarse when he finished. "I'll pick you up in the morning."

"Sounds good." I slid in the door, aware we weren't going to be talking about tonight soon or ever. But when I went to turn off the outside lights, he was still standing on the stoop, both hands gripping his hair as he stared out into the sky.

37

worried about what would happen once the cross-country season ended, but Merri ran her last race in early December and Toby and I stood by the trail in scarfs and hats. We clapped gloved hands and cheered—using the approved non-yelling words from Merri's list: "You look great!" "I'm happy to see you!" "Yay, runners!"

In the days that followed, Merri traded runs and trails for time at Eliza's or Fielding's and hours in front of her laptop—writing super-secret things that turned her pink whenever I asked about it. She didn't intrude, and since she and Toby were finally tiptoeing back to being normal with each other, I didn't try too hard to include her. I had Merri time at the store and Toby time all the days I wasn't working. I was fine with this arrangement, but it didn't stop me from being anxious about how long it would last, how long I could possibly be his substitute Campbell.

These were fears I inserted into sketches constantly. The stack of Toby drawings I'd ripped up was rapidly being replaced by a new creeper sketch pile. One I justified because I'd started drawing him in scenes with other people. Toby at lacrosse with Curtis, Lance, and Huck. Toby with Gatsby. Toby in the car with Merri and Eliza. If no one looked too closely, they might not notice the overlap, but if there were a Venn diagram of my sketches, Toby would be the center.

I was organizing these, rationalizing that friends could draw friends—I'd drawn Clara . . . sitting at a Knight Light meeting where, shockingly, I was next to Toby. And I'd drawn Huck onstage at Saturday detention . . . but at the moment Toby had crashed our cleaning party.

The doorbell rang, making me jump and then scrape the drawings into a pile I shoved under the bed before heading down to answer it.

My favorite smile was waiting on the other side of the door. Toby had changed out of his uniform into a pair of jeans and a faded green Henley. He had a gray hoodie on top and fiddled with the zipper as he asked, "What are you up to?"

It wasn't even five. Normally, we didn't do tutoring or not-tutoring for another hour. The only difference was, Merri was home. I'd seen her room light on when I went to answer the door, which meant he would've seen it from his room. "Are you that bored without . . ." I bit down on my tongue in time to amend my answer from *Merri* to "lacrosse?"

It was a weak change, because the season was over, but he answered, "Desperately." I waited for his eyes to flicker up the stairs, but they never wavered from my face. "Entertain me? What were you doing?"

I was too stunned to answer with anything but the truth. "Drawing."

"Teach me?" He stepped forward and I moved out of the way, letting him in and shutting out the cold and dark of December twilight. "You be the tutor this time, I'll be the student."

I led the way up the stairs, past the hallway gallery of Mom's humiliating photos: braces, home-cut bangs, matching sister outfits. His gaze may have lingered on my sister's bedroom, but he followed me into mine and shut the door, blocking our view of all things Merri.

Toby didn't hesitate to flop on my bed. He arranged the pillows behind his head so he was in a semi-sprawl and stared up at me. "On a scale from now to never, how long is it going to take me to master Aurora Campbell–level skills?"

I—I couldn't speak. My eyes kept flickering from where he was lounging—on *my bed*—to where I'd shoved that pile of drawings underneath it. His was the only spot in the room where he couldn't see the white paper peeking out, and if he had no qualms about sitting there, then I shouldn't either. Because we were *friends*. I'd sat on Clara's bed and painted her nails. On Huck's and done homework.

Toby was glancing around my room, studying the art tacked to my walls. He waved to my fishbowl. "Hey, Klee Five and Ariel Four."

"It's Ariel Eight now . . . It was a rough summer to be a snail."

He snorted. "I guess so. Maybe Klee Five is a bit of a bully."

"Yeah. Um, I'll get you set up." I clipped a paper to a drawing board and grabbed him a set of pencils and erasers. I gave him a quick run-through of pencil type—hardness versus darkness, graphite versus charcoal—and made him do shading spectrums down the margin of his page to get a feel for each and how they changed with pressure.

"Got it," he said, lining them up on my comforter. "You draw me and I'll draw you."

The way he glanced at my footboard made me think he expected me to settle over there, so our feet would overlap and we'd have a little artist colony on my mattress. The idea was almost comically impossible. Instead I tossed him the kneaded eraser I'd been twisting between my fingers and crossed the room to the tower. Once I was behind my easel, I picked up a pencil and said, "Sounds like a plan."

I'd drawn him more times than I counted stars, but never here, live. And here, live, was better than photographs or memory. Especially with the way he was looking at me too. It felt like performance art, because I was aware of my body in ways I normally tuned out. The way I drew my bottom lip into my mouth when I focused. The tightness in my shoulders from standing. The partial hiding place my easel provided and how its ledge was the perfect height to rest my trembling hands when the sensation of his eyes on me got to be too much. The weight of my pencils, the *scritch* of their lines. The balls of my feet and the way I shifted pressure between them. The tickle of a strand of hair against my cheek. The way my skin flushed under his gaze.

Which of these would Toby capture?

Though that was expecting too much, because while he was the most remarkable person I knew, his artistic genius began and ended with music. I'd seen his childhood crayon drawings. We'd done the whole Play-Doh thing and his had mostly ended up in Merri's hair. I'd been on his team for Pictionary. The fact that he was attempting more than a stick figure proved how bored he was.

But the expression on his face wasn't bored at all. He tucked one pencil behind his ear as he picked up the next, squinting at his page and tilting his head. The best thing about this situation was it gave me full permission to stare as much as I wanted. Or maybe that was the worst thing, because, heart, we weren't going there again. We couldn't.

His mouth was slightly open, the tip of his tongue resting to the side of his full bottom lip, like when he was really into a piece of music or driving in traffic. His eyebrows were lowered and his eyes bright as he looked from me to the board in his lap. His shoulders were relaxed against my pillows and his long legs were sprawled across my gray duvet. I didn't need a drawing to remember this scene, but I wanted to document it anyway. My lines grew in fast strokes, capturing the curves of his muscles, the tease of his eyelashes, that pencil behind his ear, peeking out from between his dark waves. The only part of him that wasn't relaxed was my favorite part—his hands. One gripped the side of the drawing board. The other drew a line, hesitated, drew again, then tinkered with his row of pencils.

We'd set a timer. It was the only way I let myself sketch on school nights. Otherwise I'd pause to sharpen a pencil and notice it had suddenly become two o'clock in the morning. I wanted to glance at it but resisted. I didn't want to know how many minutes remained of this spell, this place where I had permission to engage in open admiration and Toby's dark eyes grew darker.

The tinny, repetitive beeping made us both jump. I put down my pencil and picked up the timer, pressing the stop button.

"I don't remember what you said about shading."

It was the first time either of us had spoken since I hit start forty minutes ago. When I opened my mouth to respond, all that came out was a rusty "Oh."

"Part of me wants to ask you to come here and help—but if you do, I lose my subject."

"Take a picture," I answered automatically—because that was the art answer, not the human one. I didn't know if I wanted him taking a picture of me—here, now, when all my green light emotions felt dangerously close to the surface.

I also didn't want to go over there. To perch beside him on my bed and lean over his shoulder, my arm grazing his as I pointed out areas of his drawing he could improve.

Why couldn't I pretend he was Huck? Today Huck had stood behind me and propped his chin on my head, an elbow on each shoulder as I offered feedback in the studio. It had been . . . nothing. But imagining adopting that same pose now had me shivering.

I blinked at the computerized sound of a camera shutter. Toby lowered his phone. "And I can't figure out how to draw your easel so it doesn't look like a hulking monster attacking you."

Toby moved to sit and I held up a hand. Grinning, he eased back into the same position, looking even more like he owned that spot on my bed.

"You use foreshortening." At his what-the-what look, I elaborated. "Draw it smaller. It's all about perspective. Break the whole object up into shapes and then draw those shapes in a way that shows the distance from you."

If he'd been grinning before, he cranked up the dial now—from breathtaking to smolder. He lifted an eyebrow. "Don't take this the wrong way, Roar, but you talking art is kinda hot."

My hands closed around the ledge of my easel, gripping so tight the lip bit into my fingers. My cheeks lit up, but the lump in my throat tasted like anger, not embarrassment. *Kinda*, because that compliment needed a qualifier. And maybe he hadn't planned to kiss me at the concert, but he *had* checked me out during yoga. And we weren't five anymore, so all the casual touches to boost me on a counter or squeeze my hand—he had to realize he had more mixed signals than the outdated GPS we'd finally made Dad throw away.

"You're in my bedroom. On my bed. Telling me I'm 'kinda hot'—I know I'm not supposed to take that the 'wrong way'—but what's the right one?"

"I—I—I don't know." Toby sat up, ruining the composition I'd been working on, but the evening was already ruined. There was no way we were going back to peacefully sketching, not after that.

I stepped away from my easel, lowering myself onto the window seat. I wasn't a toy; this wasn't some game. I may not have a ton of experience with flirting or dating, but I knew Huck and Byron didn't talk to me like that. Even when Huck and I fake-dated—and a lot of people still thought we were together—there had been clear lines between real and pretend. Toby was blurring all those boundaries. "Maybe don't say things like that if you don't know. It's not fair."

He shoved the drawing board to the side and curled his legs up; the vulnerable portrait in front of me was infinitely more interesting than his casual sprawl. Not that I reached for a pencil. Instead I watched emotions drift over his face. "I didn't mean to— I should've thought before—" He dropped his chin. "I'm so confused."

"Yeah, well . . ." I wasn't going to excuse this, but I wasn't going to accuse him either. I could've made a statement about *Campbell sisters being a confusing species*—but I didn't want to group myself with Merri. I wanted to be treated as my own entity. I wanted to be seen as *me*—and if he was discovering my potential hotness, that was fine. But not if he was going to weaponize that realization and use it as weightless, careless words. Because my expectations wanted to sink their claws into any scrap of hope, and that statement was a ball of yarn dangled before a cat.

I was never the winner in staring contests. Merri dominated. Lilly too. I blinked like a first-time contact user. But if I looked away at that moment, would I ever be able to meet his eyes again?

Toby lost. He studied the paper in front of him like it was one of those hidden picture puzzles we used to be obsessed with. Only, instead of trying to find a shoe or a toothbrush, he was searching for the exit from this conversation or the answer to our unasked questions.

Finally he said, "Maybe we should just share our pictures."

"Good idea." I sagged against the window long enough for the icy glass to sink its chill through the fabric of my sweat-shirt, then I stood and faced my easel.

"How are we doing this? Like Slapjack? One-two-three *flip*?"

It was as good a suggestion as any, so I nodded, letting him start the count and joining in on "*Two. Three*—"

"Wait!" he said. "Changed my mind. I'll go first."

I froze with my hands on the side of the easel, not quite ready to see how he saw me, but even less ready for him to see how I saw him. His hands fumbled as he turned the drawing board to face me.

Oh, Toby. Despite his love for superheroes, he hadn't manifested any sudden artistic talent. I knew it was me in the drawing only because I'd been here while he drew it. But he'd tried and it was adorable—if I let myself not be offended that he'd given me a fivehead and creepishly large eyes. My hair was a dozen straight lines and I had no eyebrows. My favorite part was that he hadn't attempted a realistic mouth but had used a stick figure's half circle instead—one as wide as the smile currently on my face.

"I love it." I grabbed a sticky note off my dresser and did a quick scribble on it. Crossing the room, I stuck it on the upper corner of his paper.

"Batman," he said.

"I don't have any stickers and that's what you—"

"I used to do that for your drawings. I thought they were the best things I'd ever seen." He brushed a finger across my sticky-note sketch. "Still do. Can I see me now?"

I gripped the side of my easel, but suddenly there was a question I needed answered first. "Toby, who did you take to Fall Ball?"

He frowned. "I asked you. Don't you remember turning me down?"

"Right. But you could've gone with someone else."

"I didn't." His expression clouded. "Did you?"

"No." I laughed. "I went bowling with Huck."

"Right." His expression tightened. "Well, I went to the movies with Lance. Why?"

I didn't have a good answer, so I turned the easel instead. It was an accidental declaration in all its messy glory. Practically a billboard advertising how much I'd failed these past few months. I should have used Gatsbian green pencils, because nothing on that paper expressed friendship. It was a portrait of longing, of love.

His eyes went wide when I stepped out of the way. His eyebrows flew up and his jaw dropped. I gnawed my lip, refusing to ask the insecure artist's question *Do you like it?* I wouldn't be that needy. His eyes flickered from me to the paper and his lips formed a soft word. "Whoa."

"Do you like it?" Apparently I *was* that needy when it came to him.

"Roar." His voice was soft and gravelly. He sat up farther, leaning his elbows on his knees and still gaping at the drawing. "I never realized . . . Do you know how talented you are? That's how you see me?"

I wanted to deflect, to point to his paper and ask the same question, because hadn't we been given the same task and tools and the same amount of time to complete it? But if you sat me in front of a piano and asked me to write a song about him, I wouldn't be able to put emotion into a tune. We spoke different art languages and that was okay. I didn't need to translate; he wouldn't want me to.

"Does it not look like you?" I joked.

He stared at the paper, then patted the bed beside him. "I'm just—"

"Hey, Rory—" My sister froze with the door half open. "Oh. Hi, Toby. I didn't know you were here . . . in my sister's bedroom. On her bed? And aww—you're even wearing matching outfits."

Not really. I mean, we both had on gray hoodies, but he had on jeans and I was in black leggings. Still, my heart surged at the idea that we were worthy of a collective "aww." I could live for days replaying any comment that grouped him and me together. But I shouldn't.

And I couldn't admit to any of that, and everything inside me was stretched thin and fragile. I narrowed my eyes and snapped, "Did you want something? Or just to bug me?"

Merri raised her palms. "Never mind. I'll leave you alone."

I shut my eyes and waited for Toby to jump up and take her side, knowing his criticism would make me want to crumple even more than the self-condemnation already looping in my head. But he didn't—the sound that made me open my eyes was the door shutting as Merri backed out of my room. Toby's puzzled gaze was on me.

"Sorry," I told him. "That was rude. I need to—" I crossed the room. "I have to apologize. I'll be right back."

"I should go." Toby stood too and then we were both crammed in the space between my bed and the door. I had to step closer to make room to open it, but he didn't back up. I wanted to stay in this flustered moment of flushed cheeks and eye contact and ask him to end the sentence Merri had interrupted: *"I'm just—"*

Instead I pulled the door open and we blinked at the hallway light. All our privacy evaporated into the public space created by Merri's bedroom being across from mine—and her sitting on her bed, facing us—observing us standing way too close.

"Girls, dinnertime!" Mom called up the stairs.

"Are you staying for dinner, Toby?" Merri asked as she came into the hall. "You should. It's been forever and Dad made it. Mom just had to heat it."

I felt Toby's eyes on me, but I kept mine on my sister, focusing on the fact that I wanted to both apologize and gag her. Guilt and rage didn't mix well and I choked on the combination.

"No," Toby said. He touched my shoulder lightly as he slipped by me into the hall. "I'm heading home. I'll see you in the morning, Roar. Later, Merri."

He made it half a hallway, until he was beside a picture of all of us at a playground—a row of swings, a string of knobby knees pumping. Merri's eyes on the sky, Lilly's on the camera, his on the dirt. Mine on him.

"Oh, wait." He pulled the drawing pencil from behind his ear and tossed it to me. I caught it in the only way I knew how: uncoordinated, with both hands, against my chest, looking like some ridiculous court lady clutching a favor from a knight. He saluted us both and turned again.

I waited until I heard his footsteps on the stairs before speaking. "I'm sorry I—"

"Forget it." Merri waved a hand to dismiss the whole thing. "I should've knocked."

"You don't have to. I mean—" My cheeks were turning red as my words matched my scrambled thoughts. "You weren't— We weren't— You didn't interrupt anything."

"Hmm." Merri tapped a finger on her mouth. "Then it sounds like I came in thirty seconds too soon."

"That's not funny," I said, but she'd turned and flitted toward the stairs. "Seriously, Merri. Don't go there." But I didn't truly expect her to listen to me. When had she ever?

"Where are you in *Little Women* by the way?" she called over her shoulder. "Because . . . Never mind, zipping my lips. No spoilers."

38

Rory, a word?"

I was starting to dread the end of English class. On the one hand, it was *over*, but, on the other, being asked to stay for "a word" had never resulted in anything good. I sat back in my seat and crossed my ankles under my chair, pressing the bones together so tight that they ached.

Ms. Gregoire stayed standing, watching the classroom empty of my curious classmates. I kept my eyes on my notebook, mentally tracing the lines of all the different doodles that covered its surface. Today I'd added a new sketch, a skyscraper copied from the print of Ms. Gregoire's dress.

When the door finally shut behind Huck, who had dawdled nosily, Ms. Gregoire slid into the desk beside mine, her relaxed posture so different from my own. "I won't keep you long. I just wanted to impart one piece of advice, if I may."

Was that a question? And did I want to give permission? I nodded anyway, automatically.

"I meant it when I said you could read *Little Women* at your own pace. I gave it to you during exams and I know you had to prioritize studying and repairing some of your grades. But that was Halloween. It's now December."

"I . . ." The book lived in my backpack and I carried it with me everywhere. I hadn't forgotten, couldn't forget with the weight of it against my spine as I moved through my school day. But I couldn't make myself read it. Not just out of procrastination but something else too. Something I wouldn't or couldn't name.

Ms. Gregoire waited for me to make eye contact before continuing. "Avoiding the things you're afraid of doesn't make them go away," she said softly. "I want you to remember that. When you keep them locked inside they have power, but when you confront them, you give *yourself* the power to fix them and let go."

"I'll read the book," I promised. I'd do anything to escape the way those words shivered over my skin and settled in my throat like a lump that I couldn't swallow down.

Ms. Gregoire gave me a smile full of such sympathy that my eyes started to itch. But it wasn't allergy season; there was no excuse for them to water and no reason for me to cry. I wasn't in trouble. I hadn't done anything wrong. It was a perfectly normal day and yet I wanted to put my head down on my desk and blubber.

"Sweet girl, I don't just mean that book. You've got a lot going on—and your life's about to get much more complicated." She sighed and pressed her hand to her mouth. "I won't spoil that surprise, but I just wanted to say it's okay to be scared, but don't stay frozen in your fear."

"I'll read the book," I repeated, because the lack of context in her advice made my stomach churn. My hands shook around my notebook as I thought about Toby at the concert, Toby at yoga, Toby and a million moments in his car and kitchen . . . and the way I'd snapped at him in my bedroom last night for calling me "hot," then retreated before we could have an actual conversation. Instead hiding my feelings behind our drawings and a sham relationship with Huck—avoiding anything real.

Some fears weren't worth confronting. Some things weren't worth the risk. I stood up and pulled on my backpack, sniffing into the shoulder strap.

"Rory," Ms. Gregoire said gently. She offered me a tissue she pulled from her pocket.

I snuffled into a laugh, because every girl I knew would be thinking the same thing right now—*That dress has pockets?!* Merri called a cute dress with pockets "the holy grail," and as I squeezed my hands around my notebook, I wanted my sister here, now. To diffuse this situation with a joke and distraction. Or Clara, who kept a running log of all of Ms. Gregoire's outfits in the back of her planner and would ask where she shopped.

I wanted anyone so I wouldn't have to stand on my own and face the way her shoulders curved with such empathy. "Rory," she repeated. "I'm going to say this now and I want you to hear me—I'm proud of you. Remember that. I'm proud of you and nothing is hopeless."

39

A urora!" I'd been walking down the aisle of the Convocation Hall when a voice and an arm snagged my progress. Both belonged to Eliza, who was staring at me with calculating blue eyes like the vengeful cherub she resembled. "I need you to sit right here."

"Um, okay?" I waved to Clara and Iris. "I'll see you after Convocation?"

The "right here" Eliza pointed to was the section of bench next to her. On her other side were Fielding and Merri, beyond them Fielding's sister, Sera, her girlfriend, Hannah, and finally Lance and Toby. "Where's Curtis?" I asked. He was the last member of their squad and it was rare to see Eliza without him loitering nearby looking antagonistic.

"I believe he mentioned a restroom break. Where he sits when he gets back is no concern of mine." Eliza straightened her shoulders, making her blond ponytail sway. She always wore it back, pulled so tight it made her cheekbones appear sharper and her glares razor-edged. If I hadn't grown up with her, I'd be terrified. I bet even her teachers were intimidated by the genius power contained behind her evil angel facade. I had respect for Curtis and his unsinkable optimism that he could befriend her. I felt a little bad about stealing his seat.

"Well, don't just *sit* there, I need you to talk to me," Eliza added.

"About?"

"Anything." Her eyes were flickering over my left shoulder. "No, not anything. That's too vague. About how your classes are going. No one has updated me since we stopped carpooling together."

"Um, I'm currently passing everything. Not sure how long it'll last, but . . ."

"That sounds promising." It did? Eliza's lips flickered triumphantly. I turned to see Curtis pause when he saw me in his spot, then shake his head and chuckle as he continued past our row to find another seat.

As Eliza and Curtis continued their weird version of fight-flirting, I leaned behind her and tapped Fielding on the shoulder. "At your next family meeting, can you suggest canceling Convocation?"

He grinned. "I'll do my best. Any suggestions for what we should have instead?"

I thought about this while we sang the school song. Merri still hadn't learned it and was clearly mouthing random words. I tuned out the announcements about winter sports tryouts and leaned over again. "More Knight Lights. Study halls. Or end the day early."

Fielding was normally pretty great about paying attention when I talked. He didn't make me feel like a tagalong even though I was two grades below him and had been an unwilling third wheel on some of his first drives with Merri. But this time he cleared his throat and tilted his head toward the front of the room.

I repeated my list and added, "I'd be good with any of those."

Merri whispered my name at the same time Eliza yanked my arm.

"What? Do you need me to go deliver a *Check yes or no* note to Curtis?"

"Of course not," snapped Eliza. "But since that teacher has called your name twice now, it would be prudent if you responded."

I glanced at the front; Mrs. Mundhenk was standing at the podium. "Aurora? Rory Campbell? She was here this morning. Oh, I hope she's not an early dismissal."

Ms. Gregoire's comment about my life about to be more complicated seared my mind. I froze on the bench.

"No, she's right here," Merri called out, and I felt the room whirl toward me. My smile felt cracked and crooked. Like the face in one of Picasso's cubist paintings. Only, his were a stylistic choice and this was just the best I could do.

I hissed "Traitor" under my breath as she and Eliza pushed me toward the aisle.

"Oh good." Mrs. Mundhenk exhaled into the microphone. "Will you join me up here, please? I have some exciting news to share."

My little-big sister was a ferocious figure when she wanted to be and I watched her from the front of the room as she moved against the flow of students to make her way to me. It wasn't a path of "Excuse me" and awkwardly dancing left and right to pass and pivot. Instead she charged forward and expected people to part. They did. She'd learned that from Eliza. Fielding and Toby trailed behind her. Toby shaking his head and smiling my way, Fielding lagging to issue apologies and explanations. Not that they were necessary, but he couldn't help himself.

I braced myself for Merri's whoop of congratulations and wrecking ball hug. And she did give me those, but not until after she propped her hands on her hips and demanded, "Wait. You get to go to NYC? I want to go. How is this fair?"

I snorted into her hug—giving Toby a high five behind her back and nodding at Fielding's formal "This is quite the accomplishment, Rory. I'm happy for you."

Prying Merri's arms off me, I responded, "You do *not* want to go to New York. You'd miss your subway stop every time because you'd be too busy patting stranger's dogs. And you hate cities."

Toby opened his mouth and I prepared myself to be reprimanded for mocking Merri, but instead he joined her in laughing.

"Okay, that's true." Merri's giggles had turned her cheeks pink, or maybe that was from Fielding smiling at her like she was delicious as he laced their hands together. "But . . . still. I want some big, shiny honor too! I mean, I always get good grades and I never get in trouble."

Fielding coughed and raised his eyebrows.

"I *rarely* get in trouble," Merri amended. "And I've got straight As."

I ground my teeth to keep from flinching as her words landed with laser accuracy on my oldest vulnerability and newest defeat—but she didn't know about that. When I could keep my voice level, I sharpened it. "I guess the universe likes me better."

I didn't tell her I wasn't going. There was no way I could go, because there was no way we could afford it. The thing about doors and opportunities is they lead to each other. Just because we'd scraped together enough money for me to attend Hero High didn't mean I'd have enough to take advantage of the possibilities it offered. There'd be fancy class trips, fancy fund-raisers, fancy who-knew-whats. I'd have to get good at saying no to them.

Which wouldn't be a problem most of the time. It wasn't like I wanted to say yes. Not to anything but the Snipes workshop.

I was holding my breath in an attempt to hold in tears. Looking at the nearest stained-glass window so everyone wouldn't see them shimmering on my eyes, because there was no one to blame but myself. Ms. Gregoire was wrong; it *was* hopeless.

I'd thought if I got my GPA high enough to be a nominee, I'd be okay. It didn't occur to me that grants would also be GPA-dependent and require a higher standard. And mine didn't meet it.

"Hey." Toby had cut in closer while Merri and Fielding flirted about a someday trip to New York where he promised not to let her get lost. "You okay? After the whole stand-in-front-of-the-school thing?"

"You mean do I still want to die from humiliation?" I pulled the corners of my mouth up, because that's what I was supposed to do, but really I wanted to cover my face with my hands. "Being embarrassed in Convocation is clearly a Hero High rite of passage: Merri by Monroe, Fielding by Merri, me by Mrs. Mundhenk . . ." I widened my eyes in mock horror. "Are you next?"

He laughed. "Let's get you home, you . . . What was it she called you? 'A prodigy like she'd never seen before'? I want credit for recognizing this way back in my Batman sticker days. Watch out New York—here comes Roar."

"Heyyyy!" I looked up just in time to avoid being steamrolled by Clara's hug. "So many congrats!"

"From me and Byron too," said the pretty brunette I knew from student council and Clara's stories. It was Byron's twin, Lynnie. "He's a little disappointed he didn't get picked, but he's truly happy for you."

I believed her, but I'd also watched his face fall when I'd stood at the podium. They should've chosen him. He could've gone.

"Thank you." As they waved to go, I called out, "And tell Byron thanks too."

The acceptance form and paperwork were in the bottom of my backpack, so I kicked it. Mrs. Mundhenk had gone over the details while the rest of Convocation continued. The deposit was due next week; that alone would empty my bank account, and it was just a sliver of the total.

"When do you come home?" Merri asked.

"New Year's." I needed to stop feeding the fantasy of me going, but maybe for one night I could pretend.

"Ugh, I hate when people say 'New Year's.' Does that mean *Eve* or *Day*? Lilly is the worst with this, because one of those is her favorite holiday and they're literally different months and years. Be specific, people!" Before I could clarify, she whirled to Fielding, reaching for his hand, then twirling under his arm like a ballroom spin. She spun back in and said, "It's like a.m. and p.m. and noon and midnight. You know what I mean?"

"Not a clue." Fielding smiled down at her, then continued their dance by dipping her. It was like they were competing on an imaginary game show to win the title of Most Romantic Couple. Except that would require them to realize other couples and the rest of the world existed. They were just that smitten. Ugh.

"Like, 'midnight' has the word 'night' in it, so it should be p.m., and noon is the end of the morning, it comes right after eleven fifty-nine a.m., so you'd think it's twelve a.m.—but it's not. Or is it? I can never keep those straight. Everyone should just use 'noon' or 'midnight.' Agreed?"

Fielding smiled and kissed her cheek. "Maybe we should switch to military time."

Merri tilted her head. "Could you? I'd actually like that a lot."

"Sure. I'll pick you up at eighteen hundred hours."

"Your homework in here?" Toby's voice cut through my spying on the Merri-and-Fielding show. He seemed to purposely avoid looking in their direction as he scooped up my backpack and slung it on his shoulder. "C'mon, Roar. Let's go mix up some black bean brownies and knock out your math while they're in the oven."

"Black bean *what*?" I laughed and caught up with him, because he'd started down the aisle without me.

"Someone—Curtis—informed me I'm failing as your Knight Light because I haven't done the whole baked-goods-in-your-locker thing. Then Eliza chimed in with this recipe so I 'couldn't use your plant-based diet as an excuse.'" He held the door for me. "I wasn't planning on it, by the way. I would've googled."

"Black beans?" I asked, scrunching my mouth to the side. "Brownies?"

"Should we try it? Because if they don't work, I'd love to tell Eliza she's wrong. And good news like this needs celebrating."

I tilted my head at him, skipping down the steps in a way I wouldn't have thought possible an hour ago when I wanted to melt under the combined gaze of every Hero High student. "You'd really eat black bean brownies?"

"For you, Roar?" Toby said, and I knew I'd never stop loving the way he said my name. He'd graduated from the knee brace, but he still looked cautious as he made his way down the stairs to where I waited, grinning from ear to ear. "I'd even eat broccoli."

40

"Aurora? Can you come down here, please?"

One of these days Dad was going to discover it was easier to text than to stand at the bottom of the stairs and bellow. But the realization didn't occur to him that Wednesday night.

"One minute," I hollered back. I'd just gotten out of the shower where I'd used Lilly's fancy Dead Sea scrub to scour every inch of me. For once I was entirely paint-free. It wouldn't last long, but after telling Mrs. Mundhenk I couldn't go to New York City and study with a famous artist, I felt like I didn't deserve to have charcoal beneath my nails and acrylics and oils striped and spattered across my skin.

Mrs. Mundhenk had been devastated. I'd found myself apologizing. *Sorry we're not rich?* She wanted this for me almost as much as I'd wanted it for myself. "This workshop only happens every four years."

I'd given a weak laugh and suggested, "Well, what are the chances I won't repeat at least one grade before I graduate?"

The joke hadn't been well received. She'd thought I wasn't taking it seriously; I thought she needed to look a little closer and see I was seriously close to losing it. It'd been the worst kind of stalemate. I'd solved it by faking a migraine and having Lilly pick me up early.

I'd hidden in my room through the afternoon and dinner, faking sleep whenever Lilly came to check on me, but now Mom and Dad were home from the store, and I'd blown my cover by showering. I dragged a comb through my hair and threw on the closest clean T-shirt and yoga pants.

Mom was sitting at the table, a stack of bills, their checkbook, and two mugs in front of her. She nudged one toward an empty chair and pointed at me. Dad was standing by the sink, his hands wrist-deep in soapy water. He wiped them on the frilly pink apron he always wore while doing dishes. Merri had bought it for him as a joke last Christmas, but he wore it proudly.

"Your art teacher called," Mom began. "She told us about this workshop? It sounds like a big honor to be selected."

"Why didn't you tell us?" asked Dad.

The answer was right in front of them. I could've lifted one finger and pointed at it, but like their unpaid balances, it would have to wait. Instead I shrugged slowly, like my shoulders were full of rusty gears. "I don't want to go."

"No?" Dad's forehead was scrunched. He was the one who drove me to art classes. Who'd surprised me by having one of my first paintings professionally framed. He had them lining the walls of their office at the store. He was the one I'd told my big-city dreams to, back when I still confided things like that without feeling ridiculous.

"I'm only a freshman. I won't know anyone. I don't want to give up my whole break." These were the excuses I'd come up with while lying under my covers. I hadn't meant to blurt them out all at once, but maybe it didn't matter because Mom was nodding.

"I can't imagine my baby girl on her own in that huge city. Maybe your senior year." She took a sip before adding, "Maybe. If you're ready."

"Are you sure, Rory?" Dad's forehead hadn't unbunched.

"Sure about what?" Merri skipped into the kitchen in pajama pants with sled dogs racing up each leg. Her mismatched socks were neon green and pale yellow. She'd topped these with her hideous tie-dyed bathrobe. She went to the fridge. "Don't mind me, just getting a snack. Pretend I'm not over here, totally eavesdropping."

The bedtime munch, Toby had called it, and now I wanted one too. A bowl of cereal or a piece of toast with peanut butter. But those things would tangle with the knots formed in my stomach when Dad said, "The Snipes workshop."

Merri's answer came from deep within the fridge. "Gah, it sounds amazing. I'd kill for a weeklong workshop with one of my heroes. Can someone please reanimate Fitzgerald or Austen or any of the Brontës?"

"Rory isn't feeling ready to do the workshop this year," Mom answered for me. "But she'll have other chances."

"No, she won't." Merri stood up with a cheese stick in one hand and a roll of cookie dough in the other. I seriously hoped she wasn't planning on combining them. "What the heck, Rory? You planning on staying back a grade? Because this workshop is only held *every four years.*"

"Calm down there, pixie," said Dad. "If Rory doesn't want to go, be sensitive to that."

"Doesn't want to go?" Merri was shaking her head like she was trying to dislodge water from her ears. She pointed the cheese stick at me. "What are they talking about? You want to go. She wants to go. She stood in front of the whole school and glowed—I repeat, *Rory in front of the whole school*—when they announced she'd gotten in. She didn't even puke."

"I didn't glow—that was radioactive embarrassment," I mumbled, but no one was paying attention to me. Merri had kicked the step stool into the middle of the floor and climbed on it.

"Her room is practically a shrine to Snipes. She's been talking about art in New York since you stupidly showed her how to tour museums online when she was six. This is her shot. She's going." Now the cookie dough was in my face. "You're going."

I shrank back against my seat, tucking my knees up. "No, I'm not."

"For once in your life let yourself want what you want!" Merri was gesturing with both hands now—like an air traffic controller holding batons of different sizes. Both pointed out the open front door in the direction of the Mays' house.

I wanted to slip under the tablecloth. To crawl out of the room with my face covered. Because she knew. And I didn't know how long she'd known or the extent to which she knew, but Merri knew the other thing I wanted this badly. The other thing I couldn't have.

"Sounds like everyone in here needs to take a deep breath." Lilly dropped her purse on the table and toed off her shoes. She'd let in the frigid night air, but at least she'd shut the door behind her, so Merri was no longer pointing directly at Toby's house. "What's going on?"

Merri was the first one to blurt out a summary, and I wasn't sure why I was letting her control the narrative. Her version might have been true, but it wasn't the interpretation I wanted Mom and Dad believing.

"Rory doesn't want to go," Mom countered when Merri finished, but she'd lifted the end of the statement into a question.

"Can we borrow Rory for a second?" Lilly asked. "For a Campbell sisters huddle."

Dad nodded. "I think that's a good idea."

My stomach knotted as Merri hopped off the stool and grabbed my arm. "Let's go."

"Ow! I can walk." I squirmed out of her grip and followed both my sisters upstairs to Lilly's room. Merri shut the door behind us and leaned against it. Lilly went over to her dresser, watching me in the mirror as she removed her earrings and placed them carefully in her mother-of-pearl jewelry box. "What's going on, Rory? This sounds like it would be right up your alley."

Lilly's room was pale gray and everything was just so. Compared to the riot of color of Merri's room and mismatched inspiration walls in mine, it was soothing—boring. I walked over to her desk and began to fiddle with her pens. I'm sure she cringed when I knocked them out of precise alignment, but she didn't stop me.

"I can't go."

"At least that's finally more honest than 'I don't want to,'" said Merri.

"Rory, we just want to know what's going on in your head and why you'd say no to this." Lilly reached into her top drawer and fished out a stress ball. Handing it over, she steered me to her bed and then quickly straightened her pens. "I know we're all busy. Merri's got a boyfriend and sports and whatever Eliza's dragging her into. I've got the wedding. And you're *never* around. You're either next door or shut up in your room painting—and you hate getting interrupted, so I never know if it's okay to knock."

I blinked at her description of my life. It wasn't *inaccurate*, but it was a perspective I'd never considered. *I* was the unavailable one? Me? The stress ball dropped from my hand and off the duvet. I watched it roll across the hardwood and come to a stop by a pair of mismatched socks: yellow with pink mermaids on one foot, bright green avocados on the other. Merri scooped up the ball and tossed it back to me. "You need like a code or something—tie a ribbon on your doorknob if we can come in without getting yelled at."

"I don't . . . yell." But I used to, back when they used to come in my room . . . and I guess I had when Merri barged in on Toby and me two nights ago.

"You know you're not alone, right?" asked Lilly. "If you can't trust your sisters, who can you trust?"

I snorted and closed my fist around the ball, feeling it compress against my palm. "When have you two ever trusted me with anything?"

"Rory, I would *never* have gone to that first yoga class by myself. Do you know how important and empowering that was for me?" Lilly sat on the bed beside me and looked me in the eyes. "I needed to be in that body positive space—but I wouldn't have gotten there if you hadn't agreed to go with me and then pushed me to keep going."

I squirmed. We'd taken classes together for two years, her driving home from college to pick me up. Over the summer, we'd upped it to twice weekly. But since September we hadn't gone at all. I had no idea it was part of her eating disorder recovery. "I just thought it was fun." And that she'd done it with me because Merri was allergic to sitting still and meditation.

"It *was* fun, because you were there with me." Lilly squeezed my hand and my eyes began to itch.

"And me—" I twitched my gaze over to where Merri was standing, ruffling through our big sister's closet. "You know those cartoons with the angel and the devil that perch on the character's shoulders talking them in and out of bad decisions? Toby's the daredevil saying 'Yes' and you're the sarcastic, tattletale angel who tells me not to jump off the swings, or hitch a wagon to Gatsby, or try sledding in the pool, or—"

"You never listen to me."

"I may never admit that I listen, but that doesn't mean I don't. Remember when I wanted to build a zip line from my room to Toby's? That would not have ended well. We only stopped because you threatened to get Mom and Dad.

Seriously, Rory, with the amount of adventures you've interrupted, stealing my partner in crime to go do something
behave-y, I'm probably *alive* because of you."

Because I was the tattletale spoilsport who "interrupted
her adventures." I frowned. "I didn't steal your partner
in crime."

"Are you serious?" Merri laughed. "You've always been
able to walk into the middle of our chaos and mention something you wanted to try—building Everest in the sandbox,
melting crayons on the driveway, making your own origami
paper—and Toby would abandon me and go to you like you
were an artistic oasis."

She had that backward. I was the one left behind—paper
half-made, origami half-folded—when she barged in with
walkie-talkies and plans for a spy mission, or a map and a
treasure she'd buried.

Merri wobbled in Lilly's high heels—each of her feet in a
shoe of a different height. "Did you miss the part where I said
I'm alive because of you? Take the compliment."

Lilly rolled her eyes. "Hyperbole aside, what Merri is trying to explain is that you've been there for us and we're happy
to be here for you."

I didn't know what "hyperbole" meant and didn't ask.
"That's nice, but it doesn't matter. I'm not asking Mom and
Dad for the money." Ms. Gregoire was only half right—avoiding
things I was afraid of might not make them go away, but saying them aloud wouldn't make dollar bills magically appear.

"Is that the issue? Then ask us," said Merri. She stepped
down from the heels and put them back.

"How much is it?" Lilly's voice was quiet, not as confident as Merri's.

"Too much," I answered, standing up and taking Lilly's stress ball with me. Merri was no longer guarding the door and I took the chance to slip out. "I appreciate this, but it's not going to happen."

I avoided my sisters the next day and continually reaffirmed for Mom and Dad that not-going was what I wanted. Mom believed me because that was what *she* wanted. Dad knew I was lying but couldn't figure out why.

"Is this about a boy?" he asked me Tuesday night when we were the only two in the kitchen. "Or your classmates? Mrs. Mundhenk mentioned there'd been some jealousy issues going on. Rory, I don't want you to ever burn less brightly because others don't glow. Your talent is a gift. Don't hide it."

"I'm not," I told him. "I'm learning so much at Hero High. I don't need this. Okay?"

"I'm not sure it is okay." Dad sighed. "But I'm not going to force you to go if you're uncomfortable. We learned that lesson when we believed the camp counselor who told us Lilly would get over her homesickness if we gave her time. Do you remember? You were still in a car seat and still not sleeping through the night, so the two of us made a midnight three-hour trek to the Hudson Valley to pick her up. She made me wake and unstrap you so she could hug you before we drove home—which meant you roared the whole way back."

I shook my head. I didn't remember it, but I liked the visual so much I spun it into a reflection journal. I hadn't read any more *Little Women*, but I wanted to rethink my response to chapter seven. This time not focused on the crime of pickled limes that got Amy punished at school, but on the way her sisters reacted to her punishment. Meg cried as she bandaged Amy's lashed hand. Jo had made threats and stormed the school to get Amy's things.

Amy was hurt by what happened, but her sisters made it better. When I'd had my origami catastrophe, I hadn't told Lilly or Merri. I hadn't given them the chance to stick up for me and have my back. They would've. Merri would've stomped down from the middle school and told off my teacher and Stella and anyone who laughed. Lilly would've taken me back to the store and bought more paper with her own money.

We made a great team when I let them play, but I usually kept them on the sidelines. I thought it wasn't fair to ask for their help when I had nothing to offer in return. But they didn't seem to feel that way. And maybe families weren't a game of balancing a seesaw but of playing Red Rover. You held on as tight as you could and protected that bond from the forces that flew against you and tried to tear you apart.

41

Convocation on Friday was a dizzying rundown of all the deadlines and special events before winter break. Some people around me had fancy planners out, color-coding and sticker-charting their next week. Others were in a button-pushing frenzy on their phones as they programmed in the Candlelight Concert, final projects, holiday parties, and schedule changes.

My phone was in my locker, along with everything else. The only thing I'd brought to Convocation was a feeling of restlessness and a case of the fidgets. Both grew worse as I realized I was the unprepared fool in a sea of type A organizers.

"How did you know to bring that?" I asked, pointing to the calendar in Clara's lap.

"My Knight Light told me," she whispered back, her eyes not moving from the page in her binder as she switched from green pen to purple and added *Knight Light meeting—no Convocation* to next Monday.

"Oh." My Knight Light hadn't warned me. Maybe he would've, but we'd spent the whole drive to school discussing chickpea cookies, cashew "cheese" cake, and other plant-based dessert recipes Toby had apparently been researching with Curtis's help. Some sounded gross, but we'd licked the bowl of black bean brownie batter last week, and I'd gladly talk cauliflower rice pudding if it meant he didn't bring up the Snipes workshop.

"I'll take pictures of each page and send them to you. Or—" Her pen lifted from her paper. "Oh my stars! I finally know what to get you for Christmas. Your own planner."

I mumbled, "Please don't," because there was no way I was maintaining something like that. Hers was adorable with a monogrammed sparkly leather binder and pages decorated with washi tape, hand-lettered to-do lists, and thematic stickers. Each page was crafted. I knew myself—I'd get obsessive over the artsiness of it and neglect its actual function.

Huck, on my other side, elbowed me and whispered, "Relax, I've sent you an event invite for everything I added to my iLive calendar."

"Thanks." I exhaled as Headmaster Williams transitioned to the school song.

Toby found us when Convocation ended, making his way against the current of exiting students to reach my second-row seat—Clara's pick, she preferred the front. "Hey, Roar—"

"Thanks for the heads-up about the schedule rundown," I interrupted.

"Oh, right." He face-palmed. "Sorry, it's always the last Friday before break. You can see my notes."

"Sophomore notes aren't super helpful for freshman schedules," interjected Huck. "But I got her covered."

I waited for Clara to chime in and show off her planner, but she'd gone down the row to compare layouts with Gemma.

"Uh, great, I guess." Toby's eyes shifted from Huck to me. "Anyway, Roar, I've got physical therapy at four, but you're working today, right?" I nodded and he added, "Okay, meet me at my car and I'll drop you at the store on my way."

"Sounds good. Thanks."

Huck waited until he'd left, then elbowed me. "So, Project Green Light is still glowing?"

"What?" I stopped tracking Toby's back and glanced up at Huck. "No."

"I don't know—I just saw some glow. At least some embers." I was shaking my head, but Huck was busy scanning the room. "Let's find Clara before we start brainstorming, because you know she'll be pissed if we—"

"No. Stop." I yanked on his arm until he listened. "Sometimes I just want to be your *friend*, not your project."

His dimple flickered. "I don't know what that means."

"Let's save Rory from the mean people in art. Let's save Rory from her unrequited love." I squared my shoulders and looked at him. "Huck, did it ever occur to you that *if* I need saving, I'll do it myself?"

His dimples disappeared as his face went serious. He swallowed, weighing my words. "That's fair."

"I just—"

"No, I get it. Sometimes I get too aggressive with fix-it mode. I should wait for you to ask for advice." He sighed. "I'm sorry I made you feel like a project."

"Thank you." I tucked my hair behind my ears. "I do appreciate the help, it's just . . . I'm trying to be Toby's friend, and comments like that . . ."

"Are a reminder of why you're doomed to fail?"

"That's not fair!" Normally I'd back down. I didn't instigate arguments—not with anyone but Merri—but I'd fought too hard for this and I trusted Huck would still be there on the other side of the disagreement. "I don't swoon after him anymore. I don't giggle and go along with whatever he wants. I don't see him as this perfect person."

"The thing is, Campbell"—Huck leaned one knee on the bench so we were closer to the same height—"I don't think he sees you the same way he used to either."

"Stop. Please, just stop." Because I didn't want to hear words like those, words that might make me hope and twist my thoughts and feelings into silly, reckless knots. "I need to focus on passing freshman year, not chasing disasters."

Huck mimed zipping his lips. Then locking them. Then throwing away the key. Halfway down the row, Clara pantomimed catching it, then she marched back over. "Now that we've got him set to mute, let's make winter break plans. Tell me again what days you're away in New York? Is it before or after Christmas?"

She pointed to the spread in her planner where in each block of winter break she'd penciled in *Rory away? Rory away? Rory away?*

I felt each of those question marks like a needle in my skin. I pushed the book back. Clara tutted. "Don't tell me you don't know when you're gone. This is why you need a planner."

No, what I needed was a *plan*, a way to explain to everyone not *when* I was going, but why I was not.

42

At the store that night Merri and Lilly tried to ambush me with "We've been talking and—"

I held up a hand. "I need you to hear me." They quieted immediately, the way Gatsby did when you held up a treat, and I was almost too shocked to continue. "I don't want to talk about the Snipes workshop. I want you to respect my decision not to go."

"But, Rory—" Merri began.

Lilly clamped a hand over her mouth. "We hear you and we're here *for* you if you want to talk."

I didn't. And I'd never been more grateful for the stream of people seeking drawings of their dogs. The thing had gotten an unofficial name: Pup Portraits. And the whole night there was at least one customer waiting while I drew the dog before theirs. By the time we flipped the sign to *Closed*, I needed to shake out my wrist and crack my back.

"Lilly, do you have any of those fancy bath bombs left?" I asked as we walked to her car. "I need to find a more comfortable way to draw in the store. My spine feels like a slinky someone left unattended with Merri."

"They're under the sink," Lilly said with a laugh. "Help yourself."

But I didn't get the chance, because Mom and Dad were waiting at the kitchen table with their checkbook and store ledgers when we walked in. "Girls, take a seat."

"Are we in trouble?" Merri slid into a chair and pulled up her feet. "I didn't do it."

Lilly and I shot her a look like *Great teamwork*, but Dad laughed. "No one's in trouble. We have a question."

I grabbed the fruit bowl and put it in a bare spot among the bills on the table. Lilly grabbed a banana and I went for a pear. "What's up?" I asked.

"It started a little more than a month ago," began Mom. "We noticed the register didn't balance. At first we thought it was a one-time thing, maybe we overcharged someone. We put the money aside in case they came back. Then, two weeks later, it happened again."

"It's kept happening. Tonight I realized it's only on the nights you three are working. I bet if I get the cash bag from the safe right now, it'll be more than the amount on the register tape."

Merri looked up from the numbers she was jotting on an envelope. "I'm guessing it would be a hundred and fifty over. Maybe more. I couldn't keep up with Rory tonight because the store was super busy. The waiting customers all bought stuff."

Mom held up a hand. "Slow down and speak as if you want people to understand you."

Merri pointed to me. Lilly put a foot on one of my chair's rungs.

"I draw pictures of people's dogs." I set down my pear and folded my hands in my lap, not quite sure why I was nervous. "It started by accident, but it's grown. Tonight, there was a line of people waiting."

"They pay you?" Mom asked at the same time Merri said, "You've been putting all that money in the register?"

"How much do people pay per drawing?" Dad asked.

"I don't know. I make Merri do that part."

"Between twenty and fifty," she said. "Sometimes more, but usually in that range. I can't believe you've been putting it in the register. That's got to be at least"—she looked at her envelope math—"six hundred dollars."

"Seven-seventy is what we calculated," Mom said. "Not including tonight."

Lilly and I both gasped. Merri did too, but was quicker to make it into words. "See? I was right, I didn't do it. This was all Rory." She turned to me. "But, why?"

"Because obviously I was too stupid to realize people would notice," I mumbled.

"It's your money," Mom said. "Why wouldn't you keep it?"

Lilly got it. I could see the dots connecting on her face, which was a map of sympathy and concern. She scooted her chair closer.

"Because you guys need it. You keep saying everything is expensive and I thought . . ." I swallowed and added, "I don't deserve to be at Hero High. I'm not smart enough and you guys shouldn't be stuck paying for me to flunk out."

Dad turned to Mom. Both of them were horror-struck. "Where do we even start with that?"

Mom swallowed and fanned her eyes, trying not to cry. "With the facts— Rory, you're not even close to flunking out. Yes, you struggled with math in the beginning, but your average is currently six-tenths away from a B-minus. And all your other grades are Cs or higher."

"Wait." I felt like someone had punched me in the stomach. "How do you know all that?"

"Parent Portal," Dad said. "While we wish you'd come to us with your math troubles, we watched you handle it—we've seen how hard you're working with Toby. We're proud of all the effort you're putting in. That's worth more than all the As in the world."

My middle sister squirmed in her seat, probably horrified that they'd implied all *her* As were not as impressive, but for once she remained silent. She'd grabbed another bill's envelope and was scratching a column of numbers on it.

"As for the other thing." Mom sighed. "There's nothing we'd rather spend our money on than your education." She paused to kiss Merri and me on our heads. "And your happiness." Then she blew a kiss to Lilly.

"Someday when we're old and drooling, you'll pay us back by wiping our chins," Dad joked, but there was a layer of hurt there and his forced laugh faded into a sniff. "I wish we could give you girls everything you've dreamed of: dream schools, dream cars, dream weddings."

"But what we *can* do," Mom added, "is return the money. This is *yours*, Rory." She slid a fat envelope across the table to me. "Put it in the bank."

"And on that note, we're off to bed." Dad stood and kissed each of our foreheads. "Sleep sweet, little dreamer" (Merri), "Sweet dreams, sweet girl" (Lilly), "Dream big, little one" (me).

They headed out of the kitchen and my sisters turned to me as soon as the stair light was switched off. "So?" Merri said. "Are you going to New York?"

I spun the envelope with one finger. "I had no idea I'd made that much money . . . but it's still not enough."

"But it's seven hundred and seventy dollars," Merri said. "The cost is now too much minus seven hundred and seventy dollars—plus what you made tonight. Let us pay the rest."

"You've got books and stuff to buy, and, Lilly, your dream wedding . . . I know there's got to be things you're paying for out of pocket."

Lilly laughed. "My dream wedding would be New Year's Eve: new year, new beginning."

"Same guy?" Merri joked, and Lilly glowered at her.

"Let us do this," said Merri. "I can get books from the library or Hannah."

"And you're doing my makeup for all wedding events," said Lilly. "I was going to pay the makeup artist some ridiculous amount. You'll make me look twice as good."

"Guys . . ." My voice trailed off. "I can't." Lilly was one thing, because she was months away from marrying a gazillionaire; but Merri . . . I'd spent so long resenting her for Toby's sake when she didn't do anything but exist and be lovable.

"You're my sister," she said. "I love you. This is your dream. And I'm going to support it today and tomorrow and five years from now. If I need to empty my bank account to buy a painting at your first gallery display, I will. Because I know I won't be able to afford one at your second."

We laughed and sniffed. Merri took one of my hands in both of hers. Lilly did the same. Merri leaned close. "I don't know why you thought we wouldn't do this—and right now I'm not going to tell you how much that hurts my feelings— but I'm Team Rory. Always. You don't have to ask for my help. You get it by default."

I started to cry. Not the silent tears that were already slipping down my cheeks; those didn't count. These were messy gulping sobs that made my nose as wet as my eyes and had both of my sisters thrusting tissues my way before they gathered me in a group hug.

"Just paint me a picture for Trent's and my new apartment when you're in New York and we'll call it even," said Lilly.

"Actually . . ." I cut off a sniff and disentangled myself. "I can give you that right now. Hang on—" I darted up the stairs to get the watercolor drying on my easel. It was the sketch I'd started in the store last month—Lilly and Trent on a bounce house wearing smiles and wedding apparel. The soft colors of the paint gave it just the right glow, and it radiated with the happiness I wanted for her on her wedding day. I held it carefully facing my chest as I went back down to the kitchen. "I was going to save this for Christmas, but it's done now and . . ." I trailed off and flipped it around, wanting to die in the seconds before she reacted, because my heart was on the page along with my wishes for her future.

"Rory . . ." Lilly raised her hand to her mouth, her fingers trembling as she bit down on a knuckle.

"You did this?" asked Merri. "I knew you were good, but Rory—that's unbelievable."

Lilly's cheeks were wet again. The soft, graceful tears I never quite managed. "I love it."

"It's how I picture your wedding."

She snorted. "Can you imagine? Half the guest list would . . ." She sighed and traced Trent's face with one finger. "We look so happy. This is beautiful."

Merri looked at the stairs. "You got another one of me and Fielding?" she asked hopefully.

I laughed. "Not yet." Her Christmas present was a painting of Gatsby—the dog, not the stupid book—in a holiday sweater. But maybe I could stick her and Fielding in there too. I'd give them matching sweaters like a cheesy Christmas card. Merri would adore it.

"You'll let us do this?" asked Lilly.

"I'll pay you back," I promised. The truth of it sank in deep. "I—I'm going to New York."

"No." Merri stood up on her chair. "Like this—" She threw her head back and shouted, "I'm going to New York! NYC, prepare for me!"

Before I could copy her, which I was prepared to do, chair climbing and all, the front door opened and Eliza walked in with a quizzical expression and a binder under her arm. "You are? When? You hate the city. Also, you forgot this in my car."

"Not me," Merri clarified, making no move to take the binder Eliza held out or climb down. "Who rocks the art party that rocks the art party? Rory rocks the art party that rocks the art party."

Eliza nodded like this made sense while Lilly and I laughed.

"Well, I guess I should go tell Mom and Dad." I paused in case anyone wanted to offer to do it for me or at least come with me, but all they did was say, "Good luck."

43

On Monday, instead of Convocation, freshmen and sophomores had their last Knight Light meeting of the year. This was one of those things I hadn't written down in last week's Convocation schedule fest and it felt like the icing on a fabulous day. I'd dropped off a check to a very relieved Mrs. Mundhenk that morning. I was *going to New York to study with Snipes.* Every time I thought of it, my lips twisted into a ridiculous smile. One no one else understood, because as Clara informed me, "You've known since last week—why the sudden effervescence *now*?"

I told her a simplified version of the truth. "Because now it's real. I didn't believe it before."

She opened the doors to the Knight Light Lounge. "I'm happy for you."

Huck added, "You're going to teach me everything you learn, right?"

I laughed into a nod. *It was real.* Mom wasn't happy, but she relented; and Dad had muttered, "*Oh, thank God,*" before hugging me. They'd offered to pay for my train ticket, but that was all the money I was accepting from them. And like with Lilly and Merri, I was going to pay it back, even if it took hundreds of dog drawings.

"Hey, Roar, ready to go?" Toby's group merged with mine. "I already got our plans approved."

"Approved?" We were standing beside the blackboard wall and my fingers reached for the chalk. Just a little doodle, a sketch of this group in this moment, because some memories were worth capturing.

"Each Knight Light had to come up with a plan that was adoptee-specific, something we thought you'd like." Toby grinned as he watched the shapes come together beneath my fingers. "Then we had to write them up and get them approved."

Hannah, my sister's Knight Light, added, "It's our big first-half-of-the-year assessment—to prove we actually got to know our adoptees and to justify the mentorship program."

Lance laughed. "That's the official explanation, but I think it's just three days before break and Mr. Welch was too lazy to plan something."

Hannah shrugged. "Either way: Merri, you, me, scavenger hunt in the library."

My sister fist-pumped and followed her out of the room.

I rarely heard Fielding's sister speak, but Sera quietly said to Eliza, "Bio lab," and the two of them peeled off too.

"Yo, Huckleberry—let's roll. We've got a trophy hall to tour. Hannah made us a scavenger hunt . . . It leads to cupcakes. I made those."

Huck rolled his eyes at the nickname but nodded to

Curtis. "I'm down with cupcakes. What are you guys up to? Art room scavenger hunt? That seems to be the theme here."

"No. I'm taking Rory to the lake in the woods. I figured she might want to draw it sometime."

"Really? That's way better than trophies." It was better than anything I could think of—except maybe time to draw the Convocation Hall, but that was filled with upperclassmen.

"It sounds awfully romantic," added Huck, and I glowered as I waited for Toby to scoff or correct him, but he didn't acknowledge Huck at all.

"I've got my coat, let's get yours. It's cold."

I waved a few fingers, avoiding Huck's smug expression and Clara's hearty-eyed hope.

❧

It was close to freezing. Even with my coat zipped to the point where it covered my mouth and I was breathing and speaking through a layer of clammy fleece, I was still shivery.

"This way." Toby turned onto a path I never would've been able to pick out. What distinguished this patch of leaf-covered ground from any other in the forest?

"Is your knee up to this?" I asked.

"It's fine. I'm supposed to be using it more. Are you cold? Was this a bad idea?"

Toby's eyebrows were pulled in, forming a furrow between them that looked like the exclamation point on his concern. "Maybe Huck was right, and I should've done an art room scavenger hunt."

"It's the perfect idea." But my honesty was undermined by my traitorous chattering teeth.

"Come here." Toby reached for my hand and flinched when my fingers brushed his palm before interlacing them with his own. "Cripes."

I sighed, because nothing had ever felt more perfect in the history of perfection than his fingers alternating with mine, folding over the back of my hand. His thumb stroking patterns on my skin in ways that made me want to draw the emotions of this moment in dizzy abstract explosions of red and violet and gold—and made me itch to know what it sounded like in his head.

"Your hands are ice. Why didn't you tell me?"

Oh, maybe his "Cripes" wasn't some exclamation of blood-sizzling electric compatibility?

I sighed. "They're not so bad?"

"They're Popsicles." Toby cupped his other hand on top of the one he was cradling and brought the whole knot of fingers up to his mouth. I was too busy trying not to hyperventilate to process what was happening. Warm hands and then warmer breath as he blew on my cupped fingers. Licorice and mint—the Tobiest of combinations. Add in a dash of the earthy smell of the woods, and this was my own personal brand of cologne. My fingers probably smelled of turpentine, or art room soap, or the shea butter I slathered on in the winter. But as he leaned down again and his lips brushed my skin during another exhale, I forgot to be self-conscious, or cold, or anything but radiant.

He switched hands and repeated the process—interlaced

fingers, encircling the other hand, warm breath in puffs over my too-sensitive skin. My own exhales were visible in the air, small gasping clouds betraying how breathless this made me.

"We need to protect these priceless hands," he said while rubbing them. "Think of all the masterpieces contained within these fingers."

I pulled my hands back, tucking them inside my sleeves. I didn't want him thinking about my art—I wanted him thinking about *me*. Stepping around him, I continued across the forest floor in a straight line, which was as close as I could come to following the path. "What about *your* masterpiece-making fingers?" I asked, ducking under a skeletal tree branch. "Will we get to see them on display at the Candlelight Concert Wednesday night? Maybe playing one of your compositions?"

He laughed. "No one wants to hear that. And there are plenty of other students who can hammer out 'Jingle Bells' and 'O Tannenbaum.'"

"*I* want to hear it."

He paused with his hand on a tree branch and looked over his shoulder at me. It was a moment to frame in my memory so later I could draw it and decipher that expression: Wistful? Thoughtful? Confused? He shook his head and lifted the branch. "We're here."

Though the air temperatures argued otherwise, it *was* a sunny day. The proof of that reflected off the surface of the lake like a diamond with a million facets. It was so bright I had to blink before my eyes adjusted and could absorb all the brilliance.

318 | TIFFANY SCHMIDT

I took a few steps out of the woods and onto the rocky shore—the pebbles were smooth and round and slid over each other beneath my feet.

"Is this worth freezing your fingers?" Toby asked. He'd come to stand beside me, propping one foot up on a fallen log, which would've made a great bench if the air was warmer and it was dryer. The moss on top was the perfect cool counterpoint to the textured browns of the fallen leaves and the glistening lake, to the stark lines of the bare trees and the inky wet rocks.

"Shhh," I told Toby, because I was deep in my head, framing pieces and the whole, analyzing how it fit together and the angles and inclusions that would make the best composition.

He laughed as I took out my camera and snapped a few test shots. But the lens couldn't capture the light—not fully. And not the way it felt to stand in this place, alone with Toby and his thoughtfulness and my fingers that still tingled from his touch.

"I thought you'd like—"

"Shhh!"

He laughed louder and took a step back to give me space. I continued to take pictures. My fingers ached for a sketch pad, a notebook, a napkin. Toby walked tightrope-style along the log—not his best idea when he'd just gotten out of the knee brace and the moss looked wet. I skipped a rock to capture the ripples—three hops. Toby took it as a silent challenge and his bounced four. I leveled up at five and pretty soon art and clocks and everything were forgotten as we competed—hip-checking and laughing and interfering in all ways imaginable. It was like the best memories of our shared childhood—only with touches that lingered and sparked in ways I hadn't dreamed of when my ideas of romance started and ended with princess stories. His hand caught my wrist as I'd cocked it back for a throw, pulling me close as his other hand snaked around to pluck the stone from mine. It was practically a hug from behind and when I looked back over my shoulder to see why he hadn't let go once he'd pilfered my rock, his face was *right there.* Kissing close. Eyes serious and dark. His voice gravelly when he whispered, "Roar, I—"

My heart was a hummingbird in my chest and I'd already done this once—misread the signals and head-butted him in the stomach at the concert—so this time I chopped down those delusions before they could take root. Forcing a laugh, I stepped out of his arms. "Rock thief."

Toby looked down at his hand like he'd forgotten what he was holding. And I took the chance to jump piggyback-style on his back. He laughed—laughed harder when I tickled him while he lined up his throw, but he'd gotten six skips anyway. He cheered as he bounced me down the lakeshore before I caught sight of his watch on the wrist clutching my calf.

"Is that the real time?" I gasped. "Tell me you still haven't reset it from daylight savings."

"Why?" Toby tilted his wrist, then almost dropped me. "Mr. Welch is going to kill us! We needed to check in at the end of the day so he knew we didn't skip."

The campus had that haunted empty feeling—the one that occurs two minutes after everyone has scrambled to buses or cars or clubs or practices. An echo of the chaos lingered in the silence. My boots were much louder on the flagstone paths than Toby's loafers and he wasn't breathing as heavily. I wasn't a runner like Eliza or Merri, and weeks in a knee brace hadn't undone Toby's lacrosse conditioning. I prayed I didn't end up in an asthma attack; my lungs and cold air exertion didn't play nicely together.

Mr. Welch was waiting outside the dining hall with his arms crossed over a clipboard. "Tobias, Aurora, it's nice to see you back in one piece. I was about to send out a search party."

There were all sorts of implications in his eyebrows. Ones our appearances supported—being breathless, disheveled. I was red-cheeked and sweaty. Toby had a smear of mud on his coat where my boots linked in piggyback.

"Sorry," said Toby. "We lost track of time."

"It really was the perfect Knight Light plan," I added, hoping it helped. "I'm dying to draw it."

"Good." Mr. Welch narrowed his gaze. "Because I'd like you to turn in a sketch tomorrow to show how your time at the lake inspired you."

We agreed with nods and apologies and made it to his car before we burst into laughter. "I can't believe we were an hour late," I said. "Who would've ever guessed I'd voluntarily spend extra time at school."

"It's easy to lose track of time around you. Roar, these past couple of months, even with lacrosse and everything going on with my dad, and . . ." His voice trailed off and I mentally filled the silence with the name of the girl who slept across the hall from me. "This has been the best fall."

I couldn't reciprocate. It was my fall of failure. Fall-ure?

AutumNAH? It was a fall of teasing myself with what I couldn't have. I ducked my head and changed the subject. "If I have to do a sketch, you should write a song."

He laughed. "Sounds fair. Do you know what you're going to draw?"

You, on the log, arms out like you could fly, grinning like the world loves you most of all. "I'm sure I'll come up with something."

44

While I wanted my birthday forgotten, Merri wanted hers to be a national holiday. It started with the streamers I'd draped outside her doorframe so she could bust through them diva-style. Which meant she woke me up early so I could witness it.

Then Dad made chocolate chip pancakes, topped with whipped cream and ice cream. Toby came over in his pajamas to join in her sugar fest. Merri greeted him with a smile as she squirted chocolate syrup on both plates.

"Watching this is making me queasy," I said, and Toby gave me a chocolate-milk-mustache grin, which shouldn't have looked as attractive as it did. I realized I was glad they worked again—that they'd found a way to still fit and be silly. That maybe part of my objection to being Merri's replacement was that I didn't want her out of his life or him out of hers.

Merri responded with an exaggerated "Mmmmm, yum."

Lilly laughed and crowned her with a tiara headband, which I thought should be banned on all other days, but I wasn't going to be the one to bring it up.

Eliza joined the seven a.m. party with a bag from Donut

Hut and flowers for my parents. "Thank you for creating my favorite human."

"Jelly?" Merri asked, making grabby fingers while Eliza was being crushed in a Mom hug.

"You're going to be sick, but that's your birthday prerogative and we're not driving in my car today, so go ahead." Eliza handed over the bag and joined me by the fruit bowl.

"Candles! Singing!" Mom insisted, so we did—watching as Merri squirmed in her seat trying to think up a wish and the candle dripped onto the cinnamon sugar of her already bitten doughnut. When she blew it out, we scattered. Toby went home to shower and dress. I left to finish my French homework and pack lunch. Dad and Mom and Lilly hopped in their cars, bound for jobs or appointments.

Eliza and the birthday girl stayed put. Their giggles echoed through the house until Toby beeped and it was time to head to our last day of school before winter break.

"Ho! Ho! Ho!" Curtis swooped down on the Audi as soon as doors were opened in the Hero High lot. "Merri Christmas! No one's ever made that joke before, right?"

She laughed and swatted at the tinsel he was sprinkling in her hair, some caught in the points of her tiara. "Never."

"Happy birthday! I figured I'd go the whole *Merri Christmas* angle since we couldn't do *Sweet sixteen and never been kissed.*" He elbowed Fielding, who was leaning in to peck my sister on the cheek. The jostling meant he was almost impaled by her headband, but they laughed.

Eliza cleared her throat.

"Annnd," continued Curtis, "if some people would let me

finish, also because I refuse to participate in a conversation that perpetuates a double standard that tells women their value is based on some purity myth."

Eliza pressed her lips together, but the corner of her mouth twitched.

"But I stopped at Cool Beans. I asked them to make the most sugariffic drink on the menu." He reached behind a bench and pulled out a plastic cup.

"It's pink!" squealed Merri. "And it has sprinkles!"

Eliza and I exchanged gagtastic expressions. As I gave a wave and turned to head toward my own friends, I heard Curtis add, "I also asked for the most boring drink on the menu. They made you a chamomile tea, Eliza."

I bet her mouth corners were twitching as she took the cup. Mine were as Toby caught up with me. "Six hours 'til we're free of this place until next year. You ready?"

I had a history quiz and a painting to complete, but the rest of my classes were in holiday mode—we were watching a movie in French. The movie itself would be in French, but it was still a movie. "Yup," I told him. "Are you?"

"Very."

"I still think you should've played in last night's concert."

"How about this: I'll give you your own private concert when the lake song is done."

I kept my face still, but I'm sure my blush gave away how much I liked the idea. "Concert implies more than one song. Will you play some others?"

"I'll play as long as you want. You can bring your sketch pad over and draw."

I subtly pinched the inside of my arm, because maybe I had a secondhand sugar high from sharing a car with Merri, and these were sucrose delusions. But the pinch hurt, so I shifted my backpack up my shoulder and asked, "When?"

"It'll have to be before you leave for New York and I go see my mom in California. But you're working tomorrow—"

"And Saturday," I added.

He groaned. "And I've got Dad's company Christmas party the night after. What about Christmas Eve? Are you around?"

I nodded. We didn't have big Christmas Eve traditions because it was a hectic day at the store—people buying last-minute gifts. When my parents got home, we read a hasty *The Night Before Christmas*, hung our stockings, and went to bed. "That sounds"—*perfect, too good to be true, dreamy*—"fine."

"Can't wait," he said.

There was just one thing I needed to do before break began. I knocked on Ms. Gregoire's door at the end of the day, opening it when she called out, "Come in."

"Hi." I hovered awkwardly by the doorway, twisting the strap of my backpack. "Um, Merry Christmas . . . I mean, if you celebrate."

She smiled. "Thank you. You as well, if you do." She was sorting papers on her desk into two stacks. "This one stays," she said, pointing to the larger pile. "And this one comes home with me. But it's the fun kind of work—planning curriculums and picking out books."

Speaking of books . . . I took a deep breath and wiped my hands on my sweater. "I also wanted to say thank you. For helping me and the advice and the extra credit. I promise to read *Little Women* over break."

"I hope you do. Sometimes you find what you need waiting next door—"

I choked on air and she paused politely while I coughed and sputtered. "*W-what?* What did you say?"

She smiled that annoying smile people used when they saw more than you wanted them to. "Sometimes you find what you need waiting in the next story. Why, what did you hear?"

I shook my head. "Never mind."

She crossed the room to the window, watering the ivy that grew in pots along the ledge. "I know you're off for some big adventures over break, but the right book can help you stay grounded, keep you connected to home . . . and make things a little easier, or at least a little clearer when those you love disappoint you."

Because that didn't sound ominous at all? My heart sank. So if Merri was right about *Little Women* being some sort of prophecy, my break was going to include being disappointed by someone I loved? Well, maybe then I'd be able to let go of Toby once and for all.

I bit down on my lip and tried not to let the resignation show in my voice. "Have a good break."

"You too, Aurora. And remember . . ." She paused and turned away from the plants, pointing a pale green fingernail in my direction. "Just keep reading. Things *do* work out in the end."

45

Toby was late. I mean, maybe not truly late, since he'd said, "My dad's coming home for Christmas Eve dinner. I'll come get you after we're done eating. I'm guessing seven thirty."

It was seven fifty and the Mays' dining room windows still glowed, which made me hopeful for Toby . . . but impatient for myself. I'd followed Merri's suggestion and hung a stupid ribbon on my door to signal I was open to visitors, but neither she nor Lilly stopped by, so I drifted to her room instead. My feelings felt too close to the surface tonight, like all that effort and anguish had only kept them submerged for so long and they'd drifted back up to seep through my skin.

She was sitting at her desk, typing. Again. This was her new thing—spending quality time with her hands on the keyboard and refusing to answer any questions about the words appearing on the screen. Even my best snooping and eavesdropping hadn't solved the mystery. It had been much easier to sleuth back when her diary was paper and she thought her pillowcase was a super-secret hiding spot.

"You busy?" I asked, my hand still resting on the doorframe after knocking.

Her shoulders twitched with irritation, and she didn't take her eyes off the screen. "Yup."

"Can I help?"

"Only by leaving," she answered. Her voice wasn't hard, just distracted. "I need to finish this before stockings and cookies."

"Oh." I lingered a second or eight to see if she'd change her mind—I was leaving in two days for the rest of Christmas break!—but she shook her head to clear out my interruption and got back to work. I knew I shouldn't be mad; I got the same way when deep in draw mode, but my throat still stung as I left her bedroom and wandered back to mine. I was in the middle of organizing my paintbrushes when I heard Toby's voice in the hall and dropped them all back in the mason jar I used for storage.

I popped out of my room, sketchbook under one arm, pencil case in my hand, and an eager smile pressing up my cheeks. "Ready?"

Toby grinned when he saw me, but my own smile stuttered and disappeared when I noticed what he was carrying: a root beer in one hand, a cream soda in the other. "Sorry, Roar. Soon. Merri needs me first."

"Needs you?" I leaned against the wall and tried to pretend the bottom wasn't dropping out of my stomach.

"It's a writing thing. And since we used to do all that fan fiction together . . ." He shrugged. "I don't know how long it'll take, but I'll come get—"

"Toby!" Merri hollered from her room, and he didn't bother to finish his sentence, just mouthed *Sorry* as he walked past me toward her.

My heart was shredded, my blood replaced with fire. And she—she stood in her doorway smiling at him and me like it was no big deal. Like it was a given they'd blow me off to hang out together. I'd forgotten my role in his life was temporary.

Which was totally fine . . . except that it absolutely wasn't. I was the fool. I was always the fool. The proof of that was written in our history and stamped on my GPA.

Even Alcott had known the truth about little sisters and boys next door. I read about it before dinner: Amy March being left behind while Toby and Merri—Laurie and Jo—went to a play. Was it any wonder I'd thrown the book across the room during that scene? Amy begged to be included and Jo wasn't subtle about not wanting her there. Just like Merri had made it clear I wasn't welcome tonight.

Well, Ms. Gregoire had said those I loved would disappoint me. Was this it? Toby could keep his songs and Merri could keep all her empty claims about wanting to work on our relationship. And I was going to tell them so—I swung Merri's door open without even knocking.

Except her room was empty. Her balcony door was cracked, and from across the narrow strip of lawn separating our houses, I could see the glow of Toby's bedroom.

When we were little, Merri was the one who flopped flat on her stomach in legs-kicking, screaming tantrums. Mom said whenever she did, I'd freeze and shut my eyes—like that would make me disappear. When toddler-me got mad, I held my breath until I turned blue and occasionally passed out. It had terrified my parents, but the pediatrician had told them not to worry—I couldn't actually do any harm that way.

Tonight I wanted to do harm. I wanted to pay them back for the harm they'd done me. And it didn't take a genius like Merri to figure out how—because her computer screen was still glowing. The computer where the project she'd *needed* his help with waited. Clearly it was just an excuse.

I glanced from the laptop to the balcony. The cursor blinked in time with my shallow breathing. It taunted me as words jumped off the screen. What is it about rooftops that make secrets easier to share? My parents had a heart attack the first time they caught Toby and me up . . .

Yup, there was no question—I was reading this. I straddled her chair and scrolled back to the top with impatient fingers. You'd think a girl who's read hundreds of romance novels would recognize love when it showed up in her own life—

My eyes skipped from the balcony to the screen. My lip was firmly between my teeth and I sighed in relief when I read the rest of that sentence—but who would've pictured me with Fielding Williams? Especially after the way we met . . .

I knew both of my sisters were smart, and it seemed like there wasn't anything they couldn't do—but I hadn't expected this. I didn't even like to read, and by the end of the first page I was laughing. By the end of the second I was wishing I'd made popcorn. Ten pages in I realized I'd picked up and drank half the cup of apple cider on Merri's desk, and I hated cider. I almost, *almost* forgot to keep an eye on the balcony door, but years of snooping had made that a habit.

I was on these pages with Lilly, Toby, Monroe, and Eliza. It was amazing to read how she saw us, how much she loved us. Well, not Monroe. She had nothing but loathing for him, and after reading how he'd treated her in this room, I didn't blame her. But mostly the narrative was about Fielding—and it was cheek-heatingly personal.

I glanced at the balcony again and hesitated with my hand above the mouse. Should I walk away? Too much more of this and I'd bet I was at risk for developing a secondhand crush on him. I snorted; who was I kidding? Little sister's prerogative— of course I was going to read it all! And after the way she'd treated me tonight, she deserved it.

"Rory!"

I screamed. A full-on horror-movie noise that made my throat ache. I twirled toward the empty balcony, then screamed again when I felt a tap on my back.

My head swung from my frowning sister to the balcony. "But—you—how?"

"I can use the front door," she answered. "And *what are you doing?*"

We looked at the computer screen and then *both* of us were yelling, because somewhere in my swiveling and screaming, I'd managed to mash my fingers down on a random combination of buttons that had taken Merri's fifty pages and replaced them with waiuhgeoi.

"What did you—"

"I didn't mean—"

I shoved back from the desk to put distance between my hands and their crime and managed to run over Merri's toes with her desk chair. "Oww!" She began to hop on one foot, upending the last inch of cider into my lap. I leaned to avoid it, but her leg was still behind the chair and instead of escaping, I toppled—both of us going down in a heap of shrieks and limbs.

From my vantage point under Merri's arm, I watched Toby appear in the doorway. He took in our flailing panic and Merri's hysterical "You deleted—worked so hard—and gone—"

Without saying a word, he walked over to her desk. He calmly pressed a few buttons and then lifted the laptop to show us the story restored to the screen. "All fixed. Command-Z works wonders."

I blew Merri's hair out of my face and shouldered her leg off my back. She exhaled and went boneless with relief, which did nothing to help me get out from beneath the Rory-chair-Merri pig pile.

"Get off," I insisted.

Merri sat up on my back, but instead of standing, she bounced. "Serves you right for reading my story. Is that what a panic attack feels like? Because you almost—"

"I repeat, Command-Z," interjected Toby. "Undo. Learn it, love it, use it."

"I know what undo is, Mayday," snapped Merri, and he grinned back at her. It was the first time I'd heard that nickname in months, and it burned in my stomach.

"Get. Off." I rolled to my side and shoved her. Glowering at them both.

Toby raised his hands. "I'm guessing there's a Campbell sisters showdown about to happen and that's my cue to leave." He gave a salute from the doorway. "Merry Christmas."

I wanted to yell at him to wait—to remind him we'd had plans. But if he didn't remember, then what was the point?

Merri was still sitting on my legs, poking my side. But there was nothing playful about this tickle fight. Her jaw was locked, her fingers stiff.

I curled into a ball. "No. Stop it. Don't you dare."

"Oh, I dare!" She licked a finger and stuck it in my ear.

I bucked her off and jumped to my feet—holding the chair between us like a shield. "What are you, eight?"

"I don't know," Merri said in her best menacing voice. "What are *you*? Nosy?" Her nose wrinkled. "That didn't come out the way I planned. I can't believe you read that, Rory. It was really personal."

"Yeah, I noticed." Merri really loved Fielding. Her feelings were way deeper than I'd realized, and they'd been there for each other in all sorts of ways I'd never known. But there was one thing that wasn't in those pages at all: any romantic interest in Toby. The fact that he'd blown me off tonight to help her—that was all on him. She hadn't known. I could be angry at myself for hoping or at him for being fickle . . . but it wasn't Merri's fault. I offered her a small grin. "Did Fielding really admit to doing ballet with Sera?"

Merri's eyes lit up. "She put him in costumes! There are pictures. Headmaster Williams showed me when I went to—" She scowled and put her hands on her hips. "Wait. I'm still mad."

"You were sharing it with Toby. I didn't think it was *that* big a deal."

"I asked Toby five questions and then we went next door

because he wanted to tell me . . ." She trailed off, eyes wide as she looked at me. "Anyway, I'm still mad at you."

"Good, because I'm mad at *you*." It was a six-year-old's retort, but that didn't make it any less true. "You kicked me out and then asked Toby for help. I'd already volunteered!"

"Oh, really?" Merri arched an eyebrow. "Because I needed Toby to fact-check the part about the lacrosse game where he got hurt. I wasn't aware you were there or knew anything about lacrosse."

"Oh." I could feel the flush creeping up my neck and into my cheeks. "Sorry I read your story."

Merri tried to maintain her glower, but I watched it slip away. Finally she shrugged. I marveled at her inability to hold a grudge. I would've nursed this for weeks and brought it up for years. She tugged her chair out of my hands and said, "At least you didn't burn it."

"Burn it?" One of these days I was going to make it through a full conversation with my sister without feeling like we spoke different languages. "Yeah, um, I think Mom and Dad would have a problem with me *burning* your laptop."

She just gave me one of those supremely obnoxious smug looks as she sat back down and reached for her headphones. "But seriously, I *do* need to finish this so I can email it to Fielding at midnight. I want it to be his first Christmas present. Why don't you go read more *Little Women*."

46

did as Merri suggested. I figured I owed her for not going nuclear on me. Within ten minutes I understood Merri's book-burning reference and why people hated Amy—because in retaliation for being left home from the theater, she tossed the *only* copy of Jo's manuscript into the fireplace.

I audibly gasped and mouthed the word *No* while shaking my head at Ariel and Klee. Not that I expected them to respond; but seriously, that was unforgivable. My heart pounded like *I* was the one who'd done it, like Toby hadn't been able to restore Merri's story with a few simple keystrokes. Yeah, I guess if Merri was looking at it from that perspective, my snooping didn't seem so bad.

I curled an arm around a pillow and kept reading. How would Amy and Jo move on from this? Because, also unlike Merri, Jo was a grudge holder. I snorted when I read the answer—Amy just had to *almost die* in another Laurie-Jo exclusion mess. Well, that settled that—I was never going ice-skating with Merri and Toby.

Which is how I greeted Merri when my parents got home and we went down to hang stockings. "By the way, I'm never going ice-skating with you."

She clapped and beamed. "See what I mean about Ms. Gregoire? It's magic—you have *got* to keep reading."

I wasn't sure I agreed about the magic part, but I did about the reading. Luckily our Christmas Eve traditions were quick—and they hadn't changed since we were small. We hung the stockings, in order of age, from the mantle. I put out a plate of cookies for Santa and and a carrot for the reindeer. Merri wrote a letter about how we'd all been "good." Lilly read *The Night Before Christmas* aloud. Our parents took pictures, then shooed us all upstairs so they could go into present-wrapping mode.

Lilly paused at the top of the landing. "I'm going to watch a movie—anyone want to join me?"

"Can't," said Merri. "I'm almost done with Fielding's Christmas present, and I need to finish."

"Sorry," I said. "I need to get back to my book."

"You mean *sketch*?" said Lilly, and when I shook my head, she gaped. "What book?"

"It's her Gregoire assignment!" Merri bounced. "See, she's so magic she's got Rory reading on purpose."

"I don't think it's possible to read by accident," I countered, rolling my eyes.

"I still need to get Trent to tell me *his* Gregoire book," Merri mused.

Lilly blushed and turned toward her room. "If you finish early, come join me and *Elf*."

Merri and I exchanged glances. We might have to tag team Trent tomorrow.

Trenton Rhodes had an impressive poker face. Merri had spent the whole morning suggesting books at him and he had not so much as twitched an eyebrow. That was the deal he had made when he arrived to accompany us to church—that if Merri guessed the book Ms. Gregoire had assigned him back in his Hero High days, he would confirm it.

"Anything by Shakespeare?" I asked when Merri paused to sip cocoa.

Trent wagged a finger and laughed. "That's cheating, Aurora."

"*Othello*, *Julius Caesar*, *Macbeth*, *Hamlet*," rattled off Merri after she'd swallowed.

"Those are all tragedies." Trent laughed. "Is that how you picture my relationship with Lilly?"

"Don't answer that," interjected my oldest sister. "And get your coats on, or we'll be late. I do not want to have to stand."

Trent had driven a fancy two-seater to our house that morning. Merri swore he'd done it on purpose, even after I pointed out he hadn't known he'd be facing a literary inquisition. She just huffed and googled lists of books on her phone. During the turn-and-greet-each-other portion, I heard her whisper (in her whisper-fail voice), "Dante's *Inferno*, *Frankenstein*, *Lord of the Flies*, *Dracula*, *Antigone*."

He laughed and shook both his head and her hand. When it was my turn, I said, "Merry Christmas?"

He gave me a hug. "You get as many law school sweatshirts as you want."

Halfway through brunch, Mom shut her down. "Enough, Merrilee. Some of us would enjoy a conversation that doesn't sound like a library list."

During presents when Trent pulled out gorgeously wrapped packages from his family, Merri inspected hers. "If they're books, are they *the* book?"

Trent shrugged. "I had nothing to do with the purchasing of these gifts. I'm just the messenger."

Merri's were autobiographies by politicians. Included was an early copy of the senator's upcoming book. I'm not sure what was written inside the cover, but it made Merri's eyes well and she threw her arms around a very startled Trent. "That hug's for your mom. You just get to pass it along."

My present was a truly amazing pair of boots. The note read:

Merry Christmas, Aurora!

Every New Yorker needs a fabulous pair of black shoes. We know you're going to take the city by storm. And if you need anything, call Senator Delgado. I've passed along your name and enclosed his number below. Have fun, be safe.

The postscript below Senator Rhodes's signature took my breath away.

Let's talk about me commissioning a piece of art for my D.C. office when you get home—your painting of Lillian and Trenton was exquisite.

I folded the note and stuck it in the left boot. I'd have to rearrange the contents of my suitcase to make them fit, because there was no way I was leaving them behind—not with how Merri was already eyeing them.

When Lilly and Trent left to go have dinner with his parents, Merri pulled out her phone. Dad held out his hand. "You are not text-hassling them."

She sighed and put it away. "How are we supposed to have board game night if Lilly isn't even here?" Her protests were cut off by her pocket starting to ring. She beamed at the screen, so I knew it was Fielding even before she answered with "Did you read it? And Merry Christmas. Now tell me what you think!" while slipping up the stairs to her room.

"And then there was one," said Mom, smiling at me. "I can't believe you're leaving tomorrow for a whole week."

I gave her a weak smile and began to collect the scattered wrapping paper and ribbons. The closer we got to the trip, the more nervous I was. What if the other artists didn't like me? What if Andrea Snipes didn't? "I should probably finish packing."

Dad took the pile of paper from my hands and kissed my head. He went to stand by Mom, slipping an arm around her waist. "And then there were none."

47

'd lied to my parents. I was packed. The only things I needed
to add to my duffel bag were my new boots and a toothbrush. But I didn't want to be the only one downstairs while
Merri and Lilly were off being in love.

Some Christmases Toby stopped by. When we were little,
it was so he could show off new toys. He and Merri would
race remote-control cars around the family room or he and
I would play new board games at the table. This year I knew
he wouldn't. Or if he did, it wouldn't be a good thing. Major
May had invited his girlfriend to join them for dinner. I'd been
shooting glances at his house all day. Right now, I turned to
my fishbowl and addressed Klee Five and Ariel Eight. "Do you
think introductions are going well? I mean, how could anyone
not love Toby?"

I'd certainly tried, and I'd failed miserably. I took out my
phone half a dozen times to text him for an update, but he'd
picked Merri last night. I didn't know what he'd brought her
over to his room to talk about—some reprisal of his earlier
declaration? It clearly hadn't worked, since Merri was currently gushing to Fielding.

My fish blew bubbles in response and I sighed and flopped onto my bed, landing on the hard corners of the book I'd fallen asleep reading last night. I flipped it open.

Beth falls ill with scarlet fever and Amy is sent away. Laurie is the one who comes to visit Amy every day when she's scared and lonely. But his chapters with her are boring compared to his chapters with Jo. With Jo, he's pranks and scamps and mischief. With Amy, he tries not to laugh at her and falls asleep.

I tried to steer my thoughts differently, but my eyes watered and my throat itched. Merri was rooftops and balconies and dressing up for movie nights. I was front doors and tutoring and talking.

I read until it was Christmas again—in the book. In real life it was only eight o'clock. Dad was probably making a leftovers sandwich, and since I hadn't heard her bedroom door open, Merri was probably tethered to the wall, charging her phone while continuing her conversation. I kept reading until the end of the first volume. The last scene was supposed to be one that made the reader sigh with contentment and feel like things had been wrapped up neatly, happily. It made me grit my teeth and grab a sketch pad.

I drew the scene as described, Mr. and Mrs. March coupled up, happy he's home from war. Meg and Laurie's tutor, John, newly engaged and all shy smiles. Beth, who'd sorta recovered from being sick, lying on the couch and talking with Laurie's curmudgeonly grandfather. Jo sitting in a chair with Laurie leaning on the back as the two of them chatted.

Amy . . . she was by herself. The *only* character in the scene who was flying solo. But she—like me—had her sketch pad for company, and I guess that was supposed to be good enough.

I smudged in shadows between the family and Amy, creating an actual dark barrier that separated her from their domestic bliss. Dramatic? Sure. But it was how I was responding, and Ms. Gregoire had asked for response art. I snapped a picture and attached it to an email, typing up the requisite paragraph with hasty fingers: Amy's sent away while Beth's near dying and the only one who seems to care is Laurie. But his compassion feels like pity, the sort of pity you give the neighborhood kid who has no friends so you stop and listen to his stupid knock-knock jokes or watch his stupid magic tricks, when all you want to do is leave.

I knew I needed a final beat of personal reaction—something that aligned my own feelings with those of a character. But they were knotted so tightly in my chest that if I exposed them on paper, it felt like I'd bleed to death from vulnerability.

I hit send and turned the page.

Three years could skip in an instant in a book; I wished the same were true in real life. If so, I'd almost be done with high school. Lilly would be past her wedding panic and finishing up law school. And Merri and Toby—I didn't know where they'd be for college or in their friendship, but it wouldn't be in front of my face anymore.

The three years in the book weren't as satisfying as I'd hoped. Laurie tells Jo she'll be the next one married and agrees with his grandfather that he should marry one of the March sisters. Then he goes off to school. Amy tries different types of art and fails—I'm sure it was supposed to be comic relief, but it didn't feel funny the night before I left on my own art adventure.

Clara called from her dad's as I reached chapter twenty-nine—we were opposites this week. She was leaving the city as I was arriving. Her voice was a much-needed break from Alcott's, her words an even more needed pep talk.

"All I ask is that you don't let some fancy New York art school recruit you. I mean, if it's truly better for you in the long run, I'll act selfless and say I'm happy for you, but I need you at Hero High. Who else is going to doodle on my notes or laugh at my jokes? Because I know I'm not funny."

"I'm not going anywhere," I said. "I promise."

"So I can throw away these New York school brochures I've been collecting?"

"Yes!" I laughed. "I'm staying at Hero High." The statement didn't make my stomach turn like it once would've.

"Good!" She exhaled loudly. "Then I should get back to my dad. Have a fun week. We'll talk soon."

I went downstairs to say my good nights before I climbed back in bed and reopened the book. I cringed as Amy experienced her own version of *Isn't that your sister?* when she and Jo went on social calls. Clearly Alcott wanted the reader to sympathize with Jo for rejecting superficial social rules, but my heart went out to Amy, because Jo doing her own thing was humiliating to her sister. One good thing did come of it though—Jo's careless remarks to her aunts meant they picked Amy to accompany them to Europe . . . where she'd get to study art. I glanced at my own bags stacked by the door and at the time stamp on my phone. Which was more important—sleep or a heads-up on Amy's adventures?

I fell asleep on the book as Amy hugged Laurie. He is the one who lingers longest at goodbyes and he promises he'll come to her if anything bad happens. In my dreams, it was Toby and my dad waving goodbye, not Laurie and Mr. March. They were standing at a train station, not a boat dock, and I waved out the window feeling an oil-and-vinegar mixture of love and apprehension. It was the type of dream that clung like a memory when I woke the next morning. I'd planned to leave the book behind, but I shoved it in my bag instead.

48

rode in Toby's car every school day morning, but on December 26, we weren't driving to Hero High, so I felt awkward perched on his leather seat. And I sounded like someone's stiff great aunt when I asked, "How was your Christmas?"

"Fine. Dad's girlfriend, Monica, is actually pretty cool. She's funny. I don't think he gets half of her jokes, which I found hilarious. Yours?"

"Fine. Quiet." Which made me nostalgic for those remote-control car days of him being the fourth person jumping around in the wreckage of toy boxes and wrapping paper. "Mom and Dad and everyone missed you. I'm not sure how they roped you into it, but thanks for taking me to the train."

"I volunteered." Toby took a sip from his travel mug. "I figured it was an all-hands-on-deck retail day."

I shook my head. "Only Dad's at the store." He'd kissed me goodbye and reminded me to call or text *at least* four times a day. Mom had given me a written list of rules that made me wonder why she was letting me go if she thought I needed to be reminded: Don't wander off from the group. Don't get in cars with strangers. Don't go down dark alleys. Remember you have asthma; stay away from smokers and subway steam. I wasn't even sure that last one was a thing. I kicked the bag where I'd buried the list. "Lilly has a dress fitting, so Mom and Merri are with her. Then they're going bridesmaids shoe shopping."

Toby frowned. "Without you? Aren't you a bridesmaid?"

"Come on." I slumped down in my seat, angry he was going to make me own this rejection. "You've met my sisters—the fabulous Campbell duo! Are you even surprised?"

"Do they know you're upset?" Toby asked. "Because when you shrug and get snarky, it's hard to tell if you care."

I winced, because that felt a lot like blame and I was sick of being the bad guy in our trio. A week ago we'd been all rah-rah Team Campbell Sisters, but this morning Lilly had said, "Since you hate shopping, I figured I'd save you the ordeal."

But it wasn't an ordeal. I would've wobbled in as many heels as she wanted. Instead I'd said, "Don't do the dyed-to-match thing; it's tacky."

Fine. Toby was right. But if he wanted me to be honest, then I'd start with him. "*You* hurt me. Christmas Eve, when you blew off our plans to do stuff with Merri." I curled my arms around the tote bag in my lap.

He was silent for a block, then two. "Sorry. I thought we'd hang out after. Then the story thing happened—I thought it was better if I got out of the way so you two could fix things."

I sighed. "It probably was." But that didn't change the fact he'd prioritized her over me, or that I was the one whose plans were canceled.

"Have I told you I think this trip is brave?" He changed the topic with a flick of his blinker.

I slumped deeper into my coat, not wanting the focus on me when I was still simmering in so many hurts. "You could do something similar. I'm sure there are composer camps."

He snorted. "Now, where have I heard that before? Let's see . . . your sister."

"No." I kicked at the floor and hardened my voice. "This is *not* the same. Merri bullies and teases you to take your music more seriously. I'm not doing that. There's no point."

"I'm pointless?" He snorted. "Thanks."

"Not what I'm saying. Just—the arts are hard. No one is going to hand you success. If you want it—if you *really* want it and want to work for it—the only thing holding you back is you. I know your dad's not supportive, but he's not actively stopping you. Maybe if you took your music seriously, he would too."

"You think I could?" We'd braked at a stop sign for much longer than two seconds, but I let the moment stretch—his brown eyes searching mine to read the sincerity behind my words.

I turned my whole body toward him. "You have the talent, but do you want to?"

He looked away and began to drive. "I don't know."

I touched his arm, and we both jumped like it was a bee-sting. "That's a good place to start."

Toby cleared his throat. "I'm surprised Huck didn't come along to say goodbye." He addressed his words to the windshield. They felt as icy as the frost at its edges. "Or is he meeting you at the station or something?"

I clicked the top on and off my lip balm. "He's going to New York with his brother later in the week. I'll see him then."

"Oh. Right."

My lip balm slipped from my fingers, but it lived on the floor of his car now, because there was no way I was picking it up until I figured out why Toby's face suddenly looked like he wanted to punch someone. I didn't want to hope. After the Christmas Eve brush-off it would be safer for me to jump from this moving vehicle than it would be for me to allow my heart to lie and say there might be jealous subtext behind his gruffness.

"I know what my mom keeps saying, but Huck and I . . . we're not dating."

"But you could be?"

I shook my head. "It's not like that with us."

He pulled over and slammed the car into park. His eyes blazed, but his voice was gentle. "Like it's not like that with us? We've been 'not like that' for a long time. But . . ."

I prayed for him to finish that sentence, to share whatever was hanging on the end of his sigh. I wanted to tell him the truth, confess all the things I'd refused to put in my *Gatsby* papers and pry out my feelings like splinters that had burrowed so deep beneath my skin.

He studied me with the same intensity as in our childhood staring contests, but the heat behind his eyes felt totally different. My breathing had gone shallow and my mouth dry. A train blasted by, shaking the car and making me jump and realize we were at the station.

"Were you drawing last night?" Toby asked. "You've got a smudge of charcoal—" He didn't point or indicate where on his own head. Instead his fingers traced along my temple and I shut my eyes at the electricity in his touch. His hand danced down my cheekbones, pausing to slide my hair back before gliding his thumb along my jawline. If my breathing was shallow before, it had gone nonexistent now.

I shivered when his left hand joined the right, cupping my face, two thumbs gently lifting my chin, and in the moment before I dared to open my eyes or guess what his expression would be like, his breath ghosted over my lips—followed immediately by the shock of his mouth against mine.

You know those moments in comic books where the heroes first receive their powers and their bodies literally glow from the transformation? I felt like that. Like every cell in my body was waking up in flashes of lightning and glory. My skin sparked where he was touching my cheek, my neck, my shoulder, his fingers caressing my face and sliding into my hair. This was everything I wanted in a kiss. In a guy. And the urge to lean in, to get closer by kneeling on the seat or straddling the center console was overwhelming. My hands itched by my sides, fighting the need to grip his coat, touch his face, grasp his shoulders. But Christmas Eve had confirmed it: I was his second choice. His standby because my sister was taken. My eyes were already filling when I raised my hands—not to pull him closer but to push him away. "Stop!"

"Roar." Toby jerked his hand off my neck immediately and ran it through his hair, looking up at the ceiling instead of at me—but at least he was saying my name, not hers. "I thought—"

"I'm not the one you want to be kissing."

"No." He groaned. "That's not true."

"It *is* true. And it's not fair. I ha-hate that you did that to me." And I hated that my voice had broken and my lip was quivering. "Merri's the one you write songs about."

Toby's brow furrowed. "I have songs about everyone important to me. You have songs, so many."

I wanted to squeak. *Really?* To find the closest church or school or house with a piano and ask him to play them. I wanted to live in the giddy euphoria of that moment. *I. Had. Songs.*

Instead I swallowed and bit the inside of my cheek. Reality-check time. "Yeah, but do my songs make you cry?"

"How do you . . ." He sighed. "Aurora the spy. Never mind."

"I don't want to be anyone's backup plan. Especially not yours. I'm not a replacement sister. I want you to like *me*, not my last name." My mouth was full of sparks, yet I couldn't stop licking at the dynamite. And what was my alternative? Swallow them down to a stomach full of gasoline? Destroy us or destroy myself.

I was choosing to save me.

Toby had one hand fisted in his hair and the other clutching his seat belt like he was physically restraining himself. "Roar—no. I'm . . ." He shook his head. "I'm not sorry. That's not what I'm feeling—but I didn't mean to hurt you, and I'm messing this all up. Let me start over."

"Don't." It was a plea I whispered to my lap as I tightened my hand around the straps of my bag. I didn't want to hear some speech about *You mean so much to me, but I don't want to risk our friendship*, because that was a pretty lie that meant *I don't feel the same way, but I don't want to be the bad guy and tell you the truth.* And pretty lies hurt more, because they were knotted with permission for misplaced hope. "Please, just—don't."

"Roar—" The cracks in his voice could swallow me whole.

"You know my compass points, Toby? The things you told me would always guide me home?"

"Yeah," he said softly, his eyebrows scrunched together in confusion.

"You've always been one of mine." I shoved the car door open, holding up a hand when he moved to follow. "Maybe that's why I've felt so lost."

49

checked the time on my phone—seventy-three more minutes until the train reached New York. Which was about seventy-two more than I could tolerate spending in my head. I'd already gone through half of my tissues and made the inside of my hoodie soggy with tears. I dropped my phone in my bag and fished out *Little Women*. I wanted to distract myself with Amy's art adventures as I prepared for my own.

But what I wasn't prepared for was seeing my heart shredded on the page.

I was sickeningly disappointed with Amy. I didn't want to read pages of her tourist travels. I didn't want her to write her mother and say she'd decided to settle on a courtship with Laurie's friend Fred. It sounded like she was talking herself into it for all the wrong reasons: He's nice, he loves her, his family likes her, she'll be able to provide for her family.

But what about the art? I wanted Amy to burn brightly. I wanted her to forge a path across Europe with her paintbrush and charcoals. I wanted her to erupt with talent and success . . . not settle.

Then Jo went on this epically boring multichapter trip to

New York where she makes friends with a forty-year-old guy, starts writing, stops writing, then goes back home.

And Laurie. He had to go and propose. For once Jo and I were in agreement when she begged him *not* to spill his feelings. I was mouthing the words along with her, *"No, Teddy, please don't."* He didn't listen to either of us but proclaimed his love for Merri—I mean Jo. And he was pulverized by her rejection. I felt like I was back in the hallway outside Toby's bedroom. The white carpet under my knees as he played his broken heart into the melodies he wrote for my sister. Tears were running down my cheeks and I couldn't stop there. I had to keep turning pages.

"Miss?" I looked up from my hoodie cave, raining tissues onto the train floor. The conductor was standing at my row and the seats around me were empty. "We're at Penn Station."

I sniffed and wiped my cheeks. "Oh, thanks."

"Are you okay?"

I nodded and sniffed again, no closer to holding in tears than I was chapters earlier. "It's just—after everything, stupid Beth had to go and say she's dying. I mean, she's obnoxiously saintly and boring, but then she's like, 'I'm sorry, I'm dying,' and I'm a mess, you know?"

He took off his conductor cap and wiped his bald head. "I'm not sure I follow, but sorry for your loss."

"What?" I blinked. "No. Beth . . . It's in a book. She's not a person."

"Ahh." He squinted. "You're one of those brainy types. Maybe join a book club or something."

I snorted as I gathered up my stuff, fishing used tissues

off the floor and shoving them in my pocket. "No one has ever confused me with 'brainy' before. But sorry for being weird and not getting off."

He laughed as he stepped back to let me pass. "Young lady, this is New York. You're not even close to weird. Have a good one."

I stepped off onto the platform. I was supposed to meet two other workshoppers beneath a giant clock in five minutes. I could only hope my face would be less guess-who's-been-crying blotchy by then. And that they were nice, because this was the part I hadn't let myself think about—strangers. I was going to spend the next week surrounded by strangers. And I hated all things new and scary.

50

We came from Iowa and California. Michigan and Maine. One of the Dakotas and both of the Carolinas. Pennsylvania and Oregon. And right in New York. A spectrum of colors, sizes, religions, and genders. If I'd had to describe everyone, I would've said talented and focused first—way down the list of adjectives would be kind. Even Merri at her merriest would've had a hard time turning the other workshoppers into lifelong friends, because—thankfully—we weren't there to socialize and do late-night slumber parties. We were there to draw, paint, create. We were there to learn.

Which isn't to say we didn't hang out or talk. I'd gone to MoMA with the workshoppers I'd met at the train station. There'd been time between when we reached the dorm and the welcome dinner, and when Justin suggested, "Let's go see some art," Trinity and I had been all about agreeing. But we didn't stay glued together in the museum. No one hurried me when I wanted to linger in front of *The Starry Night*, and an hour later I passed Trinity entranced by Lichtenstein's *Drowning Girl*.

When we met out front at five, Justin had already bought a giant street pretzel. He tore it into thirds and we spent the trip back to the dorms in an effortless and overlapping discussion of the exhibits. The conversation at dinner that night was more of the same—us getting loud and louder in a pizza place as we shared favorite artists and techniques. Favorite museums and pieces. We shared the prints we had hung on our bedroom walls, the first time we'd heard of Snipes, and our reactions to being accepted into the workshop.

Marie from Michigan, whose dorm room was next to mine, paused in her doorway to say good night. Her hair was bundled up in a scarf and she was carrying her face wash and toothbrush. "It's a bit like finally finding people who speak your language, isn't it?"

I nodded, emotionally exhausted from the day but eager for tomorrow when we would enter the studio. "Exactly like that."

Call-me-Andrea Snipes had started our workshop by going over her guidelines: We had twenty-four-hour access to the studio—a white-walled space with concrete floors, an army of easels, a storeroom of supplies, long steel sinks, and a wall of windows—but we were not to walk home alone between ten p.m. and five a.m. If we felt inspired to create during those hours, we needed to call the security number and get an escort. She wasn't going to police us, but she recommended that within every twenty-four-hour period we get at least five hours of sleep, drink four noncaffeinated beverages, take three breaks to step outside, and eat two full meals.

Overall, it was a frightening amount of freedom. My parents had pictured something like summer camp, with meal hours, group activities, lights out. I didn't correct them.

Andrea didn't have a set syllabus or preplanned lessons. Instead, she let us shape our own curriculums. Before we put a single mark on our first blank pages, we each had to tell her our goal for the workshop. She jotted each student's down on a bright green sticky note and stuck it at the top of their easel.

"There are no prizes," she proclaimed. "And no penalties. While you're here, your only job is to support and learn from each other. Every one of you has something to contribute to the group. Whether you finish one piece or eight or none at all—my only request is that you respect yourself and your peers."

There was no easel kicking, no nasty glances. I was practically giddy to be in a space where the mutterings were compliments and I didn't have to hide my talent or my voice.

With every rotation around the studio Andrea asked about our progress. "How are you challenging yourself right now?" These conversations led to personalized mini lessons. Tutorials on technique or demonstrations or critiques. It was hard to wait my turn. Hard not to eavesdrop when she was working with the artists on either side of me. And sometimes hard to stop drawing when she reached my easel. We each had a yellow sticky note labeled *Do not disturb* for this purpose. All we had to do was hang it up and she'd skip us on that rotation, but I couldn't convince myself to give up even a second of her instruction.

Those around me set goals like edges, capturing white on white, scumbling.

I chose emotion. A goal that made Andrea smile and ask, "To evoke or to capture your own?"

I scraped at a spot of dried paint on my easel. "Capture my own, but in a way that translates to the viewer. They don't have to experience the same feeling I'm drawing, but I want them to be able to recognize it."

"That's a lofty goal." She considered my paper, where I'd just begun to block out the barest lines of a portrait. "Do you have an emotion in mind?"

"Love," I answered immediately.

She smiled. "Let's see what you do with it."

Andrea arrived each morning by seven thirty. She left by four. I worked so intensely during those hours that when she left, I usually did too. I'd take the stairs down from the studio and try to relax the muscles in my back and wrist, wake up the muscles in my legs by wandering until my head had cleared and my eyes no longer strained for an easel that wasn't in front of me.

The first night, I'd walked to a nearby art supply store and bought two small sketch pads—one a dignified dove gray, the other covered in pink hearts. I stuck them in the tote bag I brought everywhere, pulling them out every so often to complete a quick drawing when something caught my eye. I'd also found some takeout, then headed back to my dorm, where I ate dinner on my bed while calling home. Then I met up with Trinity to practice Andrea's mini lessons so I wouldn't forget a thing.

The second night Justin organized a group dinner. We'd crammed into two tables and it had lasted two hours. The conversation had been witty and arty, but by day three I needed air and space and privacy.

I didn't want to go back to my dorm and stare at those walls. Or my noisy phone with its stacks of unanswered texts. I didn't want to sit around a plate of fries and make small talk. And I definitely needed time away from my easel. I'd spent the day staring at the face I was drawing, and while everyone had complimented the way I'd captured it, it no longer looked familiar—in the way that repeating a word over and over turns the sounds and syllables to gibberish.

I definitely, definitely didn't want to read any more *Little Women*—because what did I do with the fact that Laurie had met up with Amy in Europe? That he found her beautiful and grown-up and yet still the girl he'd known for so long—someone he enjoyed spending time with. And what did any of these facts matter when Amy was still trying to talk herself into marrying his friend Fred and Laurie was still going sad-eyed over even a sketch of Jo?

I'd read that chapter so quickly the night before, I'd had to go back and read it again this morning. I'd skipped the next chapter. It was all old-married-boring-baby stuff with Meg and her husband. Sorry, Lilly—I mentally promised to be more interested when that sort of thing took place in my real sister's life—but anything keeping me from more pages of

Laurie and Amy deserved to be ripped out of the book. And yet, I could've turned into any of the coffee shops or restaurants along the street. I could've found a seat, ordered, and pulled the book out of my bag to find out what happened in the chapter titled "Lazy Laurence."

Instead I kept walking and made a phone call.

"Meet me at the Met?" I asked when he answered.

"Affirmative. I'll be there ASAP." He pronounced it *a-sap*, something I would've given him grief about, but he'd already said, "Huck over and out" and hung up.

51

You too good for me yet?" Huck asked as I strolled around the corner of the museum and into his hug. "I mean, on a scale from stick figures to Singer Sargent, how talented are you now?"

I laughed as we walked up the steps. "You should start trying to steal my homework now, because my signature's going to be worth something someday."

"Is that the new 'My dog ate it'? *Sorry, Mrs. Roberts, I don't have my homework because it was stolen by art fans.* I'd pay money to see you try that." We stopped at the kiosk to buy our tickets and I followed Huck around the crowds and past the gift shops. "Hey, I got something for you," he said as we approached the Medieval Arts exhibits. "Hold out your wrist."

He pushed up my sleeve and knotted on a lumpy string bracelet. "What is that?" I asked, rotating my arm to examine the gaudily bright colors and lopsided braiding.

"It's your friendship bracelet obviously. I promised it to you back in September. I gave you a few months to change your mind, but now you're stuck with me." He grinned and began to wander among the displays. "You're welcome. So, what's the famous Snipes like?"

"She's . . . great." I struggled to figure out how to capture her while standing in a museum that displayed some of her art. "She'd be a horrible substitute teacher. She's too easy to distract and get off topic. All you have to do is ask her a question, and she'll drop everything to answer it. She tells these amazing stories from her gallery shows and museum openings. One time every guest got food poisoning and the writer who was supposed to cover the event was too busy vomiting to meet his deadline. She's got so many stories about patrons of the arts and narrow-minded critics. One guy offered her a million dollars if she'd repaint *Girl, Rising* but make the subject nude—obviously he missed the point. She's told us about pieces she'd loved and then burned because they were too private to exist in this world. And pieces she hates that are hanging in major museums. And she still gets intimidated by every blank canvas. I find that so comforting."

"So I take it you still want to do this?" Huck gestured around us at art that had lasted centuries, telling stories of creators long gone. "Even though you're risking food poisoning and creepy guys and, like, jet lag from all the world traveling you'll be doing for your openings and exhibits?" He dimpled down at me. "And paper cuts. Don't forget the paper cuts."

I inhaled my shoulders up to my ears and exhaled into a smile. "More than ever."

"Then I'll start stealing your homework. Feel free to doodle in the margins."

His belief in me was complete and uncomplicated. It made me want to dance in the aisles or spin through a doorway. I mean, I would never—I'd leave all that to Merri and people who didn't mind being kicked out of museums—but for a second I wanted to. "Argh, it's too bad I don't like-like you."

Huck laughed and bumped his shoulder against mine. "One of the world's greatest tragedies. Why can't we like-like each other?"

"I'm serious. We get along. I'm not nervous around you. We both like art and have the same classes. I could learn to tolerate lacrosse. Maybe you'd try yoga?" I stepped between him and the entrance to the American Art exhibit. "We spend enough time together that we might as well be dating."

Huck's dimples were MIA and his forehead was wrinkled. I'd never seen him serious before and the expression looked odd on him. "Except, I don't like you like that. And you don't . . . Do you?"

"No."

"Good heavens, woman, don't scare me like that." He pulled a hand to his chest and stepped around me, into a small hall of paintings.

"I don't . . . But maybe we could?" This was probably the world's worst idea, stranger than the painting of a boy and his squirrel in front of us, but was it any worse than what Amy March was doing with Fred Vaughn? It would be easier for everyone if I excused myself from the secret love triangle that caused so much Campbell sister tension. If Ms. Gregoire had had a purpose for assigning me *Little Women*, maybe this was it. "I mean, would it be awful?"

"Just to be clear, you want to try dating?" He waved a finger back and forth between us and swallowed. "Each other? And for *real*, not fake?"

"Maybe we'd fall in love later. It happens in, like, fifty percent of Merri's romance novels." When Huck continued to stare at me with his mouth open, I mumbled, "It's stupid, forget it."

"Not that you've read them, because you hate books," he reminded me as he pinched his arm and mine too. When I smacked his hand, he said, "Hey there, I guess we're not dreaming, but I'm breaking up with you if you get abusive."

I gave a thin laugh. "Shut up."

"If you really want, I guess we can . . ." He gave me a grave nod. "We should at least try, right?" He pointed to the golden eagle clutching a ball that hung above our heads. "Pretend that's mistletoe." He took a step closer to me, and I copied the movement. When he reached for my cheek, I reached for his. It was like a mirrored game of Twister. Left hand shoulder, right hand cheek.

If only he weren't so stupidly tall. Him bending down so his mouth was in range of mine took a lifetime and I couldn't decide if I was supposed to shut my eyes or keep them open. Instead I blinked a lot, giving his movements a strobe effect. When his lips neared mine, they paused and the corners flicked upward. Mine did too and the air rushed out of my stomach in a giggle. One he matched and escalated until everyone around us had turned to look.

"Well, it was worth a try," I said, wiping laugh-tears from my eyes.

"You have very bad ideas. Remind me not to listen to you anymore." He bumped his shoulder against mine and kept bumping it, steering us into the small coffee shop that looked out over Central Park. It was my job to hold down the table while he came back with coffee (him) and tea (me). Once we were both seated, he flattened his palms on the table. "Now spill, Clementine. What was that about? You don't want to kiss me any more than I want to kiss you."

So I spilled. First I spilled a pile of sugar from a packet onto the tabletop, so I could use my finger to draw in it like a Zen garden. Then I spilled the truth—the feelings about Toby I'd suppressed, the kiss I'd rejected . . . and all the texts he'd been pouring into my phone since the train station that I'd been ignoring. Something else spilled too, hot and wet down my cheek. Huck stood. My breath caught because he picked up his coat and scarf from the bench beside me and I thought he was leaving. Fed up and over it.

Instead he tossed them onto the table and took the seat beside me, putting his arm around my shoulder. I blinked up at him through swollen, wet eyes.

"What?" he asked, one dimple flickering in his cheek. "Did you think you had to do this alone or something? I'm hurt, Campbell. Now give me your phone. I want to see these texts before we make a plan."

52

You busy?

I stared at the words on my phone screen. They'd arrived hours ago. Right after Huck had hugged me goodbye to meet up with his brother and head back home. It was Toby's latest attempt at getting me to respond—and he deserved a reply. Part of me wanted to play it cool and act like I had plans. But I'd never pretended to be cool before, and if I'd wanted plans, I would've joined the group going to the Empire State Building. Or headed back to the studio with Marie and Trinity. With Toby I wanted to be me. Even if that wasn't someone he was interested in as more than a friend. Even if we had to have an uncomfortable conversation about that kiss and agree to put it behind us.

The plan Huck had proposed was simple. "You take a deep breath," he instructed me, "and then ask yourself, *What does Rory want to do?* That's it. No more pretending or protecting other people. Ask yourself what you want, and do it."

What did I want? I wanted to talk to him.

I keyed in **Nope.**

I saw your iLive post at the Met with Huck. Have fun?

What did I want? To shut down any further conversation

about *Hury* or *Rock*—since that was clearly never happening. Yeah. He's a good friend.

This time Toby's pause was longer. Long enough that I brushed my teeth and washed my face before he replied with an unsatisfying **Good.**

I changed the subject: **How's CA? Tell your mom I say hi.**

The weather is great. We've talked about you a lot, actually. She'd say hi back. My stomach somersaulted with those words—if he enjoyed California too much, would he want to stay? And would it be selfish of me to not want him to? I gritted my teeth, then switched out of that messenger window and into the group family text. I hadn't sent a picture in a few hours and they'd be getting anxious. *Proof of life* my parents called them—demanding I send visual evidence that I was still alive and intact several times a day. I posed in front of statues and my dorm and with my easel. They each responded to every post—so after making a goofy face beside my bed, I had to wait for four different versions of **Sweet dreams, Good night, 'Nite, and Dream big, little one** before I tapped back over to Toby and said, **Have you tried the knee out on any beach runs?**

A short one. Sand running is no joke.

I took my phone with me to bed, plugging it in and setting my alarm, then trying to find a comfortable position where it could charge and I could type. Toby and I went back and forth. Back and forth. Until I forgot to be uncomfortable and slid back into our familiar patterns. He'd typed **I should let you get some sleep** at least five times. Each time I agreed, but then one of us asked another question and we'd begin a new conversation. I fell asleep in the middle of one and awoke to Toby's messages stacked like a tower of tippy blocks.

It was strange not having you next door. I didn't like it.

Is that weird to say?

It's stranger having you across the country.

Did you fall asleep?

Roar?

Roar?

Sweet dreams.

Also—good morning (for when you wake up).

When Merri—Miss Imagination, Nightmare Queen—was little, Dad used to say, "Everything looks different in the dark, but all you need to do is turn on the light."

Everything looked different post-kiss, but I wasn't sure I was ready for it to be illuminated. Sure, it was terrifying living in a place of limbo and expectation, of uselessly telling my heart not to grow more hopeful with every beat and text.

But.

I didn't want to ask. I didn't want to know if he regretted it. And maybe I didn't need to ask, because his texts didn't stop. He didn't seem to mind if it was hours before I responded. Like prayers, they became a part of my pre-meal and pre-bedtime routines.

Ran on the beach at sunrise today—thanks, jet lag. Thought about how you'd draw it. I tried to take a picture, but it didn't do it justice.

There are so many vegan restaurants in CA. Bet they're not as good as our Mockingburger . . .

When Marie dragged me to the famous wax museum after a day of drawing—"They're sculptures . . . that's art"—I sent him a selfie captioned Look who I met. Marie laughed at my poses and continued her running commentary of trying to decipher *why* some of the figures just didn't look right. "His jaw is too wide. Look at this picture—do you see it?"

I'd added a second figure to my drawing today and had spent eight hours staring at photos and trying to replicate features. The last thing I wanted to do was more of that.

Wait. Isn't that—you met Meghan Markle????

Instead of answering, I sent him another picture.

And the Pope?

I giggled and sent him one more, with the message: Thanks for the math help, but I've found a new tutor.

Einstein?

Oh, you're at that museum. I was so confused. I hate you.

Marie was laughing at my giggles as she analyzed the ratios of another statue, holding up her brown hands with ink-stained nails to form a frame as she deconstructed the pieces. I bit down on my lip and responded No you don't.

His response was instantaneous and settled like a glow beneath my ribs. No, you're right. I absolutely don't.

I slid my phone back in my pocket. Each text was like being blindfolded and spun around before a game of pin the tail on the donkey. It was disorientation. Vertigo. It was that feeling you get when walking upstairs in the dark and you expect there to be one more step. You're thrown off balance and feel like you're going to fall. It's only inches—seconds—before your foot finds the floor, but it lasts forever, long enough for your lungs to flatten and your heart to pound.

370 | TIFFANY SCHMIDT

My phone buzzed one more time: *It's strange to be around someone else all the time. I'm used to being mostly with you.*

I needed some time to think of a reply to that one—so I turned to Marie instead. She was twirling the end of one of her braids while she tilted her head and frowned at a blond statue. I cleared my throat. "My stomach is about fifteen minutes from some monster-style growling. If I promise to do five full-attention critiques with you, can we go get some food?"

She grinned. "Sure. I already know which to start with— can you figure out why this looks nothing like Jennifer Aniston?"

Marie had been so right that first night when she'd said being here was like finally finding people who spoke your language. Maybe things at Hero High would never be this easy, but knowing there were others like me out there gave me hope.

53

f math worked the way I wanted it to, I'd be able to hoard my bored and lonely hours—the ones where I couldn't sleep or that I spent waiting in checkout lines, or for my turn in the shower—and smush them onto days when I wanted time to slow down. My last day of workshop had raced toward me like a sunrise, at first seeming like it was far away, then peeking over the horizon, then all of a sudden it was here.

And among the good-morning texts on my phone was the latest from Toby: I head home tomorrow and it's strange how relieved I am. You still won't be back from New York, but at least I'll be closer.

I didn't know how to respond. But, yeah, I was relieved he'd be back on the East Coast too. Having an entire continent between us unsettled me in ways I didn't know how to express. I typed, deleted. Typed, deleted. I put my phone away and set up my easel, rotating it to catch the morning light and prepping for my last full day of work. I needed my head to be in the game. I needed to soak up every speck of Andrea's advice and memorize every nuance of her feedback.

I'd made so much progress this week. My hands no longer shook when Andrea stood behind my shoulder. I no longer held my breath while she spoke—even though I still couldn't accept her compliments or critique without turning bright red. I'd even managed to ask questions without stumbling over my words.

"The way you've framed this scene—it's exquisite," she'd said, pointing to the easel in front of me. I was one of those who'd worked on a single piece all week. With just hours remaining until our last night of the workshop, I was *almost* finished. I'd put the watercolors to the side and was going back in with ink to pull out some of the finer details.

Andrea tapped on the sticky note where she'd written my goal. "The energy and emotionality of this piece radiate off the paper—it would be impossible to look at this painting and *not* experience the love there. Take a step back and take it in—how do you feel about how this has turned out?"

I obeyed, setting down my pen and joining her six, then eight feet back from my easel where it was easier to observe the piece as a whole, instead of fixating on the parts. There were two photographs clipped to the corners of my easel, but I'd played with the angles and spacing and combined them into a single composition. I was at the center—a spot I was learning I was allowed to occupy—and my sisters were on either side of me. I was seated on a stack of dog beds, leaning back against the checkout counter, my head tilted up, a sketch pad in my lap. Lilly was on my left, looking back over her shoulder with a smile while her hands were busy stocking the shelf in front of her from a half-full box of dog food cans at her feet. Merri was to my right, holding court from her seat on the checkout counter, leaning forward to peek over my shoulder at the drawing in my lap, her hands gesturing, her crossed ankles swinging.

Andrea squeezed my shoulder. "Do you see it?"

I nodded, because it was true. There was love in each one of the lines on that page. These were my sisters, and no one was more important to me. I might need to join Merri in boycotting Lilly's faraway law school choices, because even going this whole week without them had felt too long.

"This is quite well done," said Andrea. "Where do you go to school again?"

"Hero High—Reginald Hero Prep." There was a middle initial too, but it had disappeared from my head in the vacuum created by her praise.

"I want you to stay in touch," she insisted. "I've got your contact information on your application, but if I don't reach out within the next week, you should email me." She placed a business card on my easel. "Don't lose that."

I nodded and immediately thought of how Merri *would* lose it—then end up on some rom-com adventure to find it or get her mentor's contact information in some other roundabout way. I took out my phone to take a picture of the card, just in case. But the screen looked blurry through my welling eyes. I missed my sisters.

Andrea had turned to the next workshopper, and I was going to be useless at my easel right then, so I wiped at my eyes and went outside. I bypassed all the other texts in my inbox and pulled up a new blank message. I knew Merri had plans with Fielding today—a fencing tournament—but I also knew that her attention span wasn't that great. After ten minutes of watching people in suits jump around with swords and buzzers, she'd be thrilled for the distraction. Especially if I mentioned the one thing she wouldn't be able to resist: books.

Is it just me, or is Professor Bhaer stodgy & boring?

I clapped when the three dots appeared on the screen almost instantly. There was such satisfaction in knowing I *knew* my sister.

It's not just you. Everyone thinks that. Literally everyone.

I laughed out loud and contemplated whether I should tell her I'd been mentally inserting her and Fielding into the spots of Jo and the professor. Better not. But *come on*, Fielding was a bit stodgy—granted he wasn't old or fatherly; he was illegally hot and played with swords—but still, he did stodgy. I'd even looked the word up to confirm the meaning.

Good to know I'm not alone.

But are you FINISHED YET????

I laughed at her shouty capitals. Imagining her mouthing the words aloud while sitting between Fielding's sister, Sera, and his father. At least Headmaster Williams couldn't be too miffed that she was texting to encourage her younger sister to complete school assignments.

Almost. I've got to get back to work. Talk soon.

Because I'd be home soon. Tomorrow. And then Merri, Lilly, and I would spend New Year's Eve like we always did, in pajamas with tubs of ice cream (nondairy for me), playing board games until it was the New Year. This time I'd call them out on inside jokes. This time I'd work to create some of my own. And when it was time for team games, I wouldn't preemptively choose Mom or Dad or volunteer to be scorekeeper—just to avoid *not* being picked by either of them. Besides, now that Trent was pretty much permanent, that evened things out.

Hurry! Merri had texted. I want to hear your thoughts on the ending. Gregoire's a genius book-life puppet master, right?

I didn't know whether to scoff, laugh, roll my eyes, or agree. I'd gotten way more out of the book than I'd intended. Though last night's chapters . . . they were the sort that made me want to blow out my breath slowly and reread to make sure I wasn't miscomprehending. First, Amy goes A-plus lecture mode about whether Laurie intends to make something of himself, sorta how I talked to Toby about his music on the way to the train station. He listens and leaves and all I wanted to do was skim the pages until he reappeared. Sure, Beth *died* in the intervening chapter, but there'd been such a long buildup to that moment, it was almost a relief to be like *Okay, I'm going to cry for this event—one last time—and then we can finally move on*. But Laurie . . . he falls *out* of love with Jo. I read those pages with my mouth hanging open.

And I bet, unlike my unromantic encounter with Huck, Amy and Fred Vaughn were not going to be buddies after she turned down his proposal. But whatever, Amy's too busy to care because she's being pen pals with Laurie. Much like my own endless back-and-forths with Toby. If Amy had had texting, she totally would've been all over it.

And then Laurie comes to her! Even standing on a slushy street corner replaying it in my mind made me beam—which earned me a creepy wink from a guy passing by. Ew. As soon as Laurie hears about Beth's death, he comes to Amy in

Switzerland. My heart was beating so hard my chest ached when I turned that page. I'd kept looking from my book to the door, like somehow Laurie's declaration of love and his proposal meant my own were about to happen.

But I was a modern girl—I had texts and all sorts of feminist progress on my side. Maybe I'd be the one doing the declaring? Maybe. Someday, way in the distant future.

But first—boats! Why was it that both Nick Carraway and Laurie were into the whole boat thing? Unlike Fitzgerald and his bummer ending, the boat Laurie asks Amy to help him row is uplifting. They were going forward—together—not *endlessly beating against the past* or whatever. Laurie wasn't going to win any Most Romantic Proposal awards with "I wish we might always pull in the same boat. Will you, Amy?"—but maybe he didn't need to. They knew each other; they trusted their love. The idea of something big and flashy for them repelled me as much as the idea of anything big and flashy for myself.

I turned to reenter the studio, but my phone buzzed in my hands.

I miss you. Toby's three-word text worked better than any pair of gloves for heating up my frozen fingers.

I'd been averaging hours to respond, so it was perfectly safe to do what I'd been doing for days: typing up my truth, then deleting it. Ms. Gregoire would be so proud—not necessarily about the deleting part—but that I was taking her advice and writing my feelings. It was a real-time response journal to my life. Only, with no actual record, unless Huck was right and the government really was monitoring our phones and everything we did on them.

I miss the way we used to be when all my energy didn't go into not wanting you.

A group of schoolboys playing tag shoved their way down the sidewalk, jostling me as they made a last-minute maneuver to avoid an oncoming stroller. My hand slipped on my phone, almost dropping it onto the slush-covered sidewalk. But when I looked at the screen I realized that might have been the better outcome.

I'd hit send.

54

didn't have time for a proper meltdown. Not with a painting to finish, goodbyes to say, and a dorm room to pack before we had to be out by eleven the next morning.

I took a deep breath and curbed my impulse to chuck my phone down the nearest sewer. Instead I powered it down and shoved it deep in my pocket. I was not going to think about that. Not at all. Cell phones? What were those? Never heard of them. Maybe Amy had had the better end of the deal with her pen pal letters.

Frenetic energy thrummed through my fingers, anxiety spiked through my blood—I had better uses for it than pacing the sidewalk. Taking one more deep breath, I turned and headed back inside. There were only four hours left of workshop time, and I wanted to make the most of them all.

We'd come from Iowa and California. Michigan and Maine. South Dakota and both of the Carolinas. Pennsylvania and Oregon. And right in New York. We'd all vacated the studio with Andrea, leaving behind easels we'd become attached to and wet paintings she promised to carefully package and ship to our homes.

I hadn't expected us to become friends. I'd thought we'd do hugs or handshakes and maybe keep in touch on iLive. But all their numbers lived in my phone. And while we hadn't had late-night slumber parties, we'd shared meals and museums and one of the most meaningful weeks of our lives. It was a different type of bond—one forged over the tears of being unable to get the perspective right, or the frustration of a color that wouldn't match, the exhaustion of wrists and backs and eyes that strained, and the exaltation of taking that step back to see a drawing from a distance and realizing it worked—the pride of knowing *you'd* created it.

In the lobby of the dorms Justin was organizing one last outing. He tapped his paint-spattered sneaker against my paint-spattered ballet flat. "Come on, Aurora. Don't you want to see the crowds in Times Square?"

No. No I did not. I *hated* crowds. And as much as I enjoyed everyone in this group, I'd reached my limit. I'd spent so much time surrounded by people, and it was taking a toll. If "introvert" could be used as a verb, I wanted to introvert so hard right then. Shut my door, turn out the lights—and breathe.

"Come, Aurora! Marie! Simon!" Trinity was making puppy-dog eyes and begging hands, but I backed away from the people tugging on their gloves and toward the group waiting at the elevators.

"Maybe we can meet for breakfast," I offered in consolation. "Before flights."

"I'll text you," answered Trinity, and I nodded, which meant I'd have to turn my phone back on.

I stepped into the elevator and the knot in my stomach loosened with every floor separating me from socializing. This was the right decision—for me—even if it wasn't one everyone approved of.

I finished packing before six. Finished my takeout by seven. And *Little Women* by ten. Then I finished dessert, vegan cookie dough, by ten thirty. I loved food delivery. Any kind I wanted could be delivered to the dorm's security desk with a few clicks on my phone. I also appreciated the number of me-friendly menus in the city.

But even delicious cookie dough didn't dislodge the lump that sat in my throat from the moment I'd closed the back cover and texted Merri: **All done!**

Jo married the stodgy professor and started a school. Meg was still married to Laurie's old tutor and nothing much had changed. Laurie and Amy were married—married!—and happy. Though there was a weird bit about Amy sculpting a statue of her pale daughter in case she died? I was choosing to forget that and focus on *married and happy*. And the sisters were still sisters. Still as different as can be and as close as can be.

I missed mine. Enough that I checked my phone five times in five minutes, but Merri hadn't responded. I called Lilly and was sent to her voicemail. "Hi, it's Rory. Will you pick me up from the train tomorrow? They leave almost every hour—so just let me know what time works for you. Okay?"

My mailbox was full of my parents' typical: **I miss you. You're being safe, right? We love you.** I shot off a quick selfie with my empty cookie dough cup paired with the message **Yum! Dinner!**

and a winky-face emoji. But there were none of the messages I'd been expecting. None from Toby and none from Merri or Lilly. Neither sister had even complimented the photo I'd sent of the painting I'd worked on all week. How was I going to know whether I'd met my goal if I didn't know whether they could read my feelings in that paint?

It was hard to shake the sensation I was missing something. But I forced myself to brush my teeth and get in bed. Finally, my phone buzzed beneath my pillow. I pulled it out expecting an essay from Merri about the book, or a train time from Lilly, or a who-knows-what from Toby. It was from Dad: **Get some sleep! Dream big, little one.**

Maybe Lilly and Merri were already asleep—resting up for board game annihilation tomorrow night. Maybe Toby was on his plane and hadn't seen my text yet. But I no longer hated that I'd sent it. Like Ms. Gregoire had told me, I couldn't stay frozen in my fear. Come what may, it needed to be said.

55

was the last workshopper to leave the dorm. I'd stayed to make sure Marie's ride to the airport picked her up . . . and because waiting in the dorm lobby seemed better than waiting in a dirty train station.

I still didn't know which train to take because I hadn't heard back from Lilly. Or Merri. Or Toby. I knew my phone was working because I'd gotten all the meet-up-for-breakfast texts and a **Happy New Year's Eve, Aurora!** from Mom. But she didn't mention being excited to see me later, and she hadn't responded to my proof-of-life selfies or picked up when I called.

I wanted to stay curled up in the rubbery lobby chair, panic-checking my cell every thirty seconds, but our deadline to turn in dorm access cards was eleven, and it was 10:58 a.m. Juggling my gloves, duffel bag, and tote, I took a deep breath—it was time for me to brave the cold and figure out a plan.

There are scenes in Merri's rom-coms where the elevator doors open and the hero's waiting there for the heroine to step off. Or he's standing at the top of the escalator as she ascends, or outside her building, lounging against a car in a studly macho pose. Or the airport baggage claim, her front porch, the counter at her favorite diner. I never bought those scenes. They seemed too perfect, with the music rising to a crescendo and the lighting narrowing to the heroine's face as everything else is filtered to a soft blur.

Except when I opened the door of my dorm, I paused on the threshold and waited for someone to cue my soundtrack, because the crowd crossing the street had thinned—revealing someone standing on the opposite corner watching my building. Those eyes—chocolate brown and full of mischief—shifted to me and he smiled like this was exactly where we were supposed to be. And even though I was sure he could compose the most gorgeous arrangement for this moment, I didn't need music to tell me how to feel. It wasn't a dream, because the strap of my duffel had slid from my shoulder and dug painfully into the bend of my elbow. It hurt worse than any pinch. Also, if this were a movie he'd be holding a ridiculous bouquet of red roses. Toby's hands were tucked in the pockets of his gray herringbone peacoat as he crossed the street toward me.

I drank him in piece by piece. His skin was darker from the California sun. His cheeks and lips were red, but that could be sunburn, emotion, or the cold of December in New York. My mouth twitched, wanting to bloom into a smile that stretched from one ear to the other. I think his did too, but he was pressing his lips together to suppress it. His eyes, though—they glowed with all the same happiness that mine echoed back.

I'd gotten to observe a lot of masterpieces this week—

both artistic and architectural—but he was the best thing I'd seen. As soon as he was within reach I threw my arms around him, pinning his to his sides. I buried my face in his coat and breathed him in. Toby let me nestle into him the way Byron did whenever anyone turned on the space heater. He extracted a hand so he could return my hug, and we stayed that way for minutes, hours, days.

"This is some greeting." He laughed against my hair. "You should go away more often."

I bit my lip and began to pull away, but he wasn't having it. He wiggled his other arm from beneath mine and held me for another lifetime.

We finally broke apart when someone cleared their throat. "Excuse me, I need to get in here."

"Oh, sorry." We shuffled to the side so we weren't blocking the doorway. I stared at the nine inches separating the toes of our boots. "What—what are you doing here?"

"I came to pick you up." Toby ducked to try to get in my line of vision, but I turned my head. It was too much. My brain was still catching up to him being *here, now*, adding licorice to the smells of falafel and roasted nuts emanating from food carts. "I stopped by your house on my way from the airport, and your parents were confused about whether you finished today or tomorrow."

"New Year's Eve or Day." We said the words together with matching eye rolls. Merri's confusion superpower struck again.

"I volunteered to figure it out and pick you up. But when I got out my phone to call you—I searched train times instead." He sighed as he had to step out of the way of a dog walker, then a delivery man. "This meant I could see you sooner. I've been climbing the walls without you."

"Lonely?" I asked, because while Toby had sent me lots of updates from California, not a lot of them had mentioned his mom.

"More than that. I missed you." He paused and spoke slower and louder so I could hear him over a group of tourists that bumbled by, phones and maps out. "I missed *you*."

"Oh." I breathed out the word in a puff that hovered in the cold air and made me confessional. "I sent that last text by accident. I was going to delete it."

"But did you *mean it*?" he asked, his gloved hand resting on my arm, a spot of warmth that heated all the air around us. "Do you know how many text messages to you I typed and deleted? Or the emails in my drafts folder? The day after you left, I even drove back to the train station and bought a ticket . . . I tore it up and went home because I didn't want to distract you while you were in your workshop. But, Roar, you've done nothing but distract me since you left. I. Miss. You."

I'd gotten so used to the sounds of the city this week. The white noise of traffic and conversations, the squeaky wheel on a delivery cart, the call of someone hawking purses or trying to hand out discount coupons, the occasional jackhammer, the hundreds of boot heels hitting sidewalks in an endless rhythm. Usually I tuned them out. But now, within the midst of this important conversation, they were all I could hear. Someone whistling for a cab. A dog barking. A baby crying from somewhere within that stroller's bundle of blankets. The *beep-beep-beep* of a truck backing up.

To all of this, I added a sigh-soft "Oh," too overwhelmed to be articulate.

Toby was studying me, trying to read my expression, but my face was like my voice—blank. I didn't know what emotion to feel, so I wasn't going to feel any. He let go of my arm and took a step backward. "Can we—can we get back in the building or go somewhere quieter? There's so much to tell you, but I should start with what happened this morning."

"I had to turn in my access card. There's a café around the corner though." Something about his expression or voice made my lungs burn from more than cold air. "Is everything okay?"

"Café," he said, taking the duffel bag I still had looped over my elbow. "Lead the way."

It was maddening that he didn't answer me until he'd ordered us tea and we'd finessed our way into a table. It was wedged in the corner, and the space was so tiny we couldn't both sit without our legs brushing and tangling, but I would think about that later. First I needed him to share whatever news had him clearing his throat and playing with the sugar packets.

"Toby!" I insisted, my nerves alive with anxiety. "Tell me now."

"Everyone's fine. It's just— Part of the reason your parents were so frazzled about when your program ended and agreed to let me get you, is . . ." He took a deep breath. "Lilly and Trent decided to elope. Your parents found her note this morning."

"Elope?" I gasped on the word, then laughed from shock. "The senator is going to be so mad. And poor Merri is on her fifth draft of her toast."

"Well . . ." He looked away from me and grumbled under his breath, "Merri will still get to give her toast."

"What do you mean?" I took a small sip of my tea. Nope, too hot. "Are they doing a reception when they get back? That's kinda cool."

"Maybe? But also . . . Merri found out before Lilly left."

"Of course she did." I snorted.

"And coerced Lilly into bringing her along to act as witness. Her and Fielding. It was in Lilly's note."

"Oh." Apparently that was my favorite word today. I gulped at my tea and it should've burned my tongue, but I didn't feel it. Toby was still talking, but his words were as blurred and distant as all the strangers' café conversations. There was no way any of them could compete with the ones screaming in my head: *Lilly and Merri, but not me. Aurora Bore-ealis— too boring to include. One day! They couldn't wait one day. Or even a few hours until I got home. I would've taken the earliest train. I would've left last night. I would've moved any obstacle to attend . . . if they'd wanted me there. But they didn't.*

When Ms. Gregoire said those I love would disappoint me I'd assumed she'd meant Toby. This was worse.

"Roar. Are you listening?" Toby's hand landed on mine and he tugged the empty cup from my fingers. I nodded, but that wasn't good enough, because suddenly Toby was crouching in front of me so we were eye to eye. He reached with both hands to cradle my face. Eight fingers on my cheeks, two thumbs at the corners of my mouth. Ten points of electricity. "This is important, so listen: *This is not about you.*"

"Clearly." I tried to scoff and shrug, because I didn't want

388 | TIFFANY SCHMIDT

to be held by his eye contact, not when I was raw and vulnerable and he saw me too well.

"No. I mean—this is on *them*. It's not on you. It has nothing to do with how amazing you are or wanting or not wanting you there. Based on Lilly's note, this is . . . It's impulse and anxiety and societal pressure and opportunity. This is not about *you*. Rory, they didn't stop to think about *anyone* but themselves. It was not done to hurt or exclude you."

I placed both of my hands over his and tugged his fingers off my face. He let me, and let me turn around, like I was suddenly fascinated by the lousy art prints on the wall behind us. "That doesn't mean they didn't though—hurt and exclude. It doesn't change that I'm not going to be in my sister's wedding photos. It didn't matter to her that I wasn't there. She didn't even ask."

"Your *parents* aren't there, Roar. It wasn't personal."

"But *Merri* is! You don't get it! It's always those two. Merri always gets picked and never me. I love her and I don't ever want her to feel this small and horrible, but . . . Just once can't someone choose me?"

"Hey." His voice was soft. It was such a contrast from the barbed tone I'd used. And his touch was soft too as he wrapped an arm around the back of my chair and leaned to rest his chin on my shoulder. "Why do you think I'm here? I did. I do."

"What?" I stopped pretending to care about the prints. They were badly drawn boats—what was there even to look at? I turned back toward him. Our noses were inches apart. It was a distance that felt like it should be temporary, that we should be moving away to give each other space, or moving forward to press our mouths together.

We did neither. I studied the fullness of his lips, the length of his eyelashes, the arc of his cheekbones. I had to look at these pieces individually because I was too close to process the whole.

"Roar—" When he spoke, the words danced across my cheeks in a song of mint and licorice. "As soon as I heard the news, it was *you* I was thinking about. How would you feel? How fast could I get here? I didn't want you to be alone. I didn't want to be without you."

I closed my eyes so he wouldn't see them well with tears and leaned my forehead against his. He reached for my hand underneath the table and squeezed it tight. "It's going to be okay," he told me.

I let myself stay there for a minute, until my breathing started to settle and my neck began to cramp. I wiped my eyes and said, "I'm going to have to walk into that house today and be happy for them."

Toby shook his head. "Be happy next week. Or next month. They're not getting unmarried, you've got time. You're allowed to feel what you feel. Frankly, I'm pissed on your behalf." He pressed his lips together for a moment, then blurted out, "Let's not go home."

My jaw dropped. "You mean run away?"

"Not forever—just tonight." He squeezed my hand again. "We'll have a secret adventure. One that's ours."

"But—" My head spun with logistics and possibilities.

"My dad's got party plans somewhere in the city. And yours . . . well, they weren't sure Day versus Eve. They've got their hands full with the senator's panic about this leaking to the press. Send a *Can't wait to see you tomorrow* text and they won't give it another thought."

"We don't have anywhere to stay. I can't get back in the dorm."

Toby laughed and stood. "It's New Year's Eve—we'll stay up all night—go home first thing in the morning."

"Can we do this?" Impulsive was never a good look on me, but he sure made it sound tempting.

He nodded. And waited, letting it be my choice. I glanced back at the framed boats. *Boats!* "Wait! You came for me—like Laurie did for Amy."

He looked between me and the wall, his forehead creased. "Are those girls in your workshop or something?"

"No . . . it's a Gregoire thing." I took a deep breath. I was not going to stand frozen in my fear. "Okay, let's do this."

He stood and held out his hands to pull me up, then began sorting our gloves and hats and scarves. Handing me my stack, he proclaimed, "Our adventure starts *now*."

56

So, we can do *anything*, Roar. Any opinions? You're the expert on Manhattan now." Toby held the door for me and we both inhaled at the sudden temperature change outside the café.

"No more museums. I'm arted out. I bet you never thought you'd hear me say that."

He laughed and slid his fingers through mine. Even though it was glove-to-glove, I still got tingles. But should I? He'd said a lot of things that were *almosts*; almost declarations, almost clear, almost enough to believe in. I didn't want to live in almost—I wanted absolute. I gnawed on my lip. "I don't have any great ideas for any big adventures—I can't come up with them that fast. We can't all be Merri."

"No," he said, pulling me to a stop and out of the flow of foot traffic so he could meet my eyes. "And I wouldn't want you to be. Please don't be anyone but you. Merri . . . she's pepper. You're salt."

"Explain," I demanded. Was this some sort of food version of rubber and glue? It did nothing to calm the energy skittering across my skin and within my veins.

"Pepper—you can't ignore it. It's spicy and demands attention. A little goes a long way, and it can overpower every-thing around it if you lose the right balance." Toby squeezed my hand. We sidestepped out of the way of a man push-ing a dolly full of boxes and found ourselves backed against construction scaffolding. "Fielding needs spice and excite-ment. He's better for it. He's so much happier since he met your sister."

"And you? Or me? What's salt?"

He stared at me with eyes blazing. "Salt enhances every-thing around it. It brings out the best in natural flavors. Makes sweet things sweeter and pretty much everything taste better."

I got that those were compliments—kinda? But whether they were about me or the spice or how this analogy applied to my personality wasn't quite clear. But if this was how he wanted to ease into this conversation, I'd follow his lead. "Salt is bad for the heart."

"Not my heart. At least, I hope not. I mean it has— you have—the power to destroy me like no one else ever could, but . . ."

I sucked in a breath because now that he was done speak-ing in spices, my body flooded with hope. "But?"

"You know what you said about songs?" he asked, bracing one hand on the scaffolding behind him. "It's your songs I hum when I'm scared. When I'm lonely. When I'm happy. When I'm falling asleep or trying to wake myself up. When I'm brushing my teeth. When I'm driving. It's your songs that are always in my head. And no, they don't make me cry. Because you make me so happy. And to be one hundred percent clear—back in my car, I knew which Campbell sister I was kissing."

"I'm not sure—" I didn't know how to finish that sentence or how to sort through my thoughts or how to convince myself to believe this could be true. I wasn't that five-year-old in the sandbox anymore. Or the ten-year-old darting from her bus stop to give him an origami star, or the first-day-of-school freshman who'd blushed at the mere thought of getting into his car. But he still gave me tingles and tangled my tongue. "Toby, what do you *want*?"

He took a deep breath. "First, I want to kiss you."

"Oh." There was my favorite word again, but the way he was watching my mouth as I said it, the way he licked his lips and his eyes darkened, made it clear he wasn't currently debating my limited vocabulary.

"I should have asked last time. Should've made it clear it was *you* I wanted to kiss, that I've been waiting and wanting to: at the concert, when you taught me yoga and drawing, at the lake, and a million times over your math book. But I couldn't tell if you—and I thought Huck . . ." He exhaled. "May I?"

I nodded and made the briefest of mental notes to tell Eliza she was right—asking for consent was *so* attractive. I closed my eyes but opened them again when no lips-touching happened. Instead Toby kept talking. "I was going to wait until midnight—but that feels like the coward's way out. I don't want you to feel like you *have* to kiss me for superstition or luck or whatever the whole midnight kiss thing means.

And I didn't want you to have any doubts or second-guess what it meant to me." He leaned closer, until his lips were brushing mine. "Everything"—it was a caress and a promise I could taste.

I shut my eyes and pressed up on my toes, closing any remaining gap between our mouths. My tote bag landed on my boots as I dropped it to wrap my arms around him. Toby's hat joined it after I pulled it from his head so I could slide my fingers through his hair. My scarf was dangling off one shoulder because he'd unwound it when he brushed his hand across my neck.

Dear Gustav Klimt, I get it. Why you used all that gold and glow and detail.

I needed a print of *The Kiss* to hang in my bedroom, but even that masterpiece didn't come close to capturing the emotion of *this*. I was aware of his hands, his lips, his skin and hair beneath my fingers—but I couldn't have told you a thing about the street or the world around us. At least not until a little kid on a scooter knocked into us, breaking our lips apart so we could smile giddily at each other while catching our breath.

"You said, 'First, I want to kiss you.'" I tilted my head and beamed up at Toby. "Was there a second? And just because we didn't first kiss *at* midnight doesn't mean we can't kiss then too, right?"

He laughed. Deep and long and full of real joy. "Go ahead and kiss me whenever you want. You have my full permission." He demonstrated this by pressing his laughing lips to each of my cheeks, my nose, my forehead, then nuzzling

THE BOY NEXT STORY | 395

against my neck until I was ticklish and laughing too. "And second, I just want you. And me. Together. Boyfriend-girlfriend, seeing each other, dating—you pick the label. I want to be *yours*."

My giggles dried up at the earnestness of his voice. "I want that too."

"Good," he answered, nodding twice. "Then let's go. There's someplace I want to show you—adventures to be had."

Toby wouldn't tell me where he was taking me. "It's a surprise," he said.

The subway was packed with the usual traffic, plus people starting their New Year's celebration eight hours early. Normally I'd feel claustrophobic and panicked in that crush of bodies shoving in and out at every stop, the layers of loud conversations and perfume and beer and sweat and city, but Toby wrapped both of his arms around me to hold the subway pole I was holding, creating a barrier between me and all the elbows and intrusions. I leaned into his warmth, feeling the path of his breath against my ear. "Almost there."

We emerged blinking into the late afternoon sun at Battery Park and were immediately greeted by people holding out brochures and asking, "Tickets? Do you have your tickets? Last boat of the day to see the statue."

"We're going to see the Statue of Liberty?" I hoped I wouldn't get seasick. Or freeze. I pulled my scarf a little tighter.

He shook his head, both at my question and at the ticket hawkers who'd started to close in. "Nope. Now stop trying to spoil the surprise. It's just over here."

The flower beds were all brown where they peeked out of snowdrifts, and the lawn was blocked off by temporary fences. But the weak sun reflected off the buildings and the water, and the white trees stretched toward a cloudless sky. New Year's Eve was supposed to be an ending, but this felt like a beginning.

The building he led me toward was round. Glass sides, with a metallic swirl on top. It looked like a flatter version of a soft-serve ice cream cone . . . or an abstract version of the fishbowl in my room. As we got closer, I saw the walls weren't actually round; they were flat panels of glass in overlapping panes. Music spilled out—and my eyes grew wide as I saw what was inside.

"What is this place?" Besides somewhere I wanted to live forever. I was already fumbling for my phone and taking picture after picture.

"It's the SeaGlass Carousel," said Toby. "It seemed like you." I squeezed his hand so tightly he winced. "Is that a yes?"

"We have to come back!" I said. "In the summer, we have to come back so I can bring paints." This was built for watercolors and ink. The carousel didn't have horses but fish—each with a round opening for the rider to sit inside. And the colors were incandescent, iridescent, pearlized. I wanted to capture the way it all glowed with its own type of magic.

"I'll bring you back, I promise." Toby grinned. "But since we're already here, do you maybe want to ride it?"

I didn't answer, just pulled him toward the line, his laughter chasing us both.

I put my phone away while we rode. I wanted to capture it all in my memory. The way some fish went up and down and others stayed still—and we'd strategized in line about picking ones that rotated together. The fish each had their own source of illumination, which bounced off the sequins and sparkles inside the pearlized plastic. The speaker in the front of each fish played old-timey songs and I laughed as we spun and Toby's smile rotated in and out of my orbit. When the ride ended, he was by my angelfish's side before I'd unclicked my seat belt. "So?" he asked.

"Again," I answered.

57

By nine o'clock my mind was more crowd than kissing. I was glad we hadn't waited until midnight to lock lips, because while I wanted it to be romantic to have a Times Square New Year's Eve moment, the reality was not measuring up.

The crowds apparently started gathering before noon and we hadn't shown up until after dinner—which meant fewer hours waiting in the cold but also that we weren't up with the good views or among the orderly, prepared spectators I'd seen on TV. Not that *we* were prepared. My toes, fingers, and nose burned with cold. I appreciated the aesthetic of it all but not the energy. The elbows rose as the glitter fell—people pulling out party crackers and pockets full of streamers at random. There was trash and confetti under our feet, and my boots— my fabulous New Yorker boots—kept stumbling over debris and getting stepped on by the strangers pushing in from all sides, like getting an inch or two closer was going to improve their viewing experience.

I turned away from the glass ball on an LED screen. I couldn't see the actual thing. I didn't care if it dropped, stuck, or shattered—as long as I didn't have to stare at it for another three hours. I didn't want to celebrate with a million strangers—there was only one person here who I cared about, and it was too loud to talk to him. People kept tugging on my tote bag and I was sure Toby would have similar bruises from people snagging on my duffel, which he had slung around his neck.

"Toby, I'm tired." And I had to pee. There were no bathrooms. I'd seen one mom tell her small son, "Just go on the street, try not to hit anyone."

I knew Merri would've been instigating an all-night adventure. She'd leave this corner with numbers from all her new friends and invitations to three different after-parties. Or she'd charm her way into a jazz club, smiling and laughing until she was onstage.

But then again, I'd be leaving the corner with *Toby*. And I didn't want strangers' numbers in my phone or to attend an after-party. I wasn't her, and I didn't want to be.

But I still *missed* her. I wished we were grouped around the Monopoly board. She was always the dog and Lillian was the wheelbarrow. Mom was the race car and Dad was the bucking horse. I was the thimble.

But all those pieces were sitting in the box, our ice cream in the freezer. Lilly was getting married . . . and I wasn't there. I hated that Merri would have that memory and I wouldn't. I hated that we'd texted yesterday and she hadn't even hinted.

I also hated every drunken part of this shouting revelry. Maybe other places in the crowd were kinder or calmer, but our corner had air horns and I had confetti in my hair, mouth, and ears. I was done.

Toby's eyes scanned my face and he grazed his lips across my forehead. "Okay, Roar. I've got you."

For a heartbeat I worried he was disappointed, but when his eyes met mine, they were smiling. He put his arm around my waist and began to push through a mob that was only too happy to let us pass if it gave them the chance to be a few cubic inches closer.

Once we were back through the barriers, I took my first deep breath in hours. We passed groups in party hats, sparkly paper tiaras, and sunglasses shaped like the new year. Noisemakers. Bottles of champagne and sloshing flasks stuffed inside coats.

People shook cowbells and blew whistles as we passed. "Happy New Year!"

And now that I didn't have to be smushed among them, I was happy to shout back "Happy New Year," because it was going to be a great one.

Penn Station was busy, groups pouring off the trains in sparkly dresses and paper hats. Our train was rowdy with revelers too, but Toby offered me the inside seat and put his arm around me. "Well, now we know that's one of those things that looks better on TV," he said.

"Agreed. But this part's pretty great." I curled tighter in his arms. "Do you think Merri and Lilly are home? There's nothing on Merri's iLive yet."

"No." Toby dropped a kiss on my head. "Fielding texted me that they wouldn't be back until tomorrow. He told his dad ahead of time and got permission. Though it sounds like he leaned heavy on the 'May I accompany Merri to her sister's wedding to the senator's son?' and didn't mention it was an elopement and they'd be the only guests."

I dropped my phone back in my pocket, then stuck my hands inside Toby's coat. They felt icy, all of me did. Fielding had had enough notice to ask permission. He'd had time today to text an update to his friend . . . but I hadn't heard from either of my sisters.

"You have to tell them, Roar," Toby said gently. He ran his hand through my hair and looked down at me with eyes so kind and sympathetic, it felt safe to let mine well. "You have to let them know it *hurts* when they exclude you."

I sniffed and wiped my eyes on my scarf. "But what if they don't listen?"

His jaw hardened but his eyes stayed soft. "Then you keep talking. They love you—but they're clueless. You have to *tell* them, Roar. No hiding behind snark and insults."

My lower lip trembled, but I nodded. He was right. Ms. Gregoire was right: *"When you keep your fears locked inside they have power, but when you confront them, you give yourself the power to fix them."*

Though this wasn't the way the book went. I sob-snorted. He lifted a curious eyebrow and I tried to explain. "At least no one is dead. When you first said you had news, I thought we had a Beth March situation. I think elopement is way better than death."

His forehead was a map of befuddlement, but he smiled. "Me too."

58

We were in his car at midnight. I was fiddling with heat vents and he was telling me his realizations about music. "I thought about what you said—about wanting it enough—and I don't know if I do, but I know I want to *try*. I'm looking at composition programs for the summer—and I already emailed my music teacher to sign me up for the spring showcase."

I squeezed his arm and smiled. "If you're happy, I'm happy."

He was smiling back when our phones began to chirp. I looked at the dashboard clock and at the red light above us—then stretched over to give him a quick New Year's kiss. "Begin as you mean to go on, right?" I sassed as I sat back in my seat.

He grinned. "Then it's going to be a good year."

I took out my phone and he handed me his to read and respond. Mine were from my parents, Clara, Huck, and even Molly, Greta, Gemma, Elinor, Iris, and Boy Byron.

Toby had the same group text from my parents—**We are so lucky to be starting another year surrounded by those we love. Happy New Year.** Seeing it on his phone made me bite my lip, because it was among messages from his teammates and friends, not his own parents.

And maybe he sensed that was why I wasn't reading them aloud, because he said, "Hey, my mom won't send one for another three hours—California midnight. And Dad thinks texting is impersonal. He'll say something when I see him tomorrow night."

I nodded and scrolled through to find some to make him smile. "Um, Curtis says *Happy Nude Rear*, and there's a picture."

"What?" Toby attempted to grab the phone from my hand, but I laughed and tugged it away.

"It's a cartoon. But it's started quite the GIF thread."

In between responding, I kept checking my own phone for the two missing texts. Finally, one came through from Lilly: **Happy New Year! I've got news . . .** I waited for her to complete the ellipsis, but she didn't. And Merri, who was in the group message, didn't say a word. I ground my teeth, then put the phone down. We weren't going to do this over text, so there wasn't any point in torturing myself.

Toby pulled into his garage and I looked in the rearview mirror at the sliver of my house and driveway disappearing as the door lowered. "Dangit, I don't want to go home," I whined. "I'd sneak in, but . . ."

"I've met your dogs." He grinned at me. "No explanation necessary. So stay here. Your parents think you're coming back tomorrow—well, later today. I'll crash on the couch or in the spare room. You can have my bed."

I blinked at him and bit the inside of my lip. This didn't have to be a major thing. I didn't *have* to freak out—but given a choice, my brain was hardwired to panic. I inhaled deeply through my nose, forcing the air down into my lungs and imagining the oxygen spreading throughout my body like I did in meditation. Then I smiled and said in a voice much calmer than I felt, "Okay."

"Wait." I paused with my hand on the doorknob. "Is it white? Tell me it's not all white." I'd spent hours imagining the room on the other side of this door—my jealousy amped by the fact that Merri had such free access to it. If I were the type of person who made inspiration boards on iLive, I totally would've had an inspiration board about Toby's room—set to private, of course. Imaginary creepy-stalker me wasn't stupid.

He laughed and closed his hand over mine. "Not *all* white, but the most colorful things in my room come from you."

White walls, white blinds, but the hallway's white carpet had changed to dark hardwood. His furniture matched. His bedspread was light gray. His pillowcases white. It would've been a boring room, if it weren't for splashes of color and personality—a Batman cosplay mask I'd made for him hung on the wall beside a framed picture of his lacrosse team. A shelf full of trophies—Hero High red and gleaming gold and silver. A white binder full of sheet music sat on his keyboard, but slipped inside the cover's pocket was a drawing from when I couldn't have been more than ten—Toby in a Beethoven wig sitting at a grand piano. It was no masterpiece—done in cartoon style and marker. It had a Batman sticker in the corner.

I pointed. "I don't remember giving you that."

"You didn't." He grinned with impish glee. "I stole it off your fridge."

Something I *had* actually given him was suspended on a thin string from the top of his mirror. Its tie-dyed print was likely the most colorful thing in this room, and seeing it made my heart fold in on itself with creases as crisp as those on the object. My hand was too shaky to point, so I nodded at it instead. "You kept that?"

It was a little girl's crush captured in paper. It was the gift that caused me to be one short when I reached my fifth-grade class—so that I stood up to Stella and was paid back in humiliation.

Toby stepped behind me, wrapping his arms around my stomach and leaning his chin down on my shoulder. His gaze was also on the tie-dyed origami star. "You were so proud of it," he told me. "And you gave it to me right at the time when we were starting to get so busy that we didn't hang out as much anymore. Different schools, and I had lacrosse and piano, you had art. I missed you—but I was a stupid twelve-year-old boy and didn't know how to get over myself and admit that. Merri and I still had the fanfics we wrote and the cosplays we did— but I didn't know how to fit you in my life when I was supposed to stop swinging on swings and playing tag. Everyone kept telling me to grow up and be a middle schooler; I thought that meant leaving you behind."

I hugged my arms over his. "Don't let me go again."

"Never." He punctuated the statement with a kiss on my temple.

I sniffed a few times and took some deep breaths, not

wanting to spoil everything by crying. Glancing around the room, I saw one other colorful item—a white vase filled with slightly wilted sunflowers sitting on the table beside his keyboard. "Who are those from?"

"Me. They were for you—they still *are* for you—but I was going to give them to you Christmas Eve." Toby spun me around to face him and cupped my chin so I had to meet his eyes. "Roar, I didn't blow you off because I wanted to spend time with Merri. She needed my help, *and* I wanted to tell her I was going to ask you out. Not because I wanted her permission or anything—but because I needed to make it clear you were never my second choice or a replacement or anything like that. I wanted to make sure Merri knew I'd moved on—I didn't ever want her to throw that in your face or say something that made you doubt us."

He paused to kiss me and I think he meant it as a dash or ellipsis or some other temporary punctuation, but I pressed up on my toes and made it an exclamation point. We were both breathing hard by the time we broke apart. He tipped his forehead against mine and exhaled the rest of his words across my nose. "The way I feel about you is unlike anything I've ever felt before. It crept up on me slowly and then I was in it so deep I couldn't breathe. And it scared me. Because if it hurt to be rejected by other people . . . You can destroy me, Roar. If you wanted to, you could pulverize me. Please, don't."

I echoed his answer from earlier, "Never," then sealed the promise with a stamp of a kiss, pulling back quickly before

I yawned in his face. As much as I wanted to stand there and hear him profess his feelings until sunrise, I was swaying with exhaustion.

Toby laughed nervously. "Aren't you going to say anything back? I really don't know how you're feeling right now."

I snorted. "Then I have a much better poker face than I thought." I pointed to the origami star above his mirror. "I gave you my heart in fifth grade. I'm glad to see you finally noticed." It was a glib response that made him grin, but it wasn't the full truth. "But . . . I also outgrew that schoolgirl crush and fell for *you the person*, not *you the idea* sometime this fall. You can thank Ms. Gregoire for that."

Toby raised his eyebrows. "I'm not even going to ask. Unless you really want to tell me."

"You wouldn't believe me if I did." I toasted with my water glass from his bedside table. "Here's to Ms. Gregoire, and Louisa May Alcott, and math tutoring, and carpooling."

Toby picked up where I left off. "And the St. Joe's defender who whacked my knee. And Mockingburger. And Knight Lights."

"Speaking of Knight Lights . . ." I held up a one-minute finger while I yawned. "Can I hear the Lake Song yet?"

"Sure. Climb into bed. I'm going to go take my contacts out, but then I'll play until you fall asleep." He winked at me. "Someone once told me I looked hot in my glasses."

I threw a pillow at him. "I didn't tell *you*, I told your dad . . . Wait, that just sounds weird."

I could hear him laughing all the way to the bathroom.

By the time he came back, I'd tucked myself in with his flannel covers pulled up past my chin. The blankets, the pillow, the sheets all smelled like him. Licorice and mint and Toby. I hoped they all would infiltrate my dreams. And his music too.

"Ready?" Toby asked from his seat in front of his keyboard, and even with his back to me, I could tell he was nervous. His shoulders were too high, his voice gruff. He cleared his throat. "And if you hate it, that's okay. You don't have to tell me. Pretend to fall asleep or something."

"I won't," I assured him, nestling deeper into his pillow. "Play, maestro, play."

He laughed and began, the notes tripping blithely over each other in ways that made me picture us going through the woods. The flirty pokes, the tree roots, the teasing. The feelings we were both feeling but not admitting. The tempo increased, the notes building and building until they gasped into tranquility—the quiet of the lakeside, the water lapping, the sun blazing off its surface. I closed my eyes to soak it all in and bring myself back to that rocky shore with a boy on a mossy log. A boy who was now mine. My thoughts snagged on that daydream made real, and it took a few moments for me to catch up when the tune shifted again.

"That's"—yawn—"*Harry Potter*"—yawn. "You didn't write that."

I heard Toby chuckle but didn't open my eyes to see his smile. "Just checking to see if you're still with me. Want to hear a few of your songs before you completely pass out?"

I think I nodded. I meant to. Because I did. I really, really wanted to hear and memorize them. See what it sounded like to make him happy. But that would have to happen some other day, because the pull of sleep was too strong. Happiness was straight-up exhausting.

59

woke up to fierce sun and fiercer bedhead. I looked like the cover of Merri's copy of *Ramona Quimby, Age 8*—my bobbed hair sticking out straight in all directions. I attempted to flatten it while searching for my phone.

I found it in my shoe: 11:17 a.m.

I hastily made the bed and gave his pillow one last creeper sniff before I headed down the stairs to find its MIA owner.

"Happy New Year!" Toby stood from his stool at the kitchen island and turned to greet me. But where our greetings before had always been words, this one involved lips . . . in a non-speaking manner. Which would've been great if I hadn't left my toothbrush down here with all my other toiletries.

I clamped a hand over his mouth before it made it all the way to mine. When his eyebrows shot up, I turned to the side and explained, "Morning breath. Where did you move my bag?"

He pointed and I removed my hand. While digging out my toothbrush I dug out my brush-brush too. And deodorant, because why not? Buried beneath these were the presents I'd collected for him in the city. "Catch!" I tossed him a small bag that had gotten surprisingly heavy. "More colorful things—for the kitchen this time."

He dumped the bag onto the counter, laughing as he turned over the bright magnets one at a time. Art and buildings and the ubiquitous I♥NY. He put them up on the fridge immediately. "This is perfect. I love them."

"Good. Can you bring me to the store?" I called from the bathroom doorway. "I want to see my parents, and they've got to already be at work."

"They are." Toby came to stand in the foyer. "I saw their car leave earlier. Lilly and Merri haven't come home yet either."

I nodded, relieved. I wasn't quite ready to see them. "Then let's definitely go to the store."

Right as I shut the bathroom door Toby asked, "Can we tell them about us?"

I figured I had at least three minutes before I had to open the door and answer, which was good because I needed all three minutes to tame my expression. I'd never known how hard it would be to brush my teeth while beaming. When my hair was slightly less horizontal, my armpits smelled powder-fresh, and my teeth arctic-icy, I opened the door. Toby was still leaning against the wall, but the relaxation had drained from his posture. He looked like Gatsby when I told him to sit while holding up a cookie. As in, his self-control was fraying. "We can tell them if you want."

He was still nodding when he kissed me.

᪉

"Aurora!" Dad shouted as the door chimes announced our arrival. "That's my baby girl—back from a week in New York!"

The customer buying an LED leash smiled politely. Mom shoved a receipt at her and barreled from behind the counter to hug me. "Let me look at you! Do you look more grown up? George, does she? Did you have fun? Were you safe?"

"Mom, we talked every day. Stop fussing." I ducked away from her and rubbed lipstick off my cheek.

"Not yesterday," Dad said, pulling me into his own hug. "I need a recap of your past twenty-four hours. What's new?"

"We're dating now," Toby blurted out, reaching for my hand as soon as Dad let go. "That's new. Me and Rory. Aurora and me. Together . . . I asked."

Mom and Dad exchanged a glance and I wondered if they were thinking the same thing I was—about the time nine-year-old Toby had announced to Major May, "Me and Rory—Rory and me—we ate a whole watermelon!" It had been at a joint cookout between our backyards. My parents had laughed and wished us the best of luck with whatever stomachaches came our way. Major May had narrowed his eyes and asked why Toby was interrupting. *Why do you think I'd want to know that?* I hoped he wouldn't have the same response if Toby told him this latest news.

But if he did, I hoped my parents' reaction buoyed him through it. Because Mom hugged him and Dad did too. Lots of "We couldn't imagine anyone better for our littlest girl."

"Excuse me one second." Mom ducked into the backroom and came back with her wallet.

"Did you make a bet about us or something?" I asked.

"No, not quite . . ." Mom's wallets were always fat things, the snap closures stretched to their ultimate limit to hold the chaos of receipts and bills and discount cards and pictures she carted around. This time she fished out the three photo bundles that sat behind her money. Each was bound with a flat hair band and contained wallet-size pictures starting with us as newborns and continuing to our latest school year. I bet Lilly's top picture was about to be updated, from college graduation to wedding. But she put Lilly's and Merri's bundles to the side and unbound mine. Paging back to the beginning of the stack, she pulled out a photograph and handed it to me. Its edges were worn soft and clearly it had been a bigger picture that was trimmed down to match all the others, but the image was clear: small Toby and smaller me. In the sandbox. Kissing.

I turned to show Toby, but he was already peering over my head. He put a hand on my hip and the other on my shoulder to anchor me as I leaned back and smiled up at him. "Pretty good first kiss," I told him.

"Turn it over," said Mom. "I don't need to say *I told you so* to your dad, if you read the inscription out loud."

I flipped it over and squeaked. It was Toby who read out the words in his deep voice: "*Rory's first kiss with Toby next door. I predict it won't be their last . . .*"

"So you'll have to excuse me for not being more surprised. Your dad and I have known this for ages. We've been waiting for you two to catch on to the fact that you're inevitable."

"But no eloping." Dad's attempt at a joke fell flat and I could see the pain in his and Mom's forced smiles. "I've got to walk at least one of you down the aisle."

I took the photo from Toby and handed it back without

saying a word. Because what were the right words for your parents telling your boyfriend of less than twenty-four hours that they've been predicting this for more than a decade?

None. There were none. So I used none. I buried my face in Toby's shirt. He chuckled. "Um, I think that's Rory's way of saying she's tired and wants to head home."

"No," Dad corrected. "That's Rory's way of saying we're embarrassing her. Sorry, pumpkin. But why don't you go ahead and take her home. I know she's impatient to see the surprise Huck and Clara left in her room."

"Call us if the wayward Campbells come home," said Mom, her voice full of forced cheer. "We'll close the store and be there ASAP."

"Wayward Campbell," I said softly. "One of them is a Rhodes now."

No one had an answer for that, so I slipped my hand in Toby's and we headed home.

60

Merri was sitting at the kitchen table when we walked in. All my plans for bringing Toby upstairs to show him Huck and Clara's project and grab a minute of make-out time vanished when she bounced out of her seat. "Do you know? Because I'm not allowed to spoil it, but if you already know . . ."

"I know."

She squealed. "Lilly's dropping Trent off, but then she'll be back. They both decided to 'face the music' with their own parents, then all six of them are doing a big ol' dinner tonight."

"Oh" was the only thing I could think to say, so I said it twice. "Oh."

Toby twisted his fingers between mine.

"Did you know you can elope to places other than Vegas? When Lilly asked me to be her witness, I assumed we'd be getting on a plane and being high rollers at some drive-through wedding chapel." She shrugged. "I was pretty disappointed until I realized eloping to Philly meant I got to bring Fielding along."

"Oh."

"Also, they had the officiant meet them at the Liberty Bell. So it was pretty amazing—especially for history nerds like them. All the trees had twinkle lights still up and the photos Fielding got are incredible."

I knew I should ask to see them, but I couldn't. Merri went on about how Lilly's dress had been ready at the fitting and hers had just needed a strap tightened, so they'd picked them up on the way. "It was super easy to buy some fake fur stoles from that boutique by Haute Dog. And Trent *owns* a tux. Apparently that's a thing you can do. You don't just rent them."

Toby stepped closer until our arms were touching from shoulder to knuckle. I couldn't turn my head to look at him. I could barely make my chin bob up and down to acknowledge Merri's words.

"And for her bouquet I got the florist to make one with lilies—duh—mixed with holly and mistletoe. I make a pretty good MoH, if I do say so myself." Merri paused to roll her eyes. "Even if I had to give my toast with cream soda at Reading Terminal Market instead of champagne at the country club. From the moment she decided to do this until we left we had less than forty-eight hours, and we pulled it off without anyone knowing."

"Yeah," I bit out. "Including *me*."

Toby switched hands, lacing his left through my left so he could step even closer and put his right hand on my shoulder, his thumb resting right over the pulse point that was racing and telling me to escape. He was the only thing keeping me in place, because my toes curled with the urge to run upstairs and hide in a sketchbook until I could plaster some bland *I don't care* emotion over all the hurt on my face.

"Hey." Lilly glided into the room, radiant with happiness. "What's going on in here?"

Toby squeezed my hand, a gentle pressure that helped me open my mouth and tell the truth. "I'm glad you got your dream wedding, Lilly—but I'm heartbroken that me being there wasn't part of it. And that neither you nor Merri thought I'd want to be." There it was. Clear and calm and true.

Lilly put her keys on the table and turned to me with a puzzled expression. "But . . . I'm honestly shocked you cared. Of course I wanted you there, but I didn't think you'd want to miss any of your art workshop. And you've been so . . . blasé about everything wedding."

I clamped my hand tighter on Toby's. "How else was I supposed to react when you made Merri maid of honor and me just a regular bridesmaid?"

Lilly crinkled her nose. "*You'd* want to be maid of honor and give a speech?"

"No. I wouldn't *want* to, but I would do it." My voice began to crumble away with all the anger I'd been clutching. "You're my sister, of course I would. And this whole thing—helping to pay for the Snipes workshop—was that just to get me out of the way? Send me to New York so I couldn't interfere?"

Lilly looked like she might vomit. Her mouth gaped open and she clasped a hand over it. Merri ran for the trash can mumbling about the "Campbell curse" and "stupid stress-puking."

"No," Lilly managed, and at first I thought she was

responding to Merri, because she was pushing away the bin. "Rory, you can't really think that. Really?"

"Why *wouldn't* I think that? You guys are always doing stuff without me. How many times have I heard you halfway down the stairs to go for a manicure or shopping or lunch or whatever and one of you says, 'Oh, we should get Rory.' I'm an afterthought at best, and at worst . . . sometimes you don't turn around and knock on my door."

Merri and Lilly were exchanging the guiltiest and palest of glances. "But you usually say no, and I didn't know you could hear us," Merri said.

"Does that matter?" I answered. "Would it change anything?"

"If we knew you *wanted* to come? Absolutely. Always. I always, always want you there, Rory." Lilly's eyes were wet, and tears spilled over onto her cheeks.

"Except for at your wedding," I replied. My fingers had to be crushing Toby's, but he didn't complain or move away. He was my steadiness in this emotional tumult. Honesty hurt.

"Rory, I can't change that." Lilly stepped forward and reached out a hand, but I didn't move. "And I apologize for not understanding and not asking, but you have to know I wanted you there. In fact, it's *because* of you that we did this."

I wanted to scoff or snap, *Yeah, right*, but I was trying so hard to curb the points on my words, to take Toby's advice to listen and be heard. "Because of me, *how*?"

"Your painting. I couldn't stop staring at the picture you drew of Trent and me and how you imagined me having this happy wedding. And then Dad made that comment about how they're sacrificing financially to give us our dreams—but the wedding I was planning *wasn't* my dream. It seemed like such a waste, them spending all that money on a wedding I hated. You almost didn't get to go to New York because of it. I don't want you to miss out on things you want . . . especially for something I *didn't* want. *I* wanted a New Year's Eve wedding—and I told Trent that if my youngest sister was brave enough to chase after *her* dreams, I wanted to be brave enough to fight for ours."

Lilly slid her wedding band off and held it out to me. "Look, I even turned that into an inscription—it's inspired by *both* my sisters."

I wordlessly accepted the ring and held it up to the light. Letters were stamped all around the inside of the band: *Dream big, live big, love big.* Her eyes and cheeks were wet when I handed it back. "I'm the big sister, but you and Merri are my heroes." She sniffed. "I'm so sorry I hurt your feelings. I never wanted you to feel left out, and I promise to be better about it going forward. Can you ever forgive me?"

I pulled my hand free of Toby's because I didn't need his courage for what I was going to do next, and I *did* need both hands. I threw them around her neck. "I forgive you. And I'll be better about telling you how I feel."

I usually felt so pointy and prickly and shrugged out of hugs, but Lilly's were the best. She didn't hold back or let go too fast. "I'm so sorry about the wedding. I wanted you there. I really did. It just— It felt like this small window of opportunity to get out of having our wedding be this big social spectacle. And you seemed so happy in New York. I didn't want you to have to leave early because of me. But I should've—"

"It's done." I shook my head. "I don't want you to have wedding day regrets because of me . . ." Because I was sure she was going to get plenty of guilt from both sets of parents. "I'm happy you're happy. And I want to hear about it at some point."

But not today. Toby was right—I didn't have to do it until after the emotional bruises had faded. The sketchbooks I'd made each of them this week could wait too. Between the hearts on Merri's cover were a dozen city dogs; Lilly's had historic buildings and monuments. They were thank yous for pushing me to chase my dreams, but I wanted to deliver them when my gratitude wasn't still tinted with betrayal.

"Thank you," Lilly said. Her wet cheek pressed against mine.

Merri had been uncharacteristically quiet, but now she was budging in, all elbows and squirm. "Middle sister coming through, don't leave me out of this. And I was thinking . . ." Lilly and I locked eyes and exchanged *Watch out* looks. "You owe Rory a major life event. So, you should take her on your honeymoon. I'll come too. We'll leave Trent at home—girls' trip—way more fun."

"Merri," Lilly warned.

"Kidding. Trent and I, we're like *this* now." She held up two crossed fingers. "I told him he should take his big-brother job seriously and threaten to bust Fielding's kneecaps if he ever hurt me." She gave us a smirk. "He said he'd think about it."

I laughed against Lilly's shoulder.

A door opened behind me and I craned my head to see Toby at the threshold. He paused and caught my eye, mouthing, *Later*, before he slipped away.

I turned back to see Merri watching me. She disentangled first and dabbed beneath her eyes. "Now that everyone's forgiven and done crying, can we get out the ice cream so Lilly can tell Rory about her wedding and Rory can tell us why Toby's making googly eyes at her and holding her hand? Not that I didn't see this coming the second you got your Gregoire assignment—*hello, Laurie*—but I still need all the swoony details." She continued to fan her eyes and take deep breaths. "Also, when did I become the boring one? I'm going to tell Fielding we need to do something exciting to keep up with you both."

"No eloping," Lilly said firmly while pressing a tissue to her eyes in some graceful way that prevented her mascara from smearing. "At least not for another seven to twenty years."

"You spoil all my fun," called Merri, already halfway to the freezer. "I bet you're not going to let me squirt whipped cream directly into my mouth either."

"Nope," called Lilly, chasing after her, but I stayed put long enough to take out my phone and text Thank you. I'll see you later. The words sounded so ordinary, so insignificant—but I'd put a heartful of sincerity in each one.

Toby's response was immediate: Can't wait.

An hour later and I was finally headed up to my room to greet my pets. Ariel Eight and Klee Five were swimming and snailing happily. "You don't even look like you missed me," I said, then turned back toward the door.

My handwriting wasn't great. I'd never have an Etsy shop with cute hand-lettered prints. I didn't know how to draw with simplicity. In art—as in life—I always overcomplicated and overthought.

But Clara had amazing handwriting. I'd watched her copy the swoop and curl of letters from the math class posters. I'd seen the locker banners she created for other cheerleaders. And when Huck found out from Clara what I'd asked her to do in my room, he'd wanted in.

I was sure they'd squabbled about the design, but I hadn't had to witness it. I'd given them free rein and a lot of trust. Mom had given them access to my bedroom, and even though they'd finished days ago, they'd both refused to send me pictures.

I stood in the middle of my rug and stared up at the quote they'd drawn onto the wall above my doorframe. Huck had outdone himself with the sketch, a dark bulbous cloud that hovered ominously on the left, transforming via a night scape of diamond stars into a nimble sailboat on the right.

In between were Clara's letters. They were the perfect balance between graceful and strong. If I ever got a tattoo this Amy quote from *Little Women* would be it: I am not afraid of storms, for I am learning to sail my ship.

I snapped a photo and attached it to an email to Ms. Gregoire.

This is my last response journal on *Little Women*. I finally get it. Why you chose this book for me. It's not because of the guy next door romance—which is what I'd originally thought. It's because it's a story about sisters. And I need mine—needed to remember how invincible we are when we're together. And how we might not always be, and our trio can exist as a duo—but we're connected by an unbreakable and invisible bond. But I'm also fairly unbreakable on my own. This year has been one nonstop storm, but I've sailed through.

It won't always be easy—I've got three and a half more years of math classes ahead of me. :) But I'll get through. Someone wise once told me sailors need three fixed points to navigate. I've spent so long trying to navigate based on others' opinions, but I'm not doing that anymore. I'm going to be my own fixed points, my own constellation. And in the darkest nights, I want to glow bright enough to guide my own way.

Thank you for picking this book for me and coaching me through it.

Happy New Year,

Aurora Campbell

61

My parents would probably have grounded Merri for her role in Lilly's elopement, but she gave them the best reason not to: "I've got plans: a double date with Fielding, Rory, and Toby."

She might have already informed Fielding, but this was news to Toby and me. I looked at him across the Connect Four grid and he smirked. We'd decided to spend the afternoon playing all the board games we hadn't played on New Year's Eve. So far I'd trounced everyone at Pictionary and Merri had kicked everyone's butt at Scrabble. Now Lilly and Trent were playing a nervous game of chess while they waited for Senator and Mr. Rhodes to come over and join my parents for dinner. Merri, Mom, and Dad were in a round of Monopoly that was rapidly becoming *Who can cheat the most obviously*—my money was on Mom because she was a totally dishonest banker. Toby and I were tied at two games each of Connect Four.

Merri rolled a three and moved her dog five spaces. She picked up two cards and discarded the one she didn't like, then read the bonus on the other. While Mom paid up, Merri added, "And don't you want us out of your hair while you talk to the Rhodes and Lilly and Trent? Because if I stay home grounded, I'm going to eavesdrop."

"Fine, go," Dad said. "But don't think we don't see right through you, pixie. You'll get a consequence for staying out all night without permission . . . as soon as I think one up."

Merri clapped and divided her savings between them. "Sorry, can't play anymore. I have to go get ready. Come on, Rory. Come back in an hour, Toby."

I expected Toby to pop up and cater to Merri's order, but instead he tilted his head and looked at me while spinning a red checker between his fingers. "You good with this, Roar?" and my heart hurt with how perfect that question was and how okay that made this moment. I nodded. Then he stood, but not until after he took his turn, sliding that red piece into the middle row and then pointing out a diagonal. "Connect Four. I'll demand my winnings when I see you in an hour."

"Your winnings?" I asked with a smile as I put the pieces back in the box. "I was unaware we were playing for a prize."

"A kiss." Toby's grin was my most favorite one—and if it had shaken me like an earthquake before, now that he was mine, it hit me like a volcano, all my feelings rushing to the surface. He waved to my family, then touched my cheek, tracing the line of my smile. "See you soon."

I could've walked out the door that minute. I didn't know what Merri had planned for her spontaneous double date, but I would've gladly gone in day-old yoga pants and the blue-gray tunic I had on. It was *Toby* and the best part of dating him— No, the best part of dating him was *him*, but one of the great

426 | TIFFANY SCHMIDT

things about dating him was not being nervous. I didn't have
to primp or dress up. Unless I wanted to. Merri wanted to so
much that her desire became infectious. I traded yoga pants
for jeans, swapped the tunic for a sequined sweater from her
closet, and finished it all with the senator's boots. "How soon
until I can borrow those?" asked Merri.

But that didn't take even close to an hour and for once
I was the one bouncing and impatient, and thinking of how
Laurie describes his relationship with Amy to Jo—*"We were so
absorbed in one another that we were of no mortal use apart"*—
until Merri relented. "Fine, see if Toby's ready. I'll text Fielding
to come over."

Eliza showed up at the door as the four of us were gathering to leave. She held up a bag of popcorn. "There's a Hallmark
movie marathon. I assumed my presence was required."

"Oh." Merri's face crumpled with guilt. "No, I can't. I have
plans. A double date with Toby."

Eliza looked from Fielding to Toby and back to Merri. She
didn't need to say a word; her expression gave whole mono-
logues about what a bad idea she thought this was. "Toby's
dating someone? He actually talked someone into going out
with him?" Even those words were marinated in skepticism.

Fielding laughed, but then when Merri screeched, "Eliza!"
he realized she wasn't joking, and it turned to a choking cough.

"Yup," I said lightly, laughingly—because I was not going
to let her ruin this.

Toby grinned at me. "It's fine. Even Eliza can't get to
me tonight."

"It's just—" She shook her head. "Sorry, that was rude. Clearly I'm processing this slowly. Who is it?"

Toby raised our hands, which had been linked the whole time.

"Surprise?" I said softly.

"Toby and Aurora?" She tilted her head and looked between us. "How did no one think of that? You two are so compatible."

Merri blew out a breath of relief and everyone laughed.

"Someone *did* think of it," I answered—and exchanged winks with Merri.

"Who?" Eliza demanded. "Because I'm kicking myself for not putting it together sooner. It was right there in front of me. And you even asked me about him and— Who?" she repeated, shaking her head, incredulous someone had been more perceptive than she was.

"Louisa May Alcott," I answered. "And Ms. Gregoire."

Merri's nod was a full-body action, and if I had to guess, I was only seconds away from her ripping my hand from Toby's so she could give me a hug or discuss all the finer points of her *Our teacher is magic* theory.

"No. Not that again. I'm not talking to you two." Eliza turned to Fielding and Toby. "You realize your girlfriends are delusional, right?"

Girlfriends. It was such a lovely word.

Fielding and Toby chuckled.

"I'm used to it by now," said Toby, pulling me closer. "It's what makes life interesting."

Fielding smiled down at my sister. He freed his hand from

hers to unbutton his coat and spread the lapels. "And I'm not going anywhere near that statement beyond saying Merrilee is my best adventure."

Merri went up on her tiptoes to kiss his cheek, and on her way back down she nuzzled against the sweater he'd revealed, which *must* have been a gift from her. It was a dizzying red-and-white-checkered print—and taking up the entire torso was a basset hound in a Santa hat.

Toby sounded like he was choking behind me. When he composed himself, he whispered in my ear, "Promise me you'd never . . ."

"Never's a very long time," I teased before turning to Eliza. "Just wait. Maybe there'll be a book in your future too."

Eliza raised her hands like she could erase my words from the air or shield herself from their meaning. "No. You take that back, Aurora Leigh Campbell. Absolutely not."

Merri was rubbing her hands together in glee. She folded them and then bit down on her knuckle. It was probably the only way she could keep herself from agreeing with me and listing a whole library full of potential titles.

I tipped my head back on Toby's chest and he brushed his lips against my hair. In all the perfect moments I'd imagined in all my years of daydreams, nothing compared to standing there with my sister and our best friend, who was no longer an obstacle between us. I tightened my fingers around his—this was real. He was mine to sketch and talk to and drive with and math with and listen to as he played music. The only thing that had changed was that I'd do those things with his hands in mine and his lips on mine. This was just the beginning, this foyer full of happiness and harmony, where I knew what Merri was thinking and went ahead and said it for her—after all, wasn't that what snarky little sisters were for?

"Why not?" I asked Eliza with a grin. "More impossible things have happened."

ACKNOWLEDGMENTS

When I was eight, my Aunt Terry gave my older sister and me a giant edition of *Little Women*. Its pages have gold edges, it has beautiful illustrations, and it's large enough to use as a step stool. I read it before my sister and promptly claimed it as my own (I still have it if you want to demand joint custody, Heather). My takeaways from that first read were: I'm some hybrid combination of Amy and Jo, pickled limes sound gross, and I badly want my own Theodore Laurence.

I'm so grateful for that book and for all the people in my life who have given me books over the years or listened when I rambled about them and my own stories. I was so fortunate to grow up in a family and community that valued reading. I'm beyond lucky to work with the people who fostered and supported the novel you've just finished reading.

Anne Heltzel and Barry Goldblatt, there are no words for how grateful I am to have you on my team. I'm a better writer and a happier human because you're both in my life. Thank you. To the rest of the Abrams crew: Andrew Smith, Marie Oishi, Tessa Meischeid, Masha Gunic, Carmen Alvarez, Penelope Cray, Nicole Schaefer, Jenny Choy, Brooke Shearouse, Jessica Gotz—endless, heart-squish gratitude.

My own older sister, Heather, who cast such an impressive shadow I worried I'd be forever lost within it—thank you for always loving me, hearing me, and championing me. Like the Campbells, our united sister powers are unstoppable. To my younger brothers, who let me read aloud to them and who participated in plays I wrote and directed—much like the March sisters—thank you for letting me boss you around while dressed up in my ballet costumes. And my parents— thank you for weekly trips to Stevens Memorial Library and pretending not to see the glow of flashlights beneath my door when I read long past bedtime.

To Jessica Spotswood, Lauren Spieller, and Bess Cozby— sorry, not sorry for making you cry. Thanks for all the walks in the woods and the late-night critiques and carrot cake at Highlights (thanks, Amanda!). To Courtney Summers, Emily Hainsworth, Annie Gaughen, Tricia Ready, Nancy Keim Comley, Jen Zelesko, Stacey Yiengst, Claire Legrand, Katie Locke, Elizabeth Eulberg, Heather Hebert, Jenn Stuhltrager, Kristin Wilson, and Karen Lash, I want to have you all over for a *Gatsby/Little Women* movie night and feed you all fun drinks and cookies and tell you how glad I am to call you friends.

To *my* Mrs. Gregoire, who is even more magical than her Bookish namesake—thank you for believing in fifteen-year- old me, and thank you for teaching me to believe in myself. I hope everyone has a teacher like you as part of their journey. I'm so grateful that my twins have found their way into the classrooms and hearts of truly gifted educators—most espe- cially Rachel Griffin-Snipes.

To the heroes in my real life: St. Matt, my Schmidtlet twins, and Rascal—you make every day an adventure. Thank you for filling our house and lives with chaos, love, and laughter. So much gratitude to St. Matt for coffee and apple deliveries when I get up at four a.m. to write, and to the twins for continuing to be the world's best sleepers. Rascal, I'm still hoping you learn to nap, but in the meantime you do an A-plus job of coloring on and ripping up old drafts while I work.

To all the librarians, teachers, bloggers, and readers who have read and recommended Merri and Rory's stories—you make my heart squish, and I can't wait to share the next *Bookish* adventure with you!

And finally, thank you to Skittles, because I cannot revise without you, and to whoever cast Christian Bale as Laurie in the 1994 version of *Little Women*.

TIFFANY SCHMIDT

Tiffany Schmidt is a former sixth-grade teacher. She lives in Pennsylvania with her family and spends her time baking cookies, chasing her sons and puggles around their backyard, and writing the kissing scenes first. Tiffany is the author of *Bookish Boyfriends: A Date with Darcy*, as well as four other books for young adults.